FAMILY ALWAYS

COMES FIRST

AN ALICIA ANDERSON STORY, BOOK 2

BEVERLEY NEILSON

Other Books by Beverley Neilson

The Dark Side of Pain

Praise for The Dark Side of Pain

Suspenseful, and moving, full of twists and turns, this is a great start for this new author. Looking forward to the next instalment in this series. M.C.

This book pulls you in and doesn't let you go. The reader becomes personally vested in what happens to Alicia and her family. Fast paced, intense right from the beginning to the end. Look forward to the next chapter in Alicia Anderson's life!!! L.B.

This is a page turner at its best! This story is fabulous! Beverley has brilliantly interwoven a storyline with gripping events, surprising twists and painfully true depictions of real life trauma. The story is grounded in her rich writing style that allows the reader to grab hold and dive deep into Beverley's imagination. The ride was emotional, awesome and eye opening. All checks were marked on my list! Great story! D.M.

This novel doesn't waste any time jumping into the action, which I like. I enjoyed the fact that it was set in Ontario and the familiar references to locations. I'm looking forward to the next novel in the series! C.J.

Family Always Comes First

Copyright © 2022 by Beverley Neilson

The following story includes strong and potentially offensive language, sexual activity, sexual abuse, violence, and drug use which may be disturbing to some.

For information contact:
Beverley.neilson.author@gmail.com

ISBN:

Kindle ebook: 978-1-7775923-4-9
Kobo ebook: 978-7775923-6-3
Paperback: 978-1-7775923-3-2
Hardcover: 978-1-7775923-5-6

First Edition: June 2022 v4

Readers - If you encounter typos or inconsistencies in the story, please send me a note at Beverley.neilson.author@gmail.com. Even with many layers of editing, mistakes can sometimes slip through. Thank you in advance for your help in eradicating such nasty nuisances.

If you enjoyed "Family Always Comes First," I would appreciate if you would help others enjoy this book, too.

Recommend it. Please help other readers find this book by recommending it to friends, readers' groups, and discussion boards.

Review it. Please tell other readers why you like this book by reviewing it on Amazon or Kobo.

For My Family

Will
(Happy 40th Anniversary)

My Favourite Sister, Heather
(I am so lucky that you are my sister, my friend!)

My Favourite Brother, Charlie
(Miss you, we don't see each other enough!)

King George
(best dog ever, I promise you'll be in the next book)

Mom and Dad
(I miss you both every day.)

Chapter 1
June 30

The club makes a subtle whistling sound as it cuts through the still night, before smashing into the girl's shoulder, creating a loud cracking sound as it shatters her shoulder bone.

"What the fuck!" she yells as she falls back on the grass, cradling her arm protectively against her body. She looks up at her attacker, her eyes searching for an answer to what is happening, why she is being assaulted, lifting her good arm to protect herself as the second blow comes crashing down on her head. She lets out a howl with the impact as a flash of red blurs her vision.

"Wait, wait," she screams as the taste of blood seeps into her mouth. "Please. No more," she begs, her arm and hands raised trying to protect herself as the weapon scrapes her skin, breaking several fingers before whacking her again on the side of her head. Her world goes black, blacker than the night sky she had been gazing at before the assault began. Streaks and specks of lights twinkle in and out, not from the stars in the sky but from the damage that the persecutor and their club are inflicting on her.

The girl is crying now, fat tears flowing freely from her scrunched up eyes. "No, no," she whimpers as a cloud of pain settles over her entire being, when another blow bashes her head. She pleads, she sobs, but the log continues to batter her. The pain is so intense that she is unsure where the blows are landing. Slowly the speck of lights, and the stars go dark, blackness taking over her entire being and there is no more pain.

The perpetrator continues to pummel the inert body, blow after blow until spent from the hard, physical work, unable to hoist the chunk of wood over their head for another swing. The killer collapses beside the dead girl, looking around to ensure that they are alone.

The executioner sits in silence, waiting for their heartbeat to slow down, for the pounding in their head from the stress of the assault to dissipate. They sit and watch the stars, the moon, the quiet until the sound of people laughing breaks through the night. A group of people

1

are walking, laughing, talking, making their way from the downtown area to the outer limits of the park, toward them.

"Shit," the killer mumbles, standing up, brushing the grass and dirt from their clothes, remaining immobile for a moment, contemplating what to do before bending down to grab the blanket that the girl had around her shoulders, dragging it over the dead body, tucking the edges in around the unmoving bulk, hiding it. The culprit looks around, spotting the dead girl's purse in the grass, her phone lying beside it. They pick up it and toss it into the water before running into the night.

Chapter 2
July 1
Alicia

Alicia strides down the hallway toward the Detectives' Den, the office space which houses all of the criminal investigation staff at the precinct. She is finally able to get out of the prescribed patrol uniform, wearing a conservative navy-blue pant suit and white blouse for her first day at her new job. Her long chestnut-brown hair is pulled back into a single ponytail which accentuates her strong high cheek bones and dimples, evident when she smiles. As she rounds the corner in the building, getting closer to her new office, Detective Chuck MacLean, her friend Liz's husband, and her ex-husband James's old partner, greets her.

"Welcome to the Detectives' Den, Alicia," Chuck says, greeting her at the doorway. The average height, heavy-set, middle-aged man with short dark curly hair and thick black framed glasses holds the door wide open, beaming at the newcomer like a little boy who received everything he asked Santa for on Christmas morning.

"Thanks, Chuck. I can't wait to get started, but I'm surprised to see you here on Canada Day. Shouldn't you be out celebrating with the whole town at the waterfront festival on this special holiday?"

"I'm hoping today is quiet and I'll be able to get caught up on some paperwork this morning. I promised Liz and the girls that I would meet them at the waterfront this afternoon to listen to some music before dinner and take in the fireworks."

"Sounds like fun. Say hello to Liz for me. I'll catch up with her next week."

"I will tell her. And now, your partner awaits," he says, waiting for her to enter the detectives' area.

Helen stands up from her desk and waves at her friend and new partner as Alicia enters through the double doors. "Perfect timing, Ally. We just caught a case. A major case. Body found at the

3

Southshore Community Centre, young female, tentatively identified as Jessica Winters."

Alicia grins as she hears the case basics. *Wow, already. A case. And it sounds like a big one.* Alicia fights hard to keep the smile on her face as she asks her new partner, "Did I hear you right? Jessica Winters?"

Helen stops and looks down at her iPad with the dispatch information on it. "Yup, that's what it says. Tentative ID is Jessica Winters. Why? Do you know her?"

"Luke's old girlfriend's name is Jessica Winters, but it can't be the same girl."

"I don't know. Let's go see," Helen replies as she picks up her iPad and moves to Alicia and the office door, still reading the dispatch. "Says here that a purse was found near the body, contained ID. Is Luke still going out with her?" she asks, looking up at Alicia.

"No, they broke up months ago. She met someone else and ended it with Luke," Alicia replies, following Helen to the parking lot.

"Was it amicable?" Helen asks as she clicks the key fob, unlocking the doors on a police SUV.

Alicia looks over the roof of the car. "Amicable? Not sure that's a word I would use for any break-up when you are 16 years old, and your girlfriend dumps you. Why? What are you thinking?"

"Nothing. I'm not thinking anything. Just asking some questions for a little bit of background, in case it is that Jessica," Helen replies, getting into the car and shoving the key into the ignition.

"Even if it is that Jessica, you can't think Luke had anything to do with this," Alicia insists, as she buckles her seatbelt, turning to Helen.

"Alicia, I don't think anything at this point. Let's go take a look. It might be her; it might not. If it is, we might have a problem with conflict of interest," Helen continues pulling the SUV out onto the road.

"There is no way Luke knows anything about this or is involved. They broke-up months ago. They've both moved on – they are 16 for God's sake," Alicia finishes as she turns her attention to the streets as the SUV races to the scene of the crime. *What are the odds that this is Luke's Jessica? How many Jessica Winters live in the city? Maybe they are wrong with the ID. It is only tentative. Who would do such a thing to her? Does Luke know? There is no way Luke is involved in this, is there?*

Chapter 3
3 months prior - April 1
Luke

"What the fuck! This can't be right," Luke mutters as he rereads the text on his phone, pushing his sandy-brown hair back from his eyes with one hand, a grimace marring his attractive face. He's standing in his next-door neighbour's garage while Dylan works under the hood of his 1969 earthy grey-green coloured Camaro.

"What's going on, dude?" Dylan asks, glancing up from under the hood. He takes a step back, still holding an adjustable wrench in his hand that he had been using to work on the carburetor of his prized possession.

"I don't know," Luke replies, looking up. "I just got this weird text from Jessica. Says we are breaking up. That it's over between us."

"That doesn't sound right, does it? I thought you guys were pretty solid."

"We are," Luke replies, punching the speed dial button for Jessica on his phone, as he walks toward the back of the garage. The phone rings four times before going to voicemail. Luke frowns as he leaves a message. "Jess, you need to call me. I just got this strange text from you, and we need to talk." He presses the end button and turns back to the front of the garage as Dylan watches.

"Maybe it's an April Fool's joke," Dylan comments leaning his hip against the front bumper of the car, his tall frame dwarfing the vehicle. His hair is cut short, similar to those in the military. His smoky grey eyes watch the kid next door closely as raw emotion covers Luke's face, presenting worry-creases on his forehead, reflecting fear in his bright blue eyes as he looks around the garage, as if the answer to this strange situation is hiding in a dark corner. "Doesn't she have a little brother? Maybe he sent it as a joke, or he's pissed off with her, so he wants to cause some problems," Dylan suggests, trying to console his new-found friend.

"Maybe, but Jessica doesn't usually leave her phone around for anyone to pick up. And he would have to know her password," Luke replies looking up at Dylan, hoping for a logical answer from this 20-something guy with much more experience in life than he has.

"Chicks, what can you do? Can't live with them, can't live without them," Dylan jokes, trying to minimize Luke's anxiety level.

Luke's eyes move back to his phone as he rereads the text message. *Could this be a joke? It's not funny if that's what it is.* He stabs the icon for Jessica's phone number and moves the cell phone to his ear, once again hearing the call fall into voicemail. "Jess, it's me. Where are you? Call me. We need to talk."

"Dude, you just left a message not even two minutes ago. Calm down. She'll call you back," Dylan offers, shuffling over to his storage chest, filled to the brim with automotive tools, opening a couple of the drawers, as he looks for a specific implement for the job at hand.

Luke stands for a moment taking big breaths trying to calm his nerves and still the foreboding thoughts that the message has wreaked on him. Tears rim his eyes as the possibility of losing Jessica sets in. He swipes his hand across his face as Dylan turns back to face him. "I'm going over there," Luke decides, picking up his jacket from the work bench.

"Maybe you should talk to her first, man. And don't you think if she could, she would answer her phone?" Dylan asks, standing up to his full height.

Luke pauses, as he reaches for the handle on the garage door. "If she's not there, maybe her mom will be home. Maybe she'll know where I can find her, maybe she'll know what the hell is going on." He pauses for a moment taking in the car, the garage. "Sorry, I can't help you with the car right now. I need to go. I'll come back when I can," Luke says as he walks through the door, letting it slam behind him.

"Hhhmmm. Fucking women," Dylan mumbles to the empty space. He smiles to himself, picturing Jessica's lean, well-proportioned body, her long soft, sexy hair, and a smile that would light up any room. He picks up a can of carb cleaner from the tool chest, shakes it to ensure there's enough for the job, and moves back to the car, wondering if this could be his chance with that luscious little girl.

7

***

Luke pulls the zipper up on his winter jacket before he grabs the handlebars of his old bike, jumps on it, and peddles frantically down the street. *Thank God the snow's gone or I would be walking. I need to straighten this out now. I didn't do anything wrong, did I? She's been a bit distant lately, preoccupied but said that was because of all the fights between her mom and dad, yelling at each other all the time, making life difficult for everyone in the house. That must be it. She's just afraid our relationship will turn out like theirs, but we love each other. This has to be a misunderstanding. There's no way. No way she really wants to break-up.*

Luke uses all his muscles to stand upright on the pedals to increase his speed up the hill. He continues to pull hard as the slope levels out, pushing as fast as he can along the well-worn path to Jessica's house.

He rounds the corner and notices that her mother's car is in the driveway. *If Jessica isn't home, at least her mom will know where she is,* he thinks as he pulls up to their front door and throws his bike on the lawn.

He knocks on the door, waits, but there is no answer. He knocks again, pounding harder with his full fist, hopping impatiently from foot to foot in anticipation of Jessica's mom answering the door. *What the hell? Her car is here. Where is she?* He holds his clenched fist up again, but before he can buffet the door, he hears shuffling on the other side of the wooden slab. He lowers his hand, pausing, anticipating someone coming to the entrance way.

The door slowly opens and Jennifer Winters, Jessica's mom, smiles as she recognizes him. "Hello Luke. How are you today?" she asks as the door opens a crack, enough for them to see each other.

"I'm good, Jennifer. Is Jessica here?" he asks, moving tentatively to the door expecting to be let in.

"No, no she's not here," she answers, moving the door to make the opening even smaller, as if she is hiding from the world.

"Do you know where she is? I need to talk to her and she's not answering her phone," Luke pleads stepping back on the front porch.

8

"I'm really not sure. Supposed to be working on a paper for school. I just got in but she's not here. Maybe at the library?"

Luke pauses. *Why would Jessica go to the library when they have internet service at home, and she could do any research she needed for the paper online here?* "She didn't say anything before going out? No idea where she might be?" Luke persists.

"No, none, Luke. Is everything OK? You sound a bit frantic to find her."

"I received a strange text from her, and I need to talk to her about it," Luke explains.

"Well, I'm sorry I can't help you. When she gets in, I will tell her you were here looking for her, if that helps."

"Thanks Jennifer. I'll try the library or maybe she went into work. Yeah, that's probably it. She's at the restaurant, that's why she's not replying to my calls," he says, looking to Jessica's mother for confirmation, but none is offered.

"Well good luck finding her," Jennifer Winters comments as she steps back into the warm house, leaving Luke on his quest to find Jessica. Luke grabs his bike from the front lawn and jumps on it, pedaling quickly toward the library.

***

Luke goes to the library, but she is not there. He stops by the restaurant where Jessica works, but she is not there either. Luke rides by the coffee shop where they sometimes hang out, cruises through the lakefront park where they like to walk in the summer, visits the bookstore where her friend Nova works but Jessica can't be found. No one has heard from her; she has just vanished. He has texted her three times and called twice more, but still no answer. He slowly pedals home, pulling his bike into the driveway, defeated and a little afraid of what she is going to say when he finally tracks her down.

***

Luke sits at the kitchen table. His mom is still at work, and he is alone with his thoughts as he clicks through Facebook and Instagram searching for some glimmer of where Jessica might be. When he can't find any current information online, he combs through his pictures of them together, displaying their happiness, the good times, their passion as he continues to reel from her blunt words 'it is over'. *Dylan may be right. Her brother, Oliver, must have sent it, playing an April Fool's joke on her. On me.* A smile emerges on his face as a picture of Jessica standing on Centennial Beach appears on his phone, her smile, her long golden-brown hair shimmering in the wind, freckles cascading down each side of her small pert nose, her watchful blue eyes. *No way, it's a mistake. It's got to be a goof. We haven't even had a fight in forever.*

His thoughts are abruptly interrupted with the explosion of Justin Bieber's love song "Anyone," the ring tone on his phone assigned to Jessica. Though he has been waiting for her call, he studies the screen displaying the picture of her smiling face. He lets it ring once more as his finger hovers over the button. He gulps, hits the button to accept the call, and closes his eyes. "Jess, what's going on?" he says instead of 'hello'.

"What do you mean, what's going on?" Jessica asks.

"That message you sent me? The one about breaking up. That's not something you should joke about. Did someone steal your phone and send it? Oliver, I bet," his voice petering out, waiting for her to deny the words from the text, waiting for her to confirm that she did not send the message that shattered his world.

"It wasn't a joke, Luke. I don't want to go out with you anymore."

"Why? What did I do?" he whines, his chin trembling as fear sets in.

There's a slight pause before Jessica replies. "You didn't do anything. It's not you, Luke. It's me. I just don't want to be tied down anymore," she explains.

"I don't understand. What happened? What's changed?"

10

"I'm just not in that place anymore."

"Is this about your parents? How crappy their marriage is? We've talked about that. We aren't them and we will never, ever be like them, you know that," Luke pleads.

"I'm sorry but it's over," Jess concludes.

"Jess, where are you? Let's meet. Let's talk. I'm sure we can work this out," Luke begs.

"There's nothing to work out, Luke. I've made up my mind."

"Just give me five minutes. Are you at home? I'll be there in ten minutes," Luke replies.

"No, I'm not at home and don't go to my house again and upset my mom."

"Where are you? I'll come there, wherever you are," Luke pushes again, holding his breath waiting for Jessica's decree. After several seconds of silence, he adds, "I think you owe me that much."

After another pause, Jessica finally concedes, "Okay, Luke, if we must. Meet me at the gazebo at the park, near the Community Centre."

"Yeah. Our place," he agrees, almost optimistically.

"Our place," Jessica sighs, resigned. "I'll be there in an hour," she adds disconnecting the call.

Luke pulls the phone from his ear and looks at the screen showing that Jessica has, in fact, hung up on him. He stares at the screen for a moment longer, like it holds all the answers to this situation. *What on earth is going on with her? What is she going to say? What can I say to change her mind?*

***

Luke is sitting on top of the picnic table under the gazebo, his coat pulled tightly around him, his hands tucked up in the jacket's sleeves, his breath forming a mist in the frigid air as he breathes in and out slowly, steadily, trying to calm his jittery nerves, waiting for Jessica who is 15 minutes late from her one-hour decree. *Where the hell could she be? Sweet Jesus, it's cold out here,* he thinks as he raises his shoulders to keep the brisk wind off his neck.

11

A brand-new lime-green Mustang Shelby pulls into the parking lot to his right, the exhaust making a loud rumbling noise against the whistle of the cold north wind. Luke turns to watch as the car turns around and stops. The engine continues to grumble as it idles, no movement apparent from inside the car until the passenger door opens wide and Jessica steps out. *God dammit! What is Jessica doing with Ziggy?* Luke scrutinizes the scene as she slams the door and moves toward him as the car sits, seeming to watch and wait for its passenger to return.

Jessica approaches him, her arms crossing her body, pulling her open coat closed against the freezing wind, her head down, watching her feet intently navigating along the pathway to the bench where he is sitting. She looks up as she nears Luke, her face calm, no sign of a smile on her lips or the sparkle that he loves so much in her eyes. "I'm here. Now what is it that you wanted to say?"

Luke is astounded at her callousness, her uncaring attitude toward him, the situation that she has created with the abrupt break-up. "What the fuck are you doing with that asshole? Is that why you didn't answer my calls?" he asks, nodding to the rumbling auto waiting for her in the parking lot.

Jessica sighs. "I didn't answer your calls because you just kept calling and calling and I had sent you all the info that you really needed in the text. And Ziggy is just a friend of mine. He's got nothing to do with this. With us."

"Are you sure?" Luke asks, trying to put the pieces of the puzzle together.

"I'm sure. He's just a friend. Now what is it that you wanted to say?"

Luke moves his focus from the car, an unwelcome intrusion into his world, back to the love of his life, Jessica. "Jess, please. I don't understand. I love you. You love me. Right?" he pleads.

"I did love you, Luke, but it's over. We're over."

"No, that's not possible. Why? What happened? What am I missing?" he moans, reaching out to take her hand as Jess pulls back, stepping away from him.

"It's been coming for a while, Luke. I'm sorry. I don't feel that way about you anymore. It's me not you," she gallantly adds.

"What do you mean, you don't feel that way anymore? You did last week. You did when we were together in bed. We made love and you were definitely into me then. Do you remember last week? What has changed in a week?" Luke's voice rises as anger starts to seep in.

"My feelings have been changing for a while now. It's over. We're young. You're young. Immature. Things change. I don't know what else to say."

Luke's eyes move from Jessica to the idling car. "Is that the reason that you've changed?" he asks, signaling to the vehicle. "What's going on with you and Ziggy?"

"He's got nothing to do with it. It's me," she answers, looking into Luke's tear-filled blue eyes.

"Bullshit. It has everything to do with him," Luke argues, turning his attention back to Jessica. "He's fairly new here. He's got a nice ride. He's got money. Is that what turns you on now, Jess? Cars? Money? I can't believe you are that shallow."

"I've grown up, Luke. I've changed. You're still just a high school jock and I need to take care of myself and my future," Jessica counters, pulling her coat tighter around her body, shaking her head, her long hair blowing in the wind.

"I'm not just a jock. You know that. I'm working on my electives so I can go to college. I'm going to be a cop like my mom and dad."

"And that's great for you. But we're done. I have moved on. You need to too. Grow up and move on," Jessica finishes turning away from Luke, leaving him in the cold blowy afternoon with no real answers. Luke watches as she makes her way back to the warm waiting car.

Luke sits on the bench for a long time after the car has roared away, trying to digest the nastiness and finality of Jess's words. He scans the frigid water of the bay, recently melted from the long cold winter temperatures. Tears puddle in his eyes, dripping down his face, freezing on his cheeks. He contemplates her words, her actions, the finality in her voice. After a while, he wipes the evidence of his pain from his face with the back of his hand and mumbles to himself, "It

13

will be a cold day in hell if she thinks we're over. She won't get away with this."

Chapter 4
April 3
Luke

"Hey, Luke. What's going on?" Dylan asks as Luke pulls the door shut behind him, entering Dylan's garage.

"Thought I would come over and see what you're doing. Still working on the carb?"

"Just giving it a tune-up, new spark plugs, ignition wires, distributor cap, rotors. I want this baby to purr when I finally get it out this spring." Dylan pauses as he reaches for the torque wrench to remove the spark plugs, searching Luke's face. "What's going on with you and that girl, Jessica? You left here the other day to go look for her. Did you find her? Did you get it straightened out?"

"She says we're done. I still can't believe it after all we've been through together."

"That's too bad, man," Dylan says, trying to comfort his young friend.

"She's hanging out with a new kid at school, and I think he's the real issue. Showing her a new world with all his family money. Maybe you've seen him around. He drives a lime-green Mustang."

This last comment captures Dylan's attention as he stands up from the engine compartment and turns to face Luke. "Tunes's kid brother? That's who she's going out with now?" he asks with astonishment in his voice.

"You know Ziggy? His brother?" Luke questions.

"You don't know Axl Tunes?" Dylan asks surprised.

"I don't. Who is he?"

"He's the big wheel in the Ruebens, the gang in town. He's got his fingers into everything illegal and criminal from drugs to hookers. Anything criminal that makes money and he's part of it."

"Really? Are you sure? In this piddly-ass town?"

"There's criminal activity everywhere, and yes, in this town too. Axl came out of the big smoke last year, promoted to VP of the Barrie chapter. He runs everything and everybody in this town. My advice to you – stay away from him and anything related to him," he warns as he leans back against his car, reconsidering his earlier thoughts about pursuing Jessica. In his mind's eye, he sees her succulent tasty body under his, them both moving to the forceful rhythm of sex. He blinks the daydream away, turns to face the car, and bends into the engine cavity.

"How the hell do you know this? Are you part of this gang?" Luke asks, standing straight to project a strong, stalwart front.

Dylan stands away from the car again and gapes at his naïve neighbour. "I've heard stuff and I've seen him around at the car shows. Axl Tunes has a boss vintage red Mustang that is mint. Looks after it like it's his baby. I've seen his brother there too with a lime-green Shelby Mustang. Beautiful car. One of his hench men, I think his name is Chevy, has a classic GTO, really sweet ride," he smiles, remembering the shiny chrome, the gleaming cars, the spotless engines.

"I don't give a shit about their cars or who his brother is. I swear to God that I will hurt Ziggy if he so much as touches a hair on Jess's head."

"I would be very careful if I was you and I wouldn't be saying shit like that to anyone. You never know who is involved in their gang. I hear the tentacles of the Ruebens even reach into the police force," Dylan says, not including the rumour that he has heard about Luke's father being an active part of the gang, an enforcer, protector in the club.

"What's with their names? Axl? Ziggy? What kind of family has names like that? And the last name Tunes?"

"From what I heard from Chevy, their mom is a bat-shit crazy old lady who was a big groupie with the band scene years ago, floated from band to band, guy to guy. She ended up with three kids, all different dads and gave them freaky-ass names to reflect her love of music. Axl was named after Axl Rose, while Ziggy is after David Bowie's famous song. I hear the sister's name is Annie Lennox, you know the chick in the Eurythmics? At least she got a fairly normal first name. The brothers are scary dudes, and they stick together. I would walk away from them if I were you, Luke."

16

The deep rumbling sounds of a car pulling in the driveway grabs their attention away from the serious conversation. Reverberations of a car door slamming, and thumping footsteps approach the side door, followed by a swift knock. Moments later the door opens without their invite, and Luke's friend Noah steps into the garage. Noah's dusty grey-blue eyes take in the space, his lips curving into a smile as his gaze lands on Luke.

"Thought I might find you here," he says to Luke. "Sorry to hear about your break-up with Jess." He nods at Dylan in acknowledgement.

"How did you hear about it so quick?" Luke asks, nodding at his school friend.

"Nova," he indicates his twin sister. "She seems to think Jess is seeing Ziggy."

"Asshole," Luke says under his breath. "Yeah, we were just talking about him and his illustrious family," Luke nods at Dylan. "Noah, this is Dylan. Dylan, Noah," he says, introducing the two.

They acknowledge each other with head nods before Noah turns back to Luke. "How about we go out tonight? Go up to Retro Planet and play some mini golf or laser tag or something? Or better yet, go up to the mall and see if we can pick up some girls. Do you want to come Dylan?" he asks, twisting back to look at Dylan.

"Not my scene, man, but drop by afterwards for a beer," Dylan suggests moving back to the engine cavity.

***

Noah pulls up in front of Luke's house in his beat-up black Mazda 3 hatchback, which he fondly calls the Chick Magnet. An old mattress and musty blanket in the hatch give the car its distinctive nickname, though Luke is not sure if it has ever been used for sexual liaisons and is certain that it is not a vehicle that anyone would flock to see. Noah gives the horn a quick honk and sits back to wait for his friend to appear.

17

Luke comes out of the house immediately, as if he was standing in the front hall waiting. He yanks the house door closed behind him before rushing to the car, opening the front passenger door, noticing Nova, Noah's sister, sitting in the back. He nods to her and looks questioningly at his friend.

"She begged me to come. Got nothing to do as her best friend has other plans, apparently."

"Hi Luke," Nova smiles genuinely at Luke, her dusty grey-blue eyes smiling, her luscious lips curved into a large grin, dark hair framing her face. "Hope you don't mind, but I was bored at home by myself," she explains.

Noah puts the car in drive and pulls away from the curb, ignoring his sister's greeting and her blinding smile. "There should be about ten of us playing, so we can split up into two teams. It should be fun. Did Dylan change his mind about joining us?" Noah asks.

"No, says it's too juvenile for him, but he did say we could come over after the game and have a couple of beers."

"What's his deal anyway?" Noah asks, driving steadily to their destination.

"Guy lives alone. He was here when me and my mom moved in. He's fairly new to the city. Comes from up north somewhere. No family, no girlfriend, no friends in town. Works as a mechanic and spends all his spare time in his garage working on his Camaro."

"Kinda strange, don't you think?" Noah asks.

"Never really thought about it," Luke replies, sitting back in the seat, watching the scenery as Noah drives.

***

Laser tag ends quickly for Luke as he is eliminated immediately after the starting bell rings, like someone was just waiting for him and used all their fire power to take him out. He is disappointed and removes himself from the floor to the glassed room overlooking the darkened field to watch the others have their fun without him. He sits

18

down and within a minute, a body plops down beside him. "Well, that was a quickie if I've ever had one," Nova laughs.

"Yeah, what a waste," Luke commiserates.

"I'm glad we have a couple of minutes alone, Luke. I just wanted to let you know that I heard about you and Jess." She pauses, watching the pain move across Luke's face with the mention of Jess's name. "I know you're hurting right now, but she wasn't good enough for you. Anyone that would dump you for that cretin Ziggy is just plain stupid."

Luke turns to examine Nova closely, her eyes caressing him with kindness. "What do you know about her and Ziggy? How long has this been going on?"

Nova sits back, aware that she may have said too much. She picks her words carefully trying to backtrack, "I don't really know. I know they've been talking for a while, but my understanding was it was just talk. You know – like between friends. I think it turned last week though. He invited her to some family party. That made it real and at least she had the courtesy to break-up with you before saying yes to him."

Luke was unaware of any communication between the two, and it hurts him to think that Jess and Ziggy's relationship had started while they were still together. He shakes his head, as tears begin to shine in the corners of his eyes as the reality of the situation sinks in.

Nova moves closer to Luke, brushing her hip against his, taking his hand, holding it in hers in her lap. "Don't worry, Luke. You won't be alone long. You know the saying 'the best is yet to come.' I honestly believe that," she smiles, leaning in to give him a soft kiss on his cheek, staying close to him as Luke's thoughts drift to Jessica and Ziggy.

***

"Well, that was quite the game," Noah announces as the three of them get into his beat-up car. "What the hell happened to you Luke? You were out of there pretty quick."

19

"Not sure, but I got hit to the max straight off the top. Like someone was waiting for me," Luke confirms as Nova beams in the backseat, smug that her plan had worked to get alone time with Luke.

"Too bad Dylan didn't want to come with us," Noah replies, his thoughts of the game disintegrating quickly, moving to enjoying a couple cold beers at Dylan's. Noah parks the car on the street in front of Dylan's house, next door to Luke's place. The three get out of the car and walk up the driveway to the front door. Luke knocks and the door is quickly opened.

"Come on in. How was the game?" Dylan asks.

"Great. I was on the winning team, but Luke got put out really quick," Noah confirms. "Hey, Dylan, this is my sister, Nova. Nova, Dylan."

Dylan steps back looking at the twins standing beside each other. "Hello beautiful," he murmurs, eyeing Nova up and down. "Welcome to my home," he continues as he opens the door wide to let them in, watching Nova intimately as she moves into the house.

Dylan leads the teens into the kitchen, opens the fridge to display a case of 24 beers and a few lone edible items. "Help yourself," he encourages, passing each of them their first beer. "Let's sit in the living room, watch some TV or listen to some music."

The four move to the front room, the guests taking in the ancient rundown furniture, the thread-bare rug, the sheet hanging over the front window standing in for a drape, the TV and stereo sitting side-by-side on the floor. Though the furniture is old, the place is spotless, no dishes or glasses sitting on the coffee table, no magazines or papers cluttering up the sitting area, everything is clean, immaculate. "Still working on decorating the place," Dylan explains as he sits in the ratty lounge chair.

Luke glances around and sits at the end of the three-seater couch. Nova sits down intimately beside him, legs touching, rubbing against him.

"Furniture might not be much, but you have a great stereo, TV combo, Dylan," Noah praises moving to inspect the equipment.

"Yeah, now that's important to me, not so much the furniture," Dylan laughs, chugging from his bottle of beer. "I have a bunch of streaming services – Prime, Netflix, Crave, almost everything you can think of. Take a look. We can watch a movie or listen to some music, whatever you want."

***

A couple of hours later, inebriated from the many beers consumed, Luke's eyes slowly flutter open. He squints from the light of the TV, his head fuzzy on where he is and what has happened. He slowly realizes that he is sprawled on a couch and that he is not alone. *It's Jess,* he thinks through the beer haze. He moves slightly and she moans, moving closer to him, drawing him in, reaching up to kiss his lips, moving her hand to his bulging crotch. He holds her, feeling her hand massage him, moaning at her touch. He moves his entire body into hers, groaning with pleasure as his hands move under her shirt, feeling the warmth of her silky breasts. "Jess," he whispers to the warm body as he begins to knead the soft skin, running his fingertips over her alert nipple as it stands up, begging for more.

Chapter 5
July 1
Alicia

"Tell me what else the call-out says," Alicia asks as Helen manoeuvres the SUV through the streets filled with people celebrating Canada's birthday.

"It's open on my iPad. Take a look," Helen replies, motioning with her shoulder toward the device sitting on the console between them. Alicia picks the computer up and reads the scanty particulars aloud. "A body was discovered about 30 minutes ago by a man out for a run with his dog. He thought it was a homeless person sleeping under a blanket near the Southshore Community Centre until his dog tugged on the blanket, exposing blood and hair. At that point, he pulled the dog back and called 911. Wonder how long she's been there?" Alicia asks, glancing up from the iPad. "All night?" Alicia reflects on the time spent last evening with Luke celebrating her new job. *He was there all night. Good. Even if it is his Jessica, no way he had anything to do with this.*

Helen continues to guide the SUV through the crowded streets of downtown Barrie, moving steadily to the lakefront park as she advises, "The coroner, Dr. Jules Diamond, has already been called and will be able to answer all of our questions, maybe not all of them today but hopefully within the next couple of weeks. Who was first on the scene?"

Alicia looks back to the iPad before answering, "Officers Edward Vincent and Davy Jones were passing the Centre when the call came in. They went to investigate and found the guy reporting the situation, the dog, and the body with a purse not far away."

Alicia pulls out her cell phone, opens Facebook, and types in 'Jessica Winters' in the search area. A list of forty-four different Jessica Winters appear. She goes back a step on Facebook and adds 'Barrie' under location and searches again. Ten potential friends appear. She closes her phone and shuts her eyes for a moment. *There's no way this could be Luke's Jessica. Ten Jessica Winters in*

Barrie – and that's just on Facebook. No way, and even if it is, they broke up months ago and he was with me last night.

The waterfront parks in Barrie ring the bay in a sideways horseshoe-shape with Heritage Park on the north side. Around the bottom of the U is the marina and children's playground in Centennial Beach. The last leg is Allandale Station Park featuring the Kiwanis Gazebo and showcasing the Southshore Community Centre, a large structure overlooking the bay, perfect for weddings and receptions. Alicia stares out the window of the police SUV as they pass the swimming area of Centennial Beach, the place where Luke is working as a lifeguard again this summer.

We had such a great evening last night, Luke, Jeff, and me. I brought home Chinese food and we celebrated the end of my patrol job and the start of my new position as a detective. It was like a hard stop to the end of the craziness of our lives after my accident, the divorce, and Luke's break-up with Jessica. And Jeff was there to help us celebrate and be part of our new reality. Luke was a bit quiet, but he's been that way since the break-up. Anyway, he's over her. He's been out a lot with his friends and even told me about a new girl that he's interested in. There is no way he had anything to do with this.

Alicia's phone makes a knocking noise indicating an incoming text. She opens the app on her phone, revealing a message from Jeff, 'The bad guys won't know what hit them. Have a great day!' She smiles, thinking of his support, his caring attitude, his strong, welcome presence in her life. She closes the note, thankful for a moment of distraction from the task at hand, hoping that she's not about to see her son's ex-girlfriend's body.

Helen puts on the car's turn signal, slowing down before pulling into the Community Centre's parking lot.

Chapter 6
April 8
Alicia

"Luke. Luke. I'm going out," Alicia yells from the front hall. She opens the front door and holds up her index finger, signaling for Jeff to wait another minute, as he sits in his car in the driveway. She steps back into the house. "Luke, do you hear me," Alicia asks, hoping for a reply.

When there is none forthcoming, she moves through the house and knocks on his bedroom door. "Luke are you okay?" she asks, slowly opening the door.

Her son is sitting at his desk, his computer and schoolbooks open in front of him, supposedly doing his homework, but he's scrolling through pictures on his laptop, pictures of Jessica, pictures of their time together. His earbuds are fixed in his ears and Alicia stands there for a moment listening to the muffled chorus of Burton Cummings' hit "Stand Tall" escaping from Luke's earpiece.

She shakes her head and moves into the room to touch his shoulder gently, knowing that he will jump with surprise as his mind wanders through the past. When he looks up, she signals for him to take out the earbuds and asks, "Are you okay?"

He slowly shakes his head, no, but verbally says, "I'm okay. Just doing some homework." They both look at the screen in front of him displaying a smiling selfie of him and Jessica, taken last summer on the dock of his dad's long-ago sold cottage.

"I'm on my way out for dinner with Jeff. Are you sure you're okay? We could order in instead of going out if you would like," she suggests.

"I'm okay, Mom. You have a good time with Jeff. Say hi for me," Luke instructs as he pushes the earbuds back in, dismissing his mother.

***

Alicia walks to the front door of the house, stops in the front hall, puts on her jacket, and picks up her purse. She opens the door, eyeing Jeff's black BMW Z4 convertible sitting in the driveway, smiles at his extravagant car knowing that it mirrors his personality perfectly – self-assured, carefree, easy-going, yet a qualified physiotherapist, one that helped save her life after the fatal car crash she was involved in at work. Months later, they ran into each other at a fundraiser for the Police Association and have been seeing each other since.

Jeff's deep brown eyes smile intimately as she jumps into his sports car and gives him a chaste kiss on the cheek.

"Do you really think it's warm enough to have the top down?" she asks buckling the seat belt.

"Sure. The sun's out, the temperature is ten degrees. It's a perfect evening for a topless ride," he laughs as he pulls the car out of the driveway.

Should have brought my frigging hat and worn my winter coat, she thinks pulling her jacket tighter around her neck, gathering her long dark hair in her hand, holding it as he pulls onto the main street.

"What's your pleasure tonight, my lady?" Jeff's smile is dazzling as the car speeds up and he shifts from third to fourth gear.

"You choose. I'm up for anything you want tonight," she smiles brilliantly, knowing that the food and their time together post-dinner will be gold star fantastic.

"Excellent. No need to rush the activities of the evening?" he asks slyly.

"We are good. No more studying tonight," Alicia confirms. "Not sure what Luke is up to, but when I left, he said he was doing homework, but really he was looking at pictures of him and Jessica, wandering down memory lane a bit."

Jeff laughs. "I think the homework stuff is a cover-up to get you out of the house. Probably a wild party planned. Girls, drinking, whoa, maybe we should join them later."

25

Alicia smiles. "I don't think so. He's been told no partying at the house if I'm not there, and he's still hurting from Jessica. I don't know what he's up to, but I think it will be a quiet night for him."

Chapter 7
April 8
Luke

Luke continues to scan the pictures of him and Jess. *How could she do this to me? We were good together. That piece-of-shit Ziggy is just going to hurt her. She'll come crawling back, I bet.*

Luke's phone shrills, and he moves his attention from his reminisces to the call display. "Hey Noah, what's happening?" he asks as he picks up the phone.

"Not much, bro. What are you up to?" Luke hears muffled sounds in the background, like Noah is covering the handset while someone talks to him. "Hold on a sec," he says as the distant conversation continues. Finally, he comes back, "Sorry about that, bro. Nova is being a bitch." Luke can hear her exasperated voice continuing to protest something in the background. "So, what's happening?" he asks again.

"I have no plans for the night. My mom has just left."

"She still seeing that therapist guy? He's kinda young for her, isn't he?"

"I think both my parents are going through some kind of midlife crisis. She's got Jeff and my dad is with a fucking hooker, 20 years younger than him."

"Well at least they are both getting some good action," Noah declares. "Unlike you and me." Again, Luke can hear a fracas in the background, ending when Noah simply yells, "No."

"What is going on there?" Luke asks.

"Bitch wants to go out with us tonight. I'm telling her no way. It's just the guys."

"I'm good with that. What did you have in mind?"

"How about your place? A couple of us could come over and play some video games or watch a movie or something."

"No way. I've been given strict instructions. No parties, especially after the last time. Next idea," he replies, smiling, remembering the small intimate party – Luke with Jessica in his room and Noah and his girlfriend, Willow, in the family room – until his mom came home unexpectedly.

"How about Dylan's? I'll grab some beer and bring my new PlayStation and we can play some games, or we can watch some TV, a movie or something. Do you want to go over and see if he's good with it?"

Luke thinks for a moment, pauses, wondering if they are starting to take advantage of their new-found friend, but decides *he can always say no if he doesn't want us there. And he's always alone anyway.* "Give me ten minutes and I'll get back to you," Luke says, hanging up the phone before he leaves the house and walking next door.

***

Four hours later, Luke staggers home from the impromptu party at Dylan's. *Now that was a fun time. Lots of music, plenty of competition with the video games, lots of beer, what more could anyone ask for. I begged off a bit early, the guys are all still there, but I wanted to get home before Mom. I want her to think that I've been home all night, that I've been good, no crazy partying, definitely no drinking, keeping it clean and easy.*

He chuckles to himself as he walks into the house and makes his way to his bedroom.

***

Alicia waves to Jeff from the front porch as he backs his car down the driveway. She looks at her watch quickly – 2am.

She unlocks the front door, walks through the house, and quietly opens Luke's bedroom door. The room is dark, and only the top of her son's sandy brown hair is above the blankets. She smiles, closing his bedroom door and shuffles to her own room at the back of the house, discarding her clothes carelessly on the floor, making her way to her bed, pulling the blankets around her naked body. She smiles remembering Jeff's lips kissing her neck, licking her nipples, making their way down her body. Alicia falls asleep with a smile on her face.

Chapter 8
April 15
Luke

Luke lounges on the couch in the living room, watching TV, bored. He keeps changing the channels searching for something to capture his attention, but there's nothing on the tube. His mom is working on this holiday afternoon, Good Friday, while most businesses and schools are closed for the day.

The rumbling of a car bleeds into Luke's consciousness. He gets up from the sofa and looks out the front window into the bright sun in time to see Noah pulling his dilapidated car into the driveway. His sister, Nova, is in the front seat and there is someone in the back, who Luke cannot see. He watches as his friend has a couple of words with the passengers and opens the door to get out. He meets Noah at the front entry way, Luke holding the door wide open.

"Hey, what are you up to? Who's with you?" Luke asks, leaning down to see the passenger in the backseat of the car.

"Nova and Tater Tot. I couldn't get out of the house without her, and I didn't want to leave without Tater. We need him as our DD. I had to talk him into it. Promised him the use of my car without any questions for a month."

"Not sure it's politically correct to call your brother Tate, Tater Tot," Luke laughs.

"Hey, Tater is not the sharpest knife in the drawer, but he's harmless and he doesn't mind the name. We've called him Tater Tot forever, since we were kids," Noah expounds, leaving out details of a conversation he recently overheard between his parents about his brother's recent diagnosis of antisocial personality disorder. His parents were discussing how this new diagnosis seemed to fit Tater - his aggression, the absence of guilt for his actions, his lack of empathy for others and the inability to understand that sometimes his behaviours and logic were not normal, and that they bordered on illegal and immoral. This new analysis topped off his already established anxiety problem which makes social settings difficult,

30

evidenced in his inability to have normal conversations with people without stumbling and stammering over his words and thoughts. "I thought we could go to the Beach. Wasaga Beach. It's a beautiful, warm day and I hear that there's a party going down at the Beachfront Motel."

"It's Easter, Noah. Why would anyone be having a party this early in the season? And how did you hear about it?" Luke asks, leaning against the door jamb.

Noah laughs, "Social media, of course. Where else would you hear about a party? Are you in?"

"I don't know. Why do we need a DD when we don't have anything to drink? What's the point?"

"O ye of little faith. I've already talked to a friend of a friend up there who has 24 waiting for us. It's on ice and everything. Come on, don't leave me with those two," he smiles, a pleading tone in his voice as he turns to look at his siblings in his car.

"What time are we coming back? My mom will be pissed if I'm out to all hours. And you're telling me Tate won't drink?"

"Nope. He's on meds and will get deathly ill if he does. He is a pain-in-the-ass, might follow us around a little too close, might ogle the girls too much, but we can be sure that he won't have a drink."

Luke pauses, weighing the options of sitting at home alone, bored stiff, with nothing to do, nothing to watch on TV or going out and having some fun with his best friend.

"Come on. No contest. Come with us," Noah pleads.

"Give me ten minutes. I need to have a shower, text my mom to cover my ass and then I'm in. Why don't you go over and see if Dylan wants to join us?"

***

The parking lot of the L-shaped motel is packed with vehicles and people wandering from room to room while others drift away from the motel toward the beach. Luke and Noah enjoy the crowd, the music, the girls, and the beer which they consume quickly. A number of the

31

partygoers have set up open bars in their rooms. The two stagger from party to party, talking with people along the way with little attention to time. A girl named Cheyenne attaches herself to Luke, following him from one room of merrymaking to the next, clinging to him, dancing with him, caressing him, throwing herself at him. Nova has been following the couple, watching closely as the girl makes a fool of herself with Luke, all the time wishing it was her that he was holding, whispering to, leaning into, rubbing his hand up her back, kissing her lips. Tears come to her eyes as she watches him make a fool of himself while blind to her love.

Chapter 9
April 15
Tate

Tate spends a lot of the time quietly watching his brother and Luke move from room to room, talking, laughing, meeting new people. *If only I was more like my brother or his friend, Luke. Not a care in the world. No inhibitions, no fear. Why can't I be more like that? Just look at them chatting up the girls, laughing, talking, not giving it a second thought.* Tate studies his hands, shaking at the very thought of approaching one of the girls or even one of the guys that he doesn't know. *Fucking anxiety makes me shy and awkward, unsure of myself, nervous all the time, unless I practice my lines and stick to the script. The meds aren't helping either. Why the hell am I the one afflicted with this? Why not Noah? Why couldn't I have at least some of his natural charisma, his uncaring attitude? No, I'm the ineffective, boring big brother, used so he can get drunk and pick up trashy girls. Why can't I have one too? Just one would be nice.*

He approaches one of the girls that has been ignored by his brother and Luke, hoping that his physical resemblance to Noah might be his way in. He smiles brilliantly at her, trying to look friendly and handsome, while still respectable, but he is unable to say anything. It's like his throat has closed up and he stands powerless to follow through on any greeting, any type of conversation. She glances at him, smiles, waits a moment for something to come from his lips. When nothing comes out, the girl turns away from him following another crowd of people going to enjoy some music coming from the next room.

His nerves are stressed to the max, and he begins to tremble all over as he concludes that he will not be able to make any new friends or meet a girl, or even enjoy the craziness at this party. He turns and leaves the room, departs the motel to walk to the beach, his angular, long-limbed body moving in the cool air. He moves up the beach to town, drawn by the sound of guitar music, finds a small gathering of teenagers sitting on the beach and sits down quietly in the sand, watching the group, smiling when people look his way, being quiet, non-obtrusive, breathing deeply to reign in his nerves which are starting to chime again. After many songs, the impromptu band breaks up and Tate wanders back to the party, deciding that it is time to go home, he's had enough loneliness, enough of being ignored. He corrals Luke, Noah, and Nova, telling them it's time to leave.

Just as they are about to get into the car, Nova announces, "I have to pee. Wait a sec," she says before running back into the last room they had been partying in.

She sidles up to Cheyenne, the girl that had attached herself to Luke, and leans into her face. "Listen, bitch. He's mine and you can't have him."

Cheyenne pushes back and begins to protest but Nova pushes in closer, shoving Cheyenne into the wall. "Do you hear me?" she demands, forcing her weight into the slight girl.

"Get off me," Cheyenne heaves back.

"One more time girlie. He's mine and you will not have any contact with him." Nova leans into Cheyenne, moving her arm against her rival's neck, limiting Cheyenne's air intake, until she starts to gasp for breath. "I have a bit of experience fighting with two brothers." Nova pauses, watching as her opponent struggles to get air. "I saw you two exchanging phone numbers. So, if he calls, what will you do?" Nova asks aggressively, sneering, spitting each word.

Cheyenne wheezes, trying to get some air into her lungs. Through clenched teeth, she whispers, "I'll tell him I'm not interested. I'll tell him he already has a girlfriend."

Nova stops for a minute to consider her answer. "No, you will not answer the phone. Don't talk to him. Don't text him. Just drop off the face of the earth. Got it?"

"Got it," Cheyenne puffs. "He's all yours."

Nova abruptly pulls away, taking in Cheyenne. After a full inspection of the girl that she thought could come between her and Luke, she leans back in for her final warning, "If I hear different, if I hear you've talked to him, told him about this little conversation, I'll be back."

34

"I won't. I won't talk to him. I promise," Cheyenne vows, rubbing her neck where Nova's arm had been pushing against her larynx.

Nova turns swiftly, leaving the room. She runs to the car and jumps in the back seat with Luke.

Dylan has been standing in the shadows watching, listening as Nova threatened the girl with the wavy brown hair, the piercing brown eyes. The girl now stands silently, watching as Nova makes her getaway. Dylan sidles over to her putting his arm around her waist. "Are you okay?" he asks, his voice dripping with sympathy and understanding.

Chapter 10
April 15
Alicia

Alicia is pacing the floor, wondering where Luke is. He sent her a text that he was going out with Noah but didn't give her any details. *Why isn't he answering my texts, my calls? Is something wrong? Has he been hurt? Stupid kid! No wonder my hair is going grey already.* She paces through the house, making another lap before hearing a car roar down the street. Alicia moves back to the front window as the car pulls into her driveway.

Alicia can't make out the driver but can clearly see Noah sitting in the passenger seat. *Who the hell is driving?* The rear passenger door opens, and her son staggers out, laughing as he slams the door closed. He wobbles to the front door and turns to wave as the car leaves the driveway. The streetlights expose the driver – *it's Tate, Noah's older brother.*

Alicia pulls the drapes closed as Luke opens the front door. *Drunk. What is he thinking*, she fumes as Luke staggers in.

"What do you think you're doing?" Alicia says sternly.

"What?" he asks innocently, stopping in his tracks hearing his mother's fury.

"Texting me was great, the best idea that you've had all day apparently, but not replying to my texts, not answering your phone. What were you thinking?" she asks, holding her hand up to stop his useless excuses. "Sending a text with no reply is not asking permission."

"Awe, come on Mom. We were just at Wasaga Beach. Tater Tot drove home."

"Does Tate even have a license?"

"Yes, he has a license and before you ask, a full license, doesn't need anyone in the car with him. He borrows Noah's car all the time."

36

"Well, that at least, was smart. But you were drinking. And don't deny it. I can smell it on you, and you can't even stand up straight. Go. Go to bed now before I say something I can't take back."

Luke turns and wobbles down the hall to his bedroom mumbling something under his breath that Alicia doesn't catch.

Chapter 11
April 16
Luke

Luke stumbles out of his bedroom into a quiet house, staggering to the bathroom, leaning into the counter to help keep himself upright. His head is pounding, feels like it is going to split into pieces as he opens the bathroom medicine cabinet looking for the Tylenol. He pulls the bottle from the shelf, drops it in the sink, cringing at the hollow noise that it makes before he can grab it. After several attempts, he opens the bottle and throws two of the pills into his mouth, dry swallowing them. *My head is killing me. Maybe the meds will work faster with no water to dilute them.*

He stands for a moment at the bathroom door, taking in the silence. He tiptoes to the kitchen where he can see his mother sitting at the dining room table, laptop open in front of her, a notebook beside it. His mom is studying for the police exam, wanting to work her way up at the precinct, to take the detective position which was opened up when his father left the force.

Alicia looks up as her son enters the room. She closes the laptop and crosses her arms. "So, you decided to get up," she says loudly.

Luke holds his head, hoping that it won't fall off, knowing that this will be a loud, difficult conversation with his mother.

"Luke, you need to stop this. You need to stop this now or you are going to ruin your entire future," she begins.

Luke puts his hand up in a stop gesture, grimacing as he sits down across the table from her. "Can you talk a bit quieter?" he whispers.

"It's my freaking house and if I want to yell, I will," she counters, raising her voice to a thunderous boom, watching as Luke moves both his hands to hold his head up. "I can't believe you are so stupid. What happened to you? Did Jessica take your brain too?"

"I'm trying Mom. I'm really trying," he declares.

"Not from where I'm sitting, you're not. You could get caught, get charged, it would go on your record and that will be the end of your police career. Is that what you want? To ruin your entire life for a girl who obviously has no sense at all."

"I'm sorry, Mom. I'm sorry."

"I don't believe you. You're sorry you got caught. You're sorry that Jessica dumped you. You're sorry that I'm being such a controlling bitch, but you aren't sorry that you went out with your friends and drank."

Luke looks down at the table examining the grain of the oak top, tracing the lines with his finger, not sure what else to say to mitigate the fight, to pacify his mother.

Alicia continues. "You are grounded. Give me your phone!"

"My phone?" he whispers, moving his eyes to his mother's face.

"Yes, your phone. It's gone for a month. You're grounded for a month."

"Aw come on Mom. It was just once. It won't happen again," he tries to bargain.

"How stupid do you think I am? Only once? Think I don't know about the other times? Give me your phone. Now!"

Luke continues to look at the table, not acknowledging the question or the request.

"Luke, I'm talking to you. Look at me," Alicia demands loudly.

"I'm sorry," he mumbles.

They sit in silence as Alicia watches her son studying the tabletop intently. The minute hand on the clock sitting on the mantel in the living room clicks several times, the silence between them stretching out. "I'm at my wits end with you," Alicia finally says, disappointment colouring her voice, her face, her expression. "Give me your phone!"

Chapter 12
July 1
Alicia

Helen pulls the police SUV into the parking lot of the Southshore Community Centre and eyes the steady stream of people who were out for their morning walks or on their way to the Canada Day celebrations downtown but are now hustling toward the lakeside of the building to investigate the commotion. "Shit. God damn looky-loos! Thank God, Officers Vincent and Jones are on the scene. I hope to hell they were able to cordon off the area before these people had the chance to tromp on our evidence," Helen finishes angrily, shoving the vehicle door closed before sprinting past the inquisitive public.

Alicia follows Helen closely, afraid of what she's about to see. *It can't be Jessica. It just can't be Luke's Jessica. It will kill him. He's tried to move on, but really, I don't think that's happened*, she thinks moving through the parking lot to the side of the Community Centre.

Alicia can hear the commands of Officer Jones telling the spectators to move back, to give them room to work. She rounds the building and sees the bright yellow police tape positioned around the back side of the entire building all the way down to the water. The back of the building is two levels high; the lower with a walk out from two large garage doors with windows centred between them housing canoes and kayaks for the local club; the upper floor is the ballroom, flooded with floor-to-ceiling windows to give partygoers an unobstructed view of the bay. Near the water's edge, there is a bundle of debris, looks like blankets tossed into a heap, ready to be thrown in the garbage, until you look closely at it and see the long golden-brown hair escaping its confines.

Alicia's steps slow to a shuffle, like a centenarian's trundle. *No, it can't be. There's a lot of people with the same colour hair, same length of hair.*

Helen turns, noticing Alicia's faltering, slower pace and asks, "Are you okay?"

Alicia can't find any words but nods in the positive. *I'm fine. I have to be fine. Even if this is Jessica, I will be fine. I'm a cop. I can do this.*

Helen mistakes Alicia's hesitancy thinking it is because of the distinct odour of the body beginning to rot in the warm summer heat. She reaches into her jacket pocket and pulls out a jar of Vick's VapoRub. "Here put a bit of this under your nose. She hasn't been here too long so it's not too bad yet. Is this your first?"

Alicia nods numbly again, taking the jar from her partner's outstretched hand, still unable to speak. Alicia stands up to her full height, taking in the body three meters away. *Steady yourself, Alicia. You can do this. This is the job that you always wanted.* She opens the small jar, places two fingers in the smelly gunk and smears it under her nose as she looks around at the scene watching the people standing outside of the ribboned area. She catches the eye of Officer Vincent and nods. Alicia's vision shifts back to the blanket lying on the grass near the water's edge. She moves forward to stand beside Helen, who hands her a pair of latex gloves, as she pulls on a pair herself. Alicia mirrors her partners' actions and pulls the skin-tight safeguards into place.

"Has the scene been secured?" Helen asks Officer Vincent, who is standing outside the police barrier, near the blanket heap.

"Yes. Officer Jones and I got here within four minutes of the initial call. That's Mr. Owens over there," he turns his head, gesturing to a lone man sitting on a park bench near the waterfront about 30 meters away, patting his chocolate Labrador, talking to him as dog owners do, watching the spectacle unfold. "Says they walked across the front of the building on their first pass, but on the way back, the dog was unleashed and came over to what Mr. Owens thought was a sleeping homeless person. The dog barked a couple of times and wouldn't come when he was called back. The dog actually pulled off a piece of the blanket and exposed the deceased. Mr. Owens came over to get his dog and saw the body and called it in."

"The coroner is on the way," Helen states.

"Yes, Dr. Diamond," Officer Vincent agrees. "Also, Dispatch has called in Sanjay Ramesh as your Identification Officer and the

41

forensic team is on their way as well." He pauses for a moment before continuing, "Officer Jones and I were first on the scene. We put up the tape to keep folks away, to preserve the site until the coroner and forensics have a look. Officer Jones and I have taken control of the scene and will manage it, record who comes and goes, ensure everything is done by the book."

"Thanks, Officer Vincent. Appreciate it," Helen responds looking around at the growing crowds.

"I marked a couple of interesting items that I saw when I checked the body," he continues, gesturing to the yellow cardboard markers on the ground behind him.

"Talk to me. What did you find?"

"Number one is marking a couple of roaches; you know, marijuana butts. Not sure if they are pertinent to this scene but wanted to mark them just in case we can get some DNA off them. Numbers two to five surround a patch of sand that may have recently been disturbed. Thinking maybe the victim and the killer had a scuffle, a brawl or maybe the killer was trying to drag the victim into the water. Number six is beside the purse," he says, nodding at the far end of the area marked off, beside the grass knoll leading to the water's edge.

"Good work, Officer Vincent. Did you confirm death?"

"I did. I checked the pulse on her neck. Accidentally touched her cheek when I was moving the blanket and she is cold. Rigor mortis has set in, so she's been gone for a while." He pauses to take a gulp of fresh air, remembering the clammy, plastic-like feel of the victim's skin. "Officer Jones noticed the purse a short distance from the body and opened it with gloves on to see if there was any ID. Jessica Winters of Barrie. There is a couple of dollars in the wallet, which would rule out a robbery gone bad."

"Phone?" Helen asks.

"No. No phone, which is strange for someone her age." Officer Vincent pauses, waiting for additional questions from the two detectives, looking around as the crowd continues to grow. After a couple of moments of silence, he continues, "There's a narrow pathway to the body across the grass that Officer Jones and I used. The coroner will be able to use that path as well, so as not to contaminate the site before you get a chance to check for any evidence."

Helen, standing outside the area cordoned off, pulls out her phone to take pictures of the blanket, the barely visible top of the victim's head, the distance between the body and the building, the distance between the body and the water, the purse, the scuffle in the sand, the marijuana roaches. Alicia watches for a few moments and then also extricates her phone from her pocket and mirrors her partner's actions, hoping to capture something that may help with the case. She zooms in on the top of the body, the hair floating in the warm morning breeze, but is unable to decide if it is Luke's Jessica.

Both detectives stop their picture-taking activities as a voice calls out from the side of the building, "I'm coming, I'm coming." Dr. Diamond rounds the corner of the Southshore Community Centre, her long flowing silk knee-length jacket floating in the wind created by her expeditious entrance and directs the growing crowd to get out of her way as she closes in on the site, extending her hand to Helen. "Hello Detective Hodges. Sorry for my delay. I was hoping for a day off to spend with the kids but hey, guess that's not happening today."

Helen nods as she shakes the proffered hand. "Thanks for coming. I want to introduce you to Detective Alicia Anderson. She's new to the team, been with patrol for a long time and has now joined us."

Dr. Diamond turns her attention to Alicia, as she offers her hand. "Any relation to James Anderson?" she asks completing the handshake.

"Yes. My ex-husband," Alicia confirms.

"Too bad he left the job. He was a good detective. Hear he's opened his own private detective agency in town," Dr. Diamond says, distracted, looking passed Alicia to the reason for their early morning rendezvous. "Well, let's get started, why don't we. Let me just get in to take a look and to confirm death and then the scene is all yours. Just give me a few minutes and we should have some answers, but probably a lot more questions."

43

Chapter 13
Apr 18
James

James sits back on the chair in his new, sterile private detective's office, with nothing to do, no work to capture his attention. He's been off the police force for six months, after a long career starting as a patrol officer and ending as a senior detective. Near the end of his career, he was coerced into working with the Ruebens. His initiation was purely innocent, to make a few extra bucks, but it bubbled over the top as he was pulled in deeper and deeper. In the end, it all caught up to him when his wife found some pretty damning evidence that would have put him behind bars. He was lucky though; Alicia believes family always comes first and gave him a number of directives with the agreement that she would keep the information quiet. He has not lived up to all the ultimatums from his wife, except for the one to leave the police force, and hopes she never finds out the truth about her other demands.

Things are very calm, if not tedious, in his somewhat above-board new world. He's picked up a few minor cases; tracking down a wayward teenager who had left town with her inept boyfriend from the wrong side of the tracks. James ended up bringing her home, to her family's joy, but he wasn't sure how long she would stay under their thumb. His other major case was getting proof that a guy was cheating on his wife so she could get their pre-nuptial agreement nullified and split their assets in the divorce.

The quiet time between cases, between doing worthless grunt work for others, gives him time to think, to reminisce about his past, his journey to this cold, lonely office.

Alicia was a bit of a shrew but always kept me honest and on the right path when we were married. I was definitely tired of our marriage and strayed a couple of times, but when she went in the hospital after that fucking accident, I wasn't able to hold it together. Never mind the pressure from Don Saunders to help him, to help the

44

Ruebens. What was I supposed to do? I was weak, I took the easy way out, and look where it's gotten me, he moans to himself as he glances around the sterile, solitary space. *But hey, I got her off my back, got me free of her and that loveless relationship, though I had to give up a job I loved to stay out of jail, but I'm still alive, I'm still bringing in a few bucks; I have the hottest female in town as a girlfriend, though her courtesan work leaves a lot to be desired, but God she's hot. And understanding. And will do anything in the bedroom.*

The door leading into his storefront office opens, the bell above the door tinkling as an older man steps in. He is dressed in dark blue jeans, a denim jacket, a blue plaid shirt, a scarf around his neck, with gloves on his hands to keep away the cold, blustery day.

"Can I help you?" James asks, looking closely at the newcomer, taking in his curly, once dark hair, now grey-streaked, his sparkling intent blue eyes. *Do I know this guy? Looks familiar, but I can't place him. Must be about 65 or 70 years old but looks good for his age.*

The newcomer reaches out to shake James's hand, and James stands to accommodate. The stranger grabs the outstretched hand and uses his other appendage to pull James in close to his chest forcing their faces within centimeters of each other. "Junior, you don't recognize me? After all this time, you've forgotten your old man?"

James looks at the newcomer closer, sees the eyes, the aging face, the dark hair with shades of grey - sees what he's going to look like in 25 years. Suddenly his childhood flashes before his eyes, a violent father, the beatings that he inflicted on his wife, his sons, how it all ended with this old man killing his brother, Sean.

James shakes his hand free from the grasp, and stumbles back quickly. "What the fuck are you doing here?" he growls, taking another step back, holding his hand like it has been burnt in an open flame.

His father laughs, a low guttural sound. "I came to see you, my favourite son," he says, stepping forward, watching as James moves back another step away from him.

"Your only son, you mean. You killed the other one."

"Yeah, but that was an accident. A sad accident. But you were always my favourite," he smiles.

45

"I can't believe you're still walking this earth, old man. How did you find me?"

"I've always kept my eye on you, James. From your first job as a patrol officer in Toronto, to your marriage to your now ex-wife, to moving up here, and becoming a detective and now your work with the Ruebens. Always watched from a distance."

James huffs and is quiet for a moment digesting the idea that his father has been watching his life from a far. "Why are you back now? What do you want?"

"Well, I'm going to be in town for a while. Got me a job working with Axl Tunes. Gave me a great title – Director of Guns. I absolutely love the acronym - DOG. Pretty good, eh? It would look great on a business card, don't you think?" he laughs.

James breathes out slowly, doesn't reply.

His father continues, "Actually, I think we might be working together in the near future."

"No fucking way."

"Yeah. I think we will. Axl mentioned your name once or twice when we talked about our new endeavour." He pauses, watching horror cloud his son's face. "But what I really want from you is to meet my grandson, Luke."

"No. No way," James says, shaking his head adamantly.

"What story did you tell him about me? Does he think I'm dead? We'll have to reinvent whatever you've told him. I want to see my grandson."

James is flabbergasted by this man who calls himself his father, who thinks he can just show up after years away, who thinks he can be part of his life after everything that he did to him, his mother, his brother. "You remember there isn't a statute of limitations on murder. One call and you're done, old man."

His father laughs. "Still all talk, I see Jimmy. I would be careful before you start accusing me of murder. Have you looked in the mirror lately, son? Seems the apple doesn't fall far from the tree."

James steps back again, his butt resting against his wooden desk. *The son of a bitch knows something. Not sure what, but something that he thinks he can hold over my head. This is about him. It's always* been about him, no one else. *He'll use whatever he can to get what he wants.*

James stands, mouth firmly clenched shut. The old man chuckles, "I want to meet my grandson. Find a way. I'll be in touch." He turns quickly, steps to the door, opens it, and leaves the quiet tomb.

James moves back behind his desk, drops into the chair heavily. "No way. You will not get your hands on my son. You piece of shit," he mumbles to the empty room.

James's thoughts drift back to the last time he saw his dad. *Sean was only 12 years old. I was eight. We were playing with the brand-new Atari 2600 that Santa brought us. Shit, I still even believed in Santa Claus back then. It had taken us hours to attach the box to the TV and finally we were able to play that new game, Pong. We had finished dinner and mom was doing dishes in the kitchen, a plate for dad, who wasn't home yet from work, was in the oven. Suddenly, the front door of the house flew open, and dad came in like a hurricane, drunk, yelling, moving into the kitchen, pushing mom around, yelling at her. Where's dinner? Why didn't you wait for me? Why don't you get dressed up when I come home from a hard day? Put on something sexy, something that I'd want to come home to. Mom always tried to protect us and told us, "Go to your room." I got up to leave, but Sean just sat there. He watched dad, tears forming in his eyes. I begged him to come with me. I pulled on his arm to get him out of the living room, to come and hide in our bedroom like we'd done many times before, but he just sat there flexing his hands, making fists. Mom is crying, dad is yelling. Sean got up. I yelled, "No." Sean walked into the kitchen and yelled at dad. "Stop. Stop hitting her." Dad turned, tells him to go to his room. Sean said, "No. Stop picking on mom. Pick on someone your own size." "Are you my size?" their father asked. Sean stood there, rooted in fear, didn't move, remained between mom and dad. Mom tried to move in front of him, begged him to leave. "It will be okay. Your Dad and I are just going to talk," but Sean didn't give an inch. Dad clenched his fist, swung hard, used his hips to generate force, moved into Sean, punched him on the side of his face, between his hairline and eyebrow, beside his eyes – the place that a cop would know will knock out your opponent instantly. Sean went down like a*

47

sack of potatoes. Mom reached out to grab him, tried to hold him, but she couldn't get her arms around him before he fell, hitting his head on the kitchen counter. He was probably dead before he hit the floor.

James's thoughts slowly come back to the present day, sitting in his barren office. He looks around, checking to make sure his father has left the building. *I can't believe that piece of shit is still alive, and he wants to be part of Luke's life. Says he's going to be working with Axl. Says we're going to be working together. No fucking way!* James pounds his hand on the desk.

Chapter 14
April 18
Luke

Luke walks slowly home from school, his mind buzzing with thoughts of his day. *Ziggy is an asshole. And Jess. God damn Jess. Holding hands with him, kissing him in the halls between classes, and then smiling at me as she sashayed into our shared history class, sitting in the back row beside me, and her quiet, sexy, "Hello Luke," as she opened her books.*

He hears the roar of an engine behind him and turns to see Dylan's car fly by. Luke picks up his speed, rushing into his friend's driveway. "Hey, sorry I've been MIA and haven't been able to help you with the car, but she sounds great," he blurts out as he comes up to the driver's door.

Dylan, smiling from ear to ear, opens the car door, a grin of satisfaction on his face. "She sounds great, doesn't she?"

"She does. Is all the work done?"

"Close. She's almost ready for the Automotive Flea Market. She's sure to win the top prize this year," he brags as he walks around the vehicle. As he rounds the trunk of the car, he looks up and asks, "What have you been up to man? Haven't seen you around for a week or so."

Luke tells him about the party he missed in Wasaga Beach with Noah, meeting Cheyenne, his hope that she'd call him, though he can't check his phone as his mother has confiscated it as punishment for the whole drinking thing, that Jess is with that son of a bitch Ziggy, suggests next time they go on a road trip to party that he should come with them, maybe they could go up to the beach and Cheyenne could introduce him to one of her friends.

Dylan smiles as the youngster updates him, not letting on that he was in fact at the party, had watched Luke with Cheyenne and had introduced himself after Nova's threats. A vision of Cheyenne's

49

sensual body passes through his mind, her form makes him hot just thinking about it.

As Luke continues with details of his adventures, they hear a car pulling into Luke's driveway next door. Alicia looks up as she steps out of the car, eyeing Luke in Dylan's driveway. "What are you doing? Grounded means grounded," Alicia growls at him as she closes the car door and marches to the house.

"I gotta go, Dylan," Luke says as he turns to walk away. Dylan gets back into his car, hits the button to open the garage door, and pulls his car in, closing the door behind him.

"Damn girlfriends. Damn mothers. So glad I don't have to put up with anyone's shit, anyone's rules but my own," Dylan says under his breath as he gets out of the car, inspecting it closely. He pulls a shammy out of his back pocket, rubs it on the car's hood to remove a speck of dirt.

***

"What were you doing over there?" Alicia asks as she throws her computer bag on the hall table, turning around, waiting for her son's reply, hands on her hips, lips squeezed together, anger radiating from her body.

"I was only over there for a couple of minutes. Just wanted to see all the work he's done on the car. I was on my way home," Luke explains.

"Again, grounded means grounded. No going out. Coming straight home from school." Alicia berates.

"I was only there for a couple of minutes, Mom. I swear."

"You start your homework. I'll start dinner and we'll do the dishes together," Alicia concludes, turning away and walking into the kitchen.

Luke follows her. "Can I at least have my phone back? I've been good, done everything that you've said," he argues.

"I don't think so, Luke."

50

"Can I at least look at my phone? See if I've had any calls or texts?"

Alicia sees her son's pleading expression and melts. She moves to her purse and pulls out his phone, handing it to him. Luke quickly grabs it and types in his password, opening the text message icon. A text from Noah, a bunch from Nova but nothing from Cheyenne. He closes it and opens the phone icon. Again, a bunch of calls from Nova, but nothing from Cheyenne. He hands the phone back to his mother, confused, wondering why Cheyenne hasn't called him.

Chapter 15
July 1
Alicia

"Let's go and talk to the guy that called this in," Helen says as she moves toward Mr. Owens and his dog, sitting on the bench at the water's edge.

Alicia falls in step beside Helen as they cross the sidewalk to the slight, short man sitting quietly in his running shorts and sweaty T-shirt. His dog sits beside him, watching the crowd intently, his tail wagging in anticipation of the possible attention he may receive as they walk toward him. "What happens once the coroner confirms death? We have to wait for Sanjay, the Identification Officer, right?" Alicia asks.

"Sanjay is usually pretty prompt, lives not too far from here – that's if he's home and not out celebrating Canada Day. His responsibility is the body, bagging the hands to protect any possible evidence, taking fingerprints, checking for DNA on her body, on her clothes, the blanket, as well as photographing everything so we have evidence for the court case, once we have a suspect. Once Sanjay is comfortable that he has everything from the body, the deceased will be moved, and Dr. Diamond will complete an autopsy to confirm cause of death and timing. We'll work the site with Connor Brooks' forensic team, scouring the area to find, bag and tag any possible evidence, document everything. Might take a day or two, but we need to be as thorough as possible to find the scumbag that did this to her."

"Gotcha," Alicia replies.

Helen extends her hand to Mr. Owens, as he rises from the bench. "Hello, Mr. Owens. Thank you for calling this in and staying so we can ask you a few questions. I am Detective Helen Hodges, and this is my partner, Detective Alicia Anderson."

"Not a problem, though I am late for work," he says, shaking both their hands in greeting. "I hope this won't take too much longer," he continues as he checks his wristwatch. His dog also stands up from his sitting position, tail wagging, anxious to get one of those outstretched hands to reach out to him and give him a pat. Alicia looks down as she drops her hand. "Is he friendly? Can I pat him?" she asks.

"Sure. Huxley is very, very friendly. Just be careful. He's also a big kisser if you let him," he advises.

Alicia kneels down and the dog moves into her body, tail thumping against her leg, his tongue ready to lick her face as her hand caresses his head. "Good dog, good dog," she murmurs, taken in by the dark brown eyes of the Labrador. She looks up to see Helen and Mr. Owens watching her. She stands unsteadily, leaving her hand on the dog's head, stroking his hair to help calm both her and the dog.

"Work? You're working today?" Helen asks.

"Yeah, I have to put in a couple of hours in meetings, conference calls, stuff I couldn't move out. My company's head office is in Europe, and they don't seem to care if it's Canada Day over here," he answers indignantly.

"Can you walk us through what happened this morning, Mr. Owens?"

"I told the dispatcher everything."

"And we did review the information on our way here, but we would like you to tell us again, in case there is anything else that you may have thought of as you waited for us." Helen smiles and includes, "Please."

Mr. Owens repeats the details he gave the 911 operator, adding a few new particulars. He and Huxley left home at 6am and walked through the parking lot before getting onto the paved path near the bay on their way through the waterfront parks. He was on the phone with an early morning business call, which he didn't finish until they were passed the building and the gazebo, already into Centennial Beach. At that point, he let the dog off his leash, and they started their exercise, running together, as they do every morning, through the park on the boardwalk to the adjacent marina, into the bordering Heritage Park and back again. They were on the concrete path on their return when Huxley discovered the yellow blanket between the Community Centre and the water's edge. The dog refused to come when called away from what he thought was a homeless person sleeping or just a pile of garbage. As he approached Huxley to leash him, the dog grabbed some of the light-yellow material, pulled it and uncovered the top of a head revealing hair with red streaks, blood, he assumed. He yelled at the dog to stop, pulling him away and tying him up before calling 911.

"Did you see anyone around the building, or the water before you started your run?"

Mr. Owens thinks for a moment, "No, no one that I recall. I was distracted on the phone, but I don't think so."

"Where do you live, Mr. Owens? How do you get to the park? Do you always run in the park?"

Mr. Owens gives his address, a couple of blocks away and confirms that he typically walks to the park with Huxley for their morning run together most every day.

"Do you remember any vehicles in the parking lot when you passed by the Community Centre the first time?"

Again, Mr. Owens contemplates for a moment before replying, "No, I don't think so but it's hard to remember. I was on the phone and involved in a conversation. There were a few cars when we came back though. I did notice them as we approached, you can see them from the gazebo area before the path dips down to the water's edge. A lot of people drive down, park and then go walking or running by the lake. And there are a lot more people today with it being a national holiday and everything."

"Have you ever seen anyone hanging around in this area before or after one of your runs?"

"No, it's usually pretty quiet this time of the day, however, if you come down at night, there's usually a bunch of kids that hang out in the gazebo. As far as I've seen, they just sit around, talk, smoke, play their guitars or listen to music. Nothing too disturbing, nothing unusual."

"Ever see anyone sleeping around here? Maybe on the picnic table or up against the building?"

"Not around here. I have seen them over in Heritage Park," he turns and points across the bay. "Closer to downtown, more of a homeless population there, I think. This side of the bay is pretty quiet, closer to the residential area," he finishes, turning back to the detectives.

"Thanks for your help, Mr. Owens, Huxley," Helen says, looking down at the dog. "Can I get your contact information in case we have any more questions?"

"Sure, no problem," Mr. Owens confirms, giving Helen the information. Just as she finishes recording the specifics, they hear a call from over their shoulders and see Dr. Diamond motioning for their return to the scene.

"Again, thank you for your help today. We will be in touch," Helen says as she starts to climb back up the sloping grass. Alicia gives Huxley a final pat and follows her mentor closely.

"What did you find?" Helen asks as the two detectives stop a meter in front of the yellow police line in front of Dr. Diamond.

"I can confirm that the victim is dead, probably from blunt force trauma. Something heavy, large hit her head a number of times. The weapon also broke her shoulder, her arm and a couple of fingers. She probably put her arm up to protect herself, ward off the blows. Her arm and hands show signs of scrapes, cuts from the weapon, probably trying to defend herself. I believe the weapon is a branch or log, as she has slivers of bark and remnants of leaves and sap on her arms and hands." Dr. Diamond pauses to catch her breath, looking out at the calm, blue waters of the bay. "As the first officers on the scene have already advised, there was a purse found not too far from the body. The ID in the purse seems to match the body, says her name is Jessica Winters of Barrie. She's 16 years old."

Alicia has been battling her internal demons, her stomach contents swirling as soon as they got the call, amplified with her first glimpse of the body, continuing to escalate at the possibility that this is a child she may know. With confirmation that this is Jessica, Luke's Jessica, Alicia turns quickly, runs toward the lake, bends over from the waist, falls to one knee at the water's edge and throws up violently.

The coroner and Helen turn to watch her. "Is she okay?" Dr. Diamond asks.

Helen grimaces as Alicia kneels beside the water, her breakfast spewing from her mouth. "This is her first dead body, her first day as a detective. Just give her a minute and then we can continue."

They stand, watching as Alicia slowly gets to her feet, hands on her knees to steady herself, wiping her mouth with the back of her hand and staggering back into the huddle. "Sorry about that," she says, wiping her hand across her mouth again. "Can you repeat that about the murder weapon?"

"I think it's a branch, a big branch from the looks of the damage to the skull and the victim's defensive marks. I'll be able to be more specific after the autopsy but those are my first thoughts."

"I think it's over there," she points to a large limb at the edge of the water, near where she lost her breakfast and her dignity.

Chapter 16
April 25

The young man walks the beach, smiling at people as they pass him, blending into the scenery, not bringing any direct attention to himself. He wants to find Cheyenne, that girl he saw at the Easter Weekend party, the one with the wavy brown hair, the piercing brown eyes, freckles dotting her flawless pale skin. He reminisces about her smile – her fat pouty lips parted slightly, curving up in the corners, and her young, firm body that she was hiding under her T-shirt and jeans.

Wonder where she is? School is out today; thought she might be down here hanging out. Maybe she doesn't even go to school. Maybe she works. I didn't get a chance to ask her about herself, her life.

He continues to wander, moving closer to town, noticing the traffic on the beach increasing, more people walking, more kids huddled together, talking, laughing. *Oh well, one more pass of the beach, then I'll go home. Maybe it wasn't meant to be.*

Without warning, he hears her smooth, deep chuckle. He turns and looks closer at the group of people he has just passed and spots her sitting at the edge of the crowd on the sand, talking with another girl. He stops, unsure of what to do. *Go over and talk to her? Just join the group and slowly move around to her?* As he debates with himself, Cheyenne glances up and recognition crosses her face, and she smiles at him. His lips part and he grins in her direction. She nods and waves him over.

He moves tentatively around the group of people and stands behind Cheyenne, smiling down at her and her friend. "Hello Cheyenne," he says quietly.

"Hey, how are you? I didn't expect to see you here," Cheyenne replies. "This is my friend Cindy," she continues nodding to the girl beside her, not offering his name. He smiles at her friend, nodding while wishing that she would leave them alone so he could sit and talk to Cheyenne. *She remembers me, but I don't think she remembers my name as she didn't tell her friend. Or maybe I'm not important enough to have a name. Maybe she doesn't want to have anything to do with me. Just a nameless soul that she couldn't ignore on the beach because of her friendly disposition.*

He pauses, trying to reign in his insecurities, breathes in, breathes out, and is finally able to say, "Hello Cindy."

"Hey," she says, acknowledging his presence, without glancing at him. "Listen Che, I need to go. My shift starts in less than 30 minutes and I'm going to have to beat it to get there on time. I'll talk to you tomorrow." Cindy quickly gets up and starts jogging down the beach to the main street.

"Mind if I sit down?" he asks.

"No, have a seat. Are you here by yourself?" she enquires, looking around.

"Yup, just me. I am glad I ran into you," he lumbers through his words of greeting.

There is silence between the two as they listen to the activity of the people around them, the laughter, the jokes, the comradery. His tongue is tied, not sure what to say or how to have a conversation with this beautiful creature. Finally, he leans in and asks, "Do you want to go for a walk on the beach?"

She focuses in on him, her eyes big, bright, and immediately says, "Sure." They both get up and brush the sand off themselves and wander down the beach, away from the town centre.

Cheyenne is an outgoing, personable companion and babbles on about the weather, the water, having the day off from school, how lucky it was to run into him. She continues a stream of words which he hardly hears, just happy to bask in the presence of this girl, this beautiful girl, this girl who obviously likes him, enjoys his company, wants to be his friend.

Their stroll continues along the world's longest freshwater beach until Cheyenne stops her verbal discourse and proclaims, "Well, it was good to see you, but this is where I get off. I live just down this street," Cheyenne says, pointing to the rural laneway which ends at the beach.

"Please don't leave yet. How about we get some pizza? I think the Pizza Hut is just over that next sand dune. What do you say?" he asks expectantly.

Cheyenne looks him up and down. She really had no plans for the evening; her friend Cindy is working; her parents are in the city and her brother is home, but he won't even miss her. She decides quickly. "Sure, pizza would be great."

The two continue to move down the beach, passing between two large sand dunes, so large the sun is almost blocked out, and the world seems to go dark. Suddenly, he reaches for Cheyenne and draws her into his arms. She is surprised and starts to push back, her hands shoving his shoulders away, pleading with him to let her breathe, to let her go. Her voice begins to rise in volume as he ignores her pleas, kissing her neck, kissing her lips.

She wants me, I know she does. We spent the afternoon together. She agreed to go for dinner. Why is she fighting me now? I know, she's playing it coy. She wants me to work for it. Well, I will. I will have you now, my love.

He pushes her back on the sand, both of them falling, forcing his body on top of hers, making it impossible for her to move, jump up, run. He grabs the lower edge of her T-shirt, shoves it up to her neck, and touches her breast tentatively through her lace-trimmed bra. Cheyenne continues to mumble, "No, no, no," as he unbuttons her jeans, shoving them down her hips. She draws up all her strength as he is distracted with her jeans and kicks him violently between his legs. He moans loudly and moves his hands to cup his bruised manhood, giving her an opportunity to run. She scrambles on the sand, is almost away from him, when he grabs her ankle and pulls her back into his grasp. She falls back on the sand, her head hitting a large rock buried in the dune, knocking her unconscious. He smiles, knowing now that she will not fight him, that he will be able to take his time, enjoy himself before she wakes up.

Chapter 17

April 26
Alicia

Chad Harper manoeuvres the police cruiser through the busy downtown area, as Alicia sits beside him, watching the people on the street, while being mindful of possible criminal activities in progress.

Alicia's personal phone rings, an unusual occurrence while on shift. She frowns and pulls it out of her pocket, looking at the display screen. "I need to take this," she comments, hitting the phone icon. "Hello, Alicia Anderson speaking."

"Mrs. Anderson, this is Mr. Lennon, the principal at Luke's school."

Alicia's blood suddenly runs cold, and fear surrounds her. "Is everything okay?" she asks tentatively. Chad hears the fear in her voice and turns to look closely at his partner as he continues to drive carefully down the city street.

"Well, Luke is fine. Physically." Alicia lets out a breath that she didn't realize she was holding. "However, he has been in a fight with another student in the hall between classes."

"And the other student? Is he okay?"

"He's about the same as your son. Both got a little roughed up. Some bruises. Some scratches. A black eye. It could have been a lot worse, but it was broken up quickly by a couple of our teachers."

"Well, I'm glad to hear that it's not too serious."

"We have zero tolerance at this school for physical violence. We will not put up with anything like this. Both boys are being suspended for three days. You or his father need to come down, pick him up, advise us what kind of punishment you are going to enforce, let us know how he's going to continue with his class assignments during his absence and give us some guarantees that this will not happen again."

Alicia checks her watch. *It's only 1pm. I've got three more hours on my shift. What the hell, Luke!* She pauses for a moment, running the options through her mind.

60

"Are you still there, Mrs. Anderson?" the principal asks after a prolonged silence.

"Yes, yes, I'm still here. I'm in the middle of my shift and it's not easy for me to just leave. Just trying to decide when I can get there."

"If you don't mind me saying, maybe that's part of the problem. Luke may need more parental control than a single parent is able to give him, especially a police officer on different shifts."

"Are you kidding me, Mr. Lennon? I am certainly not the only mother that has to work. And I'm certainly not the only single parent. I can't believe you would even go there," Alicia fumes. "I'll be there within the hour," she concludes, clicking the end button on her phone.

***

Alicia sits on the stiff, wooden chair beside Luke, in the hall outside the principal's office, still in her police uniform, as Luke's adversary Ziggy, sits across the corridor, on a similar chair, waiting. Alicia tried to get the meeting over as soon as she got there but was told directly by Mr. Lennon's secretary that all interested parties needed to be in the room together. Alicia looks at her watch again. *I have better things to do with my time than sit here. Thirty minutes so far. I give them another ten minutes, then Luke and I are leaving. I don't give a shit about Mr. Lennon and his freaking rules. This chair is killing me.* She moves her butt, trying to get comfortable, but the old, non-ergonomic chair is unforgiving.

Luke nudges her and Alicia looks up to the arrival of a tall, thin man dressed in slim, body-hugging jeans, a bright Hawaiian shirt with the top three buttons open under a black leather-bomber jacket. He stops in front of Ziggy. "What the fuck, Ziggy," he says succinctly.

Ziggy doesn't answer but drops his head even lower onto his chest.

"Where the hell is this Mr. Lennon? I'm busy. I don't have time for this shit," the newcomer continues, looking around, turning to take in Alicia and Luke. "Ha. You're fighting with Luke?" His tone changes, softens as he nods to Alicia, offering his hand, acknowledging her.

61

"Alicia," he greets as she stands, accepting the extended hand to shake.

"Have we met before?" she asks, knowing who he is from work, from James's association with him, but knowing that they have never met directly.

"No, no we've never met, but I do know your husband," he pauses with a wicked smile spreading across his face. "And I know his girlfriend Camryn. Have you met her?" He doesn't wait for a reply but continues his taunts. "She's a great girl, part of my stable, if you know what I mean." He winks.

Thankfully, Mr. Lennon's door opens, and he walks out of his office into the vestibule. "Mr. Tunes, Mrs. Anderson," he nods to them both. "Please come in." He stands back, holding the door open. Axl walks in, barging in front of Alicia. He sits down forcefully in one of the visitor's chairs, pushes back on it, and totters with only the back feet of the chair on the floor, his feet balancing on the edge of the principal's desk, casual and uncaring. Alicia stands for a moment watching Axl's display of arrogance before walking into the principal's office. Mr. Lennon gives both Ziggy and Luke a stern scowl before he closes the door to them.

"Can we get this over with?" Axl starts. "I'm a busy guy."

***

"Are you okay?" Alicia asks her son as they buckle the seatbelts in her car.

"Define okay."

"Physically – are you okay?" she asks again.

"A little sore. A little bruised, but nothing broken, so I would say I'm okay."

"Good. You're going to have quite the shiner tomorrow," Alicia says, pulling her car out of the school's parking lot. "Now emotionally – are you okay?"

There is a long pause before Luke answers. "That's a very different question. It felt good to hit that piece of shit. He took the first swing,

62

but I didn't back away. You know that old wives' tale about seeing red when you're really, really angry?" he asks, looking at his mother as she nods in understanding. "I saw red. Bright, bloody red. And yeah, it felt good to hit him," he finishes.

"And was it worth being suspended for three days? Was it worth having it go on your record, Luke? A record that college will be looking at?"

Luke gazes out the window, his shoulders stooped, pulling into himself. "That's the piece of shit that Jess is seeing. He came after me, Mom. What was I supposed to do?" he asks, turning to her for enlightenment.

"Luke, I get it. Your heart hurts," Alicia pauses before continuing, "but Jessica has made her decision and there's nothing you can do."

Luke nods numbly, turning to watch the scenery, not wanting his mother to see the emotion on his face.

Alicia continues, "In my estimation, she has made a very bad decision getting involved with Ziggy and that family, but I'm more worried about you. You need to be very, very careful. Don't let that little snot provoke you. Walk away. Don't let him and his bullshit impact your future. You are so much better than either of them."

Luke nods, knowing what his mom is saying is right, but not sure he will be able to follow her directive.

"Okay, changing the subject. When should we hear from the college about your course for the fall? Shouldn't we know by now?"

"Great minds think alike, Mom," Luke smiles through the pain. "I called last week to see what the holdup was, and they told me they had a huge number of applicants this year, three times the norm apparently, and that it would take longer than expected. They think we should know by the end of the school year."

"That doesn't leave you much time to apply to something else if it doesn't work out," Alicia comments.

"Don't worry. I'll get in," Luke replies, sounding more positive than he actually feels.

"How are you doing on your credits for community work? Do you have enough yet?" Alicia follows up.

"I'm about halfway there with the work I did at the police kiosks at the last couple of events. I need about ten more hours before the end of the year."

"You should get in touch with Katie Hart. She's coordinating the activities for the Barrie Waterfront Festival on the long weekend in May. Maybe you could help out then and get all the credits you need."

Chapter 18
Apr 30
James

James drives his black Ford Bronco through the tree-shrouded laneway to the large house overlooking the bay. The leaves have not started to bud on the trees yet, and there is a clear view through the acres of land leading up to the house as he drives leisurely toward his goal. James is meeting Axl to give him the protection money that he picked up from one of the small independently owned stores in town, Not Just Groceries.

He pulls up in front of the large building off to the right of the house that was once a garage but has been extensively renovated and turned into Axl's mancave and office, the place where he holds meetings with his senior gang members, where he sits back and watches TV, especially the Toronto teams – the Blue Jays, the Maple Leafs, and the Argonauts.

James puts his vehicle in park and slowly slides his bulk out from behind the wheel, moving unhurriedly to the ornate door on the side of office, feeling his age starting to creep up on him. He knocks on the door and waits for acknowledgement before he opens it.

"Back here," he hears Axl's voice from the depths of the building.

James walks through the living room area, through the kitchen, to the back of the structure. The door is open to the office and the VP of the Reubens is sitting at his desk, his computer open in front of him. James pauses in the doorway waiting for his invite into the inner sanctuary. "Everything okay?" the boss finally asks, looking up from the screen.

James pulls the envelope, with Axl's name scrawled across it in big red letters addressed by the client, out of his pocket and throws it onto the desk. "Yeah, everything is okay with the pickup, though I think they're getting a bit antsy, might be thinking of leaving the fold."

Axl grins. "Good for them. It won't do them any good, but good for them for at least having the balls to think about it." He examines his enforcer and after a moment of inspection asks, "Are you sure there's nothing else going on?"

James stands for a moment contemplating what, if anything, he should say to the man that holds him tightly, controls him, won't let him escape the gang, finally deciding that he needs to know the truth and asks, "What's this I hear about a new position in the gang? DOG, or something just as asinine."

Axl leans back in his chair. "So, he went to see you, did he?"

James nods his head. "Tell me how this happened."

"Well, we are expanding the business and Mack has the expertise I need."

"He's calling himself Mack now, is he? I guess you can't keep your real name when you're a child killer."

"Yeah, Mack Sommers is his moniker these days," Axl replies, smiling knowing that it is not his given name. "He comes highly recommended from the Vancouver branch. He did some good work for them. Worked his way up from an enforcer, like you, to a hitman and then got interested in computers and put together a great online presence for them. He's been there for years and decided he wanted to come back to Ontario. He trained someone to take over out there and they agreed to let him come work with us."

"What expertise does that piece of shit have other than killing little kids?" James asks venomously.

Axl smiles knowingly. "I know there's some history between the two of you," he pauses as James huffs in disgust. "But that is in the past and has nothing to do with the business expansion. Not saying that what he did was right, but maybe he paid the price." Axl puts up his hand in a stop motion as James opens his mouth to protest. "He says it was all a terrible accident. He went underground after the incident; had some contacts with the gang, and he used them to go west." He pauses, watching his enforcer closely. "As you know, we can't go back in time, James. I'm sure there are few things that you might change if you could," he smiles, knowing that James would probably include working for him and the gang as one of the things he wouldn't do if he had the chance to re-write his life. Axl continues,

66

"You will put the past, your history with Mack behind you – just like you did with the police force. It's time to move on," Axl concludes.

James stands quietly for a moment, knowing that the decision is out of his hands as one of Axl's unimportant minions. After a prolonged silence, he asks, "And what is he going to be doing? What's this new title? DOG?"

"Great title, eh? Director of Guns. DOG. Love it!"

"Director of Guns?" James questions leaning back against the door jamb as Axl expands on his father's new role.

"Yup. We will be expanding our business into gun distribution. We have a great contact in Don Saunders. You remember Don, your old Chief; you guys worked together at the precinct; he facilitated our first meeting and the start of our work together," Axl smiles before continuing. "Don's promotion to the Director of the Canada Border Services Agency is perfect and apparently, he's doing a great job, seizing loads of firearms that he should be disposing of. But you know, Don. He's a resourceful guy and very money oriented. He's got an excessive number of firearms looking for a new home and we're it," Axl concludes.

"And Mack, he's going to head this new directive?"

"He's going to manage the new division - how to get the guns from the CBSA, where and when to move them, how to sell them and price them for our buyers. He's going to set up an Amazon-type site on the darknet where anyone will be able to buy from us, starting with the guns we get from Don, but I see us expanding the site to include other stuff like porn, drugs, maybe even some contract killing. The possibilities are endless. It's going to be great."

James continues to lean against the door jamb, rolling over the information in his mind. *Son of a bitch. Kills his son. Leaves his wife with bills, no money, no support. Just disappears from the face of the earth and ends up working for a gang at the other end of the country and then makes good with them. And now he's back. And they think I'm going to work with him?*

Chapter 19
May 1
Alicia

"Hello Jeff," Alicia says, answering her cell phone as she sits in front of her open computer, papers and books strewn around her on the dining room table.

"Hey gorgeous. What are you up to tonight? Are you free for dinner? And anything else that might pop up?" he laughs, painting a picture of a typical date between the two – dinner and sex.

Alicia smiles, knowing where his mind has just gone, as hers follows suit. *Skin touching skin, lips kissing her body intimately, the joy of climaxing together, laying back in the down comforter on his king-size bed to kiss, to cuddle and wait for their heart beats to slow down, to do it one more time.*

"Hey, are you still there?" Jeff asks.

Alicia shakes her head, tossing the wanton memories from her mind. "Yes, I'm here," she pauses. "I would love to Jeff, but I've got the books open, trying to get ready for the exam that is coming up really quick."

"And you can't take a break? Maybe you could work on the cop stuff tomorrow?"

"Hhhmmm, I would love to, but I think I need to be home tonight."

"Why? What's going on?"

"Luke is struggling. I told you that he broke up with his girlfriend, right?"

"Yeah. The little tramp dumped him for some new guy with a car and money."

"Well, he's still upset, and has started acting out, been out partying too much, drinking and he's underage, hanging out with the creepy guy that lives next door. I got a call from the school's principal last week and I had to go in because Luke was fighting with Jess's new boyfriend, and he got a three-day suspension."

"That's tough, Alicia. He's going through a hard time, but he'll come out of it. We all do," Jeff chimes in.

"I'm sure you're right, but I think I need to be here. I've grounded him for a month, taken away his phone, and I need to be here to make sure its enforced."

Again, there's silence on the phone as both contemplate their relationship, and what they want out of it.

"How about you come over here? We could order a pizza or something for dinner, watch a movie on TV."

"That would be fantastic if you can spare the time to eat and hang out for a while. I'll stop and pick it up on the way over," Jeff agrees, putting a smile on Alicia's face.

Chapter 20
July 1
Alicia

Helen and Alicia walk back to their police vehicle after being at the Southshore Community Centre for over eight hours, the site where Jessica's body was found earlier in the morning. They have spent the day questioning passersby, discussing the preliminary results with the coroner, discovering the possible murder weapon when Alicia reacted violently to the scene and the reality of the identification. They, along with the forensic team, have spent hours scouring the area conducting a circular search out from the body to find all possible evidence, plus a plethora of other useless items such as bottles, candy wrappers, cigarette butts, and other junk which all had to be bagged, tagged, and inventoried. Plaster casts of depressions in the nearby grassy areas and in the sand near the body were taken. Pictures of everything from the victim to the grounds, to the placement of the large limb that may have been utilized violently to end her life, to pictures of the crowds watching their every move were taken. Once Sanjay Ramesh, the Identification Officer, was satisfied that he had secured and documented everything possible from the body, it was sent to Dr. Diamond and her team at the morgue.

"Now comes the real hard part," Helen comments as she opens the door to the vehicle.

Alicia looks at her partner over the top of the car's roof. "What do you mean - the hard part? Today has been intense, so far."

"We need to notify next of kin, her parents. We need to tell them what's happened to their daughter before they hear about it from neighbours or on the news. They also need to make plans to visit the morgue to confirm that this is Jessica," Helen finishes as she gets into the vehicle and starts the engine.

Alicia slides into the passenger side of the car and pulls out her phone. She has texted and telephoned her son intermittently throughout the day but has not heard from him. She opens the app for

70

messages and still nothing. *Where the hell could he be? Why the hell is he not answering me?*

***

Helen pulls the police SUV into the Winters's driveway as a young boy, about 12-years-old, comes out of the garage on a like-new black mountain bike. "That's Jessica's brother, Oliver," Alicia says as Helen puts the car in park. The two detectives get out of the vehicle to the watchful eyes of the youth, similarities between the two siblings stark – the bright blue eyes, the small pert nose with cascading freckles down the sides, the same golden-brown straight hair. "Hello, Oliver. Is your mom or dad home?" Alicia enquires.

"You're Luke's mom, right?" he asks, without answering Alicia's question.

"I am. And I," Alicia pauses, correcting herself before continuing, "and we would like to talk to your mom or dad. Are they home?"

"My mom is here. Dad's not," he clarifies as he hops on his bike and pedals down the street, both detectives watching his outline shrink in size as he cycles away from them.

Helen leads the way to the front door, searches for a doorbell, but when she can't locate one, knocks firmly on the door. They wait about 20 seconds, but there is no answer. She knocks again, moving to peer through the sidelight. Sounds of movement can be heard in the house and they wait, both standing straight, feet apart, preparing themselves for the unwieldly situation to come.

Moments later, a voice, sounding put out with the interruption, calls out to them, "I'm coming. I'm coming." They hear a body lumbering down the three stairs from the main level to the front door and finally the door is opened. Mrs. Winters is standing there, in her sweatpants and t-shirt, puffing like she has just run a marathon. She scrutinizes the visitors, her eyes squinting in thought trying to place Alicia. It comes to her moments after opening the door, "Alicia Anderson, is that you?"

"Hello, Jennifer," Alicia pauses unsure how to proceed with the conversation.

"Luke isn't here. I haven't seen him since graduation."

Helen butts into the conversation. "No, that's not why we're here, Mrs. Winters. My name is Detective Helen Hodges. Alicia and I are here in an official capacity with the police. Can we come in and talk to you for a few minutes?"

Jennifer's deep blue eyes, the same shape and colouring as both her children, move from Alicia to Helen and back again, assessing the situation. She pushes the door fully open, stepping back. "Yes, come in, but that doesn't sound good - official capacity," she comments, leading them up the stairs into the living room. "Let me just turn this off," Mrs. Winters says, reaching for her laptop and shutting the lid, muting the exercise video. She turns to the two intruders. "Please, sit down. Can I get you a coffee? A tea?" she asks, trying to postpone the reason for this visit from the police.

"Thank you, but no, we are good, Mrs. Winters. Is your husband here?" Helen asks, looking around the open concept area, the living room, the dining room, and the kitchen.

"John? No, he's not here. What's going on? Has Oliver done something? Jessica?" she asks, easing herself into the lazy-boy chair in front of the window.

Helen looks at Alicia before turning directly to Jessica's mom. "We have some very bad news to tell you. Your daughter, Jessica is dead. She was found early this morning near the waterfront at the Southshore Community Centre."

Jennifer immediately jumps up, her eyes moving frantically from Helen to Alicia. "No, no, that's not possible. Jessica!" she yells, running from the room, down the hallway to Jessica's bedroom, throwing open the door. Alicia follows, catching Jessica's mom as she crumbles at the doorway of the empty room, the fully made bed sitting accusingly in the middle of the quiet space. "No, no, that's not possible," Jennifer Winters cries, dissolving onto the floor.

"Jen let's go back in the living room and talk. We will answer your questions if we can," Alicia says propping up the distraught woman.

Suddenly, Jennifer coils back against the wall, pushing Alicia away. "Did Luke do this? Is that why you're here? What did he do to her?" she demands, tears running down her face.

Alicia takes a step back, stunned at the allegation, even though it mirrors her internal thoughts she has had most of the day.

Helen has heard the accusation and moves to take Jennifer's arm, leading her away from Alicia and back to the living room, back to the large chair. "We aren't sure exactly what happened yet but are investigating all possibilities. If Luke is involved in this in any way, we will definitely find out."

Jennifer folds in upon herself, tears flowing freely down her face. She looks up at Alicia. "Get out. Get out of my house. Now," she demands.

Alicia nods her head and softly says, "I am so sorry for your loss," as she moves to the front door, to wait for her partner in the car.

***

Alicia sits in the passenger seat of the police SUV and pulls her phone out of her pocket. *Still no answer from Luke. Wait. Is he working today?* Alicia hits a couple of buttons on her phone and pulls up Luke's schedule for work. She scans it quickly, confirming that he was not scheduled to work today.

Alicia is angry and doesn't understand why he hasn't replied, why he is ignoring her. *Could he be involved in this? Is he afraid? Afraid to talk to me? Afraid to tell me what happened? Is he on the run?*

Alicia dials Luke's phone once again and it goes to voicemail. "Call me now!" she yells into the phone before disconnecting.

She sits for a moment, contemplating her next steps in locating her son. *I don't want to call James. I haven't talked to him since last year, but maybe Luke is with him.*

Alicia looks at the picture of James's smiling face on her phone app, a picture that was taken over five years ago when they were still happy together. She pauses for several moments, weighing her options and realizing she has none at this point, jabs the link to James's phone and moves the device to her ear.

One ring. Two rings. Three rings. Alicia is about to disconnect when she hears, "Alicia? Is that you?" through the small speaker.

"James is Luke with you?" she asks abruptly.

"Luke? No, he's not here. I saw him the other day for a few minutes but that's all. He's probably with Jessica," James's clear, deep voice replies, no traces of emotion noticeable.

"I need you to find him. Jessica is dead." There is a long pause as Alicia stops to let this sink in. "Did you hear me, James? I need you to find him," she repeats.

"Jessica is dead? What are you talking about?"

"She has been murdered and I need you to find Luke. He's not at work and he's not answering his phone. I'm sure he didn't have anything to do with this, but it will break his heart when he finds out," Alicia continues, praying that her wayward ex-husband will be able to pull off this task. "And by the way, Luke and Jessica broke up months ago," Alicia concludes, ending the call abruptly.

Chapter 21
May 2
Luke

What the hell am I supposed to do with these, Luke asks himself as he fans the tickets for the school's prom out on his desk in his bedroom. *I should be going with Jess; we should be going together. That's why I bought the fucking tickets. Even bought a bloody suit. What was I thinking, buying a suit? Where the hell am I going to wear that again?*

Luke opens his computer and begins to shuffle through his pictures again; him and Jessica at Christmas, him and Jessica at his dad's lakefront cottage last year, him and Jessica kissing on New Year's Eve, Jessica dressed up as Day of the Dead for Halloween, a head shot of Jessica that he took on Valentine's Day. He grows hard knowing that she was nude when he took the picture, just before they made love.

What happened to us, he laments, continuing through the plethora of images.

His phone rings and he picks it up, looking at the call display. *Nova? Why the hell is she calling me?* His hand hovers over the accept button before finally deciding to pick it up. "Hey Nova," he says on the phone. "What's happening?"

"Hi Luke. What are you up to?"

"Just doing some homework," he lies, not wanting to admit that he is living in the past, missing Jessica.

"I have a proposition for you," Nova says boldly.

Luke leans back in his chair, pushing the computer away. "Okay," he says with skepticism in his voice.

"I thought we could go to the prom together."

Luke is silent, unsure what to say, as thoughts of the prom flitter through his mind again. *I want to go with Jessica. She might still come to her senses and come back to me. But will she? And will it happen before the prom? But Nova? Do I want to go with her? Noah's sister? She's all over me every chance she gets already.*

"I get that you bought the tickets for you and Jess, but honestly Luke, she's not coming back and she's going to the prom with Ziggy," Nova pauses to ensure Luke has heard this update. "And you and me, we go way back. No commitment, just some fun. Noah's going to be there with Willow, and I thought the four of us could go together." Again, she pauses, letting him weigh the options before continuing with more reasons he should choose her as his date. "It would be good for Jess to see you out with someone else, maybe wipe her nose in the fact that you've moved on too. What do you think?" she asks, holding her breath.

Nova can hear Luke breathing, but the silence seems to go on too long, prolonging her nervousness and not helping the situation. "Luke are you still there?" she asks.

"Still here. Just thinking," he replies. *Nova is good looking. I've known her forever. Always available, always fun, says she doesn't want a commitment, can be a bit pushy, always around, can't hold a candle to Jessica, but she says Jess is going to be there with that piece of shit, Ziggy.* "That might be a good idea, the four of us going together," he finally admits. "I'll talk to Noah and make some plans."

"That's fantastic, Luke. Thank you. I'll talk to Noah too. Tell him that we're going together. No pressure for anything else, Luke, but you know that I really like you. I think we could become better friends if you would just let it happen." Nova quickly hangs up before saying anything else, anything that will ruin the perfect night that she is planning with the man of her dreams.

Chapter 22
May 4

It's a bright, sunny day, though there is still a cold artic nip in the air as the dark blue fishing boat bobs in the deep waters at the mouth of the Nottawasaga River. Two fishermen, sporting the latest cold weather fishing gear including insulated overalls and matching waterproof jackets, just purchased from Cabela's Sportswear, are standing in the boat, casting their lines into the still freezing waters hoping to catch a couple of pickerel for dinner. Both are new to the sport, but they are enjoying the clear, cold weather, and their temporary escape from their wives and kids as they drink the cold beer that they added to the cooler, which was packed with sandwiches, cookies, and cans of pop by one of the wives.

After several hours, when both the beer and the food were consumed, the two are getting a little bored with their new pastime without even a nibble on the ends of their new fishing lines.

"I'm getting tired," the owner of the new boat tells his buddy. "What about you?"

"Just a couple more casts and then we'll call it a day," his friend says from the front of the boat as his line sails effortlessly over his head and hits the water. He waits, silently counting to ten, letting the lure sink in the water before he starts to reel it in. He winds the line steadily as his friend puts down his fishing pole and starts to clean up the boat, putting the spent cans and Tupperware containers into the now-empty cooler.

It's not a big grab of the lure that he feels, no big fish suddenly capturing the shiny delicacy in its mouth and swimming away, but more like hooking onto a heavy weight that hinders his ability to wind the line. "I think I got something," he tells his friend, as the tip of the rod bends to the water from the load on the hook.

"Probably weeds," his friend laughs, continuing to clean up the cans and wrappers.

"I don't think so. A lot heavier than weeds, whatever it is," he replies, using all of his strength to bring in the fishing line without breaking it. "Get the net," he yells as he pulls the treasure closer to the boat.

His friend looks up, "Really?"

"Yes, really. It's big. It's fucking big," is the reply.

The two stand at the front of the boat on the raised platform surveying the clear water, one with the net in his hands, while the other continues to wind in his line. "It's coming, it's coming," he pants at the physical exertion needed to bring in his prize.

"Holy shit," breathes the fisherman holding the net over the edge of the boat, waiting for his view of a sleek fish, but instead the bloated, translucent white face of a teenage girl floats to the surface of the water.

Chapter 23
July 1
James

James stares at his phone as the enormity of the situation sinks in. *Luke's girlfriend dead? They broke up months ago? I just saw him the other day. Why wouldn't he tell me? It's got to be fucking bad for Alicia to call me after all the shit that went down between us, but what's worse is the distance between me and Luke since I moved out. The other day was a fluke; I'm lucky if I see him once a month now. I get that he's 17 and would rather be with Jessica and his friends, but really, I should know what is going on in his life. Broke up? No way, he wouldn't break-up with her. He kissed the ground she walked on. What is going on with him?*

James picks up his phone and pushes the direct dial icon for his son. The call goes straight to voicemail, and he leaves a quick, "call me" before hanging up. He looks at his phone. *Where the hell is he? Why isn't he answering? He always has his phone with him. My God, Jessica is dead!*

He scans his contact list quickly for the best possible conduit to get the information he requires. James still has a few outstanding favours from his time on the force, and now is the time to call one in. He pushes the icon for Paul DeLuca, a dirty cop who he worked with in his past life. The phone rings, once, twice, before Paul picks it up.

"Paul DeLuca."

"Paul, it's James."

"What do you want?"

"Hey, that's no way to greet an old friend, someone who helped you out on a couple of occasions."

"What do you want James? Are you trying to set me up?"

"I need your help, Paul. My son is missing, and I'm worried about him. I need you to run a locate on his phone and let me know where he is."

"And why the hell would I do that? What's in it for me?" he asks sullenly.

"Well, I know a lot about you and your activities, like the place where you beat a couple of guys up. I might even have the hammer that we used on our last job together. I'm sure there might be some blood on it, maybe some fingerprints, maybe some of yours."

"You son of a bitch," Paul breathes into the phone. Seconds pass in silence as Paul debates his next step. He sighs. "Is it really your son that you're searching for James? Are you sure it's not one of your bimbos or one of Axl's marks?"

"Paul, it doesn't really matter who it is. You owe me. But to answer your question, it's my son. He might be in some trouble, and I need to find him."

"Give me his cell number."

James gives Paul the number, makes him repeat it before he hangs up with a promise of information within the hour.

He sits back in his office chair. What the fuck? There's no way Luke was involved in Jessica's death. No way. He would never do something like that, would he?

***

James is pacing his office 90 minutes later when his phone finally rings. He jabs the button and yells, "Hello," into the speaker.

"He's in Sauble Beach. Looks like he's on the main beach, just north of town. Been there for most of the day. Lose my number. Don't call me again." There is a loud click as the line is disconnected.

James pulls the phone away from his ear and looks at it as if answers to his many questions will miraculously appear on the screen. *Sauble Beach? What the hell is he doing there? Most of the day? What does that mean? Maybe he's been up there for a while, maybe he's been there since yesterday and has an alibi for the time Jessica was killed. Or maybe he's running. Running away from something that he did. Something that got out of hand.*

James exits his storefront office, locks the door, and jumps into his vehicle, squealing out of the parking lot on his way to find his son.

Chapter 24
May 11
Luke

Luke squints his eyes to see the time on his phone as he picks it up from the bedside table. *Holy shit. It's 10am. I can't believe I've slept in. It's my birthday. I think I'll just pull the covers over my head and rest for another hour.* Luke rolls over, pulls the covers over his head and instantly goes back to sleep.

Alicia sits at the dining room table, reviewing her notes again, getting ready for the police exam that she will be taking in the coming week. She is tired of studying, the reading, the writing, the reviewing of the vast amount of information and believes she is ready, but still, she continues to work on the materials, waiting for the birthday boy to get out of bed.

Just before noon, Luke stumbles from his bedroom, moving into the bathroom. Alicia hears the water from the shower and cleans up her books to wait for him.

***

Alicia is sitting at the kitchen table, a cup of tea in front of her, reading the news on her phone, when Luke walks into the room, all squeaky clean from his shower.

"Hello birthday boy," she says, smiling at her son. "How does it feel to be 17?"

Luke smiles, knowing his mom always likes to celebrate birthdays, anniversaries, almost anything. "Starting to feel my age, I think. My back is pretty sore this morning," he jokes.

"Smart aleck. Just wait until you really get old." She pauses, looking at Luke, her beautiful son, the one thing that she feels she has done right in her life. "Tell me what your plans are for the day?"

"Well, being grounded doesn't really give me much lead way, does it."

Alicia smiles. "Well about that. I was thinking as a special present for your special day, we could waive the rest of your sentence."

"I can go out?" Luke asks.

"Yeah, I think you've learned that you need to think before doing something stupid. You need to be smart about what you do, where you go, who you hang out with. Right?"

Luke doesn't reply immediately, so Alicia continues, "You need to be responsible, Luke. You need to grow up and get over Jessica. Remember, say it with me," she smiles. "There are plenty of fish in the sea."

Luke smiles and asks, "Can I get my phone back too?"

Alicia gets up and pulls his phone out of her purse, tossing it across the table. "I guess you'll have to charge it. Probably dead after three weeks of sitting in my purse."

Luke runs to his room and plugs his phone into the charger. He waits for the device to get a trickle of power before turning it on and searching for texts or phone calls from Cheyenne. *Nothing. She didn't call. She didn't text. Guess I thought more of her than she did of me. Oh well, too long ago to call her now. She might not even remember who the hell I am. That's okay. Plenty of fish in the sea.* He smiles to himself as he places the phone down to continue charging.

***

Luke is standing at the front window, watching, and waiting for Noah. He can hear the roar of Noah's car three blocks away as he moves to the front door, walks out, and pulls the door closed behind him, locking it, and walking to the end of the driveway. Luke notices Dylan standing in front of his garage, a smoke in hand.

"Hey, we're going up to Orillia to check things out. Want to come?" Luke yells at his neighbour.

"What are you guys planning to do?" he asks inhaling on a cigarette, the tip glowing bright red.

"Nothing specific at this point. Probably just hanging out at the docks. There's usually a bunch of people at the pavilion, playing guitars, singing. Someone usually has a case of beer that they share."

"Right downtown?" Dylan asks.

"Yeah, right at the end of Mississauga Street, the main drag. You can't miss it."

"Maybe I'll come up later. I got a couple of things to do first," Dylan replies, throwing his cigarette butt on the ground. grinding it out with his heel, then waving at Luke before he goes into the garage.

Luke turns back to the street, watching as his friend pulls his car into the driveway, noticing that Tater Tot and Nova are in the backseat. *It would have been nice if it was just me and Noah. We might need Tater to drive, but Nova is always hanging around, following me like a sad puppy.* Luke opens the door, acknowledges Noah, sits down, and turns to the backseat passengers. "Hey guys," he says, before turning forward again, pulling the seatbelt over his shoulder.

"Sorry I couldn't get out of the house without Nova. Seems I've become her best friend," Noah laughs as he backs out of the driveway. "Happy birthday, my friend," he says, nodding at a card on the front dashboard.

Luke reaches for it. "You didn't have to do that."

"Don't be thanking me until you open it," his friend laughs, driving the car out of the subdivision to the highway.

Luke rips open the sealed envelope, pulls out a raunchy card, reads it, inspects the enclosed Amazon gift card and smiles. "Thanks man," he says, stuffing them back into the envelope and shoving it into the glovebox. "Appreciate you remembering it's my birthday."

Nova leans in from the back seat and gives Luke a kiss on the cheek, "Happy birthday, Luke," she says, smiling.

"Shit Nova, I told you none of that if you're coming with us," Noah admonishes. "Here we come. Not sure Orillia is ready for us," he laughs, moving quickly into a celebratory mood, pushing the gas pedal to the floor as they race up the highway.

The waterfront is crowded with families, people walking on the boardwalk, boats tied up at the docks, people moving to the beach area. Noah parks his beat-up car behind the Port of Orillia building, the hub of the waterfront area. As the foursome exit the car, they can hear the sounds of a piano, a guitar and a low, mellow female voice singing about wanting a man with a slow hand, a lover with an easy touch. Luke looks at the docks and sees a small crowd of people standing under the gazebo near the Port office, listening to the music.

He smiles at Noah over the hood of the car and motions for his friend to follow as he starts to move to the crowd. Noah slams the car door before directing his brother and sister, "Don't go too far, not sure how long we're staying, but don't be crowding us either," he adds, staring at Nova directly.

"Hhhmm," she huffs, walking around the end of the car, following Luke to the source of the soulful music.

Luke stands at the edge of the crowd watching the petite blond sway with her eyes closed as she sings, her sex appeal front and centre. *Wow. She is good. A nice voice, a great body, simply beautiful. Wonder if she's with that guitar player? Or the piano player? They all seem to be pretty in-tune.*

Noah comes up behind Luke, putting his hand on his friend's shoulder, whispering in his ear, "Now that would be a birthday present, my friend."

Luke smiles as he continues to watch. The song ends and he, along with the rest of the audience, clap enthusiastically. The girl bows and thanks everyone as they start to chant, "One more, one more."

She laughs, looking around the ring of smiling people. Her eyes stop on Luke for a moment, and she winks at him before her gaze continues to move around the small crowd. "Okay, one more. Just a reminder about the open guitar case in front of my brother. If you have a bit of spare change, we would truly appreciate it. If you have enough to share, of course," she qualifies, before launching into another melancholy tune.

When the song is over, the crowd claps and asks for another. She smiles and replies, "Time to give someone else a chance to sing but maybe my brothers can stay?" Her gaze moves to the guitar and piano players who both nod affirmatively. "Hope you enjoyed our music this afternoon and I hope that we will meet again real soon. Our name is Longhurst," she beams moving toward Luke, taking his arm, leading him away from the gazebo and the crowd as if they've known each other for years. "Hello," she says timidly when they are a couple of meters away. "Thanks for saving me."

The two wander down the boardwalk, arm in arm, like an old married couple, as Noah and Nova watch, a smile on Noah's face, a scowl on his sister's. Dylan stands at the edge of the crowd unnoticed, scrutinizing the petite blond singer.

***

Luke leans back in the passenger seat of Noah's car. "Thanks man, that was the best birthday ever," he confirms.

"You hit the jackpot, my friend." They both hear a groan from the backseat, but neither acknowledge Nova's dismay. "You guys took off for a while. Where did you go? What happened?" Noah asks.

Luke grins, remembering Hannah's smile, her soft hand on his arm, her warm body next to his as they walked along the boardwalk, passed the boat ramp, and sat on the benches watching the lake and the boats. "Well, her name is Hannah Longhurst. She lives here in Orillia. She loves to sing, you heard her voice, it's great. She's in a band with her two brothers, Caleb, and Lucas."

"She has a great voice. And she's cute," Tater Tot adds to the conversation from the backseat, as his sister sits with her arms crossed, a pout on her face.

"That she is, Tater," Luke agrees. "Problem is she's just turned 19 and they're starting to play in the bars," Luke frowns. "There's two years between us. Not that she seemed to care but once she gets out into the bars, she's gonna meet a lot of guys. Guys her age and older. She'll leave me behind in the dirt."

There's silence in the car for several minutes, Luke deep in thought, Nova's lips turning up into a smile, knowing that Luke is still hers.

"Maybe there's a way, my friend," Noah finally says.

"What do you mean?"

"Fake IDs. I know a guy."

Chapter 25
May 17
James

James pulls his car up the winding driveway into Axl's property. He parks beside the plethora of cars and motorcycles in front of the five-car garage including Axl's vintage red Mustang, Chevy's bright orange GTO, and a car he doesn't recognize, a silver Porsche. *Nice car. Bet that's worth a bit of cash.*

He gets out of his vehicle and moves to the front door of Axl's office. Traces of music and laughter emanate from the living room area, which surprises him. He's here for a meeting of the Gun Committee, as Axl is calling the new venture. James pulls open the door and enters the main room, looking around at people lounging on the couches, talking, laughing, enjoying themselves like at a house party with Axl in the midst of the chaos.

James moves into the room, and the room starts to quiet down, as people notice his presence. Axl turns to see who has joined the impromptu festivities and greets his enforcer, "Hey, there you are, James. Glad you could make it," as if James had a choice about coming to a meeting being chaired and run by the gang's VP. Axl turns to the others in the room. "Everyone else out. We've got some important business to discuss."

The room empties quickly, people picking up their jackets, placing their empty bottles, and glasses behind the bar in the open cases. Murmurs of good-bye are heard until the door is finally closed, leaving Axl, Mack, Chevy, and James alone.

"Let's move into the office," Axl says, standing up, moving to the outer door, and locking it to ensure their continued solitude. Using hand motions, he sweeps the three men toward the back room. "Sit down," he says as he moves behind his large desk.

Axl waits a moment as his three subordinates sit down in the cushy visitor chairs in front of his desk before he starts. "We have a new opportunity and you three are going to be prime," Axl says. "Don Saunders is in charge of stopping guns from moving across the border into Canada from the US and he's been doing a great job apparently, with his team confiscating hundreds so far. The firearms that they seize are supposed to be destroyed and from what Don says, they have been doing that for some of the merchandise, but he's also been keeping some aside. I have agreed to buy the guns he holds on to and we're going to do a trial run to his warehouse in the city to pick them up. Says he has about $1M worth of weapons just waiting for us. And depending on how well the transaction goes and how many he can keep from destruction; I think we'll be rolling down the highway to Toronto on a monthly basis."

Mack and Chevy murmur their appreciation of the plan, nodding their heads as Axl continues the overview of the new business.

"Mack – your responsibility will be to inventory the guns once they come up the highway, create and manage the website, sell them, ship them, collect the money. You'll have a small team that will be able to help you with the manual labour, but you will be the guy in charge of the site, the prices and the money coming in."

"Perfect. Not a problem," Mack confirms.

"James, Chevy – you guys will be responsible for picking up the merchandise and giving it to Mack. At this point, Don and I think monthly will be good, but we'll review in a couple of months to see if we need more visits to the warehouse or less."

Both James and Chevy nod their heads in agreement.

"I see James driving; you know the city pretty well and I'm sure you won't have a problem finding the place or fitting in with the crowd of drivers on the highway. Chevy, you'll be the muscle, if needed. I don't think there will be much call for you, but just in case. You will have a bag of cash on the way down and a shitload of guns on the way back, so we can't be too careful."

"Make sense?" he asks the team of three. The trio nod their heads in agreement again.

"Great. The first trip down the highway will happen in a couple of weeks. I'll get the address and the time for pick up," Axl completes as James and Chevy nod their heads again. "Onwards and upwards into a new line of business for the Ruebens," he smiles, standing up, ending the meeting.

As James moves to leave the room, Mack comes up behind him. "I need to talk to you for a sec," he says.

James continues to walk down the hallway, through the living room, and out the door to the driveway. He stops, hands in his pockets, turning to face Mack. "What do you want, old man?" James asks.

"When can I see my grandson?"

"Never," James answers turning away from his father and walking to his car.

Chapter 26
May 21
Luke

Luke has begged off school on the Friday before the long May 24 weekend, not so he can start his festivities early, but to help set up the kiosk for the police at the Waterfront Festival to earn some of the essential community credits required to complete grade 12 and get his high school diploma.

It's a beautiful sunny day with the temperature in the low 20s, accompanied by a warm breeze coming off the bay. Luke is helping Sargent Katie Hart unload the police trailer with all the equipment required for the exhibition. He is aiding in the set-up of the table and chairs, the erection of the custom-made steel canopy with the police logo on it and stacking the boxes of brochures behind the table, that they will be giving out tomorrow.

Though Luke is in his shorts and T-shirt, sweat drips off him, evidence of the hard physical work he's doing. Finally, once the kiosk is ready for the fair, Katie sits down on one of the chairs, pulls open the cooler, and offers a bottle of water to Luke. "Sit down, Luke. Put your feet up for a couple of minutes," she says, breaking the seal on her bottle. "It's sure a warm day for doing this."

"Thanks Katie," Luke says as he sits down, opening the bottle, guzzling most of it down in one go. The little bit left in the bottle, he pours over his head, shaking it, sending droplets through the air, smiling as it cools him down.

"When are you working the booth this weekend?" she asks, slowly drinking her water.

"Tomorrow, Saturday 9am to 3pm," he answers, turning to watch as the other vendors haul their goods into the park and start setting up their stalls.

"Same time as me. It's supposed to be hot tomorrow too. I'll bring lots of water for us. Do you like butter tarts?"

The last words have Luke's attention as he nods his head and smiles at her.

"I'll stop and pick up some. We'll need lots of strength to talk to the folks and a few calories won't hurt us," she smiles, holding her bottle of water toward Luke as if toasting him.

Chapter 27
May 21
Alicia

Alicia sits in the Chief of Police, Margaret O'Malley's office waiting. *What the heck is keeping her? I know she's busy, but really I've been here for almost a half hour. Maybe it's a ploy to test my patience. If that's it, it is definitely working.* She wiggles on the chair, trying to get comfortable. Alicia reaches for her phone in her purse, opens it to read the current headlines, getting through several stories before the door opens and the Chief walks in.

Alicia stands up and thrusts her hand forward to shake the Chief's hand. "Chief," she says as the two greet each other.

"Hello Alicia. Thanks for waiting for me. It's been a hell of a day, but then what day isn't crazy around here?" the Chief asks rhetorically.

Alicia smiles at the sentiment and gives her an option to postpone their discussion. "If you're too busy, I can come back at a better time."

The Chief smiles. "Not sure when that would be, Alicia. No, if you have time to talk, now is good for me, that is unless another emergency comes up."

"Now is good for me too," Alicia agrees as they both sit down. "I appreciate you taking the time to talk with me. As you know, I'm interested in the detective position with the force. Still working on my Bachelor's in Criminology and Justice, but I did take the Police Sergeant's exam and the results came in yesterday."

"Don't leave me in suspense, Alicia. How did you do? Or do I even need to ask?"

"I passed. Got 92%," she replies, smiling.

"Good for you. That's a great score. Congratulations."

"That's what I really wanted to talk to you about, Chief," Alicia starts. The Chief nods her head affirmatively. "I would like to apply for the detective's position that has been available for the last couple of months at the precinct."

The Chief sits back in her chair, steepling her fingers. "I understand your husband, or I guess your ex-husband, was a detective in this precinct before my time."

Alicia pauses, unsure where the conversation is headed. "Yes, James was a detective here, left months back. And yes, we are divorced."

"I am sorry to hear that it didn't work out, but marriage is hard at the best of times and having two cops in the family would be extremely difficult. I think the divorce rate for us is well above the average, which is pretty high to begin with."

Alicia nods her head in agreement. There's a pause in the conversation, Alicia waiting for the Chief's next question or comment.

"Well, I am glad to see you are back on the beat, especially after the crap that you went through with the car accident." She pauses, catching Alicia's expression of surprise. The Chief chuckles. "You shouldn't be surprised. I've read the jackets on all the staff. I wanted to get a feel for what I was getting into and to be honest, when I saw your name on my schedule today, I took another look at yours just as a reminder." She pauses as Alicia nods her head in acknowledgement.

"The process is to apply in writing to the posting and then we do some internal review of the applicants before a panel interview. As you know, the posting has been up for a couple of months and honestly, we have done some interviews, but I don't think we've found the ideal candidate yet. What I need you to do is apply to the posting as per normal and send me a copy with your resume. include a cover letter that talks about your experience, your commitment to the force, your 92% and I will fast track it through to the committee."

"That would be absolutely fantastic, Chief. Thank you."

The Chief smiles and stands to end the meeting. "Not a problem Alicia. Thanks for coming in and telling me of your intentions. I think it's excellent when people want to work their way up in the ranks, especially when they do the work to prove themselves." She offers her hand to Alicia, who is now standing.

Chapter 28
May 22
Luke

The sun is bright on Saturday morning, and the park is crowded with people walking among the kiosks, admiring, and buying crafts, enjoying the carnival rides, eating junk food, and reveling in the spring day.

Luke has been at the kiosk for a couple of hours fielding questions from the kids who come by, letting Katie take the real comments like petty crimes and suggestions on additional tasks the police should be undertaking. With a break in the steady stream of people coming by the booth, Luke, reaches for his fourth butter tart, looking at Katie questioningly.

"Go for it," she says laughing, "better you than me."

Luke sits back, munching on the gooey, sweet tart, as he scrunches his eyes from the brilliant sun, watching the crowds. He sits up at attention as he notices Jessica and Ziggy holding hands as they meander down the pathway between the vendors moving toward him. They are laughing, looking at the merchandise on the tables as they wander oblivious to his presence. The hair on the back of Luke's neck goes up as he watches the two come closer and Katie notices the change in his demeanor. She follows his gaze and sees the couple. She does not know who they are, but can see Luke's animosity, his tense stance, as he stands up from the chair, crossing his arms across his chest.

"Luke, who are they?" Katie asks, moving to stand beside him.

"Well, he's a piece of shit," he replies, still watching the pair walk along the path to the booth.

As they get closer, Jessica looks up and their eyes meet. She quickly lowers her gaze and whispers to Ziggy, pulling his arm, trying to steer him away from their original course. Ziggy leans in and listens to her, glancing up to see Luke standing behind the table. He laughs and pulls Jessica back onto their original course and the couple move

95

to the table. Jessica and Ziggy stand in front of the display as Ziggy picks up a brochure as if to read it and then throws it back at Luke.

"You're just a pussy, Anderson. Probably going to be a crooked cop, just like your dad," he spits out.

Katie moves in front of Luke, protecting him from the vicious words. "Keep going," she directs, pointing up the row of booths to both Jessica and Ziggy.

Ziggy takes in the female cop and smiles, "Just like you to have a girl stand up for you, Anderson. Couldn't get mommy to come down and look after you today?" he taunts.

"One more time, move along," Katie directs, as Luke stands stock still beside her.

"Or what? What will you do?" Ziggy threatens, his glare moving from Katie to Luke to the other officer behind the table.

"Come on, Zig," Jessica implores pulling his arm, trying to move him along with the crowd.

"Another time then," he says, moving reluctantly away from the kiosk, being pulled by his girlfriend.

Luke watches them walk away, a sigh escaping his lips. Katie turns to him, "What was that all about?"

"That was just a piece of shit. Can't believe she is wasting her time with him," he replies, watching the couple walk away. "What was he talking about, my dad being a crooked cop?" he asks, moving his eyes from the couple fading into the crowd to Katie.

Katie wrinkles her lips, silent, unsure what to say. She's heard the rumours, not sure if any or all of them are true, and certainly doesn't want to have that conversation with this teenager, a kid with a potential future as a police officer.

"Katie, what don't I know?" Luke asks again.

"Not now," Katie replies as a family with several young boys walk toward the table.

An hour later, Katie and Luke are relieved as the second shift show up to man the exhibit into the late afternoon and the evening. It's been a busy day and luckily for Katie, Luke was able to push the questions he had about James out of his mind as he talked to the public, touting the advantages of the police force to the young kids that looked up to him.

"Katie, do you have a couple of minutes?" she hears, as she picks up her purse, getting ready to leave the kiosk for the day. She sees his pain, his expectant eyes, reminding her that he's only 17, and it isn't her place to shatter his dreams, his love for his father.

"Luke, it's not my place. You need to talk to your mom."

"She can barely say his name let alone talk to me about the rumours that I've heard. She always changes the subject; pretends she doesn't know what I'm talking about. Even after everything he's done to her and their marriage, she stands up for him. And yes, I've heard rumblings of something before today but if Ziggy knows, then I need to know what is going on. I'm asking you because I respect you and I know you are not biased one way or the other. I just want to know what people are saying. Help me understand what everyone knows except me," he pleads.

Katie stands there, thinking, wishing that she could plead ignorance, that she wasn't in this position, wishing that his mother would come by and take this burden off her shoulders. "Luke, please," she begs, hoping to change his mind about her having to tell him the awful things people have been saying about his dad.

"Katie, I get that I'm putting you in a bad position. I understand that it isn't your place, but if my mom won't tell me, what else can I do?" he asks innocently. "Please."

"Okay, let's go sit on one of the benches by the water and talk," she finally agrees.

An hour later, Luke is drained from the story Katie has woven about his dad. He sits alone watching the water, the boats, the blue sky, wondering how much is true, and how much of the tail is urban legend. His phone buzzes and he pulls it from his pocket, opening the text app. A text from Noah jumps out at him, 'Finished yet?'

'Done for the day' he types as he stands up from the bench where he had been listening to Katie's rendition of his father's failings, his imperfections, his deficiencies as a cop and his role in the local gang. Luke walks through the different displays and vendors at the festival, in a daze as his mind works overtime on his father's illegal and immoral activities. *Really? My dad? My dad working for the Ruebens? Is that why he left the police force?*

He stops for a moment and pulls his wallet out of his pocket, opens it, and spies the fake ID that Noah had made for him. He inspects his picture and his new birth year, making him 19 instead of 17 years old. *Am I starting down the same path as my dad? No way, it's only a fake ID and I need it to get into the bar tonight to see Hannah. Can't wait to see Hannah.* He hums to the last song he heard her sing and smiles to himself. *Tonight, is going to be fantastic. I'll worry about all this dad crap later.*

His phone chimes with a new text and he looks at the screen. 'Pick you up at 8pm.'

Luke starts to walk with purpose toward home until his phone chimes again. He opens the phone and sees a smiley face and a blue heart from Hannah. *She's excited about tonight, too.* He picks up his speed, in a hurry to get home, have a shower, change, and get to the bar to see her smile, hear her mellow voice, feel her touch on his skin.

***

The car speeds up the highway in silence. Noah picked up Luke as promised, but again, his brother and sister are tagging along. Luke could take Tater Tot's presence, in fact, would appreciate a sober driver for the ride home but he is getting tired of Nova's stares, always watching him, hovering too close, trying to hold his hand, touch his arm, trying to infiltrate herself into his life as something more than Noah's sister.

Noah looks at his friend and whispers, "Sorry man."

Luke continues to stare through the front windshield. "I understand, but really, all the time?" he questions.

"Next time. Just us. I promise."

Luke finally breaks a smile. "Don't make promises you can't keep bro. I know how close you and your sister are. It's just…" he fades off.

Nova leans into the front seat, asking, "What are you guys talking about? We can't hear you back here."

Neither Noah nor Luke say anything for a few moments, letting the quiet hang between them. Finally, Noah breaks the silence by changing the subject, "How was the festival today, Luke? Anything exciting happen?"

Luke is grateful for the new topic of discussion and tells him about his run-in with Ziggy.

***

There's a steady line of people waiting to get into the bar as the four are stopped and asked to show their ID. The overstuffed football player doorman scrutinizes each of the driver's licenses presented, looking closely at each picture, and then eyeballing the owner. He finally decides that they can come in, even if he doesn't believe the authenticity of their papers. He smiles, steps back, allowing them entry. "Enjoy yourself," he says as they move past him into the large square room.

Tables are set up in rows in the main floor area with booths along the walls at either end of the large space. The walls and floors are clad in matching barnboard. The ceiling features gold tin squares, something that could have come out of a dance hall in the late 1800s.

People are gathered around the dart boards and pool tables clustered at the back of the room enjoying themselves, guzzling their drinks and playing the games set out.

Luke is in the lead as they enter the room, and he searches the place for somewhere to sit. There is no stage, but he sees several guitars and a microphone at one end of the room. He smiles as he spies a small table next to the musical equipment and moves toward it, with the other three following him closely. They sit down as the waitress comes over. "What will it be?" she asks.

The four look at each other. This is the first time any of them have been in a bar, even Tater Tot, who has been of legal age for a while. Taking the initiative, Noah asks, "What's on tap?"

The waitress lists four different beers. Noah answers quickly, picking one of the choices, "How about a pitcher of Steam Whistle Pale with four glasses?"

"I'll have a diet coke," Tater Tot says quietly to the waitress.

"Oh yeah, a diet coke for our DD," Noah laughs.

The waitress nods as she moves to the bar.

***

Several pitchers of beer are consumed at the table before the Longhurst siblings come out of the backroom. Hannah moves to the bar stool that has been placed amid the guitars, picking up her old acoustic, pulling its strap over her head. Luke is out of his seat as soon as he sees her, moving to stand in front of her. "Hey Hannah," he greets.

Her brothers, Caleb, and Lucas, move beside her protectively, but when she recognizes Luke, a wide smile sweeps across her face and the brothers fade back. "Luke, it's great to see you," Hannah grins, stepping close to him. She leans close and whispers in his ear, "So glad you got the ID in time for tonight."

Luke murmurs, "Amazing what you can buy, isn't it?"

She gives him a quick kiss on the cheek and promises, "We'll have a beer after the set. You can introduce me to your friends."

100

"I'll be right here," Luke points to his chair, "being your biggest fan."

She smiles, moves back to the high stool, adjusting her guitar and pulls the microphone close. "Hello Orillia. Thanks for coming out tonight. We are Longhurst and hope you enjoy our music," she says as they launch into their first song.

***

Luke is mesmerized by Hannah, the band, their music, and the glass of beer in front of him, which seems to magically be full no matter how many gulps he has. Nova is watching him closely, knowing that in the end, he will be leaving with her, with Noah and Tater Tot too, but really with her, for their trip home.

***

Tater Tot is behind the wheel, with Noah passed out beside him in the passenger seat. Luke is in the backseat with Nova, eyes closed, mumbling the words of some country tune that the band played earlier in the evening. Nova moves closer to Luke, putting her hand on his leg, moving it slowly up to his crotch, massaging him.

Luke groans, whispering, "Hannah."

"Nova," she corrects, fumbling with his zipper, moving to take him in her mouth, making him groan louder as he places his hands on her head, helping her with the rhythm, the tempo. His whimpers grow steadily as she manipulates him expertly, his pleasure escalating as her mouth fills with his juices.

Luke's eyes are closed, and he doesn't move as Nova sits up and cuddles into him. She looks to the front seat and sees Tater watching her in the rear-view mirror, nodding his head with a brilliant smile.

Chapter 29
July 1
Alicia

Alicia and Helen are sitting in the Chief's expansive office, waiting for the boss as she finishes an interview with the local TV station in the front lobby of the precinct, to be played on the 11 o'clock news. The Chief is being asked about the most recent murder in the city and without any news to share, is trying to detour the conversation to the talented detectives assigned to the case while reiterating the safe, low crime rate the city boasts.

The door opens swiftly as the short, stout, whirlwind Chief rushes into the room. "Well, that was fun," she says sarcastically. "They're asking stupid questions that I can't answer, that I won't answer. Freaking press," she complains, sitting heavily behind the large desk, taking a couple of deep breaths, looking at her two detectives. "Tell me what's going on with this case."

Helen slides forward in the visitor's chair and gives a synopsis of the scene, confirmation of the victim's ID, their discussion with the passerby that called it in, their extensive search of the area for clues, the team that has been put together to assist in the case including the Identification Officer, the forensic team and getting permission to utilize Officers Vincent and Jones to assist. Helen ends her barrage of information discussing their visit to the victim's mom, concluding with Alicia being asked to leave the Winters's home.

"Why? Why was Mrs. Winters so angry with you, Alicia?" Chief O'Malley asks, turning to face her newest detective.

"Jessica and my son used to date. They broke up months ago. Both have moved on. I think she was just upset to see me there. Made the whole thing real and personal," Alicia offers.

The Chief nods, understanding the mother's reluctance with Alicia. "Is this a problem for you, Alicia?"

"I honestly don't think so. They broke up months ago. Jessica had moved on, had a new boyfriend. Luke was home with me last night. We were celebrating my new job," Alicia explains.

"Good. Glad to hear he has a rock-solid alibi, but the optics aren't good, especially what outsiders might think with the old boyfriend's mom on the case." She stops, nodding her head to herself as thoughts run through her mind. "I think you should stay on the case – stay in the background and let Helen take point, just like you were going to do anyway as the newest member of our team. You can do all the paperwork, assist with calls, book meetings, learn the ropes. If Luke's status changes for some reason, then we will talk again. If it comes to that, you would be removed from the case. We don't want any backlash from the public suggesting favouritism or nepotism in the force." The Chief pauses and turns her attention to Helen. "Have you met with the boyfriend yet? What's his name?"

"Ziggy. Ziggy Tunes. His brother's name is Axl. Axl Rose Tunes. Know him?"

"The Ruebens VP? Holy shit, that gives this case a whole new slant. Do you think it's gang related?"

"Not sure yet but Ziggy is first on our list to talk to tomorrow morning."

Chapter 30
June 4
Luke

Too bad I agreed so quick to taking Nova to the prom. I had the tickets and no one to go with and it sounded like a good idea at the time, but then I met Hannah. Wow, if I brought Hannah to the prom, the other guys would drool all over her and it would certainly have gotten Jess's attention. But it would be too juvenile for Hannah. She's been out of high school for a couple of years already. Anyway, she's playing at some bar tonight and I'm stuck with Nova. Should be a good time though, with Noah and Willow. I'll talk to Hannah tomorrow and see how her night went.

Luke nods to Noah's mom and dad as they open the door. He walks into the living room, seeing Noah, standing in front of the fireplace in the centre of the room. Luke asks, "What's going on?"

"Just waiting for her to come downstairs," his friend replies, pushing Luke fondly. "We'll have a good time no matter what she looks like," he jokes, as the two enjoy the easiness of their friendship, both decked out in suits and ties. The slim-fitting grey suit gives Luke a sophisticated air, making him appear several years older than 17. His tie is dusty rose, definitely not his favourite colour, but he was given the tie and a directive from Nova to wear it.

"Come on Nova. We're going to be late picking up Willow if you don't hurry up," Noah bellows up the stairs as the boys and her parents stand waiting in the living room. The parents want to catch some pictures of the twins all dressed up and have been instructed to get some snaps of just Nova and Luke.

"I'm coming, I'm coming," Nova replies as she starts her descent from the second floor, holding the railing tightly so she doesn't stumble on the stairs, teetering on the four-inch heels of her silver sandals. She stops at the top landing waiting to be noticed, to make her grand entrance. Finally, her mother glances up and smiles, "You look fantastic, sweetheart."

Noah and Luke's heads turn to take in the beauty coming down the stairs. Nova's dark hair has a subtle wave, falling just passed her shoulders. The dress is dusty rose with a v-neckline, which plunges to her tiny waist, allowing a substantial view of her pert breasts. The bodice is decorated with lace, beads, and sparkles. The skirt is a matching dusty rose tulle, floating about her thin body with each step. She slowly descends the stairs and does a slow pirouette at the bottom, revealing her bare back, the soft skin shimmering sensually in the light, before moving toward Luke and giving him a peck on the cheek. "Hope I didn't make you wait too long," she whispers in his ear.

"No, not at all," Luke stammers. "You look incredible," he adds, now understanding why he was told to wear the distinctive coloured tie.

"Yeah, incredible," Noah parrots. "Let's go. We're going to be late."

"Hold up for a minute, Noah," his mom interrupts. "I want some pictures. Luke can you and Nova stand in front of the fireplace," she says ready to capture a picture for her daughter's scrapbook.

***

The three pile into the back of the limo as the chauffeur holds the door wide open for them before moving around to the driver's side, sliding in, and starting the engine. They cruise over to Willow's house where they repeat the waiting, the parents, and the pictures before they can relax again in the spacious backseat.

"To the prom?" the driver asks, considering the four young people on the brink of adulthood through the rear-view mirror.

"No, let's take a couple of laps around town first. We need a bit of time to have a few drinks and enjoy this ride," Noah replies as he pulls the bottle of champagne from the mini fridge, pushing the corkscrew into the top of the bottle. Luke holds the glasses out for him to fill and passes them around. Once everyone has a glass flute filled with the bubbly liquid, they hold them up, clinking them together. Noah yells,

"Cheers," and the four gulp the ice-cold liquid down quickly. "More?" Noah asks, still holding the bottle in his hand.

"Yes, please," the three reply, smiling.

After much drinking and laughing, the driver pulls the limo up to the front doors of the Southshore Community Centre. He gets out, opens the back door and watches as the four prepare themselves for their entrance into the party. Willow links her arm through Noah's as they walk in front of Luke and Nova. Luke does not reach out for Nova's hand, so she takes the initiative and grabs his arm possessively as they make their way to the ballroom.

***

The hall is decorated with golden palm trees with white and black balloons scattered throughout. The decorations are sophisticated, giving off the impression of a summer's eve in Hollywood. As the couples walk into the room, a photographer encourages them to stand under a 'Welcome to Hollywood' banner. Nova slides close to Luke, pulling his arm around her for the picture. They smile and are joined by Noah and Willow for a picture of the four of them together.

The dining room is ringed with tables, all set for dinner with white dishes and gold silverware. The centre pieces match the room's décor, small palm trees decorated with sparkles. The north wall is floor-to ceiling windows giving an unobstructed view of the bay, with the glittering lights of the city on the opposite shoreline.

"It's gorgeous," Nova gushes to Luke, who is searching for their table number, finally finding it to the left of the stage.

"Over here Noah," he says, moving to the table with Nova in tow.

The group of four sit down and take in the beautifully decorated room. "Looks fantastic, don't you think?" Willow whispers to Nova.

"Absolutely stunning," she replies.

"Bet you're glad you asked Luke to come to the party," Willow continues innocently, putting Nova on edge.

"I did suggest it, but Luke was all for it," she justifies, cursing her brother in her thoughts.

The small talk continues until the school's principal, Mr. Lennon, takes centre stage and tests the microphone. "Testing one, two, three," he says as he taps on the device. "Can you hear me?" he asks the room, receiving nods and catcalls from the back of the room. "Okay, everyone find your table and sit down. We're about to say grace and have some dinner. Come on everyone. Sit down so we can get on with the celebration."

The room begins to quiet down as people find their tables and say hello to their table mates. "Thank you everyone. I am so excited to be here tonight, to be chairman for the festivities. It's been a hard year, a long year and it is time to celebrate," the principal finishes as the crowd begins to cheer loudly.

The photographer standing at the rear of the hall motions to Mr. Lennon, his hand in the air with his index finger raised. The principal notices the gesture, realizing that more students are arriving. He turns back to the microphone. "Whoa apparently, I started too soon. Not everyone is here yet."

The photographer nods his head to the principal. "Just give us a minute to see who the latecomers are and get them seated," Mr. Lennon says as everyone's attention moves to the doorway.

The room begins to buzz with sounds of oohs and aahs as the couple enters the room. Luke turns away from his conversation with Noah to see what all the commotion is and spies Ziggy, holding Jessica's hand. Jessica's dress is midnight black, with shimmers of blue under tones. The chiffon halter is cinched at her small waist, flowing to the floor with a glamorous slit up one side showing off a toned, shapely tanned leg.

Nova grabs Luke's hand, trying to draw his attention away from the spectacle, but to no avail. His eyes are glued on his ex as the crowd's eyes move from the newcomers to Luke, curious about his reaction to their entrance and her spectacular dress.

Jessica and Ziggy stand under the banner, where Luke and Nova stood recently, and smile as the photographer takes several pictures. Ziggy stands close to Jessica, putting his arm around her waist and drawing her in.

107

"Okay everyone. Let's calm down," the principal says, calling the hall to order. "Jessica, Ziggy, please take your seats so we can get this party started."

Luke's eyes follow the two as they walk hand-in-hand to their assigned table on the opposite side of the room and sit down.

"Thank freaking God they aren't at our table," Willow whispers to Noah. He smiles, knowing the money he spent to have them moved to another table was a good investment.

***

Dinner is delicious and a DJ starts to play loud, dance music for the crowd. Nova pesters Luke to dance, but he repeatedly declines. After several songs, Noah leans into Luke, whispering in his ear. The next song is Bryan Adams' "So Happy It Hurts" and Luke grabs Nova's hand, leading her to the floor. Noah and Willow follow and the four sway to the music together, smiling. At the end of the song, Luke leans into Nova. "Back in a minute," he says as he turns to the door following his best friend, Noah.

Luke and Noah scrutinize the crowded parking area, until they find their limo in the rear corner of the lot. They walk over and get in the back to hoist a couple of beers. "Whose idea was it to come to this party?" Noah asks. "Can't even call it a party with no booze," he laughs, chugging from the brown bottle and reaching for another.

After a couple of bottles each, there is a knock at the window and Noah lowers it to Willow and Nova's angry faces. "What are you two doing out here?" Willow demands. "Come back inside now," she says, turning and grabbing Nova to come with her.

"Busted," Noah laments as he finishes his fourth beer. "Let's go back in for a while. We can come back later when they aren't looking."

As Luke and Noah get out of the car to return to the prom, they notice Ziggy leaning against his car, beer in hand, talking with some guys dressed in jeans and scruffy t-shirts, obviously no one from the party.

As they walk by the car, Ziggy motions at them and says, "Yeah, that's the piece of shit that she used to go out with." He laughs. "She's sure come up in the food chain since then."

Luke stops, turns, stares at Jess's new boyfriend. Noah turns to him, puts his hands on his shoulders to help move him along. "Not now, Luke. There's a hell of a lot more of them than us." Luke realizes his friend is right and reluctantly follows him into the hall.

***

Mr. Lennon is back on stage asking the kids to gather around the platform. Nova grabs Luke's hand and leads him to the front of the crowd, looping her arm with his as they stand waiting for whatever Mr. Lennon has planned.

"It has been a wonderful evening. The meal was fantastic, the DJ is rocking," he says, turning to acknowledge the man centre stage wearing headphones surrounded by his turntables, mixer, laptop, and speakers. "And now it's time to crown the king and queen of this year's prom." The excitement is palpable and runs through the crowd of students before the principal continues. "For this task, I invite your student council president, Ferguson Johns up to the microphone."

The crowd claps and chants "Fergie, Fergie" as a gangly teenager wearing an oversized white suit with broad shoulders, something he may have borrowed from his father's 1980s wardrobe, walks out from the sidelines of the stage. His brassy blond hair is tapered short on the sides with the hair on top long and curly, fashioned in the day's latest quiff style.

Fergie stands behind the microphone, bowing to the crowd in acknowledgement of their chant. "I hope everyone is having a great time," he starts. The crowd cheers, giving him confidence to continue. "I want to thank the student council for all their support in putting tonight together and especially the prom committee for the decorations. Hollywood is a fantastic theme, and the room is dazzling." The crowd continues to cheer and chant supporting their student council president.

109

"So, without any further delay, let's crown the king and queen for this year." He turns to watch as the noble crowns for the winners are brought onto the stage, the king's, a solid gold-coloured circlet with red jewels embedded in the fingers rising above the band, and the queen's a glittering gold wreath adorned with sparkling diamond-like gems. He pulls a piece of paper out of his jacket pocket and opens it carefully, reading it silently. He looks up at the crowd, his mouth open, no words coming out. There is a short pause before he can collect his thoughts, still holding the piece of paper in front of him.

"Let's step back a half step, just to remind everyone that we held the vote for the king and queen in March. All students in grades 11 and 12 were given the opportunity to vote and we now have the final results," he says as he holds the piece of paper toward them as proof. The crowd continues to cheer. "Ladies first. The queen of the prom is Jessica Winters," he announces. The crowd roars, clapping and hooting at Jessica's win. Luke turns to see her as she kisses Ziggy on the cheek before making her way to the stage, standing in the middle of the raised platform as the principal places the exquisite piece of jewelry on her head.

Fergie stands back and waits for the crowd to quiet down. When he has their attention again, he glances at the piece of paper in his hand and moves up to the microphone announcing, "The king of the prom is Luke Anderson." The once rambunctious crowd is now silent, people are stunned, everyone aware that Luke and Jessica have broken up and that both have come to the prom with new dates. Luke is unable to move, surprised, stunned that his name has been called. "Luke, Luke are you here?" Fergie asks to fill in the silence.

"Yeah, he's right here," Noah yells pushing his friend toward the stage as Nova's arm slides away from Luke, letting him go to his ex-girlfriend without making a scene.

Ziggy stands at the back of the crowd, forgotten and embarrassed that he has not been voted the king, upset that Luke will be taking his place beside his girl, humiliated as the crowd turns to watch his reaction.

Luke climbs the stairs at the side of the stage and walks to Jessica, takes her hand and whispers, "See, they know we should be together."

Jessica quickly pulls her hand away. The principal puts the crown on Luke's head and stands back.

Fergie has watched the whole production and heard Luke's comment to Jessica, shaking his head as he turns back to the audience of classmates before announcing, "I present the king and queen of the prom. Time for their dance among the common folk." He turns to the pair, "Please make your way to the dance floor and Mr. DJ, when you are ready."

Jessica walks down the stairs first, followed closely by Luke. They stand several meters apart in the middle of the circle of students, awkwardly waiting for the music to begin.

Justin Bieber's "Anyone" booms from the speakers as Jessica turns around to look at Ziggy, trying to apologize with her eyes. Luke steps forward and takes Jessica in his arms, and they begin to sway to the music. As the chorus is repeated, Luke stares at Jessica's face and sings along with the words of the ring tone he still has for her, telling her that she is the only one he'll ever love, and if it's not her, it's not anyone.

Ziggy pushes through the crowd, reaches out and shoves Luke away from his girlfriend, before taking a swing, knocking his rival backwards as his fist connects. Luke shakes his head and runs forward, swinging at Ziggy, connecting with his chin. An all-out battle launches, with each placing a few more punches before they are pulled apart by the principal, Mr. Lennon.

Chapter 31
June 15
Luke

Alicia is sitting on the front porch, getting a little bit of sun, and reading a new paperback as Luke walks up the driveway carrying his overstuffed backpack filled with schoolbooks, papers, and everything else that has accumulated in his locker over the past nine months.

She looks up, smiling as he wrestles the load onto the veranda. "Hey, how was your last official day of high school?"

"Great. I'm not going back into that place ever again after exams next week," he huffs, sitting down on the top step. "In fact, not sure I really want to do that graduation thing," he confesses.

"Oh, come on, Luke. I so want to see you in your cap and gown. It's just one night. Do it for your old mom," Alicia pleads playfully.

Luke smiles at the light-heartedness of the conversation, thinking that his mother is finally happy. "Well, if it means that much to you, I guess I could go, but just for you Mom," he says, continuing the playfulness. "And you, look at you," he gestures. "It's nice to see your nose out of those textbooks, at least for a while," he laughs, knowing that his mom will be back at it again in the fall studying for her Bachelor's Degree in Criminology and Justice.

"Yeah, it's nice to get outside for a change, get some sun and read something light, something a little bit frivolous," she says, holding up the paperback.

Luke turns the conversation serious, "Way to go on the new job, Mom. I know you worked hard to get it." Luke finishes, holding his hand up for a high five with his mother. The two smack hands together, both chuckling.

Alicia smiles, unable to comment, her eyes starting to tear up, electing to change the subject. "We haven't had a chance to talk about the prom, Luke. How did it go? I need to see some pictures of you and Nova. You looked fantastic when you left here."

Luke pulls his phone from his pocket, searches the gallery app, selecting a number of pictures, and sends them to his mother.

Alicia opens her phone and oohs and aahs over the pictures. "I can't believe how you guys have all grown up. You. Noah. Nova. Unbelievable," she smiles. "I love her dress. Gorgeous. Matching right down to the sparkling dusty rose paint on her fingernails and your tie. Definitely a couple that night. Are you and Nova an item now?"

Luke smiles, remembering Jessica's beauty that night, her smile, her warm body against his as they danced together as king and queen of the prom. "Nova," he starts, hesitates, and starts again. "She's always around. A bit too needy, I think. She's pretty, I guess, but she's not Jess. Never will be."

"Don't rush into anything Luke. You have all the time in the world. If you like her, great. If not, don't hurt her but move on to someone else. And you know what my mom always said," she smiles as they both say together, "There are plenty of fish in the sea, but who wants a fish!"

There's silence for a moment before Luke confesses, "I have met someone else that I'm kinda interested in."

"Tell me."

"I actually met her on my birthday. Noah and I went up to Orillia. There's a pavilion right on the boardwalk at the town docks that people hang around in. It has a piano and sometimes people hang out and play music, and sing. Anyway, Hannah was playing with her brothers. They're in a band together. She has a great voice. We talked afterwards and then I saw her again a week or so later when they were playing another gig."

"When you're ready, I would love to meet her," Alicia says. "Just remember, you're only 17. Two years away from being legal and I don't want you to get in any trouble."

"Don't worry, Mom."

"I do worry. That's what moms do."

Chapter 32
June 18

Longhurst has been invited to play at a local trailer park for a BBQ lunch to welcome the campers back from a long, cold winter and to celebrate the beginning of summer solstice. Hannah and her brothers arrive early to set up their guitars and microphones on the raised platform in the grassy area near the park's pool. Once complete, they sit down on the edge of the stage to watch as the campers mingle among themselves, smiling, greeting their long-lost neighbours. A line begins to form for the hot dogs and hamburgers as the grill sizzles and the aroma of the cooking meat drifts through the air. The campers hold out their empty plates to the cooks, and they are rewarded with food, before they move to a table laden with many kinds of salads and condiments.

As the lineup begins to wane, the head chef asks Hannah, Caleb, and Lucas if they would like to partake in the delectable food. The three reply affirmatively with big smiles, filling their plates with burgers and salads as they move back to the edge of the platform to fill their bellies. As the crowd finishes their meals, a ring of chairs are placed around the stage, in anticipation of the afternoon's entertainment.

The manager of the park smiles and greets people as he walks through the throng to the stage. "Ready?" he asks. The trio nod in unison as they stand up and move to the back of the stage, picking up their musical instruments in readiness. The manager takes the stage, picks up the microphone and welcomes the campers back, wishes them the best summer ever, and introduces the band.

Hannah takes the mic graciously, thanking the manager for his kind words and for allowing them to join in the camp's festivities. She starts with a popular country song and immediately the crowd smiles and starts to sing along, some even get up to start a popular line dance with more people joining in as the crowd sings louder, the chorus resonating through the park.

The band plays about a dozen songs in each set and takes several breaks during the afternoon, meeting the crowd, accepting a drink or two before their last set. As the last song starts, Hannah sings the first half of the tune before leaving the stage, letting her brothers complete the melody without her. She smiles, offering the microphone to a young man in the crowd who has been singing along with every piece they have played as she steps from the stage. The man takes the microphone and croons as her brothers play.

Hannah steps away from the stage and moves toward a tall dark figure standing at the back of the crowd of partiers, places her arm in his, as they move away from the gathering, down the park's street to the lake. "I didn't know you were coming tonight. It's great to see you," she purrs.

He grins, encircling her hand with his as they walk away. He is unable to say anything, in awe of this woman.

"Are you here by yourself?" Hannah asks after several steps looking up into his dusty grey-blue eyes.

He nods, still unable to form words, happy that he is with this goddess, surprised at his good fortune.

The two wander down the street casually with country music as a backdrop to their early evening stroll. He studies the petite blond, smiling as they continue to walk slowly down the dusty roadway, stopping for several moments on the dock at the end of the street, gazing out to Lake Couchiching. "Beautiful," she murmurs, looking out at the water, the setting sun above the trees.

"It definitely is beautiful. Beautiful day. Beautiful scenery. Beautiful girl," he agrees.

"Let's walk over to the kid's park and watch the boats for a bit. I can't stay too long though. I have to help my brothers pack up," she says, pulling him along.

They walk back along the street, passing the two yurts the park rents out, to the grass of the lakefront park. There are a few kids playing on the swings and in the sandbox, but no one gives them a second glance.

"Strange that no one is swimming," he says as they sit down in the sand at the edge of the water. Hannah leans against his shoulder looking out at the lake. His arm snakes around her protectively.

"The water is too cold this early in the season," she confirms.

The two sit quietly watching the water as the boats zoom by, both smiling as a long purple speedboat zooms out of the canal hurtling toward the north end of the lake. As the two relax in the setting sun, Hannah begins to yawn, tired from a hectic work schedule. She rests against his strong shoulder, comfortable, content, closing her eyes and falling asleep. He sits unmoving, not wanting to wake her, not wanting for their time together to end, thinking about the possibilities with this beautiful woman.

***

He holds her for a long time until she slowly wakes up, watching as she shakes her head, as she tries to remember where they are, who she's with and what's happened. It's dark, the sun has set, and the kids have left the park, gone back to their trailers for the night. She looks up and the evening's activities slowly come back to her. She glances around and sees that they are alone, that everyone has left.

"Sorry about falling asleep. We've been doing so many shows lately that I am just exhausted," she explains, starting to move away from his warmth.

"Not a problem. I enjoyed our time together," he says, holding her tight, not allowing her to leave his side.

"What time is it"? she asks, struggling to get away from him, while trying to pull her phone out of her pocket.

"Not sure. It doesn't really matter, does it?" he smiles down at her.

"Yeah, I think it's time for me to go," Hannah declares.

"No, not yet," he replies, moving his head down to kiss her lips.

She allows him to kiss her, but he doesn't stop. His lips smother her as he pushes her back on the grass, moving his body on top of her.

"No, no," she murmurs through her covered lips, but he doesn't hear her as he pushes up her T-shirt cupping her breast with his hand.

116

A moan escapes his lips. Hannah begins to squirm, but he is bigger than her and he easily overpowers the girl. She pushes harder, putting her hands on his chest to shove him away.

He leans back to see her face. His hand comes up quickly clipping the side of Hannah's head, knocking her out immediately.

He smiles as he pulls off her shirt, unzips her cut-off shorts, pushes them down over her hips and mounts her.

He groans loudly, collapsing heavily on top of her, exhausted from pushing, spent from sharing his love with this beautiful creature. "That was fantastic, Hannah," he tells the motionless body.

He sits silently, waiting for his strength to come back. Finally, he heaves himself up into a standing position pulling up his underwear, his shorts and smoothing out his shirt. He looks around, satisfied that they continue to be alone.

He bends down to her inert body and yanks her underwear and shorts up, pulls her T-shirt down over her breasts, pats out the crinkles before he lays her back on the grass. Again, he takes in their surroundings making sure that they are alone.

Chapter 33
July 1
James

Taking off to Sauble Beach? What the hell? I guess it could all be innocent. He wasn't working, had nothing to do, thought he would get out of town, didn't want to hang around somewhere that he might run into his ex. I still can't believe he didn't tell me they broke up. I know he's been distant, more distant than normal, but I didn't know why. I got a lot going on with Axl and the gun thing and my fucking father coming back into town, but Luke should be my priority. I need to do better, but really Alicia should be looking after him, making sure he's okay. She's a detective now and can't even get a location on a cell phone. I guess it would have been hard to get a legitimate search for her son, especially on day one of her new job.

James is speeding toward Sauble Beach, pushing his vehicle just a little faster than the speed limit, not enough to get pulled over, just enough to shave some time off the trip. *Must be getting close. Yeah, there's a sign, 20 kilometers to go. Hope he's still at the beach.*

Traffic slows down as James travels down the hill at the edge of town onto the main street. He can see the large 'Sauble Beach' sign ahead with the wide expanse of clear blue water behind it as he travels slowly, watching the many pedestrians walking down either side of the street. It is a beautiful sunny day, and everyone is out taking advantage of the weather and the national holiday celebrating the country's birthday. He searches the face of each young man as he passes, ensuring they are not his son, Luke.

He turns right at the intersection at the beach front and moves his vehicle slowly along Lakeshore Road, continuing to watch the crowds, the kids. *There's a burger joint on the beach. Lots of kids hanging out there, someone playing a guitar, someone singing, lots of girls. Is that him? Slow down a bit, yeah, that's him.*

James pulls his vehicle into the parking lot beside the fast-food stand and gets out. He locks his SUV before moving to the crowd, sure that it is his son singing out of key, holding a bottle of beer covered with a colourful sleeve, his arm around a girl. *You've got to be fucking kidding me. On the street, underage with a bottle of beer in his hand? Thinks a koozie is hiding a beer bottle? How stupid is he? And that girl – looks like she's trying to get away from him the way she's squirming around, pushing his arm off her shoulder but he keeps putting it back on her or around her waist, almost like he's holding her against her will.*

James pushes through the crowd to confront Luke, grabbing the bottle out of his hand and pushing his arm away from the girl. Luke is startled by the intrusion. "What the hell, man," he mumbles as he turns to see the interloper.

"You need to come home," James tells him.

"Hey Dad. What are you doing here? Hey everyone," he turns to the crowd, gesturing to his father. "This is my dad."

"Now, Luke."

"It's okay Dad. We're just having a bit of fun," Luke says, looking around for the girl that he had been holding onto.

"Now, Luke. There's been an accident and you need to come home now," James hisses sternly, his face centimeters from his son's smirk. He puts his hands on his son's shoulders and moves him toward the car. "Now," he repeats, pushing him physically to the parking lot, dropping the beer bottle in a garbage can on the way.

***

"What are you doing, Luke? I thought you wanted to be a cop someday. You think drinking on the beach is a good idea? With a God damn koozie on the bottle? Did you think that would disguise it? Unfucking believable," James rants, pushing the Bronco over the posted 80 kilometers per hour speed limit as they leave the beach town. "Last I checked you were underage, too."

"What's so urgent that you had to come get me? And how the hell did you find me anyway?" Luke retaliates.

"Call your mom. Tell her we're on our way," his dad commands.

119

Luke pulls his phone from his pocket and looks at it. "It's dead," he says.

James pulls his cell phone out and throws it at his son. "Here use mine," he directs as he continues to push the speed limit.

Chapter 34

June 19
Luke

The gym at the school is filled to capacity with parents, grandparents, and students wearing caps and gowns, as the teachers urge everyone to get to their seats. The teachers are mostly successful as everyone finds their place, though they continue to talk with their neighbours, waving to each other, waiting in anticipation for the graduation service to start.

The students graduating are lined up in alphabetical order in the first couple of rows of the audience. Luke is the first student to pick up his graduation certificate on the stage, Noah and Nova are further back in the procession sitting side-by-side, laughing, talking, excited that they have both been successful. Jessica is last in line. She is turned around smiling out at the crowd of guests. Luke follows her gaze and sees that Ziggy is sitting beside her parents. *Unbelievable. Wonder why the asshole is not up here with us. Why isn't he graduating too?*

Luke continues to inspect the crowd, looking for his mom, finding her near the front of the room alone. *I guess I should have invited my dad, but he would have brought that tramp with him. She's always hanging around like a freaking virus. No, he hasn't called me for months. He doesn't really care. It's just me and mom.*

Luke shifts impatiently on the wooden chair, moving his gaze to watch the principal and teachers gathering on the stage. The principal signals the band and asks the crowd to stand before they start to play the "National Anthem."

Upon completion of the song, everyone, including the band, take their seats again. Principal Lennon moves to the podium and welcomes the crowd to the celebration. He acknowledges all of the work that the graduating students have completed over the past four years and suggests that their life work has just begun. He talks about how they need to dream big, never stop trying, continue learning throughout their life, overcome any adversity they may meet, to believe in themselves, and in the power of positive thinking.

Luke loses interest about halfway through the principal's speech and pulls out his phone, noticing a text from Noah, 'Ziggy isn't graduating. He's sitting with Jess's parents.'

Luke replies, 'Can't believe that they've accepted him. They had a hard time with me going out with their little girl and now look what they've got.'

Noah replies almost immediately, 'He'll have to come back next year. LOL.'

The end of the principal's speech is punctuated with the band standing up and starting "Pomp and Circumstance," the staple orchestral piece for all graduation ceremonies. Luke pockets his phone and listens to the familiar song. The band sits down once they have squeezed out the last note of the tune.

A cart with the diplomas is rolled onto the stage and Principal Lennon begins to call the graduates starting with Luke. Luke crosses the stage, shakes the principal's hand and grabs for the scroll. Before he can get away, Mr. Lennon pulls him in close to his chest and says, "I truly hope you were listening to my words earlier. Remember stay positive, never stop trying and you will be able to overcome any adversity that comes your way, even Ziggy Tunes."

Luke is surprised by the personal comments and nods as the principal releases his tight grasp.

"Luke, Luke, look this way," he hears as he starts to move toward the opposite end of the stage.

Principal Lennon pulls him in again and the two pose for a picture, both smiling pleasantly as his mom captures the snapshot.

Luke walks off the stage, continuing out the door into the front yard of the school, done with the pleasantries of the ceremony.

***

The rest of the graduates file out of the auditorium once they receive their diplomas, following Luke's lead. After the last diploma is handed out, parents and visitors slowly flow out of the school and the picture-taking gets into full gear with individual and group pictures of the graduates and their families.

Alicia finds Luke and they stand together, taking numerous pictures to mark the occasion.

Luke finds Noah and Nova in the crowd and poses with them as their moms take more pictures. Jessica and Ziggy, along with Jess's parents, wander over taking even more pictures of the graduates until Noah asks, "Didn't you get your certificate, Ziggy? You aren't wearing a cap and gown and I didn't see you on the stage."

Ziggy's shoulders go back, and the tension is palatable as he frowns and moves in to Noah, his fists up. Jessica steps between the two as they start to face off, answering for her boyfriend. "Zig didn't have enough credits. Some screw up from his old school. He only needs one more and he'll get it this summer."

There is silence for a moment. Noah steps back, "Thought you might not be smart enough to get it, but if it's only one credit....." He doesn't finish his thought.

Ziggy tries to sidestep Jessica, but she holds her ground. "Not now Zig. Not now," she almost begs.

Nova moves in front of her brother to help dissipate the situation. "Jess, have you been accepted by any of the universities you applied to?" she asks, trying to change the subject, and the tone of the conversation.

Tears come to Jessica's eyes as she looks at her friend, "I got accepted to all of them, just not sure that I'll be going."

"What do you mean? Why wouldn't you go?" Nova asks stunned.

"Not sure what I'll be up to next year." Jessica turns and takes Ziggy's arm. "Let's go Zig," she says, pulling him away from her old friends.

Luke, Noah, and Nova watch as the two walk away, get into Ziggy's car, the tires smoking as they pull out of the parking lot.

"What the hell was that all about?" Nova asks. "Not go to university?"

Chapter 35
June 24
Dylan

The Camaro's engine winds out to 150 kilometers per hour as Dylan glides up Highway 400 before he decides to slow down. *Don't want to get a ticket on the first day I have her out on the highway, especially with the car show in a couple of weeks.* He smiles to himself, enjoying the day, enjoying his freedom, enjoying the fact that all his hard work on the car has paid off and he can finally drive it. *It's going to be a great summer. I know it. I think I'll stop at the Dairy Queen and get a butterscotch sundae. Yeah, take it down to the park and watch the girls go by. It's nice and warm out and the little girls have taken off their sweaters and jackets, showing off their tender skin. A great day for girl watching, gives me a taste for what this summer's going to hold.*

He pulls the car off the exit ramp and glides down to the Dairy Queen near the lake. There's no line-up at the drive-thru and he is able to pull in, order and be on his way to Southshore Community Centre, where he parks so he can watch the pedestrians, see the lake. He pulls his sundae out of the cardboard container it sits in, rips off the lid, and moans as he shovels the first spoonful into his mouth. *Hhhmmm, butterscotch is just the best.*

He sits eating his ice cream treat, watching the people walk through the park, playing close attention to the young women as they enjoy the green space. *Can't wait to see them in their slinky bikinis on the beach.*

His eyes follow a couple strolling together, their dog sniffing the bushes as they mosey slowly through the open field. As his eyes move with them, his gaze falls on a lone figure sitting in the gazebo, a young woman, her coat wrapped around her as if it was the middle of winter, her long golden-brown hair blowing in the breeze, as she looks out to the water. *Whoa! Is that Jessica sitting there?* He scrutinizes the girl and is convinced that this is the beauty that has given Luke all the hassles lately. *Wonder if she's waiting for someone. Ziggy maybe?*

Dylan continues to sit and watch the pedestrians while he finishes his sundae. He scans the area again, and Jessica is still there, sitting on the picnic table, like she's waiting for someone. *Maybe she broke up with Ziggy? Maybe she's just sitting there hoping for someone new to come by and sweep her off her feet. Maybe I should take a chance. Maybe now is the right time for us.*

He opens the car door, moves his lanky body out of the vehicle, locks the door and walks toward Jessica. *My god, she is more gorgeous than I remember,* he thinks as he stumbles over his own feet. The kerfuffle brings Jessica's eyes to him, and she smiles at his awkwardness. He continues toward her, smiling, knowing that she is the one.

Chapter 36
June 26
James

The sun is shining, and the temperature is starting to climb steadily as the non-descript white cargo van glides south on Highway 400 toward Toronto. James is driving fast, well above the speed limit, but still blending in with the other vehicles in the fast lane as they barrel to their destinations. He has the window open, his arm resting on the top of the door like he's out for a joy ride.

"Damn, just lost Rock 95," Chevy says leaning forward to fiddle with the knob on the radio, looking for a new station as his lightweight, powerful Smith and Wesson Model 19 revolver sits in his lap.

"Can you put that bloody thing away, Chevy?" James asks, eyeing the gun.

"Make you nervous?" Chevy replies, smirking.

"Yeah, just a bit. Especially with you leaning on it. I sure as hell am not going to be stopping at a hospital if you shoot yourself in the gut."

"Not a problem," Chevy says, opening the glovebox and shoving the gun in. "Happy now?"

"Yeah, thanks."

Chevy goes back to tinkering with the radio, finding Q107 blasting "Life is a Highway" by Tom Cochrane. Chevy leans back in the passenger seat, smiling, and starts to sing along.

***

An hour later, James pulls the cargo van down a secluded street on the west side of the city. He slows down, checking addresses on the dilapidated buildings, examining the neighbourhood for surveillance cameras and people who may be watching their approach.

He finds the address that Axl gave him but decides to go around the block a second time before pulling the van into the driveway of the warehouse parking lot which is surrounded by a chain-link fence dressed in barbed wire at the top and a closed metal gate at its entrance. The area inside the fence is trash-strewn and encircles the large rundown brick building. James pauses, taking in the gate, while sitting in the van. He turns to Chevy. "Looks like it's not locked," he says, motioning to the chain that is dangling from the clasp. "Get out and open it," he directs.

Chevy nods, taking his handgun from the glovebox, stuffing it in his front jeans' pocket. He slides out of the vehicle, ensuring that he is alone, his hand crammed in his pocket, holding onto the gun. He moves cautiously to the gate and pushes it open.

James moves the van through the open space and stops the vehicle just inside, waiting for Chevy to close the gaping hole and get back in the vehicle. The van continues forward to the building slowly as James inspects the docks, and the doorways for some hint of occupation. *Are we in the right place? Where the hell is Don?*

As they round the end of the building, away from the street, a large overhead door opens revealing a number of large wooden crates sitting on the cement dock with his old Chief of Police standing in front of the boxes. The short, slight man with glasses waves as the van comes into view, changing his gesture from a wave to directing James into the spot in front of him.

James backs the van up to the warehouse dock before turning to his partner. "Let's be careful here, Chevy. You can't trust this piece of shit." From beneath the driver's seat, James pulls out a short Smith and Wesson 686, which he shoves into his belt in the middle of his back. He pulls his t-shirt down over the bulge, hiding it from prying eyes.

Chevy grunts as he pushes open the passenger door. Both men round the rear of the van at the same time, from opposite sides.

"Good to see you, James," Don Saunders says, greeting his former detective. "Still with Axl, I see," he chuckles before turning his attention to the passenger. "And you must be Chevy. We've never met but I've heard only good things about you."

127

"Yeah, from who?" Chevy growls, looking up from the parking lot at the little man standing on the shipping dock.

"Axl had some great things to say about you. I also recall your name coming up once or twice when I was in Barrie. Nothing that we could catch you on, but you were certainly on the radar, so you better be careful."

"Enough of this niceness. Do you have a forklift to move these?" James asks, putting his hands on the cement dock and boosting himself up.

"Not really a forklift. A bit more labour intensive than that," Don says gesturing to a manual pallet jack sitting on the dock. "I will leave that up to you two, but before you get started, where's the cash?"

Chapter 37
June 29
Luke

Luke sits in the lifeguard chair, his eyes swivelling back and forth, watching the swimmers, the kids playing in the shallow waters, the people on the crowded beach. He is attentive to all that is going on along the long stretch of almost-white sand.

Luke loves his job. It allows him to be outside in the sun while making an important contribution in the community. It's early in the year and he is ready to supervise the safety of the community and rescue swimmers as well as provide medical aid if required.

As he turns his gaze toward the beach leading to the marina and the city, he sees a couple walking on the boardwalk at the edge of the water, their arms loaded down with a cooler, a beach umbrella, towels, and a shopping bag, probably filled with goodies to enjoy as they lounge on the sand. He smiles until they get closer, and he recognizes them. *It's Jessica and Ziggy. Really? This has to be his idea. No way would she be that cruel to me. I'll just ignore them. I got a lot of other people to worry about without watching their every move.*

Jessica's gaze moves to the lifeguard chair as they get closer. She tries to lead Ziggy to the back of the beach, away from the people, the kids playing in the sand, out of Luke's direct vision, but Ziggy moves toward the water's edge, right in front of Luke's chair. Jessica gives in and throws a pretty yellow blanket accented with small white daisies on the sand, smoothing it out to sit on. As she does this, she looks up, catching Luke watching her. He moves his gaze quickly from her to the water and the people he should be scrutinizing.

"Let's put the umbrella over here," Ziggy says, moving it so that Luke has a perfect view into their small area on the beach, instead of putting the sun-blocking device where it would give them a modicum of shade. The rest of their stuff is put in place and Jessica sits on the blanket, her back to Luke, gazing out at the water, the swimmers. She holds her bathing suit cover-up tightly around her, as if cold, as her eyes watch the people, the kids playing in the water.

129

"Come on," Ziggy says, pulling his T-shirt over his head and throwing it on the blanket, holding his hand out to her, to help her up, but she doesn't move.

"You go, Zig. The water is still a bit too cold for me," she replies, clearly wanting to stay in the warm sun.

He asks again, but again, she declines.

"Fuck it," he says loudly as several parents with young children turn to see where the commotion is coming from. Ziggy stomps off to the water's edge leaving Jessica alone.

Don't make me come down there and warn you, asshole, Luke thinks as he watches Ziggy dive into the frigid water, his head coming up quickly, shaking his long hair like a wet dog.

Ziggy smiles at Jessica before his eyes move to Luke. "Hey, fuck head, what are you looking at?" he yells.

Luke does not reply and moves his focus away, watching his charges play at the water's edge. Ziggy dives back into the water and Luke's watchful eye is drawn back to him as he swims out to the buoy line.

"Stop asshole," Luke mumbles under his breath, knowing that Ziggy is trying to call him out, force him to make the first move. Luckily for Luke, his partner lifeguard Justin, who is patrolling the beach on foot, sees the situation and calls out to Ziggy. "No further," he warns, standing still, watching as Ziggy acknowledges the warning and dives under the water back in the direction of the shore. Justin watches as Ziggy moves into the shallow waters and he looks up at Luke with a smile before continuing his walk down the beach.

Ziggy comes out of the water, walks over to their spot on the beach and takes a towel from Jessica's outstretched arm. He wraps it around himself and gapes up at Luke in the lifeguard chair. "What are you doing up there, mommy's boy?" he asks as he opens the cooler and pulls out a can of beer.

Luke surveys the area for his partner, Justin, but he has moved down the beach and is not within hearing distance. He looks down at Ziggy and yells, "No beer on the beach," hoping that his statement will put a stop to an outright altercation between them.

"Fuck you," Ziggy yells as he takes a long pull of the ice-cold beer. People in the immediate area begin to pack up their belongings, shaking their heads in disgust. "Did you hear me, asshole?" Ziggy yells again. "Fuck you."

Luke gives two short blasts on his whistle, looks to Justin, who turns when he hears the call for assistance, and waves him over before he climbs down the ladder to the sand. Luke moves quickly to Ziggy, pushing his face to within centimeters of his nose. "Why the hell don't you just leave? I'm sure you could be swimming in your own pool."

Ziggy chuckles. "It's a free country asshole. My girl and I wanted to come to the beach today, so here we are. Do you have a problem with that?" he says, pushing Luke backwards. "And really you're just a pussy lifeguard, so there's nothing you can do about it even if you had a problem."

Luke takes a swing at Ziggy, but it doesn't connect. In turn, Ziggy throws a punch, hitting Luke squarely in the eye that had just healed from their last altercation, making him stagger back. He pauses for a moment before jumping forward, arms flaying, pummeling him.

Justin appears as Luke's fist connects with Ziggy's ribs, causing Ziggy to tighten up and cover his torso. A crowd of people congregate around them as they continue to throw punches, kicks, and swear at each other. Justin stands back for a moment, watching, waiting until he can safely separate the two. After several more punches, he moves between them, pushing and kicking them apart, pushing them down,

He waits another moment before yelling, "Get up." The two stagger to their feet, winded but not taking their eyes off each other.

"You," Justin points to Ziggy, "pack up your shit and get the hell off the beach." He watches, but Ziggy doesn't move. "Don't make me repeat myself," he warns. "Now."

Ziggy stands still, catching his breath before uttering, "Fuck it." He beds down and throws the blanket and towels into the bag they brought, pulls the umbrella out of the sand, and gives Jessica the look to move out before stomping away.

Justin turns to the crowd. "Nothing to see here," he confirms, putting his arm around Luke's shoulder and leading him away. "Go to the bathroom, wash the blood off your face. You have to finish your shift today, but I will have to report this." He puts his hand up to stop Luke's verbal defense. "I get that he was asking for a fight, but you didn't step back, you didn't diffuse the situation. You'll be suspended for a couple of days, a week at most."

***

At the end of his shift, Luke throws on a t-shirt and trudges over to the gazebo at the park to sit, watch the summer unfold in front of him, think. He is unsure how long he has been sitting there, time has gotten away from him when the rumbling of a car accelerating down the main street catches his attention. He turns to see a Porsche revving its engine before it pulls into the parking lot about 50 meters from him. *Beautiful car*, he laments, watching as an old guy gets out of the car and leans against the trunk. *Looks like he's waiting for someone, something. Fuck, if a young girl shows up and jumps into that car with that old guy, I have no chance. I can't compete with these rich dudes.*

Luke continues to watch, letting his mind roam, making up different scenarios for what may be going down, until he sees a black Bronco pull into the lot, drive up beside the Porsche and stop. *Is that? No that can't be. Damn, it is.* Luke watches as his father exits the sleek SUV and approaches the smiling old man leaning against the Porsche.

They are too far away for Luke to hear their words clearly, but he knows that it is an argument from the gestures, the raised voices, and the stance each man displays. Luke sits for several moments watching the encounter between the two. Finally, when curiosity gets the better of him, he slides off the picnic table and walks toward the pair in the parking lot.

He is spotted by the senior, who nods his head toward Luke and says something to his dad. James turns to look and quickly turns back to the ancient fellow with more heated words being exchanged. As Luke approaches, the two stop arguing and turn to watch his progress. There is silence as he walks up to them. "Dad?" he says questioningly, unsure of the situation, the dynamics.

132

"Hey Luke. What are you doing down here?" James asks.

Luke looks to the old guy who is silently examining him before turning back to his father. "Just got finished work for the day. I'm on my way home now," he discloses, turning to look at the man again, waiting for his dad to introduce him.

"Glad to hear you'll be working again this summer. Want a ride home?"

"Sure Dad, if you have the time." Again, he looks at the old man.

"No problem. I've got all the time in the world for you. Let's go," James confirms, ignoring the man he has been arguing with, putting his arm around his son, and moving him toward the passenger side of his car, as if bundling him away from a toxic situation.

"James aren't you going to introduce us before you go?" they both hear from the old man still leaning against his beautiful car.

James stops but does not turn around. Luke turns back, scrutinizing the man, his dark curly hair streaked with grey, his vivid blue eyes, the Blue Jays ballcap sitting on his head. His dad holds tight to his shoulder and tries to turn him around, back toward his SUV. "No one you need to meet, Luke. Just someone that I'm doing some work with," he tries to explain as he pushes Luke to the car.

Luke looks at his dad, his curiosity peaked. *What the hell is going on? Who is this guy?*

"I can't believe you're being so rude to an old man," the senior admonishes James for his lack of manners.

James stops and turns to the old gent, giving him a painful look, finally yielding to the request. "Luke, this is, ah, my uncle," he says as an introduction.

"Uncle?" Luke asks as the old man stands there not moving, a smile on his face.

James continues, "Yeah, an uncle from my mom's side of the family. Haven't seen him for years and all of a sudden, he shows up," he finishes trying to again move Luke toward his car.

Luke steps away from his father and moves to the old man, putting his hand out in front of him. "I didn't know my dad had any relatives left. I'm Luke," he explains.

The two shake hands. "I'm Mack Sommers. Good to meet you after all these years, Luke."

"Sommers? That was my grandmother's maiden name. You must be her brother."

"Yeah, her brother," he confirms beaming fondly at his grandson.

Chapter 38
June 30
Alicia

Jeff is here? Wonder what's going on? Alicia carries the heavy bags of Chinese food up the front steps, cocking her head to identify the music booming from the house. *That doesn't sound like something Luke or Jeff would listen to - it's old-fashioned, band music.* She listens more intently and hears the chorus of the song "Congratulations and Jubilations." As she opens the door, the chorus begins again and she sees the two men in her life with New Year's Eve horns up to their mouths blowing on them, making an awful screaming noise while the tassels sway. Alicia smiles as the pair continue to choke out their song, while grinning ear-to-ear.

They finally finish their exhibition and Luke grabs the bags of food from her arms. "Congratulations Mom. Last day of patrol work. Tomorrow is the first official day as Detective Anderson."

"Well thank you, I think," she laughs, walking into the living room, seeing the rest of the decorations, a congratulations banner hung over the dining room table, and a bouquet of blue balloons sitting beside her chair. She reaches out to Jeff and gives him a quick peck on the cheek and asks, "Whose idea was this?"

"Your son's, all your son's," he laughs. "But I'm glad he included me in the celebration."

"I just thought we should party a bit. You've worked so hard, and you finally made it," Luke says, walking to the dining room table with the bags of food.

Alicia looks around, smiling, impressed that her son would have the sensitivity and take the time to celebrate this milestone with her. *Life is good again;* she thinks throwing her purse on the coffee table.

"And all in my favourite colour," she says, admiring the deep blue of the balloons, the streamers, the banner.

135

Luke laughs. "Everyone knows how much the Andersons all like blue. We should have them officially rename the colour to Anderson blue."

"And you set the table. Well, will wonders never cease?" Alicia laughs, sitting down at the head of the table, noticing an envelope sitting on her plate. "What's this?" she asks, picking it up and turning it around to see the name and address. "Oh my God, Luke. Is this it?" she screams as she pulls out the piece of paper from the already-opened envelope. "It took them long enough."

"Yup, that's it," Luke agrees as his mother scans his acceptance into the college's Police Foundations program. Alicia puts the acceptance letter down and gets up to give her son a hug. They embrace awkwardly, as mothers and sons tend to do, before he finally calls an end to the theatrics. "Enough, enough Mom. Let's eat. I'm starved," he says, escaping from Alicia's embrace.

Luke and Jeff pull the containers of food out of the bag, smiling at each other.

Alicia stands back, tears in her eyes. "Life is good, Luke. It really is," she confesses.

The three enjoy the food, laughing and talking the evening away.

***

"Night Luke," Alicia calls as she passes his closed bedroom door hours later. She hears a mumbled reply coming from behind the door and continues down the hallway to her room.

Think I'll lay out my clothes for the morning. It's been so frigging long since I could wear something other than that police uniform to work. Thank God, I will almost look like a regular human being, she thinks pulling a pair of navy pants and a matching suit jacket from the closet. Hhhmmm, probably going to be hot tomorrow. How about a sleeveless white blouse to go with it? And of course, my new pair of Dr. Scholl's black leather slip-on sneakers. Made for comfort, not style. She smiles to herself, pleased with where life has finally brought her.

Chapter 39
June 30
Luke

That was a great night. Mom starts her new job tomorrow and I finally got my acceptance into the Police Foundations program. Freaking took them long enough to send the acceptance out, but I guess that's what happens when you have three times the number of people applying than available spots. Had me pretty nervous there for a while. And Jeff. He's not such a bad guy. Mom seems to like him, and he treats her like a princess, so I can't complain, especially after the shit that went down between her and dad.

I probably should have told her about the fight with Ziggy at the beach yesterday, but I didn't want to ruin a good evening. It's nothing really. She might even understand. Who am I trying to kid? No, she won't understand. She's a mom and a cop and believes you should never fight. But it's only a three-day suspension. I'll just forget about telling her for now and plead ignorance if she ever finds out.

Luke lies back on his bed with his earbuds in, listening to Tom Cochrane's "Life is a Highway". His phone signals a text coming in and he opens the app. He sits up as he reads the text from Jessica. 'Can you meet me at our place?'

He's stunned. *Jessica? After what happened yesterday? Could it be someone goofing him? Probably that jerk-off she's seeing. I need to make sure it's her. Ask her something that only she would know about, something that the asshole has no idea about.* He pauses, thinking before he types, 'When's my birthday?'

He waits patiently, looking at the screen for a reply. *Must not be her, taking way too long.*

'May 11' appears on his screen.

He types in 'where was the first place we made love?'

Several moments later, he sees the correct answer, something that Ziggy would not know unless Jessica had talked to him about it, which was highly unlikely, especially with the detail that she includes. 'At your house, while your mom was in the hospital.'

Luke's heart melts. *She wants to meet me. She wants to talk. She wants me back.* He scrambles to sit up on the side of the bed as his fingers move across the keypad, 'on my way.'

He sits for a moment listening for his mom. Jeff left a while ago, and she went to bed, hopefully has fallen asleep by now. He quietly gets up, pulls back the covers on his bed, and shoves his pillow under them, trying to make it appear like he is under the blankets sleeping. He gets dressed and sneaks to the bedroom door, opens it, waits, hears nothing, tip toes to the front door of the house, opens it, walks out into the still, dark evening, gently closing the door.

***

The evening is calm and quiet as Luke sits on the picnic table waiting. Several dog walkers and a couple on their bikes have passed through the park, but other than that he's alone as he waits for his love, Jessica. He pushes his earbuds in, turning up the volume on Bryan Adams's song "Summer of '69", trying to remain calm as he waits in anticipation for good things to come. *What a great day. Mom's last day on patrol. I got accepted to Georgian and Jessica is coming back to me. Mom is right. Life is good*, he thinks as he hears a car pull into the Southshore Community Centre about 50 meters away. *That better not be Ziggy. She better not be coming here with that loser;* he thinks as he turns to look. *Kinda looks like Dylan's car, but why the hell would he be here?*

Luke continues to sit, watching the car as the driver gets out and walks around the north end of the building out of sight. *Could be Dylan, but what would he be doing here? Probably just some guy with a souped-up muscle car that can't sleep so he's going for a walk. I'd go and see, but I'm not leaving this bench until Jessica comes. I don't want to miss her for something so stupid.*

He remains on the bench, waiting for his love. After an extended period of time, he checks his phone. *Shit. I've been here for 45 minutes. Where the hell is she?*

He decides to text her, 'I'm here. What's your ETA?' But there is only silence from Jessica, no answer to his text.

Luke punches the icon for Jessica on his phone and listens as it rings. One, two, three, four rings and it goes to voicemail. "Jess, call me," he says, before closing his phone, confused. *What's going on?*

He waits another five minutes and calls again. Still no answer. *This can't be some kind of joke, can it?* He waits another 30 minutes, calling and texting her intermittently, before sending a text to Noah. 'Want to party?' he asks.

Noah's reply is swift, 'Always. On my way.'

'I'm at the Southshore Community Centre. I'll meet you in the parking lot.'

Chapter 40
July 1
James

James studies his son, passed out in the passenger seat. *Fucking kid.*
He's playing with fire if he doesn't get his shit together. He couldn't
have had anything to do with Jessica's death, could he? He's acting
mighty pissed off at me, but what about Jessica? Is he pissed off at her
too? And he's drinking. I would have never thought he would do that,
he was so righteous all the time, doing everything his mother told him,
almost like it was the two of them against me. But guess who she calls
when she needs help? Me. I'm still the one they depend on. She could
have at least called and told me that he had broken up with his
girlfriend. I could have been there for him, but no, no one tells me
shit.

James drives steadily for over two hours before he pulls his SUV
into Alicia's driveway. He hasn't even put the vehicle in park when
his ex-wife runs out the front door of the house and yanks the
passenger door open emphatically. "Where the hell have you been?"
she yells, waking Luke up from his intoxicated-induced sleep. He
shakes his head slowly, his eyes moving from his mother to his father
and back again.

"Well, where the hell have you been all day? I've been calling you
and you haven't answered," Alicia repeats.

"My phone was dead," he says simply, unbuckling his seat belt and
sliding out of the truck.

The two walk to the house, Alicia with her arm around Luke as if
he's been wounded or lost. James shakes his head and follows as they
move to sit at the kitchen table. He sits down on the opposite side of
the table from his son and Alicia, like it's him against the two of them.

"What is going on Mom? Why did you send dad to get me? And
how the hell did he know where I was?" Luke demands, looking from
one parent to the other.

"You first – where have you been? Is that booze I smell on you?" Alicia moves her eyes to James for confirmation, and he nods.

"We were just out having some fun. A couple of drinks, listened to some music, met some new friends."

"Luke, you are underage. You shouldn't be drinking especially in public. If your dad hadn't found you, you could have been in big trouble if the police had caught you. It would go on your record, and it would ruin any aspirations you have to be a cop."

"I know, I know. We were just letting off a bit of steam. I'll be more careful in the future."

"Where were you last night?" Alicia continues changing direction quickly.

"I was here with you. We celebrated your promotion and the start of your new job."

"After that. Did you go out?"

Luke sits quietly, wondering how much his mother knows. Wondering if she's guessing that he's been out all-night partying with Dylan and Noah. After some consideration, he finally admits, "I left the house about 10pm. Met up with Noah. Went to Dylan's, had some drinks and then we decided to go to the beach. Slept in Dylan's car."

Alicia stares at her son, while James gets up and begins to pace back and forth in the constricted space.

"Why? What's going on?" Luke asks, looking from one parent to the other. "We drove to the beach, drank a bit, listened to some music, passed out. We woke up when the sun came up and decided to just hang out, go for a swim, enjoy the day. It's summer. I wasn't scheduled to work. We didn't get into any trouble."

Alicia continues to watch her son, the boy she thought she knew, who is now telling her about behaviours that up until a couple of months ago she would have said were impossible for Luke to commit, but obviously his life has taken a drastic downward turn.

"Mom, what's going on?" he asks again.

"When was the last time you saw Jessica?" Alicia asks.

"Jessica?"

"Yes, when was the last time you saw her or talked to her?"

141

Luke glances down for a moment and then up into his mother's face. "She was at the beach a couple of days ago with that dipshit she's been seeing."

"Did you talk to her? To him?"

"I didn't really talk to them, no," he hedges.

"What do you mean you didn't really talk to them?" she asks, emphasizing 'really.'

"I didn't have a conversation with them."

"Be more specific."

"Is this about work?" he asks, pausing. When there is no answer forthcoming, Luke continues, "Yeah okay, I did call Ziggy a couple of derogatory names, but he started it, he hit me first. I was just defending myself."

"And?" Alicia waits, but there is silence from Luke as he looks at his fisted hands sitting on the table. "Then what happened?" she asks as if interrogating him like a suspect at work.

Luke pauses for another moment before answering. "Justin, the other lifeguard, came over to help. He pulled us apart. It got reported to management, and I was suspended for three days. What is this about? How did you know about the fight?"

"I didn't know about it, but you should have told me, you should have manned up to what happened, what you did. And you shouldn't be slipping out in the middle of the night specially to go drinking. You are underage. If you get caught, it goes on your record. When you snuck out, did you go directly to Dylan's? Or Noah's?"

"I went to the park."

"What park? Why did you go to the park?" Alicia asks.

Luke pauses again, his attention moving from his mother to his father unsure why he is being subjected to all these questions. "I got a text from Jessica. She wanted to meet up at the gazebo, near the Community Centre, but she never showed up, so I texted Noah and he came and got me."

"And you thought going out with Dylan and Noah to get drunk was a good idea?"

"It just kind of happened." Luke pauses before demanding, "Why is this important?"

"What time? What time where you in the park?" his mother questions aggressively.

"I left here about 10pm. I walked there, took about 15 minutes. I was there for an hour, an hour and a half. Then I texted Noah."

"And he came to get you?"

"Yeah. He got there about ten minutes later. We drove around for a bit, then we saw the lights on at Dylan's, so we went there. Then we all decided to go to the beach. Why? What the hell is going on?"

"And after that, you and Noah and Dylan were together. Always."

"Yeah, we were together. Mom, what is going on? Why all the questions?" Luke pleads.

Alicia pauses, her eyes moving from her son to James, who nods his head. She turns to Luke. "Jessica is dead." She pauses watching Luke closely before continuing. "Her body was found this morning near the water behind the Community Centre in Allandale Station Park." She stops again watching pain take a grip on her son's face as her words sink in. "And now you are telling us you were at the park around the time that she died."

Luke looks to his father for confirmation, and James simply nods his head. Luke is in shock as tears begin to form at the edges of his eyes and he starts to shake uncontrollably, mumbling, "No, no, no."

Alicia sadly nods her head, reiterating the news, "I'm sorry, Luke, but she's gone."

Luke moans, groans, curses God, curses Ziggy, curses Jessica for leaving him. He rants, raves, and cries so hard he starts to hiccup as he is unable to catch his breath.

Alicia tries to calm her son, leans into him, holds his hand, rubs his arm, and hugs him. Slowly, he regains his composure and tells his parents he is going to bed. He gets up from the table, walks to his room, and slams the door shut behind him. Alicia and James can hear his guttural scream through the closed door, and they leave him to his agony, his thoughts, unable to help him or ease his pain.

Alicia turns to James, who has begun to pace the length of the kitchen again. "We need to protect him, James. They are going to come for him, I just feel it."

143

James stops in his tracks and turns to his ex-wife. "We need to keep this quiet, at least until the autopsy results come in with the exact time of death. Her death needs to be after midnight to clear him. When he calms down, we need to interrogate him again, ask him what he saw at the park, what cars were in the parking lot, anybody walking. He must have seen something without realizing its importance."

Chapter 41
July 2
Alicia

"Thank you for coming this morning and welcome to the major crime room for the Jessica Winters case," Helen says greeting the newly-formed team. "We'll meet every morning at 8am to review updates from the previous day's assignments, examine any new reports or information that has come to light, as well as allocate tasks for that day. The Chief and our Crown Attorney have joined us today," Helen acknowledges nodding at the two standing at the back of the room. "You are more than welcome to attend whenever your schedules permit. If something of major interest is going to be discussed, I will definitely give you a heads up the day before," she finishes for the Chief and the Crown Attorney's benefit.

"So, without delay, let's introduce the team members and their responsibilities for this case. Officer Edward Vincent, you did such a great job yesterday controlling the crime scene that we've borrowed you from patrol for an extended period of time to be our Case Manager. You will be looking after the case file, making sure that all assignments are completed, paperwork and reports are available to all, pictures, videos, and evidence from the crime scene is documented. You will be the keeper of all the materials related to this case and ensure we have all the evidence for the prosecution of the perpetrator, when the time comes," Helen says, turning to ensure his agreement.

"We've also commandeered your partner Officer Davy Jones, to help with evidence collection, witness reviews and field work," she adds smiling. "Davy, I would like you to work with the forensic team to go back to the park today and re-walk the area. We've left the yellow tape up with a guard overnight so nothing would be disturbed. Look for anything we might have missed yesterday. Also, in the next couple of days, this team needs to canvas the homes in the area, visit the park early in the morning and late in the evening to catch anyone

145

that may have been in the park that day. I will leave it with you guys to coordinate yourselves to get that all covered," she nods.

"Sanjay Ramesh is our Identification Officer on the case, documenting everything related to the body," Helen nods in his direction.

"We also have Connor Brooks, our Forensic Lead, to help with analysis of fingerprints, blood, everything found at the scene, her clothes, and the blanket covering her body."

"Right now, the walls are pretty empty," Helen points out as she looks around at the white boards which wrap the room. "We will collect the information, put the pieces together, post them. The visuals will help us put the whole picture together, help us see gaps or other possibilities we haven't thought of. "

"Any questions or concerns?" Helen asks looking around the room at each of her team members. There is silence so she continues, "I reached out to Dr. Diamond, the coroner, for an update on the case. They haven't had a chance to get to Jessica yet, probably won't be able to for a couple of days, but they have sent her clothing, the blanket that she was wrapped in and the log to Connor's team for analysis. I'm hoping we can lift some DNA and fingerprints to help us convict the perpetrator. I also asked Dr. Diamond to check for evidence of sexual relations. Maybe there's semen, which may or may not be her boyfriend's, Ziggy Tunes. Maybe there is someone else we should be considering."

Helen takes a breath. "Alicia and I are going to question the boyfriend this morning, see what he has to say for himself. Everyone else clear on what they are going to be doing today?"

Helen looks around at the nodding heads and smiles. "Great. Call me if you need me. We'll meet back here tomorrow at 8am," she completes, closing the meeting.

* * *

The private road winds through acres of greenery, until finally, the view opens up to a huge two storey home sitting on the bluff

146

overlooking the bay. *It is so over-the-top, like he thinks he's entitled, deserves special treatment and privileges. The VP of the Ruebens! How the hell is this right?* Alicia continues to eye the structure, the oversized windows, the view through the house to the pool and the bay beyond. A detached five-car garage is positioned beside the house. The large doors are closed and hiding its contents, leaving them to wonder if Ziggy's lime-green Shelby Mustang is secreted inside.

"Wow, this is quite the place. I guess organized crime pays well," Helen comments as she pulls the vehicle up to the front of the house on the U-shaped driveway. "Axl is pretty young to be a VP in such a big gang, but don't let that fool you. He is smart, ruthless in fact, with a great legal team behind him when he needs them."

As Helen and Alicia step from the police vehicle, the massive wooden front door is opened by Axl Tunes, dressed in his typical uniform, form-fitting jeans, a T-shirt with flip flops on his feet. He watches for a moment as the two women walk toward the house before he steps outside and closes the door behind him.

"Mr. Tunes?" Helen asks as they approach the watching homeowner.

"Yes, and you are?" he asks, standing on the top step.

"I'm Detective Helen Hodges and this is my partner, Detective Alicia Anderson," Helen says nodding at Alicia.

Axl looks from Helen to Alicia. "Alicia, how are you? That was an interesting day at school, eh? I haven't been pulled into the principal's office for years," he chuckles.

Helen interrupts, "We need to talk to Ziggy."

Axl turns his attention back to Helen. "I'm sorry he's not here right now. Why do you want to talk to him?"

"Where is he? It's important that we talk to him now."

"He's out."

"Can we take a look?" Helen asks, gesturing toward the garage.

Axl quickly counters, "Not without a warrant."

"Do you know where he is?" Helen continues trying to gain some traction in the conversation.

"He's out. Doesn't really matter where," Axl replies evasively.

147

"We hear that he's going out with Jessica Winters. Is that true?"

"Jessica? I don't know if I've ever heard him mention that name. Why?" Axl asks, privately recalling the pool party a couple of weeks ago with Jessica and Ziggy splashing each other in the pool, the two lying on the lounge chairs in the sun together very much a couple.

"What is your relationship to Ziggy, Mr. Tunes?"

"He's my brother. He lives with me."

"Where are his parents?"

"Mom is in Toronto, with her own life. My brother and sister came to live with me a couple of months ago and I am their legal guardian."

"We need to talk to him."

"Why?"

"Jessica Winters is dead, and we need to ask him some questions."

Axl pauses for a short moment, glancing at his feet before raising his head and looking directly into Helen's eyes. "I will bring Ziggy to the police precinct tomorrow morning at 9am with legal counsel."

"At this point, it's just a few questions. He doesn't really need legal counsel unless there is something that he wants to hide," Helen provokes.

Axl smiles. "Yes, I understand your standard cop rhetoric, but the fact is we will be there with legal counsel tomorrow morning. See you then," Axl finishes, dismissing the two detectives as he turns and walks back into the house.

Helen and Alicia watch him go, slamming the front door as he enters the house, leaving them standing in the driveway, listening to the two-part twill of a lone cardinal.

Chapter 42
July 2
Axl

Axl mumbles to himself as he slams the front door of his home. "Fucking kid. What the hell has he gotten himself into this time?" He stomps to the kitchen and picks up his cell phone, punching the phone icon for Ziggy.

The phone rings and rings, finally going to voicemail.

"Ziggy. Home. Now," Axl yells into the phone. He hits the end button and slams the cell onto the granite countertop. "Fuckkkkkk," he shrieks, shaking his head in disgust as he looks out of the window at the water, the trees, the gorgeous morning.

He picks up his phone and punches the icon for Sutton Fox, a lawyer who he has used several times for gang issues. The call is picked up after the first ring. "Hey Axl, everything okay?" a calm, unruffled voice asks.

"No, everything is not okay," Axl screams into the phone. "God damn cops were just here looking for Ziggy. His girlfriend is dead, and they want to question him."

"I'm on my way," Sutton confirms, disconnecting the line.

Axl puts the phone down and paces through the kitchen, through the family room, into the dining room, back into the kitchen. His movements are tense, and his heartbeat and breathing are racing as he tries to calm himself down. "Fucking kid," he repeats continuously as he paces through the house.

His phone rings. Looking at the call display, he sees Ziggy's smiling face. Axl punches the phone icon and without giving his brother a chance to say anything, he repeats his initial message sternly, "Ziggy. Home. Now," and disconnects the line.

Chapter 43
July 2
Alicia

The two detectives get into their vehicle and close the doors. Before Helen turns the key to start the car and leave the Tunes's estate, she turns to her partner. "God dammit, Alicia! What were you two doing at school together?"

Alicia buckles her seat belt before answering. "There was a small altercation, and we were called in to the principal's office."

"More, give me more," Helen demands.

"It was nothing really. Luke and Ziggy got into a fist-a-cuffs at school, and we were both called in."

"I think you should have mentioned this to the Chief. Sounds like there's more of a history between Luke and Ziggy then you've let on."

Alicia chooses her words carefully. "It was a while ago, and things have settled down. And they are 17-year-old kids. Just because Luke thinks Ziggy is an asshole is no reason to step back from the case. He is an asshole. And so is his brother," she breathes, trying to control the strain of the situation, knowing she should also confess her knowledge of the fight between Luke and Ziggy at the beach a couple of days ago.

The two sit silently in the car for a moment before Helen starts the car, puts it in drive and manoeuvres through the palatial gardens back to the street. "So, changing topics. What did you think of that?" Helen asks.

"Arrogant, piece of shit," Alicia replies, looking out the car window, taking in the trees, the gardens, while trying to temper her stress.

Helen laughs. "Got that right. But it doesn't surprise me that he's going to lawyer up. Probably has the guy on speed dial."

"Probably," Alicia agrees.

"Let's go talk to Nova Nash, Jessica's best friend. She might be able to give us some insight into Jessica and Ziggy's relationship. Do you know her, Alicia?"

150

Alicia is distracted momentarily as her mind continues to spin negative scenarios with Luke in the middle of them. She shakes these thoughts out of her head before turning to Helen, "I do. Her twin brother, Noah, is Luke's best friend. And since Jessica and Luke broke up, she's been lobbying hard to be Luke's new girlfriend. He doesn't feel the same way, though they did go to the prom together."

"Whoa, sounds like there might be some animosity between Jessica and Nova with Luke in the centre. I'll take lead on this, just like the conversation with Axl Tunes. Stand back, watch, listen but don't say anything, don't reply to any of her questions or comments. Are you good with that?"

"Sure. Not a problem," Alicia confirms, continuing to worry about her son and what he may know about Jessica's demise.

***

Helen pulls the police vehicle into the modest house just around the corner from Alicia's rental home. She turns the key off, pauses, and turns to Alicia, "Remember, I'm taking lead on this. Nothing from you. No comments, no answers, nothing. Got it?"

"Got it," Alicia agrees sullenly.

Helen pushes the button for the buzzer at the front door and the two wait on the front porch until Mrs. Nash opens the door. "Hello Alicia," she says, smiling. "What's going on?"

Helen steps between Alicia and Mrs. Nash. "I'm Detective Helen Hodges and you know Alicia Anderson, Detective Alicia Anderson," she emphasizes the position of detective. "We would like to have a conversation with Nova and Noah if they're home."

Mrs. Nash's eyes move from Alicia to Helen and back to Alicia again. "What's going on, Alicia?"

Helen answers as Alicia looks down, unable to add to the conversation. "Just some routine questions. Are they home?"

Mrs. Nash's attention moves from one detective to the other, and she finally opens the door, wide for them to enter. "Sure, they're both here. Come on in. Why don't we have a seat in the dining room," she

151

says, directing them. "Coffee, tea?" she asks as the detectives sit down at the table.

"No, but thank you," Helen replies. "Can you get Nova and Noah for us?"

"Sure, no problem." Mrs. Nash moves into the kitchen to the door to the basement. She opens it and calls down, "Nova, Noah, can you both come up here, please?" The three hear grumbling coming from the lower level. "Now," their mother directs from the top of the stairs.

Moments later they hear Nova and Noah's feet pounding on the stairs, similar to the sounds of a stampeding herd of elephants. The twins come through the basement door and both quiet down instantly seeing Alicia and Helen sitting at the dining room table. "Alicia," they both acknowledge, turning back to look at their mother.

Helen takes control of the conversation again. "Hi Nova, Noah," she says, getting up to shake their hands formally. "I'm Detective Helen Hodges and you both know Detective Alicia Anderson, Luke's mom," she continues, nodding her head in Alicia's direction. "We have a couple of questions to ask you. Can you sit down and talk with us?"

Both Nova and Noah nod in the affirmative and take chairs facing the two detectives, while their mother sits down at the head of the table. Alicia pulls out a small pad of paper and a pen, ready to take notes.

"I understand that you both know Jessica Winters?" Helen asks questioningly.

Noah answers for both of them. "Yeah, she goes to our school. She went out with Luke for a while last year. Why? What's going on?"

"What about you? I hear that you two are best friends, Nova."

Nova is intently examining her folded hands in her lap before looking up at Detective Hodges when she hears her name, but before she can answer, her mother replies, "Nova and Jessica have been best friends for years. They went to grade school together, went to high school together, had a lot of the same classes. What is this all about?"

Helen continues, "Nova, is that true? Are you and Jessica best friends?"

Nova's attention moves from her mother to Detective Hodges. "Jessica and I have always been best friends. Though lately…." She doesn't finish her sentence, again her eyes moving to her hands, away from the detectives' inquiring looks.

"Though lately what?" the detective presses.

Nova looks up at her mother, who nods her head, signaling to Nova that it is alright to tell her story, to tell the truth.

"Lately, we haven't been so close."

"Can you tell us why? What happened?"

"When she broke up with Luke, she went a little crazy and started seeing this creep at school, Ziggy." Nova looks to Alicia for a moment, before turning back to Detective Hodges. "She broke up with Luke, said he wasn't mature enough, wasn't adventurous enough, called him vanilla. Said that Ziggy was exciting, and a little wild and that it was time for some fun in life. And that it didn't hurt that his family has money." Nova stops, her eyes moving from one detective to the other before continuing, "Why are you asking me these questions? Is she okay?"

"What makes you think she's not okay?" Helen asks.

Nova looks down at her hands again, silent for a moment, before replying. "Well, the cops are here asking questions about her."

"Tell me a little bit more about her relationship with Ziggy," Helen asks, ignoring Nova's comment.

Nova looks to her mother again, sees the nod of her head, and continues. "Jessica was my best friend until Ziggy. He made her change. Made her hard. Made her do drugs. It all started innocently enough, I guess, but I think she's been doing some heavy stuff, heroin or cocaine or something that screws with her head. And he hits her. Did he hurt her? Is that why you're here?" She starts to sniffle.

"He hits her? Have you seen him hit her? Did she tell you that he hit her?"

"I've seen the bruises. I've listened to her make excuses for him. That's when we started drifting apart. Luke was such a great guy to her," Nova nods to Alicia. "A great guy and she broke his heart for a piece of shit like Ziggy. I don't understand her anymore."

153

Noah finds his voice and asks, "Why are you here? What's happened?"

Helen continues, "Just a couple more questions. When was the last time you each saw Jessica?"

The twins turn to look at each other. Noah speaks first. "I think it was probably at graduation. She was with her loser boyfriend, even though he didn't cut it."

"Cut it?" Helen asks.

Noah shrugs. "He didn't graduate. Didn't get enough credits. Has to go back, probably summer school," he snickers.

Helen turns and repeats her question. "Nova, when was the last time you saw her?"

"Probably the same." Again, her eyes move from Helen to Alicia and back again. "I've talked to her once or twice since then. Told me how happy she was with Ziggy, how exciting things were with his family, their great house, the fun they were having. I couldn't understand that, and the whole situation made me feel a bit awkward." Nova pauses for a moment before adding, "I've been seeing Luke. She didn't say anything but I'm sure she doesn't like that, me going out with her old boyfriend. I think it is the end of our friendship," Nova moans.

Helen turns her attention back to Mrs. Nash. "I understand you have another son, Tate. Does he know Jessica too? Maybe we should talk to him as well."

"Tate's not home at the moment, but he didn't really know Jessica. Only through her coming here and hanging out with Nova, so I don't think that's really necessary," Mrs. Nash counters, fear and anger beginning to seep in. "Why are you asking the kids these questions? What's happened?"

"One more question," Helen says. "Do you know anyone that would want to hurt Jessica?"

Noah shrugs his shoulders before all eyes move to Nova. She starts tentatively but gets emboldened, her voice raising in volume. "Ziggy. He's hit her. I saw bruises on her arms a couple of times. Once he got mad at her when they were up north and he took off in the car, left her to hitch hike home by herself."

154

Helen sighs looking at the twins across the table before revealing, "Jessica's body was found near the Southshore Community Centre."

"Her body?" Nova cries.

"Yes, her body. Somebody killed her," Helen finishes.

***

"How close are Nova and Luke?" Helen asks Alicia as the two pull on their seat belts in the police vehicle after leaving the Nash home.

"Well, I think Nova would like them to be very close. She has her eye on him and puts herself in every situation possible for them to be together. They did go to the prom, but from what I understand from Luke, it was more of he had the tickets and didn't know what to do with them. She suggested they double with her brother and his girlfriend, and Noah is his best friend, has been for years. I think it was more a convenience thing for him, more than anything else."

"I think we need to ask Luke a few questions," Helen says, manoeuvring the police vehicle toward the precinct.

"Is that really necessary?" Alicia asks, knowing that it is

There's silence between them, the question left hanging. After several moments, Alicia finally ends the stillness replying, "He's off with James for a couple of days, not sure when they'll be back."

"Can you call them? Ask them to come back early?" Helen persists.

"Sure, I'll give them a call tonight and let you know tomorrow." Alicia stares out the window, uneasy about the whole situation, surprised at how simple it was to lie to her new partner for her son.

Chapter 44
July 2
Noah

After Mrs. Nash shows the two detectives to the door, she returns to the dining room, sits down with her son and daughter, who haven't moved since the cross-examination and announcement of Jessica's death. "Do you guys know anything about this?" she asks.

Both shake their heads, no. "Jessica is dead," Noah murmurs. "Unfucking believable."

"Language," his mother admonishes. "Nova?" she turns to her daughter.

"What? Why are you asking me?" Nova asks getting angry.

"Do you know anything? Have you heard anything? Would Ziggy really do this to her?" Mrs. Nash persists.

"Anything is possible with him. He's a wild card, unpredictable, but it looked like he really cared about her. Paraded her around like she was something special," Noah advises.

"What about Luke? How is he handling the break-up? Didn't I hear you guys talking about him getting into a couple of fights with this Ziggy guy?"

"Ziggy knows how to push Luke's buttons. Gets in his face and Luke just reacts automatically, but he is so over her. He's moved on and he's with me now and we're tight," Nova declares before getting up from the table and running to her room.

Noah and his mom stay rooted at the table, watching her go, neither saying anything, both deep in thought.

Nova's deluded if she thinks they are a thing. She follows him around like a puppy and he's just too nice to tell her to go to hell, but he will sooner or later. Maybe Hannah will be the one. It seems like he likes her, Noah thinks. No way Luke would have anything to do with this Jessica situation, but that asshole Ziggy sure would. I bet it was him or someone from his fucking family.

Wonder why Jess texted Luke? Was that the night she died? Did she know something was coming? Was she afraid Ziggy would do

156

something to her, and she reached out to Luke for protection? But she didn't show up that night, or so Luke says. Is it a coincidence that she was found right near where I picked Luke up? What the hell is going on? I need to talk to Luke.

***

Luke's phone buzzes with a new text from Noah, 'Got a sec?'

'Not right now,' Luke replies.

'The cops were just here,' Noah texts back.

'Calling you now,' Luke types before hitting the button for Noah's phone number. "The cops were there?" he asks as his friend picks up the call.

"Your mom and some other detective. Said that Jessica was dead. What is going on?"

"That's why my dad came to get me at the beach. Him and my mom told me about it when I got home. Sorry I left you and Dylan, but I didn't really have a choice."

"We figured it was something big. What do you know about Jessica? What happened?"

"I don't know much. She was found near the water at the Community Centre by some guy out walking his dog. Fucking Ziggy tried to hide her under a blanket so no one would see her."

"Are you sure it was Ziggy?"

"Who the hell else would it be?" Luke yells at his friend.

"They found her near the Community Centre where I picked you up before we went to the Beach?"

"Yeah, that's where they found her."

"Hey…." Noah starts but doesn't know how to finish.

"I didn't do this man. No way would I hurt her," Luke confesses.

"Maybe it was an accident," Noah says, giving his friend an excuse, an out if he in fact killed Jessica.

"I didn't even see her that night. Jess texted me and wanted to meet but she didn't show. Ziggy probably found out she wanted to talk to me, wanted to get back with me and he did this to her. Probably left

157

her there as a message to me or knowing him, he found out she was coming to see me and put her body there so I would be incriminated."

Silence hangs between the two close friends as they reflect on the situation.

"Hey man, I didn't tell them about picking you up at the Centre and going over to Dylan's before we went to the beach but sooner or later it's going to come out."

"I appreciate that, Noah. My parents are waiting to hear about the time this went down with Jessica and the specifics – was she killed there or did Ziggy bring her there and dump her. I'm sure my mom will let me know when they've nailed him to the wall."

"Yeah man. I won't say anything until I talk to you first, but if they ask, I'll have to tell them, Luke. I love you man, but I don't think I can lie about the timing or picking you up."

"Yeah, I know. But I swear, I didn't do this. I didn't see her. I didn't touch her. I would never hurt Jessica."

Chapter 45
July 3
Alicia

There's no way Luke did this. No way he was even involved in it. Just a coincidence he was near where she was found. Just a fluke unless someone is trying to set him up. Ziggy probably, or Axl. Yeah, Axl would do that to protect his brother. Alicia continues to toss and turn, worried about Luke, how much he knows and what he isn't telling her. She worries that she won't be able to protect him, that something very sinister is happening, and that Axl and his brother have set him up to take the blame for Jessica's death.

Unable to sleep, Alicia decides to get up before the sun rises. She passes Luke's door on the way to the kitchen, opens it quietly and is thankful for the silence. *Hopefully he got some sleep last night.* Continuing down the hall to the kitchen, she turns on the Keurig, waits for the water to heat up and makes her first cup of coffee of the day. She sits down at the kitchen table, puts her head in her hands, as thoughts swirl through her mind. *There is no way Luke was involved. Maybe Noah. He was in the area. Maybe Jessica's boyfriend, Ziggy. Maybe someone we haven't considered. Maybe it was a random killing, but the odds of that are small. What was that stat again? Almost 75 percent of victims murdered either know the perpetrator or are related to them. And almost 40 percent of females killed are done in by their boyfriend or husband, usually during an argument. If it was premediated, the killer would have brought a weapon, probably a gun. But if the log turns out to be the murder weapon, it was a spontaneous act. Who could she have made that mad that they would kill her? Who could have been that upset with her? And why?*

A noise in the hallway breaks the silence of the early morning, and Alicia looks up to see her son stagger into the kitchen, his face puffy and streaked with watermarks from the tears he has shed. She motions for Luke to sit down in the chair beside her. When he does, she scoots over and puts her arm around him. "It'll be okay," she murmurs to him, rubbing his back as he starts to snivel again

They sit there for a long time as the sun comes up outside, as a new, difficult day dawns, as she continues to tell her son, "It will be okay," wondering silently what today will bring and if she's telling him the truth.

***

A beautiful day for a swim or a boat ride, Alicia thinks passing the lakefront parks her way to the precinct. *Can't believe my first big case is a murder investigation. If I didn't know the victim and it wasn't so close to my family, it would be a fantastic first case.* She frowns remembering her last sight of Luke rocking in the old chair on the front porch, looking like he was carrying the weight of the world on his shoulders. *Who would do this? That's what I need to concentrate on, find out who did this. That and keeping Luke safe, protected. I hate to lean on him, but James has to help. He was always an okay dad with Luke, a better dad than a husband.*

She parks her car at the back of the lot, not knowing that the parking spot is the one James always used when he was a detective on the force, nodding to the patrol officers and the office staff as she walks through the lot, into the precinct and down the hall to the Detectives' Den, which is still pretty quiet for 7am on a beautiful summer day. As the door closes behind her, Helen pops up from her desk in the back row of cubicles.

"Hey, how are you doing today, partner?" Helen says looking at Alicia closely, seeing the dark circles under her eyes, her smile more of a grimace.

"I'm okay. And you?" Alicia gracefully replies.

"Good. It's going to be another interesting day. We'll have a quick meeting with the team and see if they have any updates from their work yesterday, then we have a meeting with Ziggy Tunes and his lawyer. Sutton Fox called me last night and confirmed they would be here for 9am. I've booked one of the interrogation rooms that has recording equipment. I put together a list of questions last night," Helen says as she hands a document to Alicia. "Take a look and let me know what you think."

***

Just before 9am, after their daily meeting has concluded, as Alicia finishes reading the document, Helen's cell phone rings. She picks it up, listens and answers promptly, "We'll be right there."

Helen stands up, a big smile on her face, ready for the challenge. "They're here. Ziggy, his lawyer, and his brother slash guardian." She turns to Alicia and asks, "Any questions or concerns with the plan, Alicia?"

"It looks good to me. A great plan for the conversation," Alicia states getting up to follow her partner.

"I'll take the lead, if you're okay with that, but feel free to add to the conversation, ask questions, request clarification if needed," Helen directs. "Some of the team will be watching and listening through the two-way mirror. I'll have a microphone on to hear them, in case they have anything to add or if they see something that we don't," she says, while popping a miniature earbud in her ear.

Alicia is disappointed that she won't be leading the conversation but realizes that the Chief has instructed her to take a back seat to Helen and that it is only her third day in her new job. Alicia makes her way to the interrogation room, as Helen goes to welcome the Tunes brothers. Alicia leaves the door open as she surveys the stark space, filled with a table, five chairs – three on one side for Ziggy, his brother Axl and their lawyer, two on the other side for her and Helen. She stands silently waiting for the players to enter the interrogation room.

Alicia hears a commotion in the hall as the visitors troop toward the room. Helen, leading the trio, reaches the open door, stands beside it, smiling as she gestures for them to enter, as if welcoming guests into her home. Alicia offers her hand as Ziggy enters the room. He ignores her greeting and gives her a cocky smile as he passes, oozing

161

charm, thinking it is his best defense. He is tall, taller than Luke, with thick, styled, strawberry-blond hair grazing his shoulders. The lawyer, Sutton Fox, follows Ziggy, his aggressive and assertive personality reflected in his tailored, grey, pinstriped, very expensive suit. He grips her hand tightly in greeting, nodding as she tells him her name. Axl is the last visitor into the room. He reaches for Alicia's hand and moves it to his lips, kissing it seductively. She pulls her hand back quickly as he winks at her, like this is all a game.

Helen closes the door behind the short parade. "Have a seat everyone. Is there anything I can get you? Coffee?"

"No, thank you," Sutton Fox answers quickly for both Ziggy and Axl as they sit side-by-side on one side of the table. "Let's just get on with this charade."

Helen and Alicia sit down facing the trio, Alicia pulling out a notebook. "Not sure charade is the best word for this. A young girl has been killed," Helen counters.

"We understand that, and we are truly sorry for the family, but it has nothing to do with the Tunes," Sutton Fox volleys.

"Yes, our hearts go out to the Winters family. It is a difficult time," Helen agrees. "We just wanted to get a statement from Ziggy, understand his relationship with Jessica, understand where he was the evening of June 30."

Ziggy moves to the edge of his seat, opens his mouth to speak, but Axl puts his hand on his shoulder and pulls him back as the detectives watch the interaction closely.

"Before we begin, we do want to ensure that you are aware of your rights, Ziggy. You are here voluntarily, you have the right to remain silent and you have the right to a lawyer," Helen nods to Sutton Fox. "Do you understand these rights?"

Ziggy nods.

"Great," Helen says. "Tell us about the evening of June 30. Tell us about your relationship with Jessica Winters."

"If I could answer for poor Ziggy," the lawyer begins. "He is very upset about this whole situation. He was friends with Jessica. He cared a lot for the girl. As for the evening of June 30, Ziggy was in the city with his mother."

"His mother? I thought she wasn't part of his life," Helen questions, looking to Axl for an answer.

"I told you that his mother lived in Toronto, that Ziggy lived with me and that I am his legal guardian. I did not allude to the family dynamics other than that," Axl finishes, looking at his brother, who nods his head.

"Okay," Helen says, changing tacks. "Ziggy, can you tell me about your relationship with Jessica?"

"The two of them were friends. They went to school together. Hung out together sometimes. Nothing improper. Just being teenagers," Sutton Fox offers.

"I would like to hear the words from Ziggy," Helen pushes.

Sutton Fox nods his head and Ziggy repeats Sutton's sentiments, almost word for word. Helen shakes her head in disbelief.

"Friends? Is that how you are describing your relationship with Jessica?"

"Yes, friends," Sutton reiterates.

"And that's it? Ziggy?"

Ziggy smirks before offering, "We were in an exclusive relationship."

"So more than just friends," Helen confirms.

"That's what the boy said," Sutton clarifies.

"Okay, so more than just friends," Helen reiterates. "Going steady then, Tell me about where you were on the night of June 30."

Ziggy repeats the words that his lawyer has already offered, that he went to his mother's in the city.

"And what did you do at your mom's?"

Before Ziggy can answer, Sutton Fox objects as if they were in a court room, advising that it is not relevant.

Helen continues pushing her questions out quickly, trying to catch Ziggy in his answers, trying to get a small crack in the wall that his brother and lawyer have built around him.

"How long have you and Jessica been together?"

"About three months."

"What kind of things did you guys do together?"

"What did we do?" Ziggy asks.

"Did you go to the show? Did you go to the beach? Did you go out for dinner?" What kind of things did you guys do together?"

"Well, all of those things. We hung out, talked, went swimming, went to the beach. Had fun, you know."

"Did she have any enemies?"

"Everyone liked Jess."

"Is there anyone that would want to hurt her?"

"Maybe her old boyfriend, Luke Anderson. He was pretty sore that she dumped him. Took it out on me a couple of times," he states sneering at Alicia.

"Took it out on you? What do you mean by that?" Helen counters

"We got into a couple of fights. He always started it," Ziggy adds.

"Was she into anything illegal?"

"Jess, no. She wasn't like that."

"Did she take drugs?"

"No."

"Did she drink?"

"No."

"When was the last time you saw her?

"Before I went down to the city. We went out for lunch together."

"What about after that?"

"No, I was with my mom."

"Give me your mom's phone number."

Ziggy turns to Axl to help with a response. Axl pulls out his cell phone and rambles off a phone number, which Alicia writes on her pad of paper. The questions continue.

"Did you hit her?"

"No."

"Never?" Helen goads.

Sutton Fox interjects. "I would say you are badgering the witness if we were in court. You've asked the question and he's answered it. Do you have any more questions for him?"

"Apparently, people saw bruises on her arms after she started going out with you," Helen explains, trying to get a rise out of the suspect.

"You asked the question. He answered. Move on," the lawyer pushes.

"Did you two have a fight?"

"No."

"Was she upset when you went out for lunch?"

"No."

"Do you have a phone?"

"I have a cell phone if that's what you're asking."

"Can we have a look at it?"

Again, Sutton Fox objects. "When you get a warrant, you can have the phone."

"Where were you on the night of June 30?"

Sutton Fox stands up. "He's already told you. He was in the city." The lawyer pauses. "If you don't have any new questions, we're done here."

Helen stands as the three troop out of the room, frustrated. All of her questions were answered but with only simple, unadorned information before the fiasco of an interrogation was ended by the pompous lawyer. She continues to sit at the table for a few moments after the pack of thieves leave, replaying the meeting in her mind.

"God damn lawyer. He didn't give you an inch," Alicia offers.

"We'll just have to meet Ziggy outside of his lawyer's reach and see if we can get some real answers. Ziggy definitely threw Luke under the bus, talking about their fights and that he might want to hurt Jessica."

"There was some animosity between the two over Jessica. I told you about getting called into the principal's office because of a fight they had," Alicia defends, before adding, "You have to remember, they're just kids. Nothing too serious. No stitches, no broken bones. Sounds a lot like the TODDI defense to me."

"TODDI?" Helen asks, watching her partner.

"The other dude did it," Alicia answers, making both of them smile.

Helen gets up and the two move back to their office. "I would love to see his cell phone, the calls, texts, GPS," Helen says sitting down at her desk.

"Can we get them?" Alicia asks, her mind buzzing thing about the text that Luke received from Jessica on that fateful evening.

165

"The law is pretty grey. Cell phones are considered private and confidential, out of bounds for police; however, we might be able to get access to it with a search warrant if we arrest Ziggy for her murder. Problem is even if we get the phone with a warrant, he could still refuse to give us his password. We would have to go to the service provider for the information but there is no legal requirement currently to make them comply and give us any records, calls, texts, information." She pauses, thinking. "But we could request info on Jessica's phone. We would have to be specific on what we want, the phone records, texts for specific dates, cell site locations and sectors for all outgoing and incoming voice and data transactions. It might take a long time but at least it's a start. Are you good to put the request together?"

"Sure," Alicia replies, wondering how to delete the incriminating data trail to her son's phone.

"You start that, and I'll just give Mrs. Tunes a call, see what she has to say about her golden boy, Ziggy," Helen says sitting back in her chair. "Then I think I'll take a look at Jessica's social media. You can learn an awful lot about a person by what they post, what they comment on, pictures they share, their list of friends."

"One more question. Can we ping her phone? Maybe at least find its location?" Alicia asks.

"Good question. Our IT guys have software that should be able to give us a location. Let's go down and see them."

Chapter 46
July 4
Alicia

Alicia is in the Den early again the next morning as her worry for Luke clouds her thoughts and will not allow her to sleep. She's reviewing the recording from yesterday's interrogation of Ziggy, searching for any clues to his involvement, any conflicting answers, any gaps, but nothing jumps out at her. As she watches and listens to the video for the third time, Helen sits down at her adjacent desk. "You been here all night?" Helen asks smiling.

"No, I got here about two hours ago. Just reviewing yesterday's interrogation with Ziggy," Alicia replies before changing the subject. "It's too bad we couldn't get any info from the ping on Jessica's cell yesterday. It must be turned off or in the water, but I have the request ready for the telecom company for her phone. Maybe that will help us. Do you want to look at it before I send it to them?"

"Yes, please. Send it to me and I'll take a look just because it's your first. No other reason," Helen smiles at Alicia. "Let's go to the major crime room for our 8am meeting with the team. Maybe they've found something helpful."

The team is assembled as Helen and Alicia enter the room. Helen calls the meeting to order, and Edward gives them an update from yesterday's work – more evidence collected at the site, door-to-door canvassing underway, statements taken from witnesses that use the park, nothing earth shattering.

Helen talks about their meeting with Ziggy Tunes, and his alibi. She takes a breath. "I did call the number that his brother gave me yesterday for their mom, but the line has been disconnected. I tried directory assistance to get a number but without a full name, and who even knows if Tunes is her last name. Anyway, I was unsuccessful. We'll put that on the list of questions for Ziggy when we see him again." She pauses before asking the team, "Any questions, comments?"

"Will the coroner be able to confirm that the log found near the body is the murder weapon?" Alicia asks.

"Good question. Dr. Diamond will perform an autopsy and it should confirm the cause of death and narrow down the murder weapon. In this case, we know the manner of death was homicide, she sure as hell didn't commit suicide, and it definitely wasn't an accident. If she confirms that the death was caused by blunt force trauma, then the next hurdle is to validate what weapon was used, the log or something else. I vote for the log. I had a look at it before we bagged it, looked like blood and possibly hair on it."

"The log seemed to be pretty heavy to me, which I think would limit the suspect pool," Alicia suggests.

"Not really. History tells us that even a small woman, given the right circumstances, has the ability to use a heavy weapon, such as the log, to hurt someone. Think about the old Lizzie Borden story. She killed her father and stepmother by hitting them with an ax, 11 times for her dad and 18 times for her mom and she was a tiny little thing. Her case demonstrates that a small, not-too muscular person with lots of emotion, lots of adrenaline flowing through their system would be able to swing a weapon to kill someone. After the first blow of the axe or hit from a club, the victim would probably fall to the ground where the perpetrator could continue to swing the murder weapon in a downward motion, until they were exhausted."

"Interesting. How about blood spatter? Wouldn't the perpetrator have blood on their clothes from the altercation?" Alicia asks.

"Probably, but it's been a couple of days since the murder, and their clothes have probably been destroyed, burnt, thrown away or at the very least washed, but when we get closer and have grounds for a search warrant, that is one thing that we will be looking for."

"How long do we have to wait for the results from the autopsy?"

"We should get something within the week, or next if things are backed up at the lab. All the toxicology and histology tests that are required will take longer, but we should have the preliminary report within two or three weeks."

"What can we do in the meantime? There's got to be something that we can do," Alicia asks.

"The forensic team is going to continue canvassing the neighbourhood, talk to the people in the park – someone may have seen something. From a research perspective, we can take a look at some of the relevant databases, see if there are any other cases, criminals that we should be looking at. The YCJA, the Youth Criminal Justice Act, will give us information on any previous run-ins with the law that Ziggy may have had. The CPIC, the Canadian Police Information Centre Data Base, will give us information on previous arrests, bail, probation orders, plus photographs and fingerprints, though it won't give us anything on Ziggy as he's a minor, so maybe we should query his brother, Axl. Also, we should search in ViCLAS, the Violent Crime Linkage Analysis System which includes sexual crimes and criminals, links crimes committed by the same offender, homicides and attempts, sexual assaults, familial and domestic assaults. Again, not sure it will help us, but you never know, maybe it wasn't Ziggy. Maybe it was someone else and Jessica was just in the wrong place at the wrong time, or maybe the killer picked her out and stalked her. We should also look at Axl, maybe something will come up on him. Maybe it was the big brother trying to get rid of a pesky girlfriend for his little brother," Helen smiles at the thought.

"I'm on it," Alicia confirms.

"We also need to talk to Ziggy again and get a working phone number for his mom. We should stop by and talk to Jessica's parents once more. I had the conversation with her mom, but her dad wasn't there. We need to see if there is anything else they can tell us about Jessica, what she was up to, any discord in her life, find out where she worked and go there, consider other suspects. We should ask about alibis for her mom and dad and her brother. We don't want to limit ourselves to Ziggy. Maybe there was other stuff going on that we haven't yet discovered."

There's a sharp knock at the door, interrupting Helen's list of to-dos. The team looks up in unison as the Chief opens the door and walks in. "Glad I caught you," the Chief says nodding to the group. "I got a call from Sutton Fox, Ziggy Tunes's lawyer. He's complaining of possible bias against his client with you on the case, Alicia, because of Luke and Jessica's previous relationship and his animosity toward Ziggy."

"That was a while ago. They broke up, happens a lot to high school kids," Alicia says, downplaying the relationship.

"I hear you, but he is suggesting that the force is showing preferential treatment of your son allowing you to work the case."

"Well, you know that's not true. No way," Alicia protests.

"I hear you, but we don't want anything to interfere with a conviction, no whispers that we were prejudiced, we protected your son, we made the charges fit. Sorry Alicia, you're off the case."

"How about I stay in the background, like we had already started to do? I'll do the research, the leg work and Helen can do the real detective work," Alicia almost begs.

"Sorry, you are off the case. Chuck will partner with Helen on this one. Alicia you can partner with Fraser Weston until this case is over. Is that clear?"

Both Helen and Alicia nod their heads, acknowledging the directive from the Chief.

Chapter 47
July 4
Helen

"Hey, Chuck," Helen yells spying him walking down the hallway of the precinct. She waves him over with her hand as she sits at the boardroom table in the major crime room.

He walks into the room saying, "I heard. Just ran into the Chief in the hall. Is Alicia okay with being removed from the case?"

Helen looks around, just now noticing that Alicia has left the room along with the rest of the team. "Not sure where she is, but she was pissed off. I get it. Her first case as a detective and she's pulled off but better to do it now than to have a problem later," Helen says, shoving her laptop into her large purse. "Are you free this morning? I thought we could go see Jennifer Winters, Jessica's mom again, to see if she has any info to add. Also wanted to go back and re-interview Nova, Jessica's best friend. Nova didn't have much to say yesterday; her mom and brother kept answering for her. Then if we have time, I also want to go by the Tunes's place."

"The Tunes's place? I thought they came in yesterday with a lawyer."

"Oh, they did. The brother gave me a phone number for Ziggy's mom, his alibi for that night, but the problem is it has been disconnected. Awfully fast, don't you think, for a phone to be disconnected if he just talked to her three days ago. Coincidence? I'm not sure."

"Sounds a little strange, yeah. Give me half an hour and I'm with you. Just need to talk to Fraser about a case we've been working on before I can take off."

"Cool. I'm just going to go find Alicia, make sure that she's okay," Helen says as they both move to exit the room.

171

***

Helen finds Alicia at her desk, reviewing something on her computer. "Are you okay?" Helen asks, sitting down beside her colleague.

"Has something happened?" Alicia replies, fear etched on her face as she turns to look at Helen.

"No, no news. I just didn't see you leave and thought you might be upset about being removed from the case."

"I am disappointed. It's my first case and I know the players. I thought I might be able to help bring perspective on personalities, histories, that sort of thing."

"I appreciate that, and we may come to you with questions about some of the people involved, the dynamics. I'm sure the Chief would be okay with that."

"By all means. If there is anything that I can help with, anything like filling out warrants, doing some research on the databases, just let me know," Alicia offers as Chuck moves toward the pair.

"Hope I'm not interrupting anything," he says.

"No. We're good. I'm just going to check in with Fraser and see what he's working on, what I can help with, but remember, if I can assist in anyway, backend stuff, research, just let me know," Alicia concludes, standing up, moving through the office to Fraser's desk.

Helen and Chuck look at each other and both nod. "I'm ready any time you are," Chuck advises.

***

"We are so sorry for your loss, Mrs. Winters," Helen tells Jessica's mom when she answers her front door, sniffling into a tissue. "This is my partner, Detective Chuck MacLean," Helen continues, gesturing toward Chuck as he nods to the woman. "We were hoping you are up to answering some questions for us, help us understand Jessica, get a sense of who she was, what she did, what she liked, who her friends were. It may help us find out who did this to her," Helen continues, as she watches Mrs. Winters, who is barely able to stand up under the grief of losing her daughter.

Jennifer Winters trembles, fresh tears starting to move down her face at the mention of Jessica's name. She finally assents, "Come in. It's not going to be any better tomorrow and the sooner you find out who did this to her the better."

The three move into the house, up the three stairs to the main floor. "Can I get you coffee, tea?" Jennifer Winters asks as she waves them into the living room.

Chuck speaks first. "A coffee would be great, Mrs. Winters. Black, no sugar," hoping that giving her something menial to do will help her relax and bring some normalcy to their conversation. "Is your husband home, Mrs. Winters?" he asks.

She turns before leaving the living room area. "No, he's not here," she says simply before walking into the kitchen. Chuck and Helen glance at each other, wondering where he could be at a time like this.

While Mrs. Winters makes the coffees in the kitchen, Helen walks around the comfortable living room, looking at the family pictures; one of Jessica and her brother Oliver on a Caribbean beach, another of the family of four huddled together on a ski lift, their skis and poles dangling in the air below them, a recent one of Jessica in her cap and gown for graduation. As Mrs. Winters brings in a tray with their coffees and a plateful of cookies, Helen points out the graduation picture and asks, "When was this taken?"

Jennifer Winters smiles. "Just a couple of weeks ago."

"What were her plans? Was she going to college or university in the fall?"

"She'd been accepted at three universities. Our Jessica was smart, very smart, but she hadn't accepted any of the offers yet. Said she maybe wanted to take a year off. John and I were against that. Jess was worried about the money. The tuition is awfully expensive but we told her that we would find it."

"Talk to us about Ziggy, Jessica's relationship with him," Chuck asks gently.

"I don't know what she saw in that hellion. Luke was such a good boy, a nice boy, a responsible kid. Ziggy is just the opposite. And his family's business is wrapped up with the gang in town. He was trouble waiting to happen if you ask me, and look what happened to my sweet little girl," Jennifer Winters finishes, fresh tears clouding her eyes.

"Did Ziggy ever hurt Jessica? Did he ever hit her? Did you ever see bruises on her?"

"I saw bruises on her a couple of times. When I asked her about them, she said it was from work. Jessica was a waitress, and the trays were very heavy. Said she would bounce off the walls sometimes with the weight and that's how she got the bruises, but I'm not sure."

"Did she have them before Ziggy? Before they started going out?"

Jennifer thinks, her eyes moving to the front window as if watching a movie of the past, and finally agrees, "Maybe a little bit but certainly not anything like she's had over the last month or two."

"Did Ziggy ever threaten her?"

Mrs. Winters pauses again before offering, "Not that I'm aware of."

"Did Jessica have any enemies? Anyone that may want to hurt her?"

"You mean outside of Ziggy?" her mother asks.

"Why do you think Ziggy would want to hurt Jessica? I thought they were going steady, or whatever they call it now."

"They were going out, yes. For about three months. But as I said he was a hellion. His family are low life. Don't get me wrong, they've got lots of money. They live right on the bay, huge house with a pool. He drives a brand-new car, but he has no manners, no class, no common sense. His mother lives in Toronto, doesn't even take care of her own kids. The older brother, at least, has some sense and took his brother and sister in. I don't think the mother even knows who the fathers are for her kids. Low life is what the whole family is."

"What about anyone else that might want to hurt her?"

"Well, a while ago there was a guy that worked with Jess that was kinda stalking her. He would follow her around, showed up at strange places like when she was at the mall or out with her girlfriends, or even when she was out with Luke."

"Do you remember his name?"

"Myles. Myles something or other. I think he was a busboy or something at the restaurant."

"So, he's been around for a while then, if he was stalking her when she went out with Luke?" Helen asks.

"Yeah, the two of them worked together at the restaurant. I think Luke had a conversation with the kid, told him to back off, to stop bothering her."

"How did Jessica feel about Myles?"

"She thought he was harmless, just infatuated with her, a little immature. They sometimes worked the same shift at the restaurant."

"Other than breaking up with Luke and starting to see Ziggy, was there anything else going on? Any other changes or upsets at home or at school or at work?" Chuck asks.

Mrs. Winters sits back, deep in thought, hesitating for a moment before confessing. "I'm sure it has nothing to do with Jessica's death, but her father and I have been going through some difficult times lately, stuff that I don't think we can come back from. We are talking about divorcing."

There is a pause in the room before Chuck asks, "We don't want to pry but if something was upsetting Jessica, something that may have impacted her personally, it might help us understand her state of mind."

Mrs. Winters looks at her hands, as she shreds a tissue. She looks up, fresh tears in her eyes. "Surely, it has nothing to do with what happened to Jessica," she whimpers. The detectives wait as Jessica's mom deliberates. Finally, she pulls in a big breath, and tells the story of her husband's gambling addiction, how he has put them hundreds of thousands of dollars in debt by remortgaging an almost-paid-for house, how he has maxed out their credit cards, all while his job is uncertain with a massive reorganization pending at his company. "We've tried to keep it from the kids, but I'm sure they've overheard some of our arguments, but that wouldn't have anything to do with what's happened to Jessica. No, it wouldn't have anything to do with Jessica's death," she finishes forcefully, trying to convince herself.

"Is that why he's not here today?" Chuck asks.

"We were in a real bad way, couldn't hold it together. We fought all the time, yelled at each other. It wasn't good for the kids, so John moved out. He's been staying with his brother for a while," she finishes fresh tears cascading down her cheeks.

Chuck and Helen nod, filing the information away. Chuck changes the subject, asking, "Did Jessica like school? Did she get along with everyone at school?"

"Nova Nash has been her best friend since kindergarten. Jessica had lots of other friends too. Always a social kid. Always doing something whether it was swimming and tennis in the summer or skiing and skating in the winter. Always out with Nova and their group of friends especially Noah and Luke, that is until Ziggy came along."

"And then what happened?"

"She seemed to ignore her friends and concentrated all her time with him. She was either at school, at work or with him. Her friends called for the first month or so, but when she didn't return their calls or go out with them, they slowly stopped coming around," Jennifer Winters confesses, wiping away her tears.

"Anything else you can tell us Mrs. Winters that would help us find who did this to Jessica?"

Jennifer Winters breaks down in tears, sobbing uncontrollably. Helen walks over to where Jessica's mother is sitting and puts her hand on her shoulder for comfort. After several minutes, Jennifer Winters looks up, sniffling between words. "Talk to Luke Anderson. Jessica and Luke were together for over a year and were very close. I was totally surprised when they broke up. Maybe he knows something. Maybe he saw something. Maybe he did it. Maybe he was so upset with their break-up that he hurt her. Maybe he didn't mean it. Maybe it was an accident. I don't know." She chokes on her tears, shaking. Helen continues to hold the woman's shoulder, her heart going out to the mother of a murdered child.

The two detectives wait for Mrs. Winters to get her emotions under control, until she is able to breathe again, and the tears have stopped flowing before Chuck asks, "Can you tell us where you and your husband were the evening of June 30?"

Mrs. Winters's head pops up quickly, anger flashing in her eyes. "What the hell? Are you accusing John and I of this?" she growls.

"I'm only asking so that we can take you both off the list of suspects, so we can concentrate our time on finding the real killer," Chuck placates.

There's silence as Jessica's mother slumps back into the chair, like all of the fight has left her body limp. After several moments, Mrs. Winters shakes her head, moves to sit at the edge of the chair, like she's found a second wind. "We went to my mother-in-law's house for dinner that evening. We needed to tell them about our separation, that John was living with his brother. We stayed afterwards and went for a swim in their pool, had a couple of drinks, tried to make it as normal as possible for Oliver. Got home after midnight."

"You mention Oliver. What about Jessica? Was Jessica with you?"

"No, she was working the afternoon/dinner shift, so we went without her," agony crumpling her facial expression as she replies.

"Can you give us your in-laws' phone number? And your brother-in-law's, where John is staying?" Chuck persists.

Mrs. Winters picks up her phone from the coffee table, scrolls and recites two local numbers to Chuck.

"Thank you, Mrs. Winters. That will help us eliminate you and your husband and allow us to focus our efforts in the right place," he explains once again.

Helen squeezes her shoulder and thanks her for the time. She reaches into her jacket pocket and pulls out a business card, shows it to Mrs. Winters and leaves it on the mantel beside Jessica's graduation photo.

The two detectives leave the house quietly, leaving the grieving mother to her pain, unable to help her today but hopeful that they will be back to tell her they have caught the person responsible for this violent act, for this heartbreak.

***

Helen sits silently in the driver's seat of the police vehicle, thoughts running through her mind. After a short time, she turns to Chuck and asks, "What do you think?"

"She is hurting so bad that my heart goes out to her. I can't imagine being in her place, losing a daughter so violently, so suddenly, so young, but that aside, I think we need more information on the stalker." Chuck looks down at his notes and reads, "Myles, from the restaurant." He continues, "I think you're right; we need to have another conversation with Ziggy. He sounds like a real piece of work, a lot like his older brother, a bit of a bully, thinks he's the centre of the universe. Might not be a stretch for him to do something like this if she pissed him off, maybe wanted to break-up with him."

"It is interesting the timing of the money problems and arguments, don't you think?" Helen suggests.

"What do you mean?" Chuck asks.

"Mom and dad are fighting about money and Jessica breaks up with Luke, a steady, happy relationship from what we've heard, and then she starts going out with Ziggy – someone who is the total opposite of Luke but comes from a family of money, has a new car, lives in a great big house on the lake, probably has an in with his brother's business, all the things a poor person may covet. She doesn't want to end up like her mom and figures Ziggy is interested, he's free and he's got money. With him, she'll never have the problems that her parents have."

Chuck contemplates the idea for a moment. "Possible. And maybe Ziggy found out that she was more committed to his money than to him. He gets pissed and offs her." He pauses before continuing. "Mrs. Winters certainly has conflicting thoughts about Luke. Started with what a great guy he was but totally backtracked to maybe he did this. I think she was grasping at straws, but something else to consider."

Helen pauses. "Who knows, I guess it's possible Luke did this, but right now everything is pointing to Ziggy, until we can verify or debunk his alibi of being with his mom in the big smoke. I want to

178

talk to Ziggy again, maybe later in the day or tomorrow, catch him without his lawyer. Let's go see the Nash twins. Alicia and I talked to them yesterday, but I got the sense that they were holding back with their mother in the room."

***

Just as Helen pulls the police car into the Nash's driveway, Noah comes out the front door pulling it forcibly shut behind him. He is yelling at someone in the house and is still mumbling as he looks up at the police vehicle. He stops in his tracks and waits for the two detectives to get out of their car and make their way to the front of the house.

"Hey," he says.

"Hello Noah. This is Detective Chuck MacLean," Helen says as a way of introduction. "Is your mom home? Your sister?"

"My mom's at work but Nova's in the house," he says tentatively.

"Do you have a couple of minutes? We would like to talk to you. Ask you a couple more questions if we could."

"Do I need my mom or dad here?" Noah asks.

"No, these are just routine questions. We're just trying to understand Jessica, who she was, what she was all about, who would want to hurt her," Helen continues, watching Noah closely.

"Jessica was really a friend of Nova's. They'd been friends forever, since grade school and she went out with Luke for a while. Luke and I have been friends almost as long as Nova and Jessica," he confirms.

"Why did Jessica and Luke break-up?"

"Ziggy. Fucking Ziggy came to town with his big car, big money, big house and showed her a different life. She was impressed with that side of town and probably thought that Ziggy was the way out."

"Way out? We just came from Jessica's house. It's quite nice. Was there something else going on at home that she wanted to get away from?"

"I think her life was okay, but she said something about her mom and dad maybe getting a divorce. I think it scared her, made her start

179

worrying more about her future. She was always about better marks, a good job, saving money and her parents' situation seemed to intensify her concerns. She always wanted more, better stuff and I think that's what she thought Ziggy could give her."

"Did you ever see Ziggy hit her? Hurt her?"

Noah thinks for a moment and shakes his head. "Not that I can remember, no."

"How did Luke take it when she broke up with him?"

"He was heartbroken. You know, his first love and all, but I've been getting him out, meeting new people, going to new places. Nothing too crazy but showing him that there is more to life than just one girl."

"You sound like you didn't like Jessica," Chuck suggests.

"She was okay. I didn't really care about her one way or the other. It was Luke and Nova that were close friends with her, not me. I'm kind of a free spirit, you know."

"And was your sister still close to Jessica when she was going out with Ziggy?"

"Not so much. Ziggy kept Jess on a pretty tight leash. Between school, work, and Ziggy, I don't think Nova saw her much anymore, but you can ask her yourself. She's inside," he says, nodding toward the front door.

"One more question before we talk to your sister, who do you think did this to Jessica?"

Noah looks directly at Helen, "Ziggy. Ziggy did this to her."

"Why do you say that?"

"His family is part of the mob and I hear that they rub people out all the time. If people get in their way, they just kill them. Maybe that's what happened to Jess."

Helen and Chuck pause for a moment taking in his strong words. "Thanks for your time, Noah. Here's my card," Helen says, offering her business card to the teenager. "If you think of anything else, please give me a call."

"Sure, no problem," Noah agrees. He turns back to the front door, opens it and yells in, "Nova, the cops are here to see you," before walking past them to his car sitting in front of the house. Helen and

Chuck watch as he gets in, starts it up, revs the engine, and takes off quickly.

"Asshole," they hear in a whisper behind them. Helen and Chuck turn to see Nova at the front door, her eyes, hair colour, and stance a mirror image of her twin brother Noah. "You wanted to talk to me," she says politely.

"Yes, we have a couple of follow up questions for you."

"Sure. Go ahead," Nova says, leaning against the front of the house.

"Tell us a little bit more about Jessica. You guys were friends since public school. What was she like?"

"Jess was my best friend. We did everything together, went to the movies, went to the beach in the summer, went skating in the winter. When she was going out with Luke, it kinda turned into the four of us, with my brother Noah being Luke's best friend and all. It was great."

"You say it was great. Was it still great with Ziggy?"

"No, things changed when she broke up with Luke. Luke was perfect. Is perfect. But Jess got tired or couldn't see it or something. When Ziggy came to town, he kinda swept her off her feet. Wanted to take her to expensive restaurants, places she hadn't been to before, places that Luke couldn't afford. So, she broke up with Luke and it happened – the dinners out, fancy jewelry, shopping trips to the city, going everywhere in Ziggy's expensive car."

"Was he possessive?" Helen asks.

"Yeah, always there. We went shopping a couple of times and he would mysteriously end up at the mall like it was a coincidence or something. I think he was smothering, she thought it was romantic, that he really loved her."

"Did Ziggy ever hurt her? You told us about bruises you saw on her arms. Were the bruises from Ziggy?"

"I don't know. Jess said she got them at work. The big trays that she had to carry with the plates of food on them, but I don't think she had them before Ziggy. I don't remember them when Luke was in the picture, but I can't say for sure it was him."

"You mentioned that you thought she was doing drugs, said that her and Ziggy were experimenting together."

"That's what she told me. Said they would lie around the pool and smoke up. Said it made her mellow and made her happy."

"You also mentioned cocaine and heroin. Is that true? Was she also doing heavy drugs?"

"Well, she must have been doing something to dump Luke for Ziggy. She had to be out of her mind to do something that stupid," Nova offers.

"So, it's just your speculation that she was doing opioids? Is that correct?"

Nova looks down at her feet for a moment before answering. "Did she tell me she was doing coke? The answer is no, she didn't specifically say that. But if you look at her actions, what she was doing with her life, that's the only logical conclusion. She threw Luke away, she was about to throw away university, she was ruining her life. Drugs is the only answer to her craziness," Nova declares.

The two detectives pause for a moment, soaking in the venom from Jessica's best friend before changing the subject. "Did Jessica have any enemies? Anyone that you think might hurt her?"

"She told me about some kid that used to follow her around at work. I think he was a busboy or something. I think he was just a pain in the ass, not someone that was violent."

"Why do you think that?"

"It was just the way Jess was with him. She didn't tell her boss, didn't try and get on shifts to avoid him, was always nice to him, but he just had it bad for her and wouldn't give up."

"Why would Jessica be down at the park so late at night?"

"My guess is she was meeting someone. Probably Ziggy. I know her mom and dad didn't really like him. Maybe they were giving her a hard time and she had to meet him away from the house."

"Ziggy was supposedly out of town that night so it couldn't have been him. Anyone else you can think of that Jessica would be meeting?"

Nova pauses but is unable to give them another possible suspect for Jessica's murder.

"Thoughts?" Helen asks starting the car and backing out of the Nash's driveway.

"Everyone seems to be leaning to Ziggy doing the deed – Mrs. Winters, Noah, and Nova. They obviously don't like him, feel like he's an interloper but he's got an alibi for the night of her death."

"He says he does, but I still can't get in touch with his mother to confirm," Helen replies pulling up to the stop sign in the subdivision.

"Yeah, it is a little fishy, that we can't get in touch with Mrs. Tunes. Not too many people are without a cell phone in this day and age. I was surprised by Nova's analysis of her best friend's actions, saying that everything that Jessica has done lately can be explained with her use of drugs, but when pressed she admits that it's only her opinion that Jessica must have done something mind-altering to make such decisions about Luke, Ziggy, and university."

"Yeah, she did seem to take a lot of liberties with her friend's state of mind, just because she didn't agree with her life choices. Strange best friend if you ask me," Helen summarizes. "I think we need to talk to Luke. His name has come up again this morning. I mentioned talking to him yesterday to Alicia and she said he was away with his dad for a couple of days. I forgot to ask her if they're back." Chuck sighs heavily, gazing out the front windshield. "What's that about? You don't think we should talk to him?" Helen asks.

"No, you're right, we need to talk to Luke, no doubt about it, but you've got to remember who his parents are. I was partners with his dad for a long time and his mom is brand new in our department, your partner in fact."

"What are you saying, Chuck?"

"I think we need to give them a bit of respect, maybe not official, but a little respect. That's all."

Chuck pulls out his phone, scrolls until he finds James's cell number, and sends a short text, 'on my way for coffee to A's,' as Helen watches him. "Who did you text?" Helen asks, already knowing the answer to the question. "What did you say?"

"Just a note to an old friend. Told him I was going for coffee."

Helen shrugs, not understanding the vague message but assuming that it was probably some code from their past working relationship. Within minutes, James replies, 'coffee sounds good. Thanks.'

"Looks like they're in the city. And speaking of coffee, why don't we stop for one. I haven't had a caffeine fix for a couple of hours," Chuck suggests, wanting to give James time to get to Luke before they do.

***

James's vehicle is sitting in the driveway when Helen drives up the street toward Alicia's home. Helen smiles at Chuck and says, "Well he understood your message," as she parks the car on the street. The two get out and walk up the driveway. As they approach the front stairs, James opens the door.

"Chuck, Helen," he greets.

"James," Helen replies standing on the first step. "We would like to talk to Luke. Is he home?"

"He is. He's only got about 30 minutes before he has to leave for work though. He's lifeguarding at the beach again this summer," James says proudly. "Come on in," he continues, holding open the door for the two detectives. "He's in the front room," he directs.

Luke is sitting in the middle of the couch, his hands shaking a little in his lap. His eyes dart from Helen to Chuck as they walk through the doorway. "Hello Luke," Chuck greets. "It's been a while since I've seen you."

"Hello Chuck," Luke replies politely.

"Come in, sit down, can I get you guys a coffee?" James asks even though he doesn't live in the house.

"No, no we're good. Just had one," Chuck confirms.

"Luke, we have a couple of questions for you about Jessica. We understand that you two were together up until recently," Helen starts, sitting down on the chair across from Luke so she can watch his movements, his eyes, his reaction.

184

"We went out for almost a year. We broke up in April," Luke replies succinctly.

"Why did you break-up?"

Luke looks down at his lap and when he looks up again, his eyes are moist with tears. "She said she wasn't into me anymore."

"So, it wasn't your idea?" Helen persists.

"No, it wasn't my idea," Luke confirms.

"And when did Jessica start going out with Ziggy?"

"I don't actually know, maybe Nova could tell you. Those two are best friends."

"It seemed kinda quick that she started with Ziggy after you two broke up, didn't it?" Helen forces.

Luke pauses before answering, studying his dad, who nods his head. "I don't know when she started going out with Ziggy. We didn't talk about that."

"When was the last time you saw Jessica?"

"I saw her and Ziggy at the beach a couple of days before she died," Luke chokes up with the last word of his statement.

"Did you talk to her?"

"Not really," Luke answers.

"What do you mean not really?"

"I didn't have a conversation with Jessica, no," Luke clarifies.

"Did you have a conversation with Ziggy?"

"Why are you asking me these questions? You need to nail that son of a bitch for killing her," Luke demands.

James sits down beside his son, putting his arm around his shoulder. "It's okay, Luke. They are just trying to understand Jessica, her relationships, any tension that might have been in her life, that kind of stuff. It will help them find out who did this to her."

"Who did this to her?" Luke replies, almost yelling at his father. "It was that fucking asshole Ziggy who did this to her. Ziggy killed her."

Helen sits back in her chair and asks, "How do you know Ziggy killed her? Do you have any proof?"

Luke looks down at his hands again, before looking up directly at Helen. "You just have to look at who Ziggy is. He's a gangster, him and his brother. And I heard that he had roughed her up a couple of times. I heard that she had bruises all over her arms. I also heard a story about a time he got really mad at her and made her walk home from like Orillia or something. Who the hell else would it be? Ziggy did this. You need to arrest him."

There is silence in the living room as everyone digests the accusations that Luke has thrown out savagely, unsure if they are true, but knowing they need proof, substance before they can even think of charging anyone with the crime.

"Okay, let's calm down a bit Luke. I understand that Jessica's death is upsetting. Were you still in love with her?" Helen asks.

Luke pauses, his father squeezing his shoulder. Luke nods his head in the affirmative, unable to find the words.

"You were upset that she broke up with you?"

James squeezes Luke's shoulder again, as if giving his son a signal. "Yes, I was upset when she broke up with me, but she had moved on and I was trying to do the same."

"Moved on? How have you moved on?"

Luke is perplexed by the question initially, thinking for a moment before explaining, "I'm spending time with my friends. With Noah. With Dylan next door. I met a girl in Orillia that I would like to see more of. I finished high school. I just got accepted to college in the fall. I'm working this summer. I've moved on."

James makes a show of checking his watch. "Sorry to rush you guys, but we need to leave soon if Luke is going to make his shift at the beach. Any more questions for him?" he asks, moving to the edge of the couch ready to get up.

Chuck puts his finger in the air. "I have one. Where were you the night that Jessica died?"

"Do we know exactly when that was, Chuck? Are the autopsy or the medical examiner's reports in?" James asks, knowing from his time on the force that this information would not yet be available.

"Good question, James. We are assuming Jessica was killed the night before she was found, the night of June 30. There is a lot of foot traffic in that area during the day and there was no report of a body, the blanket or anything suspicious during the day of June 30." Chuck turns back to Luke, "Where were you the night of June 30, Luke?"

Luke looks directly at his father's old partner. "I was here with my mom and her boyfriend. My mom was starting her new job with you guys the next day and we had a celebration dinner," he finishes, leaving out a number of important details.

Chuck and Helen nod in unison, getting out of their seats. "Thanks for your time, Luke. If anything comes up and we need your help, I'm sure you'd be okay if we came back with some more questions," Helen smiles.

"Sure," Luke replies positively, standing to walk them out.

***

As the police vehicle reaches the stop sign at the end of the street, Chuck looks out the passenger window. "He's got a solid alibi, no doubt about that."

Chapter 48
July 4
Luke

Luke sits high in the lifeguard's post once again, on this bright, sunny day watching all the people in the water and on the beach. Luke is saddened by Jessica's death, and he has no doubt that if Ziggy shows up at the beach today they will get into it again. *But this time he won't be walking away. They'll have to carry him away in a body bag.*

As Luke watches the crowd on the beach and in the water, his cell phone, sitting on the seat beside him, vibrates. It's against the rules to have a phone with you while on duty, but he has set it to silent and only brought it up on the pedestal in case his mother calls. *Maybe they arrested Ziggy. Maybe they have that asshole behind bars.*

He glances around to ensure no one is watching him before he picks up the phone displaying Nova's face on the screen. He declines the call and sets the phone back down, again looking around to ensure he isn't being watched. He hears the chime for a message being left, ignoring it.

An hour later, he climbs down from his post, giving the responsibility for the beach to Justin. "Going over to the concession stand to get something to eat. I'll be back in 15," he confirms jumping down the last rung of the ladder. As Luke walks away, he opens the phone and checks the voicemail message that Nova left him. "Oh my God, Luke. I heard about Jess. The cops have been here twice. Please call me," she ends with a tearful gasp.

He walks toward the boat docks and hits the call back button. Nova answers before the first ring is complete. "Luke where are you?" she asks, speaking through sniffles from crying.

"I'm at work," he says, simply trying to keep his emotions in check as he studies the crowd of people.

"Work? You're kidding, right?"

"No, I'm not kidding. I'm at work. It's a beautiful day and they needed me to come in, so here I am. Nothing that I could have done at home except cry," he replies, smothering a sob.

188

"I guess you're right. I'm going a bit crazy here. Your mom and that other detective came by yesterday and then the other detective came back without your mom, but with another guy to talk to me and Noah today. They asked all kinds of questions about Jessica, about our friendship, about us."

"Yeah, two of them came by to see me this afternoon, too."

Nova pauses before asking, "Do you know what happened? How did Jessica die?"

"I don't know any details. The investigation is ongoing. No answers yet."

"Who would do this to her? Who would hurt Jessica?" Nova asks, digging for information.

"You're kidding, right? Ziggy did this. They probably had a fight or something stupid. He fucking killed her," Luke says, tears starting to pool in his eyes as he wipes them away with the back of his hand.

"Ziggy? Are you sure? Is that what your mom said?" Nova pushes, looking for answers.

"My mom's not saying anything. She can't, but I know. I know in my heart that Ziggy did this to her."

"I know you're upset, Luke, but you guys have been over for a long time. She moved on with Ziggy and you and I have been seeing each other," Nova reminds him.

Luke is silent for a moment, trying to find the words to explain to his best friend's sister that they are not together, not a couple.

"You still there Luke?" Nova asks as the silence lingers on.

"Yeah, I'm here. Listen Nova. I like you. You're a great person and I've been friends with you and Noah for years, but we aren't together. It's way too soon for anything like that," he tries to explain, without hurting her feelings. "I gotta go back to work. I'll talk to you later," he finishes, disconnecting the line. He sits for a moment longer, trying to calm himself, smooth away the tears, press down the frustration of Nova always pushing them together, thinking they are a couple.

Chapter 49
July 4
Alicia

It's been a long day for Alicia as she pulls into the driveway of her home. She closes her eyes and sits for a minute in the car, listening to the quiet, the birds singing in the trees, but her reverie is interrupted by the sound of Dylan's car revving in the garage next door. Slowly she gets out of her car, shoves the door closed and makes her way up the steps to her front door.

"I'm home, Luke," she yells coming into the house. More silence. "Are you home, Luke?" she asks, moving through the kitchen and down the hall to his bedroom door. The door is closed, and she opens it quietly, in case he's sleeping. The room is empty. She is alone.

Alicia moves back to the kitchen and pulls a beer out of the fridge, sits down at the table, and opens her laptop, taking a sip of the golden nectar as she waits for the computer to boot up. She signs in and types into Google search 'how do you permanently erase data from a cell phone so it cannot be recovered'.

Chapter 50
July 5
Helen

The restaurant is busy as Helen and Chuck wait to be seated. As the hostess approaches them with menus in hand, Helen pulls out her badge and flashes it. The hostess steps back, moving her hand to her mouth in surprise. Helen smiles. "We would like to sit down and have some lunch, thank you, but we would also like to speak to your manager."

"No problem. Let me seat you and I'll go find him," the timid young women replies, leading them to a corner table. She places the menus in front of them and asks, "Coffee?" to which they both reply simultaneously, "Yes, please."

They both look around and take in the clean, half-full restaurant. "I've never been here before," Helen says opening the menu.

"Looks like a nice neighbourhood gathering place," Chuck agrees as he scans the list of lunch options.

A short, stout man with a stark white beard and hair, someone who could be mistaken for Santa Claus if he wore a red suit at Christmas, walks over to their table, and pulls out a chair. "Officers," he says as a greeting. "I'm Dominic LaRosa, owner and manager of this establishment. What can I help you with today?"

The detectives put down the menus as Helen introduces herself and Chuck, explaining that they would like to ask him a couple questions about Jessica, her job, and the people that she worked with at the restaurant.

"Whatever you need. We were all so sorry to hear about Jess. She was a great kid. Great worker. Good with the customers. Always on time. We miss her already," he replies bowing his head as if in prayer for the lost girl.

"How long did Jessica work here?"

"I would have to check her file for specifics, but I would say about six months off the top of my head."

"What was her job here?" Helen asks.

"She was a waitress and a good one."

"How did she get along with the other people that work here? The other waitresses? The busboys? The kitchen staff?"

"Jess got along with everyone. She was friendly, picked up extra shifts if we were busy, changed shifts with others if asked, was always here on time."

"And what about the busboy staff? Any issues?" Helen leads.

"Well, I did hear that Myles, one of our busboys, had a crush on her. What you need to know about Myles is that he is intellectually disabled," he pauses to ensure the detectives understand before continuing. "Apparently, he followed her around a bit, but it was harmless. I heard the old boyfriend talked to him, and I think things calmed down after that, until they broke up and the new boyfriend came around. I heard the new guy beat the crap out of poor Myles when he found out that he fancied Jess. Freaking stupid if you ask me. Myles isn't a threat to anyone," Dominic confirms.

"Beat the crap out of him?" Chuck asks.

"A shame really. There was no need for any of it. That's when I told the new boyfriend not to come into the restaurant anymore. To wait outside."

"Myles? What's his last name? Is he here today?"

"Myles Stewart. No, he only works on weekends."

"Tell us about her boyfriends."

"The first guy, when she first started here, he came by every once in a while, but didn't make a nuisance of himself. The second guy, though, was different. When they first started going out, he would come into the restaurant and hang around while she was on shift. I told him that had to stop as he was interfering with the customers, they were worried about why a young punk like him was hanging around. And then the incident with Myles. After that he waited outside in that bright green car of his. You knew he was here when he revved the engine. He never honked for her but he sure as hell revved that engine, so she would hear it and hurry up."

"Were there any changes in Jessica when she started going out with the new boyfriend? How often she worked or how she interacted with the other waitresses or the customers?"

"No, she was the same loveable, nice girl. The customers loved her. but when it was getting close to the end of her shift, Jessica would hurry to get everything done so she could walk out of here on the stroke of the hour."

"We hear that Jessica had a lot of bruises on her arms. Did you notice any bruises or injuries while she worked here?"

Dominic chuckles softly. "Jess always complained about the size of the trays and their weight. She was strong, but sometimes she would pile too many full plates on the tray and would stagger into the wall or the door. I told her time and time again to slow down, take her time, put less on the tray, and make a couple of trips. I mean she had to serve everybody but if she dropped a tray of food, it would have been a hell of a mess and the customers would have had to wait longer for their meals."

"Can you give us Myles' home address and phone number, please?"

"Sure, just give me a minute to check the files," Dominic says, shoving himself away from the table and getting to his feet. He gestures to the menus. "Lunch is on me. Try the soup. Homemade from my wife's recipe." He smiles as he walks away, nodding to the waitress who has been waiting to take their order.

***

The Stewart's live outside of the city on a big farm. Helen pulls the police vehicle into the dirt driveway, noticing the beautiful yellow brick farmhouse in the distance. The fields have been cleared and both cows and horses graze on the green grass in separate fenced areas.

"I sure wouldn't want to shovel this driveway in the wintertime," Chuck laments as they continue up the kilometer-long laneway.

"They probably attach a plough blade to one of those horses," Helen laughs pulling up beside the pristine century home. "Nice place," she says turning the car off.

"Beautiful. Someone has done a lot of work on this place," Chuck agrees as he opens the car door and takes in the immaculate surroundings.

The side door of the house opens as a short grandmotherly type, drying her hands on a towel, steps out. "Can I help you?" she asks politely.

"We're looking for Myles Stewart," Helen answers.

"Myles is out in the barn with his dad. They're mucking out the stalls for the horses," she replies, nodding to the huge building behind the house. "Is there something wrong? I'm Mary Stewart, his grandmother. Can I help you?" she asks, walking to the edge of the porch to get a better look at the visitors.

Helen introduces herself and Chuck and asks if they can walk back to the barn to talk to Myles.

"By all means. It's a bit far for me but you are welcome to walk out there."

The ground is dry and hard as the two detectives make their way to the large barn, walking in the sunlight, taking in the fields, the animals, the world to which neither are very familiar. As they approach the barn, a man-door opens on the side of the building and a dusty, dirty man in jeans, high rubber boots and a sweat-stained T-shirt steps out. He pushes his baseball cap back on his head, noticing the two strangers. "Can I help you?" he asks.

Helen introduces herself and Chuck, adding that they would like to talk to Myles.

The man pushes his cap back further on his head to get a better look at the visitors before introducing himself. "I'm Warren Stewart, Myles's dad. What's this all about?" he asks.

"We're investigating the murder of Jessica Winters and we understand that Myles worked with her," Helen explains.

"And you think my boy had something to do with her death?" he asks with astonishment.

194

"We're trying to understand Jessica, who she was, what she did, who she hung around with and we understand that your son worked with her," Helen explains.

"Yeah, they worked together. Is that all this is? Should my son have a lawyer?"

"We just want to ask him a couple questions about their relationship, if there were any issues," she answers, side-stepping the question.

"Their relationship was fine. He had some designs on the girl for a while until her boyfriend beat him silly. Myles is intellectually disabled, immature for his years, a sweet kid, not worldly. Come in and I'll introduce you to him. He can tell you all about her," Warren Stewart says as he turns and opens the door. "He's down on the right, working in one of the stalls."

The three tramp over the packed dirt floor to the opposite end of the barn finding Myles in the last stall, the floor clean of hay and horse manure, as he uses the hose to put clean water in the trough.

"Myles," Warren Stewart calls as they stand in the corridor outside the stall.

The young man turns as he hears his father. "Almost done in this one, Dad," he confirms with a smile.

"Let's take a break for a sec," his dad replies. "These two detectives want to talk to you about Jessica." Instantly, Myles steps back and reaches his hand out to the wall of the stall for support.

"Jessica," he breathes out slowly. "Jessica is dead."

"And that's what they want to talk to you about," his father confirms, stepping into the stall beside his son. "It's okay, Myles. They just want to know about you, Jessica, work, how you got along," he says. Warren Stewart turns to the detectives. "Can we talk here, or would you prefer the house?"

"This should only take a couple of minutes. I think we're good here," Helen replies, turning to confirm with Chuck as he nods his head. "Myles, we understand that you worked with Jessica. Is that correct?"

"Some shifts we worked together, yes," he confirms. "When she worked days on the weekend," he adds.

195

"And how did you two get along?"

"I liked Jessica. She was really pretty and really nice to me," Myles smiles.

"We heard that there was a problem with her boyfriend. Can you tell us about it?"

Myles shrinks back against his father for support. "He was mean. He said I was interfering with them and to take a hike. And he hit me. Hit me hard."

Helen and Chuck watch as Warren Stewart puts his arm around his son, protecting him. "A real piece of work that one," he confirms.

"Do you know his name, Myles?" Helen asks.

Myles looks up as his father nods his head affirmatively. "Ziggy. His name is Ziggy," he replies.

"Did Jessica have any other friends come into the restaurant?"

"I liked her other boyfriend. His name was Luke," Myles confirms.

"How about him? Was he mean to you too?"

"Well, he did talk to me. Told me that he was Jessica's boyfriend and there wasn't room for two boyfriends. He was fine, I guess. She seemed to like him."

"Why did he have that conversation with you?" Helen pushes.

"Said I was following her around. I wasn't. I wasn't following her, not really. I just knew where she was going to be, and I went there too. But I would never hurt her. We were friends," Myles declares.

"Where were you the evening of June 30?"

"Wow, you've got to be kidding me! You think Myles did this," his dad replies, stepping in physically between the detectives, pushing his son behind him, the allegation large between them.

"It's okay Dad," Myles tells him, moving back beside his father, facing the detectives. "You remember. We went out for dinner to my restaurant. Remember, you had the shepherd's pie. That was the first day it was on the menu, remember?" he questions his dad, who nods. "Then we walked down to the waterfront and watched them set up the fireworks. The ones that were going to go off on Canada Day. They had all kinds of rockets, and stuff. It was a great display. Remember? We went the next night to see it!"

"Yes, Myles. I remember. It was a great fireworks display."

196

"What time did you get home on June 30?"

"Oh, it was dark. We went to bed but then my dad woke me to come out to the barn to help him with Dusty. Remember Dad? Dusty had hurt his leg. You thought that he had pulled a tendon and we had to ice it. Remember, Dad?" Myles asks his father.

"That's right, Myles. I forgot all about Dusty." His attention turns back to the two detectives. "Myles and I spent the night with Dusty taking turns with the ice. It's Myles's favourite horse. I'll give you the vet's number. He can confirm everything. He came that evening about 10pm to give Dusty a needle for the pain and then came back the next morning about 7am to see how he was doing."

***

"Well, we're batting zero on this case so far, Chuck."

"I don't think that boy has a mean bone in his body, and I don't see him hurting anyone even by accident."

"I agree with you. I'll call Dominic at the restaurant to confirm the new menu item and the date it showed up. Then I'll give the vet a call just to confirm the story about the horse."

"Kinda leads us back to Ziggy, the kid with the unsubstantiated alibi."

"It's been a long day. Let's go see him first thing tomorrow morning. Catch him before he gets out of the house. Maybe even catch him before he gets out of bed," Helen laughs as they drive back to the precinct through rush hour traffic.

197

Chapter 51
July 6
Helen

There are a bunch of cars parked in front of Axl's home when the detectives pull in the driveway. "Wow what a car show! The vintage Mustang belongs to Axl. Absolutely gorgeous. The GTO convertible belongs to his henchman Chevy. The lime-green Mustang is Ziggy's. Beautiful car but one freaking ugly colour," Chuck comments as Helen manoeuvres the police vehicle to the front of the house.

"Well at least we know that Ziggy is home. Let's see if we can talk to him without his lawyer," Helen comments as she parks the car and pulls the key from the ignition. "And look at that, already coming out to greet us. Bet they've got cameras at the gate so they can see who is coming and going."

Axl walks out from the separate building, once a garage but now an office or mancave. He walks toward the visitors. "Detectives," he greets. "More questions?"

"As a matter of fact, we do have a few more, Mr. Tunes. Seems the number that you gave us for your mother has been disconnected. Can we double check to make sure I have the correct one?" Helen asks, pulling out her phone, finding the contact and repeating the phone number to Axl.

"Yup, that's the one that I have for her," Axl confirms without even glancing at his phone.

The two detectives stand in the driveway, silent for a moment, waiting for more information from Axl. When nothing new is offered, Helen asks, "Do you have an address for her?"

"No, no I don't. She's pretty fluid, moves around a lot," Axl explains, nonchalantly shrugging his shoulders.

"Can we talk to Ziggy?"

"Not without his lawyer."

"We just want to ask him about his visit with his mother, get a viable phone number for her. Ask him where he stayed? How did he arrange the visit in advance? Just the logistics so we can understand where he was and get the right contact information from him."

"You are more than welcome to ask him those questions with his lawyer present. I'll call Sutton when you leave and have him make an appointment for us to come in again, if you would like."

"These are really quick questions with probably very simple answers. Couldn't we just do it now?" Helen persists.

"Sorry, no Detective. I'll have Sutton call you to set up a time," Axl responds. He turns when he reaches the doorway, standing still, watching, and waiting as the two detectives get into their police vehicle and drive back down the laneway to the road.

Chapter 52
July 7
Helen

"This is like déjà vu," Helen jokes with Chuck as they walk out to the main lobby of the precinct to greet Sutton Fox and the Tunes brothers.

"Yeah, we need to nail this kid so we can stop wasting our time," Chuck replies forcefully.

"Whoa, we don't even know that he did it yet," Helen warns.

"Don't we?" he asks as they round the corner to the lobby. Chuck puts on a smile and holds out his hand to the three waiting for them. "I'm Detective Chuck MacLean. I will be assisting Detective Hodges on this case," he says, nodding to his partner.

"Good you took that bitch off the case," Ziggy says before he gets a stern look from his brother.

Sutton Fox grabs Chuck's hand and introduces himself and the Tunes brothers. "Apparently you were at the house yesterday with some more questions," he nods toward the two detectives.

"Let's walk back to one of our rooms to talk," Helen says, turning to lead them out of the lobby. The five enter the same interrogation room that they used previously and sit down around the table before Chuck continues the discussion.

"Yes, Detective Hodges has had some issues locating Mr. Tunes's mother. We need the correct contact info for her so we can confirm the young boy's alibi," Chuck replies, smiling at Ziggy across the table.

"Young boy. What the hell," Ziggy mutters under his breath.

"Not a problem, Detective," Sutton Fox replies, turning to Axl. "Do you have another phone number or address that you can give the detective?"

Axl pulls out his phone and looks at it intently. "I've got a couple for her. She moves around a lot and tends to change her number a lot too." He takes a couple of minutes to inspect the numbers before saying, "Here try this one," reciting a phone number.

"Thank you. Can you share the other ones with me as well?" Helen asks. "That way if this one doesn't work out, we don't have to meet like this again."

Axl smiles, looks at his phone again, and agrees to give her two other possible phone numbers.

"An address would be good too. Just in case none of the numbers work."

Axl glances at Sutton for his approval, as Ziggy sits quietly, his shoulders up and arms crossed defensively. Sutton nods his head and Axl dictates a Toronto address.

"Is that the address that your mother was at when you went to visit her, Ziggy?"

Ziggy nods in the affirmative.

"What is your mother's name?"

"Now why would you need that? You have phone numbers and an address for her," Sutton objects

"Just in case we can't locate her with the phones numbers or the address that Mr. Tunes has given us. Seems she moves around and changes phones a lot and any additional information that you can give us to locate her would be helpful. I would think you would want us to talk to her to confirm Ziggy's whereabouts, his alibi," Chuck explains.

There is lull in the conversation before Axl offers, "She uses a variety of names, depending on the day, the situation."

"Please be more specific. What names does she use?" Chuck pushes.

Axl sighs before answering. "Her maiden name is Clarke, Clarke with an 'e'. Her first husband's surname was Ashland; the second was Hoolahan."

"And what about Tunes?"

"Not sure where that came from, but it is our legal name, on our birth certificates. She uses that one the most, I believe."

"And her first name?"

"Her given name is Elizabeth. Elizabeth Clarke. She's pretty consistent with her first name, though she does use the shortened versions as well - Liz, Beth, Betty," he says sullenly.

There is a silence in the room as if each person is contemplating this unique mother and her plethora of names and identities. Helen breaks the stillness. "Ziggy, can you tell us about your visit with your mom?"

Ziggy turns his attention away from the window and shrugs his shoulders. "I went down to Toronto. Sat around with her. Had some food. Watched some TV. Nothing special," he replies sullenly.

"How did you set it up with your mom?"

"She called me, asked me to come down. Gave me the address and I went. Call her. My mom will confirm I was there."

"Can you give us the number off your phone that she called from?"

"I don't have my phone with me, but I'm sure it's one of those that Axl just gave you," Ziggy explains.

Helen and Chuck look at each other, giving the other time to ask more questions or reframe the ones already on the table. After an extensive pause, Helen closes the conversation. "Thanks for your time today. If we have any other issues getting hold of your mom or getting her to confirm that you were in fact there, we will let you know."

Sutton Fox and the brothers get up and leave the room quickly.

Chapter 53
July 7
Luke

Why the hell is she not answering my texts? I know its been a while since we talked or texted, but things have been crazy here with Jessica, the cops, fucking Ziggy. I'll check the band's Instagram and see what's going on. Maybe she's been busy too. Maybe I will just show up at her next show and explain myself if she won't talk to me.

This can't be right. It says she's missing. Missing! What does that mean? I'll call her brother, Caleb. No, I don't have his number, only Hannah's. I'll use messenger. Ask him to call me.

What is taking him so long? Okay, there's an answer. He's given me his phone number.

"Caleb, what the hell is going on?" Luke bursts out as soon as Hannah's brother picks up the phone.

"Luke, when was the last time you saw Hannah?" her brother asks, not answering his question.

"The last time was at that bar in Orillia. Remember, I was up there with a couple of friends and you guys were playing."

"Yeah, that was a couple of weeks ago. Have you talked to Hannah since?"

"I did but it was just after that night. There's been a lot of shit going on here. The last I heard you guys were going to play at some trailer park on the lake. She invited me up, but I couldn't make it." Luke pauses. "What is going on? Your Instagram page says Hannah is missing?"

"We played the gig, and you know at the end of our last set how Hannah sometimes goes out into the crowd, walks away with someone that she knows, and we finish the last song without her? Well, that happened, but she didn't come back to the stage, didn't come back to help us pack up which is totally not like her. We didn't see who it was that she walked away with, thought that maybe she hooked up with someone, but she didn't show up the next day either."

"Wow. Unbelievable," Luke says. "What can I do to help, Caleb?"

Luke hears a sniffle over the phone, knowing Caleb is worried and distressed about his sister. "There's not much you can do. The cops organized a couple of search parties, and we combed the park but didn't find her. One of the campers said they saw her walk down the road with some guy, but they didn't know who it was, didn't get a good description, didn't know where they went. It's just like a dead end, man," he says, his voice catching on his sobs.

Chapter 54
July 8
Alicia

As Alicia walks down the empty hallway of the precinct to the Detectives' Den, she notices the door to the major crimes room for Jessica's case is open. She stops and looks in, noticing the beginning of an evidence board, already filled with a collage of pictures, newspaper articles, media reports, investigative reports, and diagrams of the crime scene. She steps into the room for closer inspection and glances quickly over the names and pictures, following the various colours of string connecting important details of the case. *At least Luke's picture isn't up there. Hopefully it never gets to that.* Jessica's prom picture is at the top of the collection, a big grin on her face. *She was so proud of herself for completing high school. She had such a bright future ahead of her*, Alicia reminisces. A candid shot of Ziggy hangs beside Jessica's photo, a snap taken when he was walking into the police precinct with his brother and lawyer. Beside his picture is a synopsis of his alibi that has still not been corroborated.

Before Alicia can review all of the materials, the sounds of someone coming down the hallway toward her resonates in the small meeting room. Alicia holds her breath, knowing that she shouldn't be in this room, shouldn't be looking at what they've collected so far. The footsteps stop at the open door. "Dammit! This shouldn't be wide open," Alicia hears as Helen steps into the room. "You shouldn't be in here," Helen tells her sternly as she places her coffee and briefcase on the central table.

"I know, Helen. I'm sorry but the door was wide open, and I couldn't help myself," Alicia explains.

"I get it, Alicia. You should be on this case, but the Chief has made the decision, with the help of Ziggy's scumbag lawyer, so you're out."

"I get it. I really do, but if there's anything I can help with, just let me know," Alicia offers moving toward the door as her phone chimes with an incoming message. She opens the message and looks up to her friend. "Fraser and I just got another case. Seems a resident up at the college dorm just called in an attempted sexual assault."

"Sounds interesting, Alicia. Good luck," Helen comments as Alicia exits the room, walking to the Detectives' Den at the end of the hallway.

***

Fraser parks in the roundabout in front of the main entrance of the residence at the north end of the college campus and the two detectives get out, walk into the front lobby. Fraser Weston is about a decade younger than Alicia, on the taller side of average height, short dark hair closely cropped on the sides and back, a little longer on top with a short, thinly trimmed beard and mustache. His charcoal grey suit is a classic fit, dressy, comfortable, appropriate for all situations.

There's a directory just inside the main door, and Alicia searches for Frankie Mason's room code, finds it and pushes the corresponding numbers. The resident answers quickly and buzzes them into the building.

They take the elevator to the seventh floor. When they reach the floor and the doors open, they hear a hushed voice calling out to them, "This way officers." They turn to see a petite, young woman dressed in baggy sweatpants and an oversized sweatshirt, unusual attire for the hot summer weather. They move toward the young woman as Fraser introduces himself and Alicia.

"Can we come in and you can tell us what happened?" Fraser asks.

Frankie pushes back on the door that she has been leaning against and ushers them into her small but neat living room. She lives alone and is in her third year of a four-year program, taking some extra courses during the summer months so she can finish the program earlier than most.

Fraser and Alicia continue to stand until Frankie sits down on the love seat, leaving a matching chair and ottoman for them to sit in. As they settle, Fraser pulls out a notebook and a pen to take notes, signally for Alicia to take the lead. Frankie begins to cry, tears rolling down her cheeks. Her hands begin to shake as her shoulders slump forward. Alicia gets up from the ottoman and moves to sit beside Frankie, putting her arm around the girl's shoulder, letting her move in for comfort, for support.

"When you're ready, can you tell us what happened?" Alicia asks softly.

Frankie takes a moment to slow the tears and clear her throat before she starts. "It was a couple of weeks ago. I was accosted in Heritage Park. Some big guy came out of nowhere and tried to rape me."

"Why did it take so long for you to call us, Frankie?" Alicia enquires, her arm still around the frail, shaking girl.

"I was afraid. Afraid that he knew who I was, and where I lived. I was afraid to go out, afraid to go to class, but this morning, I decided that this guy couldn't run my life, that I needed to take it back and this is my first step. And technically nothing happened. I stopped him before he could do anything," she confesses from the safety of Alicia's side.

"Very understandable to be shaken up and you're right, you can't let this guy intimidate you. Tell us what happened from the beginning," Alicia requests.

Frankie sits up to the edge of the couch, getting brave with the support of the police in her apartment. "It was Saturday night. I went to the Queens for a couple of drinks to unwind. I met a guy at the bar. We danced, we drank and decided to leave together. We walked over to the park, to the point that looks out to the bay, near the boat docks and sat down on the grass. I really liked the guy and we started to make out but then Murph, that's the guy's name that I was with, Murphy Baldwin, got sick. Started to throw up, probably from too many drinks. I got out of there quick and started to walk back to the road. I was going to catch a bus home but then this guy jumped out of the shadows, like he had been watching us and was just waiting for me. He started to touch me, tried to kiss me. I struggled to get away and I finally did, but then he grabbed me around the waist, and we fell to the ground. He was on top of me, and he undid my pants, tried to push them down." Tears stream down Frankie's face as she relives the horror. "I fought back hard. Somehow, I was able to knee him in the groin. Took the air out of him," she smiles a bit, "and I got up and ran."

"Good for you," Alicia says, patting Frankie's shoulder. "Good for you."

"Definitely quick thinking on your part," Fraser agrees, nodding his head in the affirmative.

Alicia asks Frankie a plethora of questions. What did he look like? How tall was he? What colour was his hair? What colour were his eyes? What was he wearing? Did he have any tattoos? Did he say anything? Did he have an accent? Did he smell like he'd been drinking? Did he smell like anything, cologne maybe? Have you seen him before at the bar or maybe at school?

Frankie answers each of the questions but is unable to give the detectives any substantial information to identify the perpetrator.

Alicia then asks questions about the man she went to the park with, Murphy Baldwin. Did you meet him at the bar? Did you know him before? Did you get his phone number? What do you know about him? Does he live in Barrie? Have you seen him since?

Again, Frankie answers each of the questions but doesn't have a lot of information on him either, their time together interrupted when he started to get sick, and she bailed on him.

"Can you take us to the park and show us where this happened?" Fraser suggests.

"How will that help?" Frankie asks.

"Might be some evidence left behind or maybe you'll remember other details that may have slipped your mind. Let's go take a look and make sure," Fraser confirms standing up.

***

Frankie takes them to the water's edge, where she sat with Murphy Baldwin from the bar, but there is no evidence of their tryst. The grass is no longer bent or pushed down, and anything ejected from Murphy's stomach has dissipated long ago. They walk over to the area

208

where she was accosted by the perpetrator, but the same thing, no evidence of the incident, no cigarette butts or candy wrappers on the ground, no footprints, nothing.

Alicia considers the area closely, taking pictures of where Frankie was sitting on the ground with the guy from the bar and where she was jumped by the assailant. Alicia turns and looks to the main street, at the bar where Frankie had been drinking and takes several more photos.

Disappointed, Fraser and Alicia drive Frankie back to the residence and tell her to call them if she sees or hears from the suspect again or if she remembers anything that may help them identify the perpetrator.

Driving out from the residence, Fraser asks, "Thanks for taking lead on that. I think you got more out of her than I would have. What do you think?"

"Well, a crime has been committed - sexual assault – even though he didn't get to complete the act, but unless this guy does it again or we find some kind of evidence to identify him, it will be next to impossible to bring him to justice."

"Agreed. It is good that she reported it though. Less than four percent of sexual assaults are reported in Canada while available data suggests that one in three women will experience some form of sexual assault in their lifetime. Research also shows that up to 25 percent of college and university-aged women will experience some form of sexual assault during their academic career. Frankie is lucky that she acted so quickly, so decisively, to get away from him, and that she found the strength to report it. It will help her overcome the scars that this piece of shit has left."

"She is a smart girl and kept her wits about her."

"Definitely. When we get back to the precinct, can you do a bit of research on these kinds of cases? Maybe you'll find similar incidents that will help us get a lead on this guy. You never know, maybe we'll get lucky."

"Definitely," Alicia confirms.

Chapter 55
July 8
Luke

It's early evening, a week since the discovery of Jessica's body, and Luke is sitting on the picnic table at the gazebo where he used to meet Jessica when they were a couple. He's watching people walk along the path near the water's edge, a lot of them carrying flowers, teddy bears and balloons on their way to the rear of the Community Centre, where a memorial is being created for Jessica.

As Luke watches the procession of people paying their respects, a loud distinctive grumbling sound of a V8 muscle car echoes over the area. He turns to see Ziggy's car pull into the Community Centre's parking lot. It stops and the engine is shut off, but nothing happens for several moments until the driver's door opens and a red running shoe lands on the cement.

Luke watches as Ziggy gets out of the car, opens the trunk, and pulls out a huge floral arrangement, one that would be appropriate at a funeral home, and is way over-the-top for the makeshift memorial. *What an asshole. Again, he's making this about him. Not about the perfect girl that he killed. He's a piece of shit. This is his fault. He did this.*

With this last thought, Luke is off the picnic table at a full run toward Ziggy as he moves to the rear of the building, flowers in hand. Halfway to Ziggy's destination, Luke tackles him. The two go down hard and the flowers are tossed aside as Luke pummels his head, his shoulders, his ribs. "You son of a bitch. This is your fault. You did this," he yells as he thrashes violently.

A uniformed cop, who was watching the mourners and the creation of the memorial for Jessica, hears the yelling, the commotion, and comes around the side of the building to see the two teenagers on the ground, fists flying amidst the coloured flowers. He runs over to the pair and pulls them apart with the assistance of several men who were on their way to pay their respects.

"Boys, boys, what the hell is going on here? You need to show a little reverence, a little respect," he starts to lecture them.

"Reverence? Respect?" Luke spits out in anger. "From the piece of shit that killed her? I doubt that very much."

The crowd reacts to his harsh words, a gasp rising from them in unison.

"I didn't kill her. She was my girlfriend. I loved her," Ziggy defends himself, trying aggressively to get away from the men holding him back.

"But she didn't love you. Jessica still loved me," Luke continues to goad Ziggy. "She was coming back to me," he declares.

"Now boys, both of you. Stop this. Stop it right now or we can all go down to the precinct for a conversation. Invite your parents too," the cop intervenes.

Both Luke and Ziggy shrink back with the threat of going downtown, both for very different reasons; Luke concerned with his mother's reaction to his accusations, his violence, his involvement in the case, and Ziggy frightened of his brother's wrath for being anywhere near the site where Jessica was found and for showing any emotion to the outside world.

"That's better," the officer says as the two seem to regain their civility, enough so that the men holding them are able to let their arms go free.

A police car pulls into the parking lot and Officers Katie Hart and Ian Parkes get out, looking at the crowd. Officer Hart walks over to Luke, while Officer Parkes moves to Ziggy.

"You okay, Luke?" Katie asks, standing in front of him, blocking his view of his opponent.

"This fucker shouldn't be here. It's his fault she's dead," he says, raising his voice so that Ziggy can hear him.

Ziggy's reply is to push against Officer Parkes, trying to get to Luke. "Let me at him," he shouts. "Jessica left him for me. She was mine," he yells, agitated again.

Officer Hart puts her arms up in a stop motion and turns to Ziggy. "One more from either of you and both of you are going to the precinct," she declares, which quiets them again. She turns back to

Luke. "You know that Detectives Hodges and MacLean are on this. They are the best. They will find out what happened to Jessica. You have to be patient and give them time to find the truth."

Luke nods as he steps back. "Go home, Luke," Officer Hart concludes before turning to the crowd. "This is over now. Go back to whatever you were doing. Have a good evening," she directs, as the crowd starts to break-up.

Chapter 56
July 9
Luke

Luke's alarm rings at 7am and he rolls over in bed pulling the covers over his head. *Just a few more minutes before I get up. I couldn't sleep last night. My mind just wouldn't shut down with the memorial, with fucking Ziggy trying to look like it was all about him. My head is killing me. Just a few more minutes*, he thinks as he falls back into a fitful sleep until the alarm blares again ten minutes later.

Okay, okay, getting up now. He picks up his cell phone, pushing the button to stop the loud, incessant music, noticing an incoming text. He clicks the icon and sees a note from Noah sent last evening, 'Heard about you and Ziggy. Are you okay?'

Luke sits at the edge of the bed and types, 'I'm okay. A bit sore. Bet he's in a hell of a lot more pain though.'

'Good,' Noah replies instantly.

'Just getting up. Working at the beach today. What are you up to?'

'Working with my dad. He's got a big job north of the city. A new house.'

'Cool,' Luke replies, phone in hand as he moves to the bathroom.

'Don't forget about the BBQ for my birthday. I know the timing sucks, but Nova is already making plans for our big day.'

'Count me in,' Luke replies, though he is not feeling the excitement of the celebration.

Chapter 57
July 10

"Come on, Dad. You said we could go down to the park this morning," little Teddy nags his father, who is sitting on the front deck of their trailer. "We need to go before the swings are all taken," he reasons.

His father sips his coffee and smiles at his son, remembering when he used to enjoy going to the park with his dad, how they would spend hours at the water's edge, looking for crayfish, hunting for frogs. "Give me a sec to make a fresh cup of coffee, and I'm with you," he finally agrees.

Teddy raises his two arms in victory. "Yes," he yells beginning to hop from one foot to the other in anticipation. Teddy tries to wait patiently for his father but can't and starts to pace the length of the deck, muttering to himself, "Come on, come on." Finally, his father appears at the trailer door, and the boy takes off, skipping down the dirt road of the trailer park toward the playground and the water.

"Slow down a bit Teddy," his father yells, struggling to keep up to his energetic son. "Grab a swing and I'll be there in a sec," he instructs, as Teddy is halfway down the street. "Don't go near the water without me," he adds.

The park is filled with kids of all ages – some climbing on the jungle gym, some constructing castles and roads in the sandbox, others swooping down the slides, while a couple more fly high on the swings. There is one swing with no one on it and Teddy has snagged it, holding on to it until his father gets to the park. His dad lifts him up onto the seat and pushes him, making him go higher and higher, as he squeals with glee, reaching for the sky.

After a time, his dad suggests, "How about we look for crayfish for a while?"

"K Dad," Teddy agrees before jumping fearlessly off the swing that is still in motion, onto the soft cushion of the rubber flooring surrounding the play area.

"Teddy, be careful," his dad admonishes as Teddy runs to the water's edge, knowing that at his age he used to do the same thing.

Teddy's dad follows his son around the shoreline as the boy wades into the cold water up to his knees, bending over to look closely at small rocks, and sand on the lakebed. He oohs and aahs at a school of minnows speeding away from him, the skeleton of a crayfish lying on the bottom, a dead fish floating upside down. Teddy continues to search the water as his father casually watches his son's slow trek away from the groomed swimming area to an overgrown swampy patch.

"Be careful," his dad warns as a family of ducks escape their nest as Teddy rambles toward them.

The boy continues his exploration, until suddenly his father hears him yell, "Dad, Dad!"

He looks up and sees Teddy standing in the water, knee deep, a once-white sneaker in his hand, fear filling his eyes. Teddy's dad moves quickly to his son's side in the water, wading through the water, not sure what his son has discovered, until he is beside him and follows his son's gaze to a bloated, nibbled-on body trapped among the bulrushes.

Chapter 58
July 10
Jeff

Alicia's long hair is pulled back with a single clip but the strong wind is enticing whisps to escape and fly in the breeze. Jeff reaches for her hand sitting in her lap and smiles at her as he guides the convertible up the highway to Fern Resort. *Wish she would have agreed to the whole weekend away, but I guess I get it with all the shit that's going down with Luke. Can't imagine being 17 and someone killing my girlfriend. Or even my ex-girlfriend. I get that Alicia wants to be with him, to support him, make sure that he's not sucked into the chaos around the case. She's a good mom. Maybe we can do this again once the case is settled and they find the real killer. Stay for the whole weekend instead of just for a nice dinner. Guess that's what I get for falling for an independent, strong, beautiful woman. I'm so glad that we met at that benefit and got reacquainted after her medical troubles. She was definitely worth waiting for and I will wait, as long as it takes. At least we'll have some good food, some good conversation, some time together over dinner before going back to the realities of her life as a mother and a police detective.*

Chapter 59
July 11
James

James smiles as he sails down the highway. *Another beautiful day. Too bad I don't have that cottage on the French River anymore. Now would be the time to be there. Go fishing with Luke. Sit on the deck and watch the sun come up, the sun go down. It was perfect.*

Too bad Chevy couldn't make it today. Damn appendicitis has got him in the hospital for a couple of days. He'd been sick for a while, but ignored the pain, the nausea, the vomiting until he couldn't stand it anymore. Lucky for him that he got in just before the fucking thing ruptured. I should go see him tonight. James chuckles. Go see a fellow enforcer? A guy from the gang? What am I thinking? He's not really a friend. Just a co-worker. Though he's turned out to be a good guy. Trust him with my life.

James cruises down the almost empty street, turning into the driveway of the large factory, getting out of the vehicle to open the gate. He gets back into the van, pulls into the garbage-ladened parking lot, leaving the gate wide open, too lazy to get out and close it.

He pulls the truck around to the warehouse dock noticing the door is closed, making him wary, but he backs up to the dock anyway. He looks at his watch to check the time. *Am I early? What is going on?* He pulls his gun out from under the seat, secures it under his belt and jumps from the truck.

As he approaches the back of the van, the sliding door on the dock starts to rise. James stands back waiting, watching as the door lifts to reveal Don Saunders, dressed in a pair of shiny black dress shoes, trim black pants, topped with a white shirt, a bright blue tie, and a matching black suit jacket.

"Hey James. You're a couple of minutes early," he says, moving out of the building into the sunlight. "Where's Chevy?"

"He couldn't make it," James confirms. "Had an appendicitis attack and is in the hospital for a couple of days."

217

"Hope he's okay. And what about you? See you're doing really well for yourself. Maybe a bit of a come down from a senior detective to a flunky driver, but hey, life is strange sometimes, don't you think?"

James holds his breath at the insult, saying nothing.

"What's wrong? Cat got your tongue, James?" Don chuckles watching James begin to squirm.

"Enough shit, Don. Let me get the stuff loaded and get out of here," James finally says, jumping up onto the dock.

"Whatever you say, loser," Don replies stepping back as James grabs the pallet jack, moving it toward the wooden crates full of firearms. Don watches James push the forks under one of the large wooden boxes. "Yeah, you're pretty good at this manual labour shit. Maybe this was all you were ever cut out to do," he laughs.

James keeps his head down, trying to concentrate on this simple job, trying to ignore the jeers from his old boss. *Idiot. You are living on the edge, asshole.*

"You couldn't even keep a junkie in line. What a cop you turned out to be," Don continues.

James pushes the first box into the rear of his van and turns to his old boss. "What the fuck is your problem, Don? My personal life has nothing to do with our business here, so why don't you just stop your shit before I make you," he warns, moving back onto the dock to pick up the second container.

"James, I'm just trying to point out some of your character flaws. Things that you could work on. Things that, if you changed, would help you become more like me. Someone that could afford to buy shoes, like mine," he goads turning his ankle, like Dorothy showing off her ruby slippers in the Wizard of Oz, giving James a look at his very expensive Louis Vuitton Manhattan Richelieu kid leather shoes. "Just saying, James. You could be so much better if you put a little effort into life and stopped just skating by. You could be more like me if you tried. Look where you ended up," he laughs. "And me. I was in it as much as you, but I came out the other side. Got a promotion, opened up the new agency and look at me now. Making a cool million every month on the merchandise that is supposed to be destroyed. And that's just for starters. Just wait, I'll be making twice that much a year from now. No, I couldn't have written a better life for me if I tried. Life is good, isn't it James?"

James's patience has abruptly come to an end, and he pulls his Smith and Wesson pistol out, pointing it at Don. "I would stop now if I were you," he cautions.

Don laughs. "Oh James. You have no fucking backbone. We both know that. There's always someone behind you pulling the strings. Your wife or should I say ex-wife, me for a while, now Axl and that hooker chick. You're always kowtowing to someone," Don states.

James has lost his patience and he won't, he can't take it anymore. He aims the gun at Don's head and pulls the trigger before his target can move. The tormenter falls, dead before he hits the ground. Blood spreads out around his head as his blank eyes face the sky.

"Fuckkkkkk!" James yells. "You deserved that."

James stands for a moment as his present situation sinks in. *What the fuck! Can't believe I actually killed the bastard. He deserved it. All his shit about how great he is, how my life is shit and his is perfect. I'm under a lot of stress with the gang stuff and now with Luke involved in a homicide. Fucker should have just minded his own business and let me pick up the guns. What should I do? Call Axl? Just pick up the guns and leave? But what about the body? Close the door and just leave it?*

After several moments of consideration, James restarts his work, moving the remaining cartons of guns into the back of the van. When he finishes, he closes the warehouse door, checking to ensure that the blood has not seeped onto the dock where it would be visible to a passerby. He looks around closely, ensuring that he is alone, and no one is watching him before jumping into the van and driving out of the parking lot, leaving the gates wide open.

James moves the vehicle steadily, manoeuvring through the start of rush hour traffic and coasts up the highway toward home. *Son of a bitch deserved it. Always ragging on me. Getting me involved with the gang in the first place. This is all his fault. He deserved to die for what he did to me.*

But what am I going to tell Axl? I can't tell him I killed Don. His death is the end of the gravy train of guns, and Axl will definitely kill me for hitting his bottom line so drastically.

Think, James, think.

I know, tell him that everything was fine. Everything went down the way it was supposed to. I left Don alive and standing on the dock. I got the guns, gave him the money, and left. Don't admit to anything. Yeah, yeah, that will work. And when it finally comes out that the bastard is dead, deny everything. Stick to the story. Somebody else must have come in and killed him after I left.

I need to hide the money. Need to put it somewhere no one will find it, especially Axl. Once he finds out Don is dead, he'll be watching me. I can't keep it at home, knowing Axl he'll have the place searched. I'll stop at that storage facility just off the highway before I hit Barrie. Rent one of their small lockers and leave it there. Yeah, that's it. Pay in advance for six months so I don't have to go there all the time. Pay cash. He'll never find it. James smiles and looks at the bag of cash sitting on the passenger seat.

The traffic is heavy on Highway 400 from the city, with all the nine-to-fivers rushing home after a long day of work, extending James's drive time. James operates the van effortlessly, blending into the steady flow of cars, almost as if on autopilot.

Wow. A million dollars. Maybe I can buy back that cottage on the French River. Not this year, but maybe next. Yeah, that would be great.

220

Chapter 60
July 11
Alicia

Alicia and Fraser are standing in front of Murphy Baldwin's pick up truck as the bell rings signifying the end of the day shift at the large manufacturing plant. The two detectives wait patiently as hordes of workers leave the building, talking, and laughing among themselves as they move to their vehicles for their drive home.

Frankie Mason gave Alicia and Fraser a description of Baldwin, and the detectives smile at each other as they spot him exiting the large brick building, waving, and saying good-bye to his fellow labourers as he walks toward them. He looks up, noticing them when he's about ten meters away, his pace slowing down as he contemplates their presence.

"Mr. Baldwin? Murphy Baldwin?" Alicia enquires as he gets closer to his vehicle.

"Who are you?" he asks, stopping in his tracks.

"I'm Detective Anderson, and this is my partner, Detective Weston. We're hoping you have a few minutes to talk," Alicia says, offering her hand in greeting.

Baldwin ignores her out-stretched hand as he demands, "Talk about what? I haven't done anything wrong."

"Not saying that you have, Mr. Baldwin," Fraser chimes in. "We just want to ask you a couple of questions. We understand that you were at the Queens Hotel on June 25. Is that correct?"

"I don't know. I go there a few times a week. I might have been there. What happened on that night?" he asks, moving closer to the detectives, so the others walking to their vehicles cannot hear their conversation.

"Do you recall going to the bar and meeting a young lady by the name of Frankie Mason?"

He stands for a moment, looking like he's reaching back into his memory and finally asks, "Short, small, little thing, going to Georgian College?"

"Yes, that sounds like her," Alicia confirms.

"I didn't do anything to her. What is she saying I did?"

"She's not accusing you of anything. Can you tell us how you guys met? What happened at the bar? What happened afterwards?"

Baldwin kicks his foot in the dust of the parking lot like a child who has been caught stealing candy at the corner store. He tells them the same story they heard from Frankie – how they met at the bar, had some drinks together, danced.

"And then what happened," Alicia leads.

Again, he kicks the sand around with his boot before finishing his story. "We left, went to the park across the road. We sat down in the grass, and I was hoping to get lucky, but the beer and the tacos suddenly had different ideas. I was sick and when it was over, she was gone," he concludes.

"And then what happened," Alicia asks again.

"I got up, dusted myself off and went home. I looked for her, but she was gone."

"Did you see anyone else in the park?"

"There were a few people around, walking, smoking, whatever. Why? What's going on?"

"Was there anyone else with you? Did you have a friend waiting for you in the park?"

"No, I was alone. Went to the bar by myself. Hoping to meet someone, to get some, you know. And I met Frankie. Really liked her until I barfed, and she high tailed it out of there. What is she saying about me? I didn't do anything wrong. Didn't get the chance."

"Frankie Mason is saying that she was sexually assaulted after leaving you, that she was jumped by a man in the park. Do you know anything about that?" Fraser asks pointedly.

Baldwin's jaw drops. "Shit. Is she okay?"

Fraser and Alicia don't answer and let the silence hang between them until Baldwin continues, "I liked her, thought she was cute and smart. I thought we might be good together, but I didn't call her after that. I threw up. I ruined it. Who the hell would want to go out with someone who couldn't even keep their dinner down?"

Chapter 61
July 11

"Look, it's open," the 12 year old points to the metal gate, gesturing to his friend. "Let's go in and check the place out. Vans come and go all the time. Something's got to be going on in this place," he says, walking into the parking lot.

"I'm in," his friend agrees, following him closely.

The two boys run to the building, kicking empty cans and debris in the parking area. "Let's see if any of the doors are unlocked, maybe we can get in. There's got to be something in there, maybe something that we can sell in the neighbourhood."

"Great idea," his friend confirms as they move from loading dock to loading dock, trying to open the roller doors, but they do not budge. The boys continue down the line, trying each until they come to the last door. One of the boys pushes against the door, and it opens slightly.

"Together, we can get it if we push together," he tells his friend, waiting for him to get into place at the other end. The door is very heavy, and they hoist it together, giving it a last tremendous shove, which locks it in the open position. They smile at each other until they spot the body just inside the dock area, lying in a pool of blood.

Chapter 62
July 12
Alicia

The Detectives' Den is empty as Alicia enters the cavernous room. She wonders where everyone is when a ruckus of laughter breaks out down the hall. She steps back through the door and follows the noise to the major crime room that has been set up as the centre of information on Jessica's death. She peers in, spying all of the detectives from her department sitting around the boardroom table. "What's going on?" Alicia asks.

Helen, who is standing at the front of the room rifling through a stack of papers, looks up. "Hey, Alicia. We got some results back from the medical examiner and forensics on Jessica, not all but some of the info. Wish our labs were half as fast as the ones on TV," she smiles at her comment before continuing. "Typically, we get together as a full team and review what we have, ask questions, throw some thoughts out on the table." She pauses unsure if Alicia should be included due to the Chief's directive to remove her from the case.

As Helen ponders Alicia's inclusion, Chief O'Malley appears at the doorway. "Come in, sit down," she directs as she moves into the room. "I just caught the end of what Helen was saying but yes, the team usually get together to review the information from the medical examiner. I know you're not on the case, but I don't see any reason why you can't be involved with this. It is highly confidential, like everything else we do. And if things change, if things get closer to your family, we can revisit that decision. Helen, back to you. Sorry I'm late," she says moving to the back of the room and sitting down.

Helen opens the document and starts to review the results from the coroner's office with the team. The estimated time of death is between 11:30pm June 30 to 1am July 1. *Shit. Luke said he was at the park from about 10pm for an hour, an hour and a half which is within the coroner's estimate. Not good. Leaves him in as a possible suspect.*

Jessica was killed by blunt force trauma to the head, with a total of twelve hits, and it is believed the sixth bash was the killing blow. The first strike was administered when both Jessica and the perpetrator were standing, with the following eleven hits administered with Jessica on the ground and the perpetrator standing above her, thrusting the weapon in a downward motion. It was confirmed that Jessica's blood and hair were found on the log that Alicia discovered near the site, verifying that it was the murder weapon. The forensic team are still running some tests on the log, scouring for DNA from the person that swung the weapon ending Jessica's life, though it is extremely difficult to get anything from an organic substance with very rough surfaces.

The team did determine that Jessica recently had consensual sex, not sure of the timing yet. If semen is present, it will be examined for DNA and once there is someone in custody, DNA comparisons could be done.

The other major finding was that Jessica was pregnant. Initial examination indicate the fetus at 12 to 16 weeks old, which will allow for a paternity test. There's a pause in the room as some eyes turn to Alicia, who stifles a gasp and continues to look forward, showing no outward reaction as she works the timelines in her mind. *Beginning of April to end of June – that's three months. It may be Luke's baby, which could be construed as probable cause. Get rid of her; get rid of the baby. Shit. They're going to pull him into this investigation. But it also gives Ziggy probable cause too – maybe he found out she was pregnant with Luke's baby or maybe it was Ziggy's baby, and he didn't want it, so he killed her.*

"Wasn't the boyfriend fairly new? Maybe there was someone before him and it was his kid," comments one of the senior detectives.

Alicia turns red, knowing that half the room was now looking in her direction. She decides to face the issue head-on. "Jessica Winters did date my son Luke, prior to Ziggy Tunes. They broke up months ago. Jessica would need to be at least 16 weeks along in her pregnancy for it to be his," she explains exaggerating the dates slightly to Luke's advantage.

There's a prolonged silence after Alicia's comment until Helen breaks in. "Well, that's all we have right now. Comments?" she asks, looking out over the room.

"Question - could the perpetrator have worn gloves? That might limit DNA on the log," asks the Chief.

"Possible. We didn't find any gloves left at the scene. Depending on the type, they may have left traces of fibre, latex maybe. Connor, can you make a note for the team to look for traces of latex or other materials on the log?" Helen asks as Connor Brooks nods in the affirmative. Helen continues, "The thing with gloves is the weather. Not something that people would have on their person in June. If they brought gloves with them, it would lead me to believe the killing was premeditated. If the killing was planned in advance, you would think the perpetrator would have brought their own weapon and not just picked up the closest thing. Just my thoughts at this point. We'll see what Connor's team finds. Any other thoughts or questions?" she asks, looking around the room. The group is quiet, and she moves on asking Connor Brooks to review the forensic results to date.

He smiles at the crowd as he steps to the front of the room, "Thanks Helen. It's still early for us but we are running tests for DNA and fingerprints on the yellow blanket that was draped over the body and the clothes that Jessica was wearing."

He continues his summary advising that his team are also reviewing fingerprints and finger and hand smears taken from the railings of the Community Centre, but the number of prints were astronomical, especially with the good weather and walkers out and about. They were not hopeful that they would get any results that would help with the investigation, but the results could be used to confirm the perpetrator was present at the location once there is someone in custody.

There were no footprints at the site to examine, even though they did try to make casts of the sandy area surrounding the body. They were examining some of the sand for DNA, sweat, fibres but at this point, nothing has been found.

The group is silent as Connor looks up from his tablet. "That's all I have at this point. We should have more in a couple of weeks."

"Thanks Connor. Comments?" she asks, moving back to the front of the room.

Initially, there is silence from the team of detectives, until the Chief asks about the suspects. Helen tells the team about Ziggy Tunes, that Jessica's friends have all suggested he is the one to look at, he has a violent streak, may have hit her before, but he does have an alibi which as of yet, they have been unable to substantiate.

"You still haven't been able to track down the mother?" the Chief asks.

"She seems to move around a lot, sleeps on friend's couches. We've given the Toronto police the address where Ziggy says he met her that weekend but haven't received any word from them yet."

"Anyone else you're considering?" the Chief asks.

"Honestly, no. We were able to eliminate her co-worker from the restaurant. It was suggested that he was stalking her for a while. We talked to him, and he has a substantiated alibi for that night so he's off our list. We were also able to eliminate the deceased's parents, who were together at Mr. Winters parents' home until midnight. I think with the info from the medical examination team, Chuck and I will take another run at her friends, her boyfriend, see if anything jumps out at us."

"Did you find her cell phone?" one of the detectives asks from the back of the room.

"No and apparently, she carried it everywhere with her, like every other kid her age. Her purse was lying near her, and you would have thought it would have been in there. Alicia put together the paperwork to get call and text info from the telecom provider," Helen nods to Alicia in acknowledgement. "It will take a while, you know the telecoms can be as slow as molasses, but we will keep on their backs."

"Can they ping the phone to see if it's still working? Maybe get a location?"

"We had the phone pinged, but no info returned. That can mean a couple of things – the phone could be turned off, but that should give us the last location, the last cell tower before it was powered down. Or it could mean it's in the water. RF doesn't work in water, so no signal,

227

no information. I'm betting that it's at the bottom of Kempenfelt Bay."

"How about social media?"

"What kid is not on at least one of those?" Helen laughs. "Jessica used Facebook and Instagram a lot, but also Messenger, WhatsApp, TikTok and YouTube a lot. Most of her posts are about Ziggy, work, things she was going to do this summer. I'm still reviewing her contacts in each of the apps, but not much to go on yet."

There's silence after this information is given, like the team is contemplating the impacts of social media on today's youth. Helen waits for a moment before asking again, "Any other questions, suggestions to help us find out who did this?"

The Chief stands up and starts to walk to the doorway, readying to leave the meeting room. "Can we get a DNA sample from her current boyfriend? It would be nice to test it against the fetus. If it's his or even if it's not, gives him motive. Also, see if it's on her clothes and the blanket."

"Tunes has lawyered up. Sutton Fox has advised him not to speak to us, not to answer any questions, give us nothing without him present. When asked about giving DNA, it was a blatant no."

"I hear you, but there are other ways to get a DNA sample," she says leaving the meeting room.

Helen turns to Chuck. "We could do that, I'm thinking. Get a sample from a bottle or a cigarette butt or something that he throws away. Can't use the sample legally but it might give us a direction for the case." Chuck nods in agreement. Helen turns back to her colleagues. "Thanks for coming. Don't hesitate to let me know if you think of anything to help with the case."

The detectives slowly get up and exit the room. As Alicia heads for the door, Helen calls her over. "How do you feel about us collecting a DNA sample from Luke?" she asks.

Alicia pauses, her eyes moving from Helen to Chuck and back again. "When there's a warrant for it, we will gladly comply," Alicia replies standing straight, standing her ground.

"It would eliminate him, Alicia. We could spend all of our valuable time finding the real perpetrator if we could eliminate Luke," Helen pushes.

Alicia pauses for a moment, and then leaves the room without replying to the plea. She walks directly into the women's washroom and texts James. 'They are asking for Luke's DNA. I said not without a warrant."

Chapter 63
July 13
Alicia

Alicia has spent the morning reviewing numerous databases searching for any similarities to the sexual assault reported by Frankie Mason but found nothing that has the same MO. As she runs out of options for Frankie's situation, Alicia decides to input information about Jessica's death to see if there are any hits. Just as she starts to enter the information, Helen comes through the swinging doors of the Detectives' Den. Alicia quickly closes the database.

"I heard about the case that you and Fraser caught – the sexual assault in Heritage Park and was just wondering if you thought Jessica's death and that one could be related?" Helen asks sitting down at her desk beside Alicia.

Alicia thinks for a couple of moments and then answers decisively. "That's a good question. My first instinct would be no. No, I don't think it's the same perpetrator, but Jessica did have sex prior to her death. What if it was really a rape gone bad? But the number of blows and the force that was used to kill her seems to make it pretty personal. The thing in the park was probably a younger perpetrator, someone starting out on his career as a rapist. I think Frankie was lucky to get away before the act was actually committed. She kicked him in the nuts, hurt him I think, and hopefully her actions will deter this guy from trying again with someone else."

"You're probably right, probably not the same guy, but something to keep in the back of our minds. I do think you're being a bit optimistic if you think getting kicked in the nuts once is going to deter the scumbag. I think it will make him more determined next time, smarter, more prepared. I don't think we've seen the last of him, probably just the beginning."

Alicia's phone buzzes. She looks down and sees an incoming note from Fraser of a new case assignment. She reads it quickly and sends

230

a quick 'got it' reply. "Sorry, I have to run. Fraser and I just got a new case."

***

Fraser, Alicia, and the store owner of Not Just Groceries get settled in one of the many meeting rooms in the precinct. The owner of the store, Tina Lopez, is in tears, as she tells the detectives that she wants to report extortion by the local gang, the Ruebens. They are making her pay a monthly retainer for protection to ensure that no one robs her store and that her business is not harassed by other hoodlums in the city. Mrs. Lopez is afraid that the Ruebens will hurt her and her family if she refuses to pay but, she is coming forward now as they have just doubled their price, and she wants to take a stand against them and their illegal, neanderthal-ways.

The store owner wants the police to arrest the guy that comes into the store every month to pick up the envelope for his boss, hoping that his arrest and putting pressure on him will help stop the monthly payments. She wants his boss prosecuted for his actions against the small store owners who are only trying to make ends meet, sure that her store is not the only one in town that is being targeted.

The three sit discussing the issue, the detectives asking questions specific to who and when the money is picked up, the store owner asking for protection for herself, her family, and her store against these rotten scoundrels taking advantage of her and her business.

Fraser asks if she has been threatened with physical harm. Has she seen a gun? The storeowner confirms that on the opening day of business the gang boss came around and told her she would be required to pay a monthly fee. He threatened her, her family, her livelihood before explaining that the amount of money he was requesting was almost reasonable, something like taking out an insurance policy. Then he showed her his gun, which sealed the deal. She wasn't sure if the guy that comes in monthly carried a gun, but he does have a taser. He threatened her with it the first time he came in for the cash.

Fraser asks for a description. The boss is tall, lean, with shoulder-length sandy brown hair. He was dressed in form-fitting jeans and bright red running shoes, probably mid to late 30s. The guy that comes every month is tall, heavier set but not fat, with fairly long dark hair, sparkling blue eyes that are always watching, probably late 40s.

James, Alicia thinks. *James and fucking Axl Tunes. I told him to stop working for that piece of shit and he didn't listen to me and now look what's going to happen.*

Fraser asks if there are any cameras in the store and is advised by the owner that there are none. He asks about cameras on the street or on other stores in the vicinity. The owner is not aware of any. Fraser then asks her to sit with a sketch artist, and Mrs. Lopez agrees quickly to do that.

Shit, shit, shit. It's going to be James.

Fraser talks to the storeowner about a sting operation, explaining that the police will be there when the man comes in for the monthly payment, Tina Lopez would need to wear a wire to capture the conversation and the evidence against the extortionist. The police would be on site when it goes down to arrest him immediately.

After back-and-forth discussions about timing, safety and requirements, the storeowner finally agrees to the plan, and they set it up for the last Friday of the month when the thug typically comes in just before closing time.

***

Alicia is at her desk an hour later when the sketch artist comes into the Detectives' Den looking for her, handing her two sketches. A shiver runs through her body as Alicia gazes at the two portraits that Tina Lopez has helped the artist create – one of her ex-husband, the second of Axl Tunes.

232

Chapter 64
July 13
Axl

"Fuck, fuck, fuck!" yells Axl as he paces his office. He has a Toronto Star newspaper in his hands; he still likes to get the printed paper version, a supplement to what he reads online. A picture of a smiling Don Saunders takes up the top half of the paper above the fold on the front page of the evening's edition, a prestigious location in the news industry. The accompanying article tells of the discovery of his dead body by two kids at a warehouse on the west side of the city. There is speculation that the current Director of the Canada Services Border Agency Task Force was killed to get to the stockpile of guns collected at the border and housed at the warehouse before they are destroyed. The article doesn't mention anything that could be traced back to Axl or his gang, but the VP of the Ruebens knows that the police would not be publicizing any leads or evidence they have on the case.

Axl picks up his cell phone and scrolls down, jabbing hard on the icon for James. The call rings but James does not answer. "God damn piece of shit," Axl mumbles waiting for the voicemail greeting to end. "James. Meeting. 4pm. Today," he says.

Axl hangs up and calls both Mack and Chevy, speaking to them both, verbalizing the same terse message.

***

Mack, Chevy, and James are sitting in front of Axl's large desk in his office, waiting for Axl, who has left the room to take a phone call. They sit in silence; James examines his fingers; Chevy presses his hands into his lower abdomen to help control the pain; Mack watches something intently on his phone.

Axl throws the office door open, moving back into the room. He sits down behind his desk and looks at the three men in front of him. Axl throws the newspaper with Don's picture on the front page across the desk. "Anyone know anything about this?" he asks, his menacing eyes moving from face to face to face.

James is closest to the thrown paper and picks it up, scanning the front page, breathing normally. "What the fuck, Axl. I don't know anything about this. He was fine when I left him." He tosses the paper to Chevy, sitting beside him.

Chevy turns it right side up and reads the first couple paragraphs of the story learning that Don's body was found at the warehouse. "No idea, Axl. I didn't go last time," he explains, nodding at James. "I was in the hospital. Appendicitis."

Chevy hands the paper to Mack, who looks at the picture and the headline. "Damn, and we just got started," he comments.

Axl stares at James. "What went down the last time you were there?" he asks threateningly.

"I drove down; I drove over to the door; Don opened it; I loaded the guns in the van; I gave him the bag of cash; I left."

"And?" Axl questions.

"And nothing. It happened just like I said."

"And why were you alone?"

"Chevy was in the hospital."

"Why the hell didn't you tell me? Someone else could have gone with you. Mack, for instance."

"No way, I wasn't going with Mack."

"Somebody else then."

"Axl, it was a straight drive down to pick up the stuff and come back. I didn't need anyone to go with me," James declares.

Axl sits back in his chair, looking intently at his enforcer. *Could he have killed Don? Why after all this time? What would he gain from it?*

"Did they find the cash?" Mack asks.

"They sure as hell wouldn't mention that in the paper. Whoever killed him has the money would be my guess. What I can tell you is that someone has cost me a big bunch of cash. We only got two months' worth of guns out of Don. We were set up to do this monthly, for years to come. The piece of shit that iced Don has cost me a shitload of money and when I find out who, they will be put on ice, just like Don," Axl finishes, staring at James.

Chapter 65

July 13
Luke

The backyard is decorated with bright helium birthday balloons, red and white streamers have been strung from tree to tree with matching checkered cloths on each of the tables, which are laden with party favours – one table with every non-alcoholic drink imaginable including a watermelon that has been scooped out and used as a container for some very sweet lemonade, another table piled with dishes of chips, popcorn, chocolates for people to munch on, another table featuring a plethora of condiments for the burgers and hot dogs that Noah is flipping on the BBQ. Noah's favourite playlist is streaming loudly as he sways to the music, pretending that he knows what he's doing at the grill.

Luke enters the backyard, amazed at the transformation, surprised by the work that has been put into the festivities and the number of people milling around, talking, laughing before walking toward the BBQ area and greeting his friend. "Hey Noah. Happy birthday."

Noah turns as his sister Nova scampers to them leaving the crowd of people that she was talking with. "Luke, you made it. Great," she greets pulling him close and giving him a kiss on the cheek.

"Happy birthday," he replies handing her a pink envelope.

"Oh, you shouldn't have, but thank you," she purrs, taking the proffered gift. "I'll put it on the table with the others."

"Here take this one too," Luke suggests handing her an envelope for Noah.

"Come over and meet my friends from work," she suggests smiling brilliantly at Luke.

"I need his help here," Noah interrupts, giving Luke an excuse not to be paraded around to his sister's friends.

"Sorry, I'll meet them later," Luke confides. "The chef needs my help."

"Later then," Nova suggests as she sashays away, exaggerating her hip thrusts, trying to appear sexy, hoping that Luke is watching.

Luke turns to his friend. "Thanks man. You're the chef tonight?" Where's your dad?"

"He's been delayed at work, that big house I was telling you about."

"Cool. Hope you can BBQ as good as he can," Luke laughs pushing his friend's shoulder playfully.

***

Throughout the festivities, Nova returns to Luke many times, holding his arm, snuggling up to him like they are a couple, whispering in his ear. Luke doesn't want to be rude, especially in front of the guests and on her birthday, but he is losing his patience with Nova, her familiarity, constantly overstepping the boundaries of friendship. He disentangles himself for the fifth time and turns to see Tate sitting by himself at the back of the yard watching the activities. Luke moves to sit beside the quiet man. "How's it going, Tate?" he asks.

Tate smiles, nods, but doesn't say anything. The two sit in silence for several minutes until Tate is able to utter several words, "I liked Jessica. She was pretty."

Luke is surprised by his comments and agrees. "I liked her too Tate. I liked her too." He looks to the crowd of friends celebrating and wishes that she could be here, here with him, here with her friend Nova to celebrate her birthday.

The two sit in silence, both lost in their own thoughts.

Chapter 66
July 14

Think I'll go downtown and check it out. They've got it closed down and lots of people will be walking around, looking at the shops, stopping to have lunch. There's sure to be lots of cute girls out in their skimpy shorts and tank tops, showing off their skin for anyone who wants to look. And hey, there's no rule against looking. Yeah, that's what I think I'll do on this summer afternoon.

***

As he rounds the corner to the main street, the sounds of a band, people clapping, shouting for more filter through the air. The streets are filled with tables set up by the vendors displaying their wares. Restaurants have also set up tables, chairs, and stand-up bars along the thruway. There are many colourful umbrellas above the tables to shade the throngs of people having lunch or enjoying a couple of drinks. *Wow, this place is really happening*, he smiles as he walks confidently along the sidewalk cautiously observing the crowds, eyeing the young women.

About halfway down the main street, he hears a loud group of people laughing. One laugh stands out to him – it's a boisterous, wholesome heart-felt female laugh. *No, it can't be. It can't be*, he thinks as he slowly turns to inspect the cluster of people sitting together around the two tables that they have pulled together. *That's her. I can't believe that's her.*

He steps back into the shadows of the doorway of one of the stores, moves to the opening of the alleyway beside the store, leans against the brick building and watches the girl from the Queens Hotel. *She's just as gorgeous as I remember her. A beautiful smile. A delightful laugh. Just a little thing.*

Chapter 67
July 16
Alicia

Alicia opens the ViCLAS database once again, entering information specific to Jessica's case, her description, the crime scene, the murder weapon, and the location of the body, completing the majority of the 156 questions required for the search. She waits as the database takes time to sift through the 400,000 plus records comparing Jessica's circumstances with other cases in Canada. Finally, the system sends back its results, two cases with many similarities, that may have been committed by the same perpetrator.

Alicia examines the two instances closer: Cheyenne Bailey of Wasaga Beach was reported missing by her family and found in the waters of the Nottawasaga River ten days later by a pair of fishermen. The weapon utilized in her death is suspected to be a rock, stick or possibly a log, which was used to beat her to death before she was dragged into the water.

The second case is Hannah Longhurst from Orillia who was found in the waters of Lake Couchiching a week ago by a father and son at a trailer park, where she and her band had recently played a concert.

Cheyenne? Cheyenne? Isn't that the name of the girl that ghosted Luke? Wasaga Beach? Was that where she was from?

Hannah? Luke definitely told me about her. Met her on his birthday in Orillia. And Jessica makes three. Oh my God, is this a serial killer? Three girls, all killed with a bat, a stick, a rock, something that the killer grabbed at the scene; all found in or near the water; all about the same age; all in the same geographical area; all within a couple weeks of each other. And Luke knew all three of them. Could it be Luke? Luke a serial killer? No, no way it's Luke. But then who is setting him up? That kid Ziggy and his brother Axl? I wouldn't put it past them in their attempts to take the suspicion away from Ziggy for Jessica. Oh my God, that would mean they killed two other innocent girls.

239

What to do? What to do? Should I show Helen? Won't she just think that Luke did all three of these terrible crimes?

Who was with Luke when he went to Wasaga Beach? Orillia? Who is around him here in Barrie? Noah? Could it be Noah? He's always been a bit jealous of Luke, but no, no, it couldn't be him. Who the hell else could it be?

Alicia picks up her phone and sends a text to Luke, 'need to talk to you. Be home for dinner.' Within a minute, Alicia receives his reply, 'no problem.' She sits back and sighs. *I'm sure there's a logical explanation for all of this. I'm sure there is. Maybe they aren't connected.*

I'll leave this alone for now. Think about it. Talk to Luke and see what he has to say. I'll work on Frankie's case – the sexual assault.

Alicia deletes the parameters for Jessica's case and enters the information for Frankie's situation, her physical description, information about the park and being accosted, but is unable to answer a lot of the pertinent questions required before hitting enter. She waits for a moment for the database to run through its many stored incidents, but there are no matches for the specifics of her case.

Alicia sits back in her chair and pulls out her phone, opening the gallery app, and reviews the pictures that she took at Heritage Park, the site where Frankie and Murphy sat, the area where Frankie was attacked, the views to the main street of town, the front doors of the bar they were drinking in.

What about pictures from that night? Maybe there are some cameras showing the two leaving the bar and someone following them. There's got to be some cameras at the bar, maybe inside and out, some stores nearby, maybe a couple of traffic cams.

Alicia accesses the two traffic cameras in the area first, but they are not within sight of the bar and are not helpful.

Next, she opens the Security Camera Registration and Mapping database, a registry of security cameras and their locations in the city. She examines the map of cameras near the Queens Hotel and Heritage Park, noting the contact information so that she can call to ask for access to their videos for the night that Frankie was accosted. *Might take a while to go through the videos, but at least it's something,* she thinks dialing the first number on her list.

***

The Queens, the bar where Frankie had a couple of drinks before going to the park with Murphy Baldwin, is on the list. Alicia places the phone call and is advised that they do have an outside camera and video is stored in the cloud for 90 days. The manager also mentions that they have an internal camera for the cash and bar area near where Frankie was sitting. Alicia requests the videos from the two cameras and sits back, satisfied that she is at least making some headway on the complaint.

A couple hours later, links to the videos come in and Alicia spends the afternoon reviewing them, searching for any glimpse of the man that accosted Frankie. The video from the bar shows Murphy Baldwin talking her up, and on occasion leading her off camera, probably to the dance floor, buying her drinks, and finally captures the two leaving together. The video at the front door shows them crossing the street, going into the park but it is dark outside, and the images are grainy and poor quality, allowing only limited visibility of their outlines into the edges of the park.

She begins to review other videos that shops near the bar have sent to her. One of the cameras from a store across the street includes a view of the front door of the Queens and shows Frankie and her new friend leaving on the night of her assault, running across the street, leaving the scope of the camera. Alicia is frustrated and lets the video run for several minutes watching the people walking by on the sidewalk in front of the bar, until a man comes out of the front door of the watering hole, looking around as if trying to find someone or something. *Is that the guy that was sitting at the end of the bar? He looked like he was watching the dance floor a lot. Maybe he was watching the couple. Could be the guy. He's going over to the park. Maybe following them.* Alicia sits and continues to watch the video. Ten minutes later, as she's about to stop the recording, the shadowy

241

figure comes back into view, rushing back across the street and jumping into a car at the edge of the picture frame. *What kind of car is that? Shit, it looks like one of those classic hot rods. Maybe a Mustang. Maybe a Challenger. Shit. These pictures are so blurry I can't tell. I need an expert to see this, see if we can nail down the car, the year, the model and maybe zoom in on the license plate.*

Alicia jumps up from her workstation, unplugging her laptop, picking it up and running to the IT department. *Maybe they can help me. Maybe something will come of this. I know that's him, the scumbag that accosted Frankie. I just know it.*

***

Alicia smiles at the patrol officers and other precinct staff as she walks from the building to her car. She gets in and starts the vehicle, ready to call it a day. *Long freaking day. I just don't have the energy to make anything for dinner. Think I'll stop at Subway and pick up a couple of sandwiches for me and Luke.*

Alicia pulls the car into the driveway, noticing Luke sitting on the front step, looking at his phone. When he hears the car, his head comes up and he stands to greet his mother. *What is up with him? I know I told him I wanted to talk, but there must be something else going on if he's sitting waiting for me.*

Alicia gets out of the car, pulling the sack of sandwiches behind her. "Look, I cooked," she smiles at her son, holding up the bag. "What's going on? Are you okay?"

Luke moves from the front porch, silently grabbing the bag from her, as Alicia turns back to get her briefcase. She slams the car door, locks it, and turns to Luke again, seeing his facial scowl, and repeats, "What's going on?"

The two walk up the front steps, into the kitchen without an answer to her question. "Luke?" Alicia asks again. *This must be bad.* She pulls the sandwiches from the bag and sets them on the table, looking up at her son, waiting.

Luke sits down, his tear-filled eyes moving to his mom as he starts his story. "Remember, that girl I told you about, Hannah Longhurst?" he pauses, as his mother nods affirmatively. "I found out a couple of days ago that Hannah was missing, that they were looking for her, and then today on Instagram, it says they found her dead." He sniffs, trying to hold on to his tears. "Hannah was playing a concert with her brothers and at the end of the show, she walked away with some guy that they think she knew, and they didn't see her again."

Alicia pats down the paper her sandwich is sitting on, listening to the angst in her son's voice, taking in his troubled face. "Start from the beginning," she asks.

"I texted her a couple of times, called her too and she didn't answer, didn't reply. I thought maybe Hannah was pissed at me as I hadn't gotten back to her. With Jessica and everything else going on, I just didn't get back to her right away, and she could have been mad at me. When I didn't hear anything, I went onto the band's Instagram and read that she was missing. I talked to her brother Caleb, who confirmed that they had been looking for her, had a couple search parties at the park and in the area, then somebody found her in the water near the park where the band last played."

Alicia is silent, listening to the torment in her son's voice.

Luke picks up on her silence and asks, "Mom, do you know anything about this?"

Alicia takes a big breath and starts. "That's why I texted you. I wanted to talk to you about some work I was doing today in one of our databases, the one that we use to link similar crimes, similar MOs. Anyway, I was searching around trying to find some connection with the way Jessica died and I found Hannah Longhurst's case." She stops, watching her son closely. *There's no way he had anything to do with either of these deaths. No way. Look at him. Distraught. Upset. Tears. He's not that good an actor.*

"What? Jessica and Hannah were killed by the same guy?" Luke demands.

"That's what the information in the database is suggesting. From the murder weapon to the way they were found, I would say yes, that it is possibly the same perpetrator." Alicia pauses. "Luke, you can tell me anything. Anything. You know your dad and I will protect you. We'll help you. I promise," she stops, as her meaning sinks into her son's brain.

"Whoa, Mom. You think I did this? To Jessica? To Hannah?" anger evident in his words, his tone, his mannerisms.

"I don't want to think that, Luke, no, but I need you to tell me the truth," Alicia waits, watching.

Luke gets up and starts to pace the small kitchen area. *Just like his dad. When the conversation or situation gets too hot, they pace, move. Helps them think, I guess.* Alicia watches him move back and forth several times, waiting for his answer.

He stops mid-stride and looks at his mom. "I didn't do this. I loved Jessica, even though she was with that shithead Ziggy. I loved her and would never have hurt her."

"And Hannah?"

"I just met her on my birthday at the pavilion at the waterfront in Orillia, and I saw her again at a bar where she was playing with her brothers. But to answer your question, no, I did not hurt Hannah. I couldn't hurt either of them. You know that about me, don't you Mom? I'm not like that."

"No, you're not like that Luke but it's very suspicious that you knew both of them and they died in similar circumstances." Alicia stops and takes a deep breath. "Do you also know Cheyenne Bailey, from Wasaga Beach?"

"Cheyenne?" Luke asks angrily. He starts to pace again and stops after rounding the table three times. "Yeah, I know her. That's the girl that I told you about. I was supposed to call her, or she was going to call me, and then you grounded me, took my phone away and I never heard from her. I thought she just wasn't interested in me when she didn't call me, so I let it go. What is going on Mom? What happened to Cheyenne?" he asks.

"I don't know what's going on. Cheyenne is gone too. Her case is similar to Jessica and Hannah's," Alicia confesses, pausing to think.

"Do you really think I did this? Are you calling me a murderer?" he asks angrily, smacking his fist down on the table beside her.

"That's not what I'm saying, Luke but if something did happen, something that you didn't mean to do, an accident, you could tell me," she says as he continues to move around the table.

"You think I did this! My own mother thinks I killed these three girls!" he yells.

"Luke, slow down. I don't think that. I definitely don't think that, but if it was an accident…" she peters off, unsure where she was going with this train of thought.

"Three times? You think I had three accidents? I can't believe you're asking me this."

Alicia stands up, moves to Luke and puts her hands on her son's shoulders facing him. "Look at me," she tells him as his gaze falls to the floor. "Look at me," Alicia repeats. Luke slowly raises his head to his mother. "I don't think you did this. I know you. You couldn't do this," she says as Luke slowly nods his head in agreement. Once sure that he understands that he is not a suspect in her eyes, she asks, "Tell me about Cheyenne, tell me about Hannah. How did you meet them?"

Luke lowers his head, not wanting to go into the details about the party in Wasaga Beach, how Noah suggested they go after he finagled an invite from someone he knew online, how Noah drove up and Tater Tot drove home, how the four of them wandered from room to room at the motel, but he did. He told her everything he could remember about Cheyenne and their very limited time together.

Luke sits for a moment and then begins the saga of Hannah, how they met by accident at the Orillia waterfront, how they spent time together that first day, how the four of them went up to see her and her brothers playing, how he knew about the gig at the trailer park but was unable to go because of work.

"Luke, who was with you when you went to Wasaga Beach? Who was with you when you went to Orillia? Who knew you were interested in these two girls?"

Luke breathes in deeply, thinking back to Wasaga Beach, back to the dock in Orillia. "Noah, Nova, Tater," he says in a whisper. "But no way it was any of them; Noah is my best friend, Nova keeps showing up just so she can pick up the pieces when these girls shoot me down and Tater, well Tater isn't even able to talk to them, let alone get close enough to kill them."

"Anyone else hanging around? Anyone suspicious?"

Luke shakes his head no.

"Anyone else you told about the girls? The parties?"

"Might have told Dylan. He didn't seem that interested though."

Chapter 68
July 17
Axl

Axl paces as his mind whirls. *What happened to Don? Did James kill him? Maybe someone came by after James did the pickup and killed him, took the money. Who would know that Don was even there? Whoever helped him get the guns up from the border would have known. Maybe whoever helped him transport the guns to the warehouse did it. There's no way Don would have done that manual labour himself. Or maybe someone from the Agency figured out what he was doing, figured out that he wasn't destroying all of the guns. Maybe they had an altercation, and it went bad. Maybe someone else figured out what he was doing and wanted a cut. Who the hell would know? Who can I call? Someone needs to pay for this. Somebody needs to compensate me for the money I could have made selling those fucking guns over the next couple of years.*

Axl continues to pace and after several laps of his private office, he stops in front of the large window in the living room area. He takes in the summer colours on the trees, the green grass, the peacefulness of the location. He pulls out his cell phone, reviewing his list of contacts. His finger waivers over the picture of the Ruebens's VP in Toronto. *I don't want to owe this guy, but I need to know what the hell happened.* He quickly punches the button and holds the phone to his ear before he changes his mind.

The phone rings once and he hears the smooth, deep voice of his previous boss. "Axl, how the hell are you?"

"I'm good, Archie. And you?"

"Life is good. No complaints." He pauses, before continuing. "What can I do for you Axl?"

"I need some info on the killing of Don Saunders."

Archie chuckles. "What kind of information are you looking for?"

"Whatever you can get. Do you still have your contact on the force?"

"I do. In fact, I have a couple of them."

Another pause in the conversation before Axl continues. "I had a deal with Don, and somebody has fucked it up. I need to know who was responsible for his death."

Archie chuckles again. "I heard about your deal. Good for you. It would have put you in a great place financially."

"Yes, it would have and that's why I need to know what happened, who killed him."

"Let me see what I can do, Axl. I'll get back to you."

The line goes dead.

Chapter 69
July 17
Alicia

I don't want to call him, but I have no choice. Alicia hits the speed dial number for her ex-husband, chanting to herself, "family always comes first, family always comes first," waiting for James to pick up.

The phone rings once and he answers. "Alicia?" uncertainty in his voice.

"James. We need to talk about Luke," she states quickly, before losing her nerve.

"Sure. Where and when?"

***

Alicia sits in the coffee shop waiting for James. The door opens and a warm breeze pushes into the air-conditioned seating area. Alicia glances up and unwittingly smiles at James as he moves to the counter. He pantomimes drinking a coffee, and she shakes her head, no, holding up her half-finished ice cap. He orders quickly and moves to Alicia's table.

"What's going on?" he asks, sitting down, blowing at the steaming cup of coffee.

"I'm on another case, sexual assault, and was looking at ViCLAS. I didn't find anything for my case but decided to take a look for similar MOs for Jessica's murder," she stops, taking a sip of her highly caffeinated drink.

"And?" he asks curtly.

"There are two other murders in the database that are similar to Jessica's. Same MO, similar disposal of the body, girls the same age as Jessica."

"And?" he asks again.

"Both are out of town. One in Wasaga Beach, found in the water near the mouth of the Nottawasaga. The second in Orillia," she pauses, afraid to continue and say the words aloud, making them a reality. Alicia takes a deep breath and continues before James can ask his one-word question again. "Luke was in Wasaga Beach before Cheyenne Bailey went missing. He met her at a party up there and when he came home, I grounded him and took his phone away from him so he couldn't reach out to her." She pauses again, watching James's poker-face, something he developed from his years on the force. "Hannah Longhurst was a singer that Luke met on the boardwalk in Orillia. He actually went out to a bar to see her. Her body was found in Lake Couchiching just outside of Orillia." Alicia stops, her voice starting to catch with emotion.

"Fuck," he whispers. "Does Helen know about this?"

"I haven't told her. I was taken off the case, conflict of interest. And really, I shouldn't have been looking around in the database, but I couldn't help myself."

"She'll find it sooner or later. Probably just busy with the forensics, other stuff at this point, but she will check all the systems available," he confirms. "We need to get ahead of this Alicia. Luke needs to get ahead of this," James declares, glancing over Alicia's shoulder to the outside of the cafe.

"How? How can we get in front of this?"

"He needs to go in and tell his side," James states, putting his hand up to stop Alicia from protesting. "You know how suspicious this looks and you're his mother. What do you think people that don't know him are going to think? He needs to go in and tell them everything from being at the park that night, to knowing these other girls." He stops, contemplating the situation. "I'll go with him. Who is Tunes's lawyer?"

"Sutton Fox," she tells James.

"Impressive. He's one of the best in town," James confirms, his forehead creasing as he thinks. After a couple of sips of coffee, he says, "Bryan. I'll call Bryan Reid. He's an experienced attorney. I've worked with him, and against him, a couple of times and he's pretty good." James looks up to ensure Alicia agrees.

Alicia's face reveals her elevated stress level, and concern for her son. James reaches out and takes her hand, "It's going to be okay, Alicia. I won't let anything happen to Luke," he tries to comfort her, adding, "Family always comes first."

She pulls her hand back and puts them both in her lap. "You're his father. You need to take care of your son," Alicia snarls.

Chapter 70
July 18
Alicia

Alicia sits on the front porch of her house, a paperback open in her lap. She has read the same page half a dozen times and still doesn't know what it says. Her mind is swirling around the deaths of Cheyenne, Hannah, and Jessica and the fact that her son knew each of the girls. *There's no way Luke is involved in this. No way. But who? He said Noah, Nova and Tate went with him to Wasaga Beach and Orillia when he met Cheyenne and Hannah. But Noah? He's known him forever. He might think of himself as a bit of player, might be a bit of a bad boy with his wanting to party and drink, but murder? I don't think so. Nova? Little, Nova? What would she have to gain by hurting those two girls? Nothing. She and Luke are still friends, always have been. Tate? No Tate can't even talk to another human being, never mind get close enough to kill them. He said he told Dylan. Might be him. He lives alone, doesn't seem to have any family that visit him, seems kind of creepy to me. Could he be a killer? Maybe he's jealous of Luke. Maybe he went and talked to each of the girls, and they blew him off. Might be stretching a bit, but maybe. I'll have to take a look and see if I can find any history on him.*

"Hello Alicia," she hears startled out of her reverie, looking up to see Nova walking up the driveway. "Sorry if I startled you," the girl continues,

Alicia smiles. "No, my bad. I was just sitting her daydreaming. How are you, Nova? I haven't seen you for a while. Everything okay?"

Nova stands at the bottom of the steps and beams at Alicia. "I'm good. Well, as good as can be expected after the Jessica situation."

"The Jessica situation?" Alicia asks.

"You know, her death and everything," Nova clarifies.

"Yes, a very sad situation. I know she was your best friend. You must be missing her terribly," Alicia consoles the girl, amazed at her blasé, unconcerned attitude.

"Yes, very sad. I miss her terribly," Nova says bending her head down to her chest in a thoughtful manner. After several moments of introspection, she raises her head, smiles and asks, "Is Luke home? I just wanted to thank him for the birthday present."

"No, no he's not home right now. He's at work," Alicia replies, looking at her watch. "He should be home in about half an hour. Want to come in for a lemonade or diet coke and wait for him?"

"That would be nice. Thank you, Alicia," Nova responds climbing the stairs and following Alicia into the house.

Chapter 71
July 18
Mack

Mack leans against the front bumper of his silver Porsche parked in the beach lot, watching his grandson, Luke, patrolling the beach, talking to the kids, smiling at the parents, ensuring that everyone is safe both in and around the water. *He's quite a kid. Guess he's not really a kid anymore. Turned 17 a couple of months ago. I missed everything but I'm here now even though he thinks I'm a long lost uncle. That's okay though. I just want to get to know him, spend some time with him, do all the things with him that I couldn't with James or Sean. My second chance at making a difference in a kid's life.*

Mack stands watching, hoping that Luke will look up and see him, give him an opening to go over and talk to him, but he is laser focused on his job, his responsibilities.

He's smiling, talking to everyone doing the right thing but there's an air of sadness around him. Must be the shit with his girlfriend. Wonder what the story is there. Luke? Ziggy? Someone else? Who knows? Hope James is looking out for him.

Mack shoves off the front bumper and folds his tall frame into the compact car, turning the air conditioner to full before he drives away, leaving his grandson to watch the day-trippers at the beach.

Chapter 72
July 19
Luke

James and Luke stand in the front lobby of the precinct, along with Bryan Reid, who has been retained as Luke's legal counsel. The lawyer is aware of the whole story, from Jessica to Cheyenne to Hannah, and has sworn his support. He called Helen last evening to set up this meeting quickly to ensure Luke's story is known before the police start to insinuate or fabricate that he was involved in any violence against these young women.

James is anxious, pacing the small area, not used to being on this side of the questions, afraid for his only son, knowing that Luke couldn't have done these dreadful things, even if provoked.

Alicia walks through the doors from the office area to the lobby, directly to the lawyer and introduces herself. They exchange a couple of pleasantries while waiting for Helen and Chuck to make an appearance. James starts to pace the small area again, until Alicia puts her hand on his arm as he passes her, and she shakes her head, no. He realizes the display of stress that is emanating from his body, his stance, and movements, and tries to reign them in by moving to his son's side, who seems mesmerized by the traffic out the lobby window.

What seems like hours later to the group, but is only five minutes, Helen opens the door and steps into the lobby, her hand out to the visitors, going from one to the other. "Good to see you, James. Luke. Bryan, it's been a while." She stops at Alicia and simply smiles before leading the team back through the doors and into a meeting room, decked out with coffee, tea and muffins sitting at the end of the table.

Luke reaches out to pour himself a cup of coffee, but his mom puts her hand on his arm, shaking her head, and he lets his arm fall to his side before Alicia steers him to a chair next to his lawyer. Helen and Chuck take their time getting a coffee and a muffin, asking the visitors if they are sure they wouldn't like to partake. The lawyer replies for the Andersons. "No, we're good but thank you."

Helen and Chuck sit down directly across the table from Luke before the conversation starts and Helen says, "Good to see you again, Luke. Before we begin, we just want to ensure you know your rights. You are here voluntarily; you have the right to remain silent and you have the right to a lawyer." Helen nods toward Bryan Reid. "Do you understand these rights?"

Luke looks to his father, who nods his head in the affirmative. Luke mirrors this gesture at the detectives, saying, "Yes," quietly.

"Thanks, Luke. Now, is there something specific that you wanted to tell us that you didn't when we came by your house?"

Luke looks at his lawyer and lets him answer the question. "Thanks for sharing your valuable time to see us, detectives. We know you're busy with this investigation, so we won't keep you too long. Luke did answer your questions when you came to the house, he answered all of them truthfully. I'm sorry that I wasn't there but we wanted to make sure that you have the full picture, hence our visit today to clarify and add a few things."

Helen's attention moves from the lawyer to Luke. "Go ahead, Luke. What is it that you want to tell us?"

"One more thing before we begin," the lawyer interrupts. "We realize that you are recording this meeting and that a witness statement will be given to Luke to review and sign. I would like a copy of both when we're done, the recording and the statement. Just for the files, or in case of a discrepancy. I'm sure you understand," he smiles at the two detectives.

"Not a problem," Helen replies. "Why don't you start Luke? What didn't you tell us the last time we talked?"

Luke, who has been looking down at his clenched hands in his lap, looks up at his father's old partner, Chuck, who smiles at him, encouraging him to speak. Bryan Reid puts his hand on Luke's shoulder and says, "Go ahead, Luke. Tell them what you told me."

Luke begins his statement to the police, starting with Jessica breaking up with him on April 1, how he didn't believe it initially, how she told him implicitly that it was over, and how she started

256

going out with Ziggy Tunes immediately, or maybe even before they broke up. Alicia puts her hand on Luke's shoulder, and he shrinks back for a moment before picking up his story, telling the detectives how upset he was, how he started to hang around more with his friend Noah Nash and his next-door neighbour Dylan Wheatley. He tells them about going up to Wasaga Beach and meeting a girl and that he never got to talk to her after that as his mom confiscated his phone. He talks about his work with the police force during the spring festival in May before telling them about the night of his birthday, how he and his friends went to Orillia where he met Hannah Longhurst and her brothers. He reveals his interest in Hannah and how he went to a bar with fake ID to see her a couple of weeks later, but how they lost touch after that, with all the craziness that went on.

"What craziness are you referring to Luke?" Chuck asks.

Luke lowers his head for a moment before continuing. "Fighting with Ziggy, starting work, Jessica dying, the aftermath of that," he replies.

There is silence in the room as everyone pauses.

Luke continues his story. "The day before Jessica died started off normal. I went to work, I'm a lifeguard at Centennial Beach. I was on the tower, and I saw them walking toward the beach, Jessica and Ziggy. I kept working, trying to ignore them but he called me out and we got into a fist fight. My partner at the beach, Justin, broke us up. Ziggy left and I went back to work." He stops, pausing to think back to the incident. "The next day I decorated the house, bought some balloons, a banner to put up for my mom. Jeff and I wanted to celebrate her promotion. I set up the decorations before my mom came home. I checked the mail and finally got my acceptance to Georgian College," he stops for a moment before continuing. "My mom brought home take-out food and we ate and hung out together."

"And that was the evening of June 30, correct?" Helen asks.

"Yes," Luke confirms.

"And then what happened?" Helen plies, wanting Luke to continue.

"I went to bed, and I was just checking Instagram when I got a text from Jess. I was surprised. Really surprised. She wanted to meet me at our usual place. She wanted to talk to me."

"And where's your usual place, Luke?" Helen asks.

"We always used to meet at the gazebo, the one near the Southshore Community Centre. I went there. I waited. I called her. I texted her but Jess didn't answer, and she didn't show up, so I left," he finishes.

"You left? You walked home?"

"No, I called my friend Noah to pick me up. We drove around for a bit and then went to Dylan's, the guy that lives next door to me. We hung out there for a while and then went to Sauble Beach," he answers.

"Sauble Beach?" she repeats unsure why he would go to the beach at that time of night.

"Yeah, Sauble Beach," he reconfirms.

Bryan Reid interjects at this point. "So that's the whole story. Luke did see both Ziggy and Jessica the day before at the beach, but he didn't see either of them after that. Jessica reached out to him via text but didn't show up at their spot. He waited, he called her, but she didn't reply. He was near the Community Centre, but his timing is off. He was there and left before the time of death estimated by the medical examiner," he stops, knowing that the detectives will have more questions, trying to trip up his client with their convoluted words.

"Interesting story, Luke. Why didn't you tell us all of this the other day?" Chuck interjects.

"I was afraid," Luke says.

"Afraid of what?"

"Afraid that you would think I did it. Afraid that whoever killed Jessica would come after me. Afraid that her fucking boyfriend would put me next on his list," he finally spits out.

"Why do you think Ziggy did this? Do you have any proof?"

"No, he doesn't have any proof," his lawyer butts in. "But given Ziggy's violent nature, picking on and calling Luke out at every chance and the history of bruises on Jessica's arms that may or may not have come from Mr. Tunes, Luke had every right to be afraid of this bully. And then there's the family relationship that I'm sure you're aware of," he finishes, watching both of the detectives.

258

"Family relationship?" Helen questions.

"Ziggy's older brother and guardian is Axl Tunes. It is well known that Mr. Tunes is the VP of the Ruebens," the lawyer answers.

Helen glares at James, knowing the rumours of his involvement with the gang, including his girlfriend's affiliation with the VP. James does not reply, simply returns the glare at Helen and his former partner, Chuck.

"So, you want us to believe that you sat on the picnic table under the gazebo right beside the Community Centre and you didn't see Jessica?" Helen demands.

Luke looks at his lawyer, who nods his head, "It's the truth. I don't know where Jessica was. I don't know when she got to the Community Centre or how she got there. I did not see her when I was sitting on the picnic table waiting for her," he finishes.

"Where did you get the log from?" Helen presses.

Luke stops for a moment, trying to understand the question. When it finally hits him that he is being accused of killing Jessica, he blurts out, "I didn't do it. I didn't see Jessica. I didn't see anyone. I didn't pick up a log, a stick or anything. I just sat there waiting, like an idiot."

"Why like an idiot?" Helen asks, changing direction quickly.

"Maybe it was Ziggy that texted me," he proposes. "He knew where Jess and I used to meet. I saw him there once before when Jess first broke up with me, waiting for her. He probably tried to set me up," he suggests.

"And the log?" Helen pushes.

"I didn't see a log. I didn't touch a log. I didn't see Jess. I didn't do this," he says clenching his fists on top of the table. Alicia moves into her son and puts her arm around his shoulder again, as Luke leans in, taking all the support being offered.

The two detectives continue to question Luke, and he answers their questions succinctly, while trying to keep his emotions in check. As their questions about Jessica and the night of her death peter out, Chuck moves the conversation back to the information Luke offered earlier. "Why are you telling us about Cheyenne and Hannah now?"

he asks glancing down at his notes, ensuring that he gets the names correct.

Bryan Reid jumps in, "It has come to light that these two girls have died within the last three months. We wanted you to know about Luke's relationships with them, to put your minds at ease that he didn't have anything to do with their deaths."

Chuck and Helen were not aware of these two women, unaware of their deaths. They pause for a moment before beginning another barrage of questions. Who was with you when you met Cheyenne in Wasaga Beach? Who was with you in Orillia when you met Hannah? Where else have you been? What other young women have you met? Who are you seeing now? Who will be the next dead body? You expect us to believe that you knew all three of these women and you had nothing to do with their deaths?

After all questions have been asked and answered, the detectives finally dismiss Luke and confirm that he will be asked to sign a witness statement outlining the information he offered during this meeting, and that a copy of the video recording and the document would be available to Bryan Reid.

Chapter 73
July 19
Helen

Helen and Chuck retire to the major crime room dedicated to the case and close the door. Alicia walks James, Luke and the lawyer to the front lobby, hugging her son tightly before letting him go. She turns and walks back down the hall, knocking tentatively on the major crime room door.

"Yes," Helen says as Alicia steps into the room.

"Thanks for letting Luke come in and get the whole story out," Alicia starts before Helen puts her hand up in a stop sign manner.

"I know this is hard for you Alicia, but you can't be involved with this case. We let you sit in that discussion as his mother, not as a police detective," Helen explains.

"I know and I appreciate that but before you kick me out, I have a couple of things that you need to see," Alicia says, moving into the room, setting her laptop on the table, and turning it on. "I was looking at ViCLAS for the Frankie Mason case, searching for anything similar. I didn't find anything, but I had a couple of minutes and put in the parameters for Jessica's case. That's how I learned about the other two girls."

"Whoa, Alicia. You stepped way over the boundaries by doing that. When the Chief finds out, you will be in a shit load of trouble," Helen preaches to Alicia.

"I get it and I know that I shouldn't have, but I need you to see what I've found." Alicia displays the two comparable cases, Cheyenne Bailey of Wasaga Beach and Hannah Longhurst of Orillia on her laptop. Helen and Chuck review the information on the screen and sit back in their chairs simultaneously.

"So, this is why you brought Luke in today, so you could get ahead of this before we found it. But your son could still be responsible for these two murders as well. This is not playing out so well for Luke, Alicia."

Alicia looks up. "There's more you need to know. While working on the Frankie Mason case, I looked through the SCRAM database, you know the list of security cameras and their locations in the city that have already given us permission to access their videos for police business. I was searching for Frankie and Murphy Baldwin, and them going over to the park. There is one guy of interest," she advises pulling up the video of a young man coming out of the bar moments after the pair, following them to the park and quickly returning ten minutes later, getting into a car parked in front of the bar. "I have IT working on the car to see if we can get any info on it, make, year, any identifying marks, whatever," she pauses.

"What does that have to do with this case? I don't get it," Helen comments.

"Well, then I thought about cameras around the Southshore Community Centre. Maybe I could get some info from them for Jessica's case, but there are no cameras at the building or even in the park. The closest building is the Go Station across the road, so I contacted them, and they sent me links from their four cameras on the property." She conveniently leaves out the part about creating a warrant and sending it to a judge without advising either Helen or Chuck, who are the assigned detectives on the case. "I have video from the four surveillance cameras from 9pm on June 30 to 9am on July 1 and I will send it all to you, but have a look at what I found," Alicia says pulling up the video showing Luke walking into the park, sitting on the picnic table at 10:18 pm; a guy parking his car and getting out to take his dog for a walk at 10:25; a couple near the water walking from the city to behind the Community Centre at 10:27. Alicia stops the video at this point and zooms in. "The picture is grainy, maybe IT can help, but I think this is Jessica and someone walking toward the Community Centre." The three detectives look closely at the screen, unable to confirm the identity of the pedestrians, so Alicia continues the stream, and they watch a couple on their bikes traveling from one side of the park to the other at 10:33; another man walking his dog to the marina at 10:44; the arrival of a hot rod at 10:48 which parks in the lot, the male driver getting out of the car and walking to the water, returning to his car, sits there for several minutes before leaving at 11:16. They continue to watch as the realities of that night unfold in front of them. A beat-up Mazda roars into the parking lot at 11:31 pm, flashes its lights, and Luke runs from the picnic table, where he had been sitting for the last hour, to the car and jumps in. As the Mazda leaves the parking lot at 11:33pm, a Mustang arrives – the two cars almost colliding at the entrance way. The driver of the Mustang pulls into the parking lot, stops suddenly, jumps out of the car, and moves toward the water, out of sight of the camera as he rounds the corner of the Community Centre. They continue to watch the video with no action on the film. "Wait for it," Alicia advises as she fast forwards the video. After 37 minutes, the male returns to his car and throws up a cloud of dust as he leaves the parking lot quickly.

Alicia's attention moves from the screen to the senior detectives. "Now I didn't check the plate but look at the car. You know it's Ziggy's. And I think that blows his alibi all to hell, don't you? Unless you think someone else was driving his car, but then how would he have gotten to Toronto to see the mother that you can't find?" Alicia pauses before pleading. "Luke didn't do this. I know he didn't do this. You both know him. You've known him for years. You know he couldn't, wouldn't do anything like this," she pauses for a moment. "We, sorry I mean you, need to find out who did this to Jessica and these other two young women. The MOs are the same. It's the same guy. You need to find who did this to these three innocent women and put him away for life. And this video puts Ziggy at the scene. Maybe the last to see Jessica alive."

***

Helen and Chuck are shell-shocked after Alicia packs up her laptop and leaves them to their thoughts. "Wow, the Chief is going to rip her a new one," Helen says trying to break the tension.

"That she is. I've been there a couple of times, not with this Chief though. We'll have to wait and see what happens to her," Chuck agrees. "Right now, I think we need to take the information that Alicia has found and run with it. I'll call the OPP in Wasaga, and you can

263

call Orillia. Let's see what additional details they might have. And we need to share with them what we have on Jessica. Shit, this is starting to look like a serial killer. And if it's not Luke, it's someone pretty damn close to him."

Helen nods her head as she pulls out her cell phone.

***

Helen sits back in her chair, scribbling notes from her phone conversation with the OPP Sergeant in charge of Hannah Longhurst's case, waiting for Chuck to complete his call.

As Chuck disconnects the line, Helen asks, "What did you learn?"

Chuck tells her that the police are still waiting for full information on the death of Cheyenne Bailey but believe the cause was blunt force trauma and that she was pushed into the water, after being killed. The theory is that the killer was disposing of the body in the water in the hopes that it would float out and away from the shoreline and not be found. The medical examiner also stated that she had forceful sexual relations prior to her death.

"Forceful?" Helen asks.

"The genital area was examined revealing tears in the lower part of her hymen, but the intensity of the injury could be within parameters of consensual sex."

"Okay, so at least we know she had sex. Any DNA left by the perpetrator?" Helen asks.

"Probably. Cheyenne was in the water for about seven days, so hopefully they will be able to retrieve enough sperm to complete the DNA test to identify her sexual partner, but then they would have to prove that the sexual partner and the killer are one and the same."

"Do they know where she went in the water?"

"They traced her activities, and the water currents the day she went missing, and they believe they have it pinpointed. They collected some physical evidence at the site, but it was days between her death and her being found in the water, so not sure how much of it was actually there the day she was killed. They took a lot of pictures, tried

264

to make some molds of the sand, but not sure it will come to anything."

They both sit back for a moment, mulling over the facts presented by Cheyenne's death before Helen talks about the findings in the Hannah Longhurst case. A lot of the details are similar to both Cheyenne and Jessica, death by blunt force trauma, young woman, found in the water, sex within hours of their death, killed within weeks of each other and all located in the same geographic area. The medical team are still trying to retrieve DNA from Hannah's sexual liaison, however she was in the water too long, so it is doubtful that they will be able to identify the partner conclusively. Similar to Cheyenne's case, they believe they know where she went into the water and the area was scoured for evidence. Helen lists the materials collected at the murder site: cigarette butts, an empty bag of chips, a couple empty bottles of water, some fishing line, a chocolate bar wrapper, a small piece of fingernail.

"Fingernail?" Chuck asks.

Helen flips through her notebook and stops at the particulars. "Yeah, a fingernail, a real one, not one of those gel stick-ons. From the shape, they suggest it's a piece off the pointer finger of a woman, sparkly nail polish on it. But it might not have anything to do with this case. Pretty hard to tell until we get a suspect that we could compare it to."

They both stop to think about the facts, mulling over what they both have just learned about the two victims as Alicia pokes her head into the room.

"I just wanted to come by and apologize again for overstepping, but I hope some of it will help you out."

"When are you meeting the Chief?" Chuck asks sincerely interested in Alicia's wellbeing.

Alicia smiles. "Just got a message from her Admin. I have a 9am meeting tomorrow morning. Hope she doesn't fire my ass."

Chuck grins. "I don't think she'll go that far, but definitely a formal reprimand. I've had a few of them in my day too. She has to do something just in case Sutton Reid tries to call foul and nail the department to the wall. This way she's covered her ass and yours."

"That's another way of looking at it," Alicia agrees. "Did I hear you guys mention fingernail when I opened the door? Possibly the killer's?" she questions the pair of senior detectives.

"Yeah, you did, but we shouldn't be talking about this, Alicia," Helen says strongly.

"I hear you. I understand. Are they analyzing it?"

Chapter 74
July 20
Alicia

Alicia is sitting in the Chief's office, waiting; it's been 25 minutes so far with no sign of the boss. She gazes out the window behind the Chief's large wooden desk and watches the cars zoom up and down the highway, getting bored. She checks her watch again, getting anxious to get the meeting started, wondering how bad the reprimand is going to be. *I hope to hell that I don't lose my job over this, but I had to. I had to look. I had to protect Luke. Well, it was a good run as a detective, even if it was short. I really don't want to have to look for a new job, but if that's what it comes to, I would do it all again.*

The door opens suddenly, and the Chief breezes in, hand in the air like a stop sign. "Don't get up," the Chief says moving behind her desk. "Give me just a sec to finish something," she continues as she opens her laptop and starts to type. Finally, she finishes her task and folds her hands on the top of her desk, looking directly at her newest detective. "Alicia, what the hell were you thinking?"

"Chief, I'm sorry. My research started in earnest. I was looking for similar cases for the sexual assault."

"And you didn't find anything, so you changed the search parameters to the Jessica Winters's case?"

"Yes."

"And then you continued down the path of flagrant disregard for my authority, insulted the two senior detectives on the case and requested video from the Go Station for the time of the girl's death."

"Yes."

"You do recall that you were removed from the Winters's case, correct?"

"Yes," Alicia answers succinctly.

The Chief sits watching her detective squirm for a moment. "Alicia, you disrespected my direct order. You investigated a case that you were no longer assigned to, a case to which your son is now a person of interest." The Chief pauses, choosing her words carefully. "I know that this case is very close to your heart, but one of the things that you need to learn as a detective is to disengage emotionally, disassociate yourself from the people involved. You need to be detached, objective at all times and you need to listen to me. When I tell you to do something, even if you don't like it, you do it. Do you understand?"

"Yes, Chief," Alicia replies, stinging from the rebuke.

"I know you are new to the position, but you did not take my direction and in fact, did exactly what I told you not to do. A written reprimand will be put in your file to reflect my disappointment with this situation," the Chief finishes.

"I understand," Alicia replies.

"Be aware that three such reprimands would leave me no alternative but to dismiss you."

"I understand, Chief," Alicia replies, lowering her eyes from the Chief to her hands in her lap.

There is silence for a moment as both let the seriousness of the situation sink in.

"Dismissed," the Chief advises.

"Thank you, Chief," Alicia says standing to leave the office.

Chapter 75
Frankie
July 20

The cupboards are almost bear. I'll pick up a few things. Just enough to carry me through to the long weekend in August. Going home that weekend and I'm sure Mom will send a shitload of food back with me.

Frankie casually walks up and down the aisles of the Not Just Grocers store picking up a few essentials to tide her over. She puts a couple cans of Campbell's Scotch Broth soup in her basket, adds some sesame seed bagels, a jar of pickles, a package of sliced turkey, a small Greek salad, a six pack of diet coke and a bag of Miss Vickie's Salt and Vinegar chips

She pays for the groceries, picks up the two bags from the checkout counter and leaves the store emerging through the front door onto the main street. She looks up as the door closes behind her, stopping in her tracks, spotting a man across the street, leaning nonchalantly against the edge of the building, almost in the shadows. *That guy looks familiar. Wait! Is that him? Fuck, is that him? Is that the guy from the park? Son of a bitch, he's smiling at me. Walk, Frankie, walk. Get the hell out of here.* Her first several steps are difficult as she staggers from the shock of being watched and it takes several moments to regain her balance. *No, that can't be him. Why would he be watching me? After all this time, it can't be him. No way.* Her gait becomes steady as she hikes up the street, away from the downtown area, continuing to berate herself for having an overactive imagination. *Probably just some innocent guy waiting for his girlfriend, and I've blown it all out of proportion in my mind. This needs to stop. I need to take my life back. I need to get past this, forget about that piece of shit.* She looks around occasionally during her walk back to the dorm, ensuring that she is alone and not being followed as she continues to chastise herself for being afraid.

Chapter 76
July 21
Helen

It is a hazy, overcast summer day as the police vehicle winds its way slowly into the Tunes's estate. The door to the club house beside the palatial home opens and Axl steps out, leans against the door frame waiting for the two detectives to arrive, expecting more asinine questions and innuendos from the pair.

Helen gets out of the driver's side of the car, taking in the surroundings once again as Chuck exits from the passenger side. The two walk toward Axl together, a pleasant smile on their faces, taking great joy in what they are about to do.

"Detectives," Axl greets. "What can I do for you today?"

"Is your brother here?" Chuck asks.

"He is," Axl replies nodding at his car sitting in front of the garage.

"We would like to talk to him," Chuck continues.

Axl chuckles quietly. "You guys are certainly persistent, but nothing has changed. If you want to talk to him, we'll get his lawyer and meet you at the station."

Helen steps forward within centimeters of Axl's nose. "That's where you are wrong, Mr. Tunes. Things have changed," she says shoving a piece of paper into his hands. "We have an arrest warrant. Where is he?"

Axl steps back, away from Helen and holds the paper up for inspection. He reads it slowly before looking up at the two detectives still standing in front of him, a look of astonishment on his face.

"Well, are you going to get him, or should we just go in and look for him ourselves?" Chuck asks, turning to the main house.

Axl moves swiftly to physically get in front of the detectives. "You guys don't know what you're doing. You don't have anything on him," Axl rants as the detectives follow him closely. Axl opens the front door of the mansion and bellows, "Ziggy." He pauses, listens and when there is no answer forthcoming, he yells again, "Ziggy. Now."

The trio wait for a moment but don't hear any movement or sound from within the house. "You wait here, Mr. Tunes and we'll go get him," Chuck offers, stepping into the foyer.

Axl quickly moves forward. "No, you guys are not trashing my house. He's probably in his room with his fucking headphones on listening to some crap," he says, starting up the stairs.

Helen and Chuck follow Axl closely up the open wooden staircase to the first door on the left, where he stops and pounds loudly with both fists. The three wait for a response, but there is no sound, no movement from the room. Axl, stress beginning to show on his normally placid face, grabs the door handle, tries to twist it but it doesn't move. "He's locked the door," he tells the detectives, pummelling on the wooden slab again.

"We can get it open," Chuck advises turning to his partner. "Helen, can you grab the crowbar out of the trunk?"

"No, no wait," Axl pleads. He pulls his phone out of his pocket and pushes the button to call Ziggy, but it instantly goes to voicemail. Axl ends the call quickly, pushing the button again. He does this four or five times with the same outcome.

"Helen, crowbar," Chuck instructs, to which Axl starts pounding on the door nonstop, yelling at the top of his lungs, repeatedly, "Ziggy. Now." He is trying to reign in his aggravation but is unsuccessful as the door vibrates against his strength.

Helen turns back to the staircase and is down several steps before they hear shouting coming from behind the door. It opens suddenly. "What the fuck, Axl?" Ziggy says, holding his earbuds and cell phone in his hands. Surprise is plastered on his face as he takes in the two detectives and his brother's red face flushed with anger. "What's going on?" he asks.

Chuck steps forward, places his hands on Ziggy's shoulders, and turns him around, pulling Ziggy's arms behind his back, causing him to drop his cell phone and earbuds. As Chuck puts the cuffs on him, he recites, "You are under arrest for the murder of Jessica Winters. You have the right to retain and instruct counsel without delay. You have the right to telephone any lawyer you wish. You can apply to the Ontario Legal Aid Plan for assistance. Do you understand?"

271

Ziggy struggles initially but stops as the cuffs click closed. He looks up at his brother, who is leaning against the hall wall for support. "Axl, do something," Ziggy demands.

Chuck bends down and picks up Ziggy's phone and pockets it. He pushes the boy to the stairs repeating, "Do you understand?"

As Ziggy's foot hits the top stair, he swivels back to his brother. "Axl?" he begs.

Axl shakes his head, bringing himself back into reality. He looks at his cell phone, hits a button, and moves it to his ear. "I'm on it, Ziggy. Don't say anything to anyone. Nothing unless Sutton is with you."

Chuck and Ziggy are halfway down the stairs as Chuck repeats, "Do you understand?" rattling Ziggy's cuffs to get his attention.

"I understand," Ziggy mumbles as he stumbles on the stairs, almost falling. Helen waits until Ziggy's foot lands on the dark wood of the front landing before reaching out and grabbing one arm, as Chuck moves to the opposite side, holding on to the detainee.

Chuck continues with the Charter of Rights as they lead Ziggy out of the house and move to the police cruiser. "You must clearly understand that anything said to you previously should not influence you or make you feel compelled to say anything at this time. Whatever you felt influenced or compelled to say earlier, you are now not obliged to repeat, nor are you obliged to say anything further, but whatever you say may be given as evidence. Do you understand?"

Helen opens the rear door of the vehicle and Chuck physically pushes Ziggy around so he can get in the backseat, as he repeats, "Do you understand?"

Ziggy gazes up at the house looking for his brother, his lifeline, to fix this. Axl steps through the front door, his phone at his ear and yells, "Nothing. Say nothing to anybody, Zig. I'll follow you in my car. Sutton will meet us there."

Chuck repeats, "Do you understand?" looking at Ziggy sternly.

"Yeah, I understand," he mumbles as Chuck puts his hand on his head, pushing down, propelling him into the backseat of the car.

Ziggy sits, a vacant look on his face, baffled at the situation. Chuck leans in with Ziggy's phone in his hand. "What's the password?" he asks.

His brother's words of warning are floating around in his head, and he shakes his head, no, settling back against the seat to wait for help.

As Chuck slams the vehicle door shut, two additional police vehicles pull up. Chuck waves them in and they park in front of the house, where Axl is still standing on the front steps, his phone still at his ear. Two police officers get out of each car, all resembling line backers for a professional football team, their shoulders and arms almost bursting out of their cotton shirts. As a team, the four men move to the house, climbing the stairs. One of them hands Axl the search warrant and asks him politely to leave the premises while his team does their work.

***

Ziggy sits at one end of a large cell, trying to create as much distance as possible from the other man in lock-up, who is twitching, and talking between snores. The acrid stench from his body permeates the entire room as Ziggy scrunches up his nose. He sits alone, afraid what the detectives may have on him as he waits for his brother, for his lawyer, for his freedom as he relives the terrorizing procedure of being booked, being physically searched, having his picture taken in numerous positions, his fingerprints inked, and his mouth swabbed for DNA before being thrown in this cage.

After what seems like days to Ziggy, an officer comes to the locked gate and calls his name. He stands up quickly, ready to leave this black hole as soon as possible, as the policeman directs him to turn around before hand cuffs can be secured. They walk down the hall and out into the main corridor of the precinct to a small interrogation room where his brother and Sutton Reid are waiting. Both stand when the door opens, and he is led in. The officer once again asks him to turn around and he takes off the cuffs before leaving the room.

Ziggy gives his brother a big hug, even though emotional demonstrations are not common between them. Axl hugs him back tightly before pushing him to arms length and asking, "You okay?"

Ziggy nods affirmatively.

273

The three sit down at the table, Sutton and Axl bookending Ziggy, their heads together discussing Ziggy's arrest, questioning Ziggy on what evidence the police could have found or manufactured to justify such a bold move.

After an extended time, in which Sutton repeatedly tells Ziggy not to say anything, to let him do all the talking when the detectives come in, there's a knock at the door. Helen and Chuck, with files in their hands, open the door, move into the room, and sit facing the Tunes brothers and Sutton Fox.

"Detective Hodges, Detective MacLean, why are we here? What do you think you have on my client?" Sutton asks.

Helen looks up from the paperwork and pronounces, "Ziggy Tunes has been arrested for the murder of Jessica Winters in the late evening hours of June 30 or early morning of July 1."

Ziggy opens his mouth to deny the charges as Sutton's hand moves and rests on his shoulder.

"Let me finish," Helen requests looking up at the trio. "Your rights were read to you this morning at your home. Do you recall, Mr. Tunes?

All eyes are on Ziggy as he looks at his lawyer, who nods his head, yes. In turn, Ziggy nods his head in the affirmative, stating, "Yes, I remember."

Once the formalities are completed, Sutton Fox breaks in, "We've had this discussion already. He was at his mother's in Toronto," Sutton replies, his eyes moving from detective to detective, hopeful that this is enough information to get his client released.

"Yes, we heard that, however we were unable to corroborate his story," Chuck replies.

"Still no need to arrest my client. I'm sure we can get a hold of Mrs. Tunes and she can confirm that Ziggy was with her."

"It would certainly be helpful to understand the timing of his visit to his mother's, but there is new evidence that has come to light, which puts Mr. Tunes at the scene of the crime," Chuck says, staring intently at the lawyer.

Again, Ziggy moves as if he is going to reply, and Sutton thumps his hand on his shoulder to stop him. "And what evidence is that?" he asks.

"Sutton, you know we don't have to share this information with you right now," Helen begins, putting her hand up to stop the man from breaking in. "We can charge your client, have a bail hearing, which I'm sure will find him being remanded in custody and staying in jail for a while, and then bring the evidence out at disclosure."

Sutton sits back in his chair. "Yes, Detective Hodges I am aware of the process. Is that what you're going to do? Sounds like a big conspiracy to me, just a way of holding him when you really have no evidence."

"Actually, we would like to circumvent the typical process too. We would like your client," Helen moves her eyes to Ziggy, "to tell us the truth. To tell us what he did that evening. To tell us where he was. To tell us whether he was the father of Jessica's unborn baby."

Ziggy thumps his hands down hard on the table, making a loud noise like a door slamming, making the other four participants in the room jump a little bit as the sound reverberates through the small room. Tears begin to slide down Ziggy's face as he tries to utter words, but the sounds are only guttural noises.

"Can you give us a minute," Sutton asks, putting his hand up as a stop sign to Ziggy and his brother.

"Sure, not a problem," Chuck says as the two detectives gather up their papers and leave the room.

***

Fifteen minutes later, Sutton Reid opens the interrogation room door and gestures for the two detectives to rejoin the conversation.

As the five sit around the table again, Sutton starts, "I have advised my client of his rights to be officially charged, have bail set by the courts and that disclosure of evidence on your part would follow." He puts his hand up, similar to a crossing guard telling the cars to stop, as Helen and Chuck push out their chairs to get up. "He has however, agreed to give you the full story of his whereabouts, his actions and information on the baby's paternity now, after we see the evidence that you have to charge him. He would like to clear his name sooner rather than later and in fact, we would like to see the person that actually did this to Jessica caught and charged with her murder."

There is silence as everyone takes in his preamble.

Helen turns from Sutton to Ziggy. "We appreciate your co-operation, Mr. Tunes. Tell us what happened that day."

Sutton interjects, "Your evidence first."

"No, your co-operation first and then our evidence," Helen says, standing her ground.

"That's not the deal," Sutton repeats.

Helen pauses, looking from Sutton to Ziggy to Axl and back again, addressing the lawyer. "We will show you our evidence once we hear Mr. Tunes's account of that day. If his story is true and complete, the evidence we have will be part of the story that he tells us."

Sutton contemplates the statement for a moment, before nodding at Ziggy, who sits upright, squares his shoulders, and starts his dissertation. He took Jessica out for lunch; they had a quickie in the back of his car out on some dusty road north of the city before he dropped her off at work. Then he went to his mother's in Toronto. He gives them the address where she was staying with friends. He talks about his mother sleeping on the couch at her friend's house and that though they spent the afternoon together, he returned to the city by about 9pm. At that point, he called Jessica, but there was no answer. He drove around for a bit looking for her, went to her house, went to the restaurant where she works, went to a couple of coffee shops that they like to frequent, but couldn't find her. He admitted to installing a GPS tracker on her phone previously and though he didn't want to use it, knew it was wrong to use it, he did finally and located her walking in the waterfront park, away from the city, toward the Community Centre. He watched the app for a while, watched her move, but then she stopped. Stopped for about 30 minutes and he began to wonder who she was with, afraid that Jessica was with some other guy, but he didn't want to believe that. Couldn't believe that. So he drove down to find her, thought they could sit at the edge of the water, watch the sun go down together.

He pauses, and Chuck asks, "And then what happened? Did you find her?"

Tears puddle in his eyes as Ziggy continues. "I did, but before I even got in the parking lot, I saw that asshole Luke and his idiot friend Noah leaving. I was mad. I'm sure they were together, that she was screwing around on me."

He pauses again as Axl puts his arm around his shoulder giving him time to take a couple of big breaths before continuing. "I parked the car. I got out and walked to the water as that's what the app showed. I found her around the back of the building, sitting on the steps near the water crying. I asked her what was going on, why was she with dickhead. She was surprised to see me, said she was just out walking, said she hadn't seen Luke, but that she wanted to talk to him. I asked her why, what did she have to say to him. She wouldn't answer me, just cried. I yelled at her, accused her of screwing around on me. I hit her. Just once. It surprised me as much as it surprised her. I stood there looking at her, afraid that I had ruined everything. I had to leave before I did something even worse. I left her sitting there, got in my car and drove home." Ziggy is exhausted from his confession, sniffling with tears.

"And the baby?" Chuck asks.

Ziggy looks up. "I swear I didn't know she was pregnant. I would have married her. I love her," he chokes.

"Did Jessica tell you that's why she wanted to talk to Luke? That it was his baby?"

Ziggy stands up quickly, his chair flying back hitting the wall. He glares at the two detectives. "It was mine. It had to be mine. We were together for over three months. I would have done right by her. I swear," he groans, flopping back into the chair that his brother has retrieved.

Chuck continues, badgering him. "Then why do you think she wanted to talk to Luke? What else would she have to tell him?"

Ziggy sits slumped forward in the chair, shaking his head. "No way, it wasn't his. It was mine, had to be mine," he replies, without answering the question.

"I think she was there to meet Luke. To tell him about the baby. That it was his and you found out and killed her."

"No, no, I didn't hurt Jessica. I loved her," Ziggy wails. "I would never hurt her. Never."

"What about the blanket? Why did you bring a blanket when you thought she was screwing around with someone else?"

Ziggy's mind wanders back to the day that he purchased the blanket set for Jessica. She loved it. Daisies were her favourite. But instead of putting on her bed, she had kept the blanket in Ziggy's car so they could use it to lie on the grass and watch the stars or go to the beach. The matching pillowcases were on his bed, so every morning when he woke up his first thoughts were of Jessica. He shakes his head to bring himself back to the present. "Before I saw that asshole Luke leaving with his friend, I had convinced myself that maybe she was just watching the stars, the moon. We sometimes did that. I thought we could lie on the blanket together. I guess I just got out of my car and picked it up automatically."

"You're talking about the blanket that you covered Jessica with after you killed her, right?"

"I swear I didn't hurt her. I loved her," Ziggy argues, tears covering his cheeks.

There's a pause in the conversation as everyone collects their thoughts. Helen looks at Axl. "Did you see your brother that night at home?"

Axl shakes his head. "I did not see him, but that's not unusual."

Helen asks Ziggy a flurry of questions; what time he got to the Centre; about the weather; did he talk to Luke or Noah; did Luke and Noah see him; what was Jessica wearing; what did Jessica want to talk to Luke about; why was she meeting Luke at the Centre and not at home or somewhere else; where did he go after he talked to Jessica; did he go home that night; what time did he get in; did he see anyone else nearby before or after he talked to Jessica.

278

Ziggy answers all of the questions, answering in grunts or one-word answers until Helen asks, "Was Jessica alone?" Ziggy stops, thinks. "She was alone sitting on the steps to the water when I got there. She stood up when I yelled at her, when I hit her. She gasped when my fist connected. She covered her cheek with her hand, and I thought I heard rustling behind me in the flowers, in the garden. I turned to look but it was dark, and I didn't see anything. When I turned back to Jessica, the look on her face, the redness from where I hit her, I couldn't take it. I ran."

There is an extended silence in the room as everyone takes in Ziggy's new claim.

"Now you're suggesting that someone else was there? Someone hiding in the garden?" asks Chuck.

"Yeah, the person that killed Jessica must have been there, they must have been there, hiding," Ziggy suggests shrugging his shoulders.

"Anything else you want to add, Ziggy?" Helen asks.

He shakes his head, no.

Sutton Fox takes control of the conversation. "Well, you've got it all. He did not do this. There was someone else there. You need to find out whoever was lurking in the shadows. Maybe another friend of Jessica's. She seemed to get around a lot." He puts his hand up as Ziggy turns to him, fists clenched like he's going to hit his lawyer. "It wasn't my client. You need to do your work, detectives."

Helen nods not convinced that there really was another person at the Community Centre that night.

"Can I go home now?" Ziggy begs.

Chuck looks at the boy. "No, you won't be going home for a while Ziggy. Only if everything you said is true and we can prove that Jessica was alive when you left, then you will be able to go home." He pauses. "You will be held here until the bail hearing."

"What about the evidence that you have against Ziggy? You said you would share that with us," Axl asks, coming to the defense of his brother.

Helen pulls two pieces of paper from her file folder and throws them across the table. The first page contains a black and white picture of Ziggy's car, license plate in full view, pulling into the parking lot of the Southshore Community Centre at 11:33pm on June 30, passing a beat-up Mazda with Noah Nash and Luke Anderson in it. The second picture was taken seconds later of Ziggy, a scowl on his face, tromping away from his vehicle, carrying a light coloured blanket adorned with small flowers, the blanket that was used to cover Jessica's dead body.

Chapter 77
July 21
Axl

Axl does laps in the clear blue water of his heated swimming pool. He touches the cement wall at the end of the pool and turns gracefully under water, like an Olympic swimmer. *When the hell is that fucking Archie going to get back to me? I don't want to seem needy or unable to run things up here, so no way am I going to call him, but I need to know what the cops know. If it was James, I will string him up, make an example of him, something spectacular, to remind everyone that I run this city, I am the boss, and they are just minions.*

His fingers touch the cement at the opposite end of the pool, and he turns once again. As his head rises post-turn to get some air, he hears his cell phone ring. *Shit. I better check that,* he thinks changing direction and swimming quickly to the ladder. *Maybe it's that asshole, Archie, with some news.*

He scrambles out of the pool, grabbing a towel off the glass table, draping it around his shoulders as he reaches for his cell phone. He quickly sees the call is from Archie and hits accept on the screen, plopping down in the lawn chair.

"Hey, thanks for getting back to me," he starts as he looks out at the perfect view, the sun reflecting off the water, a sailboat going by in the subtle breeze.

"Not a problem," Archie replies, "but I did have to pull in a couple of favours."

"I understand," Axl retorts, dreading the repercussions of his ask.

"The cops don't have much. The fence around the warehouse is almost three meters high with barb wire. The property does have a gate, which is normally locked but whoever killed Don was in a hurry when they left and didn't close it properly. The kids, being typical 12-year-olds, saw the gate open and went in to explore. They found the body and ran home. Mom called the cops." Archie pauses for a moment in his commentary.

"Was he killed with one of his guns?"

"Wouldn't that be almost fitting if it was one of his own," Archie laughs. "But no, they've checked the few guns left on site and nothing matches the 38-caliber used to kill him."

"What do they know?"

"Not much. There are no cameras at the warehouse, but they did find a business not too far away with one – the corner store. It showed a bunch of cars and trucks coming and going around the time of the incident. They are looking at one specific vehicle, a plain white van, that they can't trace. Seems the license plate is unreadable. They think the plates were covered with some kind of substance that makes them indistinguishable by cameras. Who knew they sold such a product?" he jokes.

Plain white van? That sounds like James. But something on the plate? What the hell? He asks, "Do they have the times for the van coming and going?"

"They do. Apparently, it went into the neighbourhood at 4:23pm and left exactly 31 minutes later." Archie pauses, waiting for more questions.

"Do they have time of death?"

There is silence for a moment, before Archie answers. "They do. The white van driver could have been the doer."

"Do they have any other suspects?"

"I hear they are still tracking down a few other leads, but nothing that I could get more information on."

"Do they know why he was killed?" Axl asks, changing tactics.

"The dock where he was found is rented out to his Agency. Apparently, they were using the warehouse to house the guns that were confiscated at the border before they were destroyed. Only a couple of guns were found on site when there should have been hundreds. They are thinking that whoever took Saunders out, stole the guns."

"What's the activity on the case? Are they searching for the missing guns?"

"They are, but their problem is no documentation to tell them what guns were in lock up or what guns had already been destroyed. The

282

Agency's records really suck or maybe that's the way your friend, Don, set it up. Hide the evidence."

"So, they have nothing to go on? No idea who did this?" Axl asks, blowing out his breath slowly.

"At this point, they are in the dark. Not unusual for the cops," Archie confides.

There is silence for a moment as both men contemplate the workings of their biggest adversary. "Thanks for the info, Arch. Appreciate it," Axl finally says.

"No problem. I'll be in touch," Archie promises as he disconnects the phone call.

Axl sits back in the lawn chair, going over the information that Archie has shared. He gets up suddenly, shoving his feet into a pair of sandals sitting on the stone deck, and walks to the garage to check the license plates on the white van.

Chapter 78
July 22
Axl

"What do you mean you don't know what kind of gun James has?" Axl screams at Chevy as they sit in his office, the VP sitting behind his big heavy desk, looking intently at his enforcer sitting in one of the cushy visitor's chairs.

"I've never really looked, Axl. I know it was a small one, one he kept under the seat if we were in a vehicle, tucked in his belt in the middle of his back when we were out. I always knew he had it and that was enough for me."

"God damn useless," Axl breathes out as Chevy sits immobile. "Unfucking believable," he continues. Axl watches his trusted sycophant, shaking his head. "I don't believe you, Chevy. You're the guy that remembers minutia about anyone that we've shaken down over the years, to the colour and type of engines in every car ever produced," Axl pauses looking closer at the giant sitting in front of him. *Where the hell does your alliance lie, you piece of shit? I can't believe all the time you worked together with James that you never noticed, never thought about what kind of gun he had to back you up. Should I be worried about you too? Maybe the two of you are in this together?*

"Axl, I don't know what to tell you. He never brandished his gun, that's not something that anyone would do. Did I see him with it? Yes. Did I look closely at it? No. I was satisfied that he had one and that he knew how to use it." Chevy pauses looking earnestly at his boss. "I'm sorry I just don't know." He pauses again before adding, "What can I do to make this right, boss?"

Axl continues to eye his enforcer. *All the right words, Chevy. All the right words. Maybe he didn't notice. Maybe James kept it hidden from him so he couldn't see it. I can't be sure one way or the other, and Chevy has been with me forever.* His mind bounces back and forth, he believes him, he doesn't believe him, until he finally stops.

284

What I need is proof. One way or the other. Let's find the proof. Let's find the gun.

"I want you to toss his place. Toss his office. Camryn's place too. Toss his wife's place if you have to. Find the gun. Bring it to me and then we'll see if it's the one that killed Don Saunders."

Chevy is silent for a moment and then confirms, "Not a problem. I'll get on that today. Might take a day or two for his wife's place though. I want to do it when she and the kid aren't there." He pauses, watching his boss's face. "Are you good with that?"

"Yeah, let's not get that bitch on our backs. Do it when no one is there, but don't take too long or I'll wonder what the fuck you're up to," Axl says, moving his eyes back to his computer, dismissing his henchman.

Chapter 79
July 22
Alicia

At last, the info on the car that was sitting in front of the Queens when Frankie was assaulted. Alicia opens the email and reads it carefully. Upon finishing the correspondence, she sits back in her chair, rage starting to cloud her face. *My God, I didn't expect this. How can this get any worse?*

As Alicia contemplates next steps, Fraser walks into the Detectives' Den, moving to his desk on the opposite side of the room. Alicia gets up and moves quickly to his workspace. He looks up as he opens his laptop, turning it on. "What's going on? Looks like you've seen the devil."

"IT was finally able to clean up the video of the car in front of the Queens the night that Frankie was assaulted. The results have come back, and you won't believe it," Alicia replies.

As Fraser opens the email and reads the results, Alicia turns back to her computer, pulling up the National Sex Offender Register, searching for the name of the driver. *Nothing.* She sits back, turning to watch Fraser as he continues to read the email, noticing that his right hand has started to clench. *Wait, what about that other database, the Vulnerable Sector Check. It has records of police contact, mere allegations, withdrawn or stayed charges, acquittals, and mental health information. Maybe he's in there.* Alicia signs into the program and punches in his name and hits enter. *Son of a bitch!* She quickly reads the notes on previous interactions with other police forces, all similar to Frankie's predicament, some going a lot farther, too, but there wasn't enough evidence to prosecute. *Son of a bitch, it's him. It's him.* She sits back in her chair and waits as Fraser continues to read, watching as his right hand starts to softly pound the desk.

Fraser slams his laptop shut, stands up. "Let's go talk to this piece of shit."

***

Luke is laughing as Alicia and Fraser walk into the garage. He turns as the door opens, startled, "Mom?"

"Go home, Luke. We need to talk to Dylan," Alicia tells her son as Dylan stands up from the engine cavity of the Camaro, tools in his hands from working on the car. He leans his hip into the front bumper, crosses his arms, silent.

Luke looks from his mother to Dylan and back again. His forehead crinkles as he tries to understand the presence of his mom until he is told by his mother a second time to go home.

He walks to the door and gives his neighbour a final salute. "See you," he says before the door closes behind him.

There is silence in the garage as the three watch each other carefully. After several moments of standoff, Fraser asks, "Are you Dylan Wheatley?"

Dylan, who is still standing nonchalantly against his car's front bumper replies, "I am. And you are?"

Fraser introduces himself and Alicia formally. Dylan nods at them both and waits for the purpose of their visit. Fraser asks if he's been to the Queens Hotel. Dylan replies in the affirmative, that he has been in the place for a drink or two. Fraser asks if he was there on June 25, the night that Frankie was assaulted. He answers that he is unsure, he goes there occasionally, but doesn't keep track of the dates. Fraser leans forward and shows him a picture of his car, which he is currently leaning against, parked in front of the bar. He asks if this is his car and Dylan smiles replying, "Well, you can see that it is. I'm leaning against it and yes, that's the plate that's on my car. Again, what's this all about?"

Alicia steps up and asks, "Why did you go to the park?"

"The park?" Dylan replies. "What park? When? You're going to have to be clearer with your questions, Alicia," he smirks.

"That's Detective Anderson, Dylan," she corrects. "After you spent time in the bar, why did you go to the park?"

287

"I'm assuming you've put this together from some cameras on the street," Dylan replies, delaying his answer.

"Just answer the question," Alicia presses.

"I honestly don't recall if I went to the park on that night, but seeing that it was summer, it was probably hot in the bar. I probably went over for a walk to get a breath of air after being inside for a while," he confesses.

"And what did you do in the park?" Alicia pushes him.

"I don't recall exactly but probably walked out to the point by the transient docks. Took in the scenery, the sky, the boats. Got some fresh air in my lungs. As I said, I don't remember that particular night but probably that's what I did."

"Why did you follow Frankie Mason to the park?"

Dylan blushes slightly at the name but continues his ignorance of the night, denies following anyone to the park, and negates knowing or meeting anyone by that name.

After several more minutes of questions and denials by Dylan, Fraser and Alicia leave the garage and regroup in their vehicle.

"Son of a bitch was there. I can see it in his eyes. He's playing with us," Fraser says as he puts the car in reverse. "Let's put together a six-pack for Frankie. See if she can identify that piece of scum."

***

Fraser knocks on Frankie's apartment door as Alicia stands beside him. Just as Fraser is about to knock again, they hear movement inside. The detectives stand back and wait as Frankie comes to the door and opens it, surprise on her face.

"Hello Frankie. Do you have a couple of minutes to talk?" Fraser asks, as he barges into the apartment, followed closely by Alicia.

"I guess," the young woman says, closing the door behind them. "What's going on?"

Fraser turns to her, holding out a document. "We would like you to take a look at a photo-lineup and tell us if you see the guy that assaulted you."

Frankie takes the piece of paper from the outstretched hand and makes a show of scanning the photos, not really looking at the faces, overlooking the face of the man who was standing outside the Not Just Grocers store the other day. "No, none of them look familiar," she says, handing the paper back.

"Can you take a closer look, please?" Fraser urges wondering what has changed for Frankie, who seems unenthusiastic about the task.

Frankie pulls the paper back and makes a show of studying each of the six pictures before handing it back to Fraser again. "Sorry, none of these guys look familiar. You've got to remember it was dark and I was in a hurry to get away from the creep. I didn't get a really good look at him."

Fraser takes the report from her and scrutinizes the pictures for a moment before looking up at Frankie. "I'm getting the impression that something's changed. Are you having second thoughts about pressing charges against the man that sexually assaulted you?"

Frankie looks like a deer caught in head lights and lowers her gaze as if she had been caught doing something wrong. After several moments, she raises her head and explains, "I didn't get a good look at him. It was dark and I'd had a few drinks. Nothing really happened. I kicked him and got away."

"And you were very, very lucky Frankie," Alicia pipes in, "but we need your help to get the piece of trash who jumped you, who would have raped you if he got the chance, off the streets."

"I appreciate everything you guys have done for me. I really do, but I just want this to go away. I don't want to think about him anymore; I don't want to be looking for him in the shadows. I don't want to have to testify; I don't want to go to court and have my reputation raked over the coals. I want to forget this ever happened. Nothing really happened to me, anyway and I'm almost finished my course. I'm going home in a couple of months, and I just want to forget it all," she finally confesses.

"I understand, Frankie," Alicia says, putting her hand on the girl's shoulder. "But can you really forget? Especially with this guy running around free and probably going to do it again to someone who isn't as smart or as quick or as strong as you?"

Frankie's face tightens, sweat starting to glisten on her cheeks. "I'm sorry, but none of these guys look familiar. And if you bring another bunch of pictures, I will say the same thing. I want this to go away. I want this to stop."

Both Alicia and Fraser try to persuade the young woman to help, to go through with what she started when she originally reported the assault, but to no avail.

Chapter 80
July 22
Dylan

Shit. Shit. Shit. What do they know? What can they prove? Nothing from that chick in the park or they would have hauled me in by now. And it was dark that night. No way that bitch could identify me from a lineup. And I couldn't have left any DNA, or they would have been all over me. Hardly had a chance to touch her before she kicked me in the balls.

Did she see me the other day at Not Just Grocers? No, I was in the shadows and even if she did, so what? I was just standing on the street doing nothing. Didn't talk to her. Didn't wave to her. Didn't follow her.

This was a good town, lots of action with the college girls, lots of bars to choose from, lots of pretty little things looking for a good time, with no complaints. But I think it's time to get out of here before that detective tries to pin something on me, something that might stick. I don't have a record, never had anything stick before, but this is calling it too close. It's time to go.

Yeah, let's pull out the computer and take a look for a new job, far, far away from here. So glad that I can work on any kind of car. I will have no problem finding another job in another city far away from their prying eyes.

Chapter 81
July 23
Chevy

James is sitting at his desk in his storefront office, his head down, looking at his computer as Chevy drives by the shop's window. *Well, that's good. He's in the office. Must be playing a good game on his computer. Didn't even look up with the sweet rumble of this masterpiece of a car going by.* He smiles, knowing that James is not busy with clients or work and that his showing up later will be a surprise. *I'll go to the apartment first. Hope to hell that bitch Camryn is not there. She's still got her own place, but she could be anywhere if she's not working.*

Chevy moves through the traffic easily, keeping his speed under the limit, following all of the road signs, aware that the cops would love to pull him over for any minor infraction. He pulls up to the dirty, brown apartment building that James lives in. *Not sure what the hell went down between James and his nosy wife, but something big if she could have forced his hand to move into this dump, after the fantastic condo he had when he first left her. Another reason not to get tied down. This place is disgusting. Dumpsters overflowing with garbage. Way too many screaming kids for my liking.*

He parks his car a couple of buildings down and walks over to the front entrance looking into the lobby, noticing the floor number on the elevator and its directional arrow indicating that it is coming down from one of the higher floors. He casually pulls out his wallet and looks through it as if searching for something. The elevator finally stops on the main floor with a dinging noise signifying that it has reached its destination. Chevy continues the pretense, waiting as a woman with a baby in her arms exits the elevator, walks through the lobby to the front door and starts to push it open with her hip. He grabs the door handle and holds it open for her, smiling casually as she thanks him. Chevy returns her smile as he steps into the empty lobby. *I'm in. That didn't take too long.*

Chevy glances around ensuring no one is watching him and that there are no cameras in the lobby recording his movements. He advances to the end of the hallway and opens the door to the stairs. *No security at all. This is a burglar's paradise. Someone could come and rob almost every unit in the place. But hey, who would want to? Probably nothing worth taking in any of them anyway.*

Chevy reaches the fourth floor and stops to catch his breath, waits until his heartbeat has normalized and leans into the door, opening it a crack to view the hallway. *Nothing. No one. Good.* He opens the stairwell door quietly and walks calmly down to the second door on the right, while pulling on his leather gloves. He stops, leans into the door, and listens for a moment. *All's quiet.* He knocks gently, not wanting to alert nearby residents in the building that he's there, but loud enough that if someone is in James's apartment, they will hear. He waits, looking around to ensure he is still alone in the hallway, as he pulls out his lock picking kit from his inner pocket. He inserts the hook of the stainless-steel pick in the lock and moves it cautiously, listening for the click of the deadbolt's internal mechanisms. *Think he would have something stronger than one single deadbolt, especially knowing what goes on in this neighbourhood.*

Chevy opens the door cautiously and steps into the apartment. He waits a moment, ensuring no one is going to appear from the kitchen or bedroom area before he steps fully in and closes the door. *Same furniture as the old place, but its fucking cramped in here, though it is clean and tidy. Must be Camryn who looks after the place. I can't see James pulling out a vacuum*, he smiles at such a vision. Chevy walks through the apartment, double-checking that he is the only one there. *The place is clear. I'll start in the bedroom.*

Thirty minutes later, Chevy is finished with his search. He's looked in every cupboard, every drawer, under every piece of furniture, including flipping over the mattress and box spring in the bedroom. He looked in the toilet tank, in the air vents, checked for phony electrical outlets and air returns. He searched the kitchen garbage, the bathroom garbage, James's dirty laundry basket, and every box and container in the closets, pulled off the table legs, checked the fridge and freezer, emptying goods and cereal boxes into the sink to ensure

293

nothing was hiding. He even looked for loose floorboards knowing that it wasn't too practical in a fourth-floor apartment as a hiding place. He did find James's gun safe, probably left over from his time as a detective. It took him a few minutes to open it, but the steel box was empty.

Chevy stands with his back to the apartment door, appraising his work. *Where the hell else could he have hidden the gun? I checked everywhere. He must have it on him.* Chevy pulls out his phone, checks the time and leaves the apartment. *Fuck it. He'll know I was here anyway. Need to get to his office before he leaves for the day.*

***

The blinds on the front window are closed. James sits straight in the chair as Chevy ties his arms and torso, before pushing him up against the outer door to ensure no one enters the office while he is searching the place.

"Chevy, if you told me what you're looking for, maybe I could help you," James suggests, knowing exactly what Chevy has been tasked to do by Axl.

Chevy ignores the offer of assistance, searching everywhere, looking in everything, pulling down ceiling tiles, looking in the vents and the exhaust system for the unit. Finally, after all the hiding places have been uncovered, he turns to James. "Where's your gun?" he asks.

"Is that what you're looking for? It's in the inside pocket of my suit coat. The one I have on," James says, moving his shoulder, his eyes moving down to his chest. "Don't you think you should have checked there before you started making all this mess?" he taunts Chevy.

Chevy smiles. "You're right. I should have tossed you first. Maybe thrown in a couple of upper cuts, a couple well placed punches like I did before. You remember, don't you?" he goads, moving closer.

"Yeah, I remember. Hurt for a month," James confirms.

Chevy is standing directly in front of James, watching him closely. "Don't move," he commands as he leans over and pulls James's gun from the inside pocket of his suit jacket. He examines it closely and

294

turns it to show James. "This is a Glock 26. Where's the Smithie?" Chevy asks.

"Smithie?" James parrots. "Don't think I ever had a S&W."

"Yeah, you did - the 686 model. It was a 38-caliber, fit in the palm of your hand," Chevy pushes.

"Maybe when I was back on the force, I had one. I don't rightfully remember. If I did, I would have gotten rid of it when I left the force," James reasons.

Chevy stands for a moment contemplating his next move. "I'm taking this," he says as James begins to protest. "Up to Axl whether you get it back or not," he completes, pushing James away from the door.

James smiles knowing that the Smith and Wesson Chevy is searching for is at the bottom of the bay, knowing that Axl suspects him of killing Don Saunders, knowing that Axl is making a case to blame him for the loss of millions of dollars in gun sales.

Chapter 82
July 23
Alicia

Alicia wrangles three grocery bags and her purse as she moves to the front door of her house, sets the bags down, pushes her key into the lock. The door opens wide, and she gasps at the mess. *What the hell*, she muses stepping into the house, stepping over the couch cushions in the front hall, around the emptied garbage on the kitchen floor.

"Luke, Luke are you here?" Alicia yells moving further into the house. *What happened here? A party? There's no way Luke would have a party and leave it like this. A robbery? But what were they looking for? And to trash the place like this? They were definitely looking for something.*

She hears a noise behind her and turns to see her son climbing the stairs of the front porch, picking up the bags of groceries left behind. As he pushes through the door, he sees the chaos and looks up into his mother's eyes. "What the hell happened here Mom? Are you okay?" he asks, moving into the front room, looking around at the debris, everything overturned, everything out on the floor.

"I'm okay," she replies. *Could it be something to do with work? But my cases are typical, nothing too crazy. Maybe Dylan? Maybe he's trying to throw me off my game. No, what would be the point? I don't have anything here to incriminate him. Definitely not Luke by his reaction. Maybe the Tunes brothers, but again, what would they be looking for? Freaking James. It's gotta be him. What is he involved in now?*

***

James drives his Bronco into the rear parking lot shared by the Best Western and Quality Inn on Hart Drive, looking intently around the area, searching for anything out of place but the parking lot is barren

296

in its far reaches, with only a few cars parked close to the motels. He backs in beside Alicia's personal vehicle, the rear touching the fence at the back of the lot between the motel parking lot and an industrial area of town. He turns off the engine, pulls the key out of the ignition and steps from his vehicle.

Alicia is leaning against the front bumper of her car, and he walks up to her. "Strange place to meet, don't you think? What's happened now?" he asks, inspecting his ex-wife closely.

"Have you extradited yourself from the Ruebens?" she asks.

James looks at her incredulously but doesn't reply.

"Just what I thought," Alicia responds.

"What's going on? Is this about Luke?" he asks.

"Who tossed my place? What were they looking for?" Alicia continues to badger.

"I have no idea, Alicia. Maybe it was the cops looking for something they could hold over Luke," he says off the cuff, trying to turn her accusations away from him.

She turns slowly to face James, searching for remnants of the man she married years ago, but finds none. "Yeah, no. I know it has something to do with you. And Axl." She pauses again before continuing what she came to tell him. "What I'm about to tell you is because you are Luke's father. You understand, I'm doing this for Luke." James nods. "There will be a raid this Friday evening at closing time at the Not Just Groceries store."

"What? Why?"

"No more info, James. If you don't know what I'm talking about, good. If you do know, do not, I repeat, do not be anywhere near that store on Friday evening." Alicia tosses copies of the two sketches that the manager of Not Just Groceries assisted the police sketch artist in developing at James. She turns away and gets back in her car, starts it, and pulls out of the parking lot, leaving a cloud of dust in her wake.

Chapter 83
July 23
Chevy

Axl and Chevy look at the gun that sits on the desk between them – James's Glock 26.

"That's it? That's all you found?" Axl hisses.

"That's it, boss. That's all I found. I tossed his apartment, his office, his ex-wife's place. Even did a number on Camryn's."

"And what did he say when you told him you were looking for the 38-caliber?"

"Said he might have had one when he worked on the force, but he would have gotten rid of it when he left," Chevy replies.

"Fuck. I know it's him. I know he killed Don. I know he was the one that fucked up that sweet deal with the guns and lost me millions of dollars. Asshole," he yells, beginning to pace his office.

Chevy sits quietly, not moving, waiting for new instructions from his boss.

Chapter 84
July 25
Helen

"What came back from the search of the Tunes's house? Ziggy's car?" Helen asks Chuck as he sits at the table in the major crime room reviewing the police report.

"The typical stuff," Chuck replies reading the list from the search team. "Ziggy's laptop, a large amount of his clothes that might have blood residue on them, leather gloves which may have been used to cover up DNA when he picked up the log that killed Jessica, hair samples for DNA testing, bed sheets being examined for remnants of sexual activity between Ziggy and Jessica and possibly other partners. Hey, look at this. The pillowcases on Ziggy's bed match the blanket that he was carrying when he got out of his car at the Community Centre that night, the one that was covering Jessica's dead body." Chuck smiles, handing the report to Helen.

She reviews the list quickly and pauses on the picture Chuck is referring to, the pillowcases with the little white daisy pattern on the soft yellow background. "Yup, same pattern. I would say that's another nail in Ziggy's coffin."

"What about his story that someone else was there?" Chuck asks.

"Bullshit," Alicia replies quickly.

***

Shortly after lunch, Chuck and Helen receive the final forensics report for the death of Jessica Winters. The room is quiet as they both study the results, nodding and making "Hhhmmm" sounds occasionally.

The report confirms that the baby was not Ziggy's. *Must be Luke's kid. They broke up about three months before Jessica died. Bet it was his and that would have definitely set Ziggy off. He admitted to hitting her once. Maybe he did something else. Something more drastic.*

DNA from Jessica and Ziggy were present on Jessica's clothes and on the blanket that covered her dead body. DNA from an unknown was also found on the blanket. "Hhhmmm," Helen says again. *We need to test Luke's DNA against the blanket. He's quickly becoming more than a person of interest in this case. Alicia is going to freak out when we ask for it, but we can get a warrant now, specially him as the possible father.*

"We're going to have to pull Luke in for a DNA sample," she muses continuing to read.

Chuck's only reply is "Hhhmmm" as he continues perusing the document.

Helen finishes the detailed report and turns to her partner, "Thoughts?"

"Why was Ziggy's DNA on her clothes?" Chuck asks.

Helen thinks for a moment before suggesting, "Ziggy confirmed a sexual tryst with her the afternoon before she died. Probably happened then."

"Well, we now know the baby isn't Ziggy's. Might be Luke's. Probably is from their history which brings him into the picture, but is that probable cause to kill Jessica?"

"I would say yes," Helen replies.

Chuck closes the document he's been reading. "Jessica told Luke about the baby, he wanted to get back together, Jessica said no, maybe told him she was going to get rid of it. It's possible. But he was seen leaving the scene as Ziggy was coming into the parking lot who confirms Jessica was alive when Luke left, so it can't be him. Still leaves Ziggy. He found out, he killed her."

"I hear you Chuck, but I think we need to understand who the father of this child was. We could also have his DNA tested against the unknown on the blanket. I'll start the paperwork for the warrant. If it matches the unknown on the blanket, he still could be toast. Maybe he came back. Maybe his friends are covering for him," Helen replies, opening her laptop.

Chapter 85
July 26
Alicia

Alicia, Luke, and Bryan Reid are sitting in the living room quietly waiting, trying to prepare Luke for Helen and Chuck's arrival, trying to calm his nerves, telling him he has nothing to worry about. The detectives have a warrant for Luke's DNA, and they have agreed to come to the house as a courtesy to Alicia to get the sample. Luke is pacing, unable to sit in one place as he mumbles, "I swear I didn't know. I didn't know." Alicia has told him of Jessica's pregnancy, and he is upset, beating himself up for not being there to help her, for not stepping up as he believes he should have, for saving her from Ziggy that last fateful night.

The police vehicle pulls into the driveway and Alicia gets up to let Helen and Chuck in before they have the opportunity to knock on the door. "Helen, Chuck," Alicia says formally as she opens the door to her two co-workers, knowing that they are doing their job but hating them for it.

The two detectives greet Alicia solemnly as they walk into the living room, catching the fear in Luke's wide-eyed stare. They shake hands with Bryan Reid, the lawyer. "Where's James?" Chuck asks.

"Don't know," Luke answers quickly. "He's fallen off the face of the earth," he adds bitterly.

Chuck turns to Alicia, his eyes questioning. "I honestly don't know what's going on with him. He doesn't answer his cell or his office number," she confirms.

"That's strange," Chuck replies, knowing that James, for all his faults, is a caring father and would be there if at all possible.

"The warrant," Helen says handing the paperwork to Bryan Reid. "Luke, can you sit down over here?" Helen asks, motioning him to the chair as she pulls out swabs and plastic bags from her pocket. Luke complies as Alicia moves to stand beside him. The lawyer folds the

301

papers, shoves them into his pocket and steps over to watch the process as well.

Helen swabs the inside of Luke's mouth, opens a plastic bag, puts the specimen in, and writes the particulars on it. She then tells Luke that they would also like a hair sample, as she pulls out a pair of tweezers from her pocket, disinfecting them with a sterile wipe before pulling out a couple of strands from Luke's head, putting them into a second baggie, writing on the container and pocketing both samples.

"Thanks Luke," Helen smiles. "Appreciate your co-operation," she finishes as she turns to the door. "See you back at work," Helen says to Alicia moving passed her in the doorway, leaving the house.

***

The door to the major crime room is closed as Alicia walks toward the Detectives' Den. Alicia stops and knocks, waiting for an answer. She hears "come in," from Helen who is standing in front of the visual story of Jessica and her death. Helen turns as Alicia enters the room, surprised. "Alicia?" Helen questions moving away from the monstrosity on the walls.

"I just wanted to drop by and thank you for letting Luke give you the samples at home instead of making him come into the station. He is upset by the whole situation, and we appreciate the additional respect that you are showing him."

"Not a problem, Alicia. Officially Luke is a person of interest even with the arrest of Ziggy. We need to prove who killed her and finding the father of her baby might be the key information we need."

Alicia pauses for a moment. *Or it could be the turning point from looking at Ziggy as the murderer to Luke.* She shakes her head to disengage the awful thought from her brain, but the fear, the doubt won't go away easily. *And what happens with the knowledge that it's Luke's child? More anguish for Luke. More feelings of guilt for not being there for Jessica. More remorse over their relationship, her death, the death of his child. Other than tying the case up with a bow, the results of the DNA test on the fetus could be very destructive and*

302

wounding for Luke, but if it helps put that scumbag Ziggy away, it might be worth it. "I have a favour to ask. Well, two really."

"If I can, Alicia," Helen says, sitting down at the boardroom table to listen to her associate.

"When the results of Luke's DNA and the baby's come back, please let me know. I would like to be the one that tells Luke, one way or the other," Alicia asks quietly.

Helen thinks for a moment before replying, "I don't think that's a problem. What else is on your mind?"

Alicia turns to the pictures on the wall, focusing in on Jessica's prom picture, letting her eyes wander down to another image from graduation of Jessica, Nova, Luke, Willow, and Noah, all smiling, all happy looking forward to their futures. She turns back and hands two small baggies to Helen. "Can you run DNA tests on these two samples?"

Helen looks at the writing on the plastic bags and then up into Alicia's eyes. "You think this person is involved? Should I ask how you got these?"

"It doesn't matter how I got them. If the DNA matches, we'll have to find a reason to get new legal samples, to prove they did it. If they don't match, then my hunch is wrong. No harm, no foul."

Helen sits quietly for a moment, reflecting on the request, turning the small bags over in her hand, examining them closely. Finally, she looks up, "I'll send them along with the samples we collected today from Luke."

"Please ask that the results be compared to this case, as well as the Hannah Longhurst murder."

Helen is surprised by the request but agrees.

Chapter 86
July 28
Alicia

Fraser holds the door open as Alicia enters the Not Just Groceries store. The two detectives look around for Tina Lopez, who called into the precinct an hour ago cancelling the sting they had set up for the end of the month.

"I don't see her, do you?" Fraser asks as they approach the cash counter.

"Must be in the backroom," Alicia says before catching the attention of the cashier and asking, "We're looking for Tina Lopez. Is she in?"

The young woman blushes slightly and advises that the owner of the store is working in the office.

"We'll just go back, if you're okay with that," Fraser advises halfway to the storeroom door.

"Sure," the cashier agrees, moving her attention to the next customer in line.

Alicia and Fraser push through the storeroom door and walk down the short hallway to the office. They knock on the door and wait for a moment before hearing, "Come in." Tina Lopez is sitting at the scuffed-up wooden table, a laptop open in front of her, as she looks up at the visitors. "Thought you guys would show up," she comments as she closes the laptop and sits back on the wooden chair, folding her arms across her chest.

"We just want to talk to you. Understand what's changed. Understand why you don't want to catch the scumbag that's been extorting money from you," Fraser says stepping into the room crowded with boxes of merchandise that hasn't made it to the storefront.

Tina sits placid, quiet as the two detectives enter the space and drag over two chairs that were sitting on either side of the door. Once Fraser and Alicia are ensconced on the chairs in front of the desk, Fraser asks again, "What's changed, Tina?"

"I don't want to do it anymore. That's all," Tina replies quickly.

"Why? What's different now?" Fraser persists.

"No reason. I just changed my mind," she replies defensively.

Fraser asks the same question several times in different ways, but the conversation is at a standstill with neither giving an inch, neither willing to discuss the issue calmly, rationally, both staring at the other defensively. Alicia moves to the edge of her chair, looking directly at Tina. "If you say you're afraid, I will totally understand. What you're doing is brave, going up against the Ruebens but we'll be here to support you, to make sure no one gets hurt, to make sure this stops."

Tears begin to pool in Tina's eyes as she nods her head in agreement. Alicia continues, "It took a lot of guts to come to us in the first place, to tell us what's been going on, and it's time that we did something about it. You shouldn't have to pay protection money, insurance money to the gang and that's going to stop this Friday."

Tina continues to nod until she finds her voice, "But what if they come after me? My family? The store?"

"We will make sure that doesn't happen. On Friday night, they'll be at least three of us in the store and a fourth outside watching to let us know when the asshole shows up. We've got this. You have nothing to worry about," Alicia declares confidently.

"And what about after? You get the guy on Friday but what about Saturday? What about after you leave, and the gang leader shows up again?"

"We'll have someone on site as long as you need us. We won't just take the guy in on Friday night. We'll stay until you feel safe, until the threat is really gone," Alicia reassures.

"Are you sure? As long as it takes?" the manager asks.

"As long as it takes," Alicia confirms, nodding her head affirmatively.

Tina sits for a moment, contemplating the plan, the possibilities, takes a swipe at the tears on her face and looks up to Alicia, "Okay, let's do this on Friday."

Chapter 87
July 30
Alicia

The Not Just Groceries store is busy on Friday evening with customers coming and going right up until closing. Alicia is stocking shelves near the cash counter while the owner, Tina Lopez, runs the check out, ringing purchases through and wishing her customers a good weekend. *I hope to hell James does not come through that door. I told him. I warned him, but he is so hard-headed he probably didn't believe me.* Fraser is posted outside in an unmarked vehicle watching the people come in and out, comparing them against the artist's sketch of the perpetrator. He has a microphone and earphone on to give Alicia and the team a heads up when he sees the tall, heavy set man entering the store. There are also two patrol officers in the store in their civies, blending in with the customers, just in case extra manpower is required.

The time creeps closer to the 6pm closing and the store begins to clear out naturally. At two minutes after 6, Tina advises the customers still wandering about, that the store will be closing and to bring their purchases to the cash.

As the last customer is ushered out the door, Tina turns to Alicia pleading, close to tears, "He always comes in on the last Friday of the month. I don't know why he isn't here."

Fraser enters the store and the team group around the cash counter. "That's okay," Alicia tries to comfort Tina. "I think we're done here for tonight, but I think we'll come back tomorrow and if we have to, a couple more days after that. I don't mind stocking shelves," she laughs to ease the tension. Looking at the two plain clothes officers, Alicia asks, "You guys good for tomorrow afternoon?"

The two nod their heads and it is decided that they haven't given up trying to catch the person demanding protection money.

Chapter 88
July 30
Axl

Axl looks at the time on his phone as he paces his office. *Where is James? He usually gets here by 7pm. The store closes at 6 and he goes in just before closing. What the fuck is he up to now?*

Axl throws himself in his chair, tossing his phone on the desk. *Five more minutes. He's got five more minutes.*

I'll check my stocks in the meantime, see if I've made any money today. He opens his computer and signs on to his account, tapping his fingers, waiting for the internet connection. Axl loves to play the stock market and has set aside $500,000 to play with. He checks his account, noticing his bank stocks have fallen a couple of dollars today. *What the hell are they doing? Everyone uses the bank and the fucking interest rates have just gone up.* His attention moves to his Tesla stocks, which have been extremely volatile lately but are showing a substantial gain today. *Maybe I should move all my money over there. Maybe they are finally on the upswing again.*

After making a few adjustments to his portfolio, Axl closes the app, notices the time on the computer screen, and signs off. *Seventeen minutes and still no call from James. Something is going down. I know it. He's doing something stupid.*

He reaches for his phone and hits the icon for Chevy, who picks up after the first ring. "Hey boss," he says tentatively, worried about why he is getting this unexpected call.

Axl huffs into the phone, "Chevy, I need you to find James. He always comes by on the last Friday of the month, drops off a payment and he's not here yet."

Chevy knows instantly what Axl is asking and why. "No problem, boss. I'll go find him," Chevy replies, disconnecting the line.

Axl leans back in his chair. *Fucking guy. First the Don situation, now this. We're done, Mr. Anderson. You've taken one too many liberties and you are history.*

Chapter 89
July 30
Chevy

The '69 GTO glides down the street as Chevy smiles to himself remembering George Carlin's comedy routine about driving - have you ever noticed that anybody driving slower than you is an idiot and anyone going faster than you is a maniac? *Well today, I'm neither. Just someone out to run a couple of errands,* he thinks as he pulls into the strip mall that houses James's office.

He parks his car by itself in the back of the lot to keep it safe from dings or scratches made by other people's stupidity. He gets out and saunters up to the door, pulls on it but it is locked. He cups his hands together and looks through the window. *Nothing out of place*, he thinks, surveying the room until his eyes fall on the desktop. *Dust. Is that dust on the desk? And the message light on the phone is blinking.* His eyes continue to move, looking at each item in the room. *How long has it been since he's been here? What the hell?* He steps back, noticing the mail slot in the door. He looks through the window again, angling himself to see a pile of mail that has accumulated inside on the floor. His eyes roam to the closet at the end of the room. He squints at the door that isn't quite closed, looking at the vacant space within. *Empty. Something's going on here. I need to find this guy.*

Chevy makes his way back to his car quickly. He starts it and burns rubber leaving the parking lot, his spidey senses tickling as he moves toward James's apartment.

He parks down the street and walks back to James's place at a rapid pace. *He wouldn't. Would he? Does he think running is going to stop Axl from finding him? He knows about the Ruebens's network across Canada, doesn't he?*

A grandfatherly type sees Chevy walking swiftly to the entrance way of the apartment and holds the door, smiling at the newcomer. Chevy nods his head as he moves into the lobby, makes a right in the main hallway to the stairwell. He takes the steps two at a time, barrelling through the steel door from the stairwell to the fourth-floor and stomps to the second door on the right.

He knocks loudly, not worried about neighbours as he puts his ear to the door, listens but hears nothing. *Fucking guy. He's got to be smarter than this.*

Chevy pulls his lock pick set from his inner pocket, shoves it into the key cylinder, jimmies it around until the bolt retreats. He pushes in the door, all caution gone.

The furniture is just as I left it when I tossed the place a week ago. Chevy steps into the room and pulls the apartment door closed and walks through the apartment, looking a little bit closer at the mess. *Where are the pictures that sat on the end table? The one of Luke, the one of James and Camryn. Gone.* He walks through the apartment into the bedroom where the mattress and box spring are still leaning against the wall before opening the closet door. *Empty.* He marches into the bathroom and checks out the bathtub where he had dumped everything from the medicine cabinet. *Everything gone.*

Chevy runs through the apartment door, grabbing the door handle and pulling it closed hard behind him. The boom of the door slamming vibrates loudly through the empty apartment hallway as he hurries down the stairs.

***

Calm down, calm down, Chevy tells himself as he leaves Camryn's apartment. I can't believe that she's that stupid that she would run with this guy. Axl's going to kill them both when he finds them. And he will find them.

***

Chevy sits quietly in the plush visitor's chair in front of Axl's desk, trying to make himself small and insignificant as his boss rants and raves about the possibility that James is trying to run from his clutches. He waits for a short break in his boss's antics before suggesting, "I didn't call Mack. Maybe he knows where James is."

Axl stops short, examining his enforcer. "Did you know this was coming?"

"Me? No, I didn't know anything."

"Are you sure? You guys have been together a lot over the last year. He was your protégé when he first came to us. You taught him how to be an enforcer."

Chevy lifts his hands from his lap, palms up innocently. "I swear Axl. I know nothing. And yeah, I helped him when he first got here but that was because you told me to. And you have to remember the beating I put on him last year when he owed you that money. I've always been loyal to you," he continues, watching his boss carefully.

Axl doesn't acknowledge Chevy but picks up his phone and hits a speed dial number, still mumbling expletives under his breath. The phone is picked up and he instantly asks, "Do you know where James is?"

He listens for a moment before ending the call. "He's fucking gone. Mack doesn't know where he is either, but he won't stay gone for long. I'll find him. The Ruebens will find him," he promises, opening his laptop and typing maniacally.

Chevy continues to sit in the visitor's chair waiting for his boss to dismiss him or to use his expertise.

Chapter 90
July 30
Mack

Mack disconnects the call from Axl, slowly setting his phone on the table beside him. *What the hell? The fucking idiot. Don't tell me he's done something stupid and run. Killed Don, stole the money and ran? Are you kidding me? Not the sharpest knife in the drawer.*

He saves the spreadsheet that he's been working on, calculating the money that has been made on the darknet from the two shipments of guns they got from Don Saunders. *Too bad this gig is almost over. We were turning a tidy 500% profit on the guns. Can't believe my son would be stupid enough to cut off the gravy train. Asshole.*

Mack leaves his small flat, gets into his car and drives down to the beach. He scouts out the area, looking for his grandson Luke, spotting him walking the beach carrying the red meter-long rescue buoy, watching the activity on the sand and in the water. He parks his car and walks through the sand toward his grandson. When he gets within hearing range, Mack calls, "Luke."

Luke looks around, searching for who is calling his name, hesitating for a moment trying to place Mack's face, until it comes to him. He smiles, standing still as Mack approaches. "Hey Mack, wasn't it?" he asks when the newcomer is within speaking distance.

"Yeah, that's right. Mack Sommers," his grandfather agrees. "I'm looking for your dad. Have you seen him lately?"

A shadow of doubt clouds Luke's face as he wonders about his dad's relationship with this guy, why he's looking for him and why he never heard of this relative before. "Haven't seen him in a while. Not sure what's up with him. It's like he fell off the face of the earth," Luke confirms forcefully, his anger at his father's absence pushing into his mannerisms. "Do you know where he is?"

"No, I don't, Luke," Mack offers.

The two stand for several minutes, unsure what else to offer the other until Luke finally advises, "I have to go back to work," and

311

walks away to watch his charges on the beach, leaving Mack standing alone.

Chapter 91
July 31
Alicia

The team is in place again on Saturday afternoon in the Not Just Groceries store, with the two undercover officers wandering the store, picking up items, putting a few in their baskets. Fraser is outside once again as Alicia marks down items on a special rack for a sale starting on Monday.

Just as the store is about to close and the last shopper has left, a tall burly biker-looking man enters. He walks around the shop looking at different things on the shelves before sauntering over to the cash counter. He looks the owner in the eye and says, "Hello Tina."

Tina doesn't recognize the man and asks, "How can I help you sir?"

"I'm here to pick up the package for Axl," he explains quickly.

Tina is startled and blurts out, "You aren't the normal guy." She looks around the store, trying to signal someone to help her.

Chevy follows the manager's gaze, eyeing the person stalking the shelves, who is moving a box to the back room and is unaware of their conversation. His attention moves back to the store owner, and he smiles. "He called in sick. Give me the money."

Tina hesitates, unsure what to do.

"Give me the package," he reiterates sternly.

Again, she hesitates, tears starting to form in her eyes as she begins to shake in fear. Chevy pulls a gun from his pocket provoking Tina to scream. Alicia turns to the commotion at the cash counter, sees the weapon, and yells, "gun, gun, gun" into her microphone, as she pulls her gun and rushes toward the altercation.

Fraser throws open the front door, brandishing his revolver, as he rushes into the store. The two plain clothes officers pull out their weapons and move to the big man at the cash.

"Drop it," Alicia yells moving toward the big man, gun aimed at him.

"What the fuck," Chevy says looking around at the arsenal pointed at him. He slowly places his gun on the counter and steps back.

"Hands behind your head," Fraser advises.

"That's not the guy that normally comes," Tina cries. "That's not him."

"Maybe not but we got this one for extortion," Fraser says securing the cuffs around Chevy's wrists, as he starts to recite his rights to the large man. At the completion of his dissertation, Fraser asks, "Do you understand?"

The big man replies calmly, "Yes, I would like my call now. The phone number is 705-555-0525. Tell the gentleman that answers where you are taking me."

"You can call him when we get to the station," Fraser advises as he grabs the cuffs and begins to steer the suspect to the door.

"No, now. I want my call now," Chevy insists.

"I got it, Fraser," Alicia advises as she dials the phone number on her cell phone. It rings once before being answered.

"Hello Alicia. To what do I owe this pleasure?" asks Axl Tunes at the other end of the phone call.

Chapter 92
August 10
Alicia

Alicia walks down the hallway to the Detectives' Den wondering what her day will bring. The door to the major crime room opens just as Alicia passes. She turns when she hears "Good morning," from behind her, as Chuck stands at the door, smiling. "You got a few minutes?" he asks.

"Sure. What's going on?" Alicia replies, turning mid-stride, noticing that the pictures, diagrams, and evidence has grown across a third wall as she enters the room. Alicia scans it quickly, eyeing a picture of Luke at the edge of the visual chronicle of Jessica's death. Helen is standing in front of the additional documents at the far end of the room and turns as Alicia says, "Good morning, Helen."

"Hello Alicia. Glad Chuck was able to find you. The DNA results came back, and we need to talk about it," she explains, pulling out a chair and sitting down.

"Sure," Alicia replies, nervousness evident in her demeanour.

The three sit down around the boardroom table. Alicia sits at the edge of her seat, unsure of where the evidence will lead, while still confident that it will exclude Luke from any wrong doings.

Helen shuffles a couple of pages before beginning. "Luke's sample was not evident on Jessica's clothes, the blanket or the murder weapon." Helen looks up, watching tears form in Alicia's eyes. Chuck reaches out and puts his hand over Alicia's on the table, a sign of support. Helen continues to watch adding, "Luke is the biological father of Jessica's baby." With this news, Alicia breaks down and tears gush down her face.

They sit for a few minutes, letting Alicia digest the information as she fights to control her emotions, wipes her eyes with the back of her hand. "So, what does that mean to the case?" Alicia finally asks.

"Well, it gives both Ziggy and Luke a reason to kill Jessica; Ziggy out of jealousy, his girlfriend is carrying someone else's child and Luke, maybe he doesn't want the child, maybe Jessica told him it

315

wasn't his, who knows." Helen sits in silence for a moment before continuing, "but the good thing for Luke is no DNA on Jessica, her clothes, the blanket, the murder weapon." She stops again before continuing. "For Ziggy, I would say the traces on the blanket and her clothes could be explainable. If she told him about the baby and who the father was, it would definitely be another twist of the knife, a reason to pick up something and hit her." Helen stops looking from Alicia to Chuck.

"But he swears someone else was there. Someone was hiding," Chuck adds.

Helen nods. "Now for the interesting results. The DNA that you asked us to test? They found remnants of it on the blanket, on the murder weapon and it also matched the fingernail found in the Hannah Longhurst murder." Helen breaks off for a moment, letting the findings resonate with Alicia. "How did you know who the murderer was? And how are we going to get evidence to convict them? We can't use these samples that were collected illegally and without cause."

Alicia sits back in her chair, thoughts of Luke still front-and-centre in her mind. *Luke was the father of Jessica's baby. How will he cope with this knowledge? Will he be able to forgive himself for not being there? I can't think about this now. How the hell can we get a DNA sample legally and prove who really killed Jessica?*

The three toss ideas around for several hours trying to cover all scenarios, all outcomes, to ensure that the evidence is attainable, irrefutable, and legal. At the end of the discussion, the three are satisfied that their plan will work.

"Let's get the Chief and the Crown Attorney together, get their approval and then set this up," Helen says excited to have a plan that will work to nail the killer.

"I'm in," Alicia says standing up, ready to discuss their plan with the boss.

***

After some flak for collecting and testing samples anonymously as well as being collected illegally, the Chief and the Crown Attorney listen to the team's plan. They shoot a few holes in it, suggest a few changes but by the end of the meeting, with their blessing, Helen, Chuck, and Alicia are excited to proceed with their proposal.

Alicia stands first, ending the conversation quickly once they have an agreement. "Everything okay?" asks the Chief.

"Everything is okay, Chief. I just need to talk to Luke. He needs to know about the baby before we do anything else," Alicia replies, taking her leave of the Chief's office.

Chapter 93
Aug 15
Luke

Luke sits on the picnic table near the Community Centre watching the boaters on the water as they speed away to enjoy the beautiful summer weather. He can hear the shouts and laughter of the kids on the beach even farther away as he sits quietly, thinking of Jessica, missing her, wishing that he had actually talked to her on that momentous evening, knowing that he would have supported her in anything she wanted to do with the baby, maybe even pushing just a bit for her to have it, for them to get married. *If I had seen her, found her that night, none of this would have happened. Jess would still be with us, and we would be together.*

He sits quietly with his thoughts until Nova appears, moving through the park toward him, dressed in a low-cut top and Daisy-Duke cut-off denim shorts, so short that the bottoms of her butt cheeks are exposed. He smiles, knowing that she dresses this way to get his attention, so he will lust after her and maybe allow himself to cross the line from friends into something more.

Her smile is brilliant as she walks up to him. "Hello Luke," Nova breathes, planting a kiss on his cheek.

"Hello Nova. You look dazzling, as usual," he replies.

Her smile grows even bigger with the compliment as she sits down beside him on the picnic table, hip-to-hip. "Thank you, Luke. It was such a hot day, just trying to keep cool," she responds, even managing to blush a little bit. "What's going on? Why did you want to see me? Wanna have some fun?" Nova continues, putting her hand on his knee, as if she owns him.

Luke lowers his head for a moment. When he lifts his face to hers, tears glisten in his eyes. "What's wrong Luke?" she asks quietly.

"I just found out that Jessica was pregnant and that the baby was mine. That's why Jess wanted to see me that night," he says, starting to choke up.

318

There's silence for a moment, both looking out at the water, putting their thoughts in order. "Did you know?" he asks.

"I'm sorry that she's gone. Jessica was my friend too, but she made it plain to you, to everyone that you two were over. She had moved on with Ziggy. You need to let this go, Luke. Life is short, as we've now seen and it's our time, not hers," Nova says, placing her arm around his back, pulling him in tight to her.

Luke doesn't fight her protectiveness but allows Nova to hold him. "Did you know?" he repeats.

There's another lull in the conversation before Nova answers. "She's gone. It doesn't matter anymore. Jessica is gone. The baby is gone. It's just us now and we are good together, Luke. So good," Nova declares, snuggling up to him.

Luke asks again, "Did you know about the baby?"

Nova doesn't answer.

After an extended period of silence, he continues. "The police are saying that Jessica was going to kill herself, that she had taken a bunch of pills."

As if talking to herself, Nova mumbles, "Pills. No fucking way."

Still looking at the water, trying to hold his emotions in, Luke asks, "How do you know? Did you see her?"

Nova hesitates before finally confessing. "Yeah, I saw her. She told me about the baby. She said she was confused, that she didn't know what to do. She said she really cared about Ziggy, thought it would turn into love in time, like she had with you, it just hadn't been long enough yet. Said that was her plan when she broke up with you, learn to love Ziggy who could look after her with his family's money, their status, their big house." Nova snorts. "What was she thinking putting money and security in front of love, especially when she had you. But then she found out she was pregnant and started to re-think the plan. She thought Ziggy was wild, too self-centred to be a father. Said that he was tender and loving when they were together and wanted to build a future with her, but a baby? What would he do with that? She thought about telling him it was his kid, but she was afraid that he would find out it was yours and then what? She would be left with nothing. She decided that she was going to tell you about the baby, see

319

what you would say, see if you would take care of her. But I couldn't let her do that. That would have ruined everything. Everything for us. You see that, right Luke?"

"Tell me what you did, Nova." There is silence. Again, he asks, "Did you plan to hurt Jess, Nova? Or was it an accident?"

Nova moves away from Luke, puts her hands in her lap. "I didn't mean to hurt her, but she wouldn't let you go. She was going to saddle you with a baby, make you look after her and the retched thing. She didn't deserve you. I couldn't let her do that. Not to you. Not to us. I had no choice," Nova sniffles, trying to justify her actions that evening. "We are so good together and in time, you'll love me like you loved her. I know you will."

"Where were you guys? I waited at the gazebo for hours and I called her, I texted her. She didn't answer me."

"I met her as she was walking to the park. I walked with her, and she told me about the baby, about what she was going to do. We walked right by you. We were down near the water where you couldn't see us. We kept walking, talking until we reached the Community Centre and then hung out there," she stops for a moment, looking out to the bay before continuing. "Her phone kept ringing. You kept calling. But I told her to figure it out before she talked to you, on the phone and in person. We argued for a long time until Ziggy showed up. After he left, I knew she had made up her mind and that she was going to take you away from me. I had to. I had to, you can see that, right Luke?"

After Nova finishes with her excuses for the violent actions causing the death of Jessica and her unborn baby, the two sit in silence, each deep in their own thoughts. Finally, Luke asks, "Did you hurt Hannah?"

"Hannah?" Nova asks, looking at him.

"Yeah, the girl from Orillia. You remember, we met her at the pavilion, went to see her band at the bar."

More silence from Nova as she looks out to the bay.

"I didn't even really know her, Nova. Why would you hurt her?"

Nova smiles. "That wasn't for you. That was for Tater."

"Tater?" Luke questions.

"You guys always thinking with your dick! You with Jessica. Tater with Hannah and that chick in Wasaga Beach. What the hell is wrong with you guys?" she asks putting her hands on her hips, showing her confidence and disdain for all males with one gesture. "Fucking animals, that's all you really are. You need someone to look after you, so you don't screw up your lives," she continues to rant.

Luke is still, tears falling freely from his eyes, waiting for the detectives who are listening to Nova's confession to come and take her away.

Epilogue – four months later
New Years Eve

James is sitting in a lounger on the sandy Caribbean beach, watching Camryn as she swims in the clear, blue waters. *Beautiful. Simply gorgeous. Still can't believe she's here with me. What a lucky guy I am. Can't wait to kiss her at midnight and celebrate another year together, away from the craziness of Axl and the Ruebens, though I do miss Luke.*

A shadow crosses his face blocking out the bright sun. He looks up at a tall man, standing beside his chair, unable to make out his face in the dark shade. "Can you move a bit, mister? You're in my sun," James asks nicely.

The man moves slightly out of the sun, allowing James to see his face. "Dad?" he questions, moving up into a sitting position, as Mack Sommers smiles down at his son pulling a gun from under the beach towel that he is carrying, aims the large silencer at his son's head and pulls the trigger. James falls back in the chair, blood trickling from a hole in the middle of his forehead. Mack reaches over and pulls James's large Tilley hat down over the wound, before standing back, looking out to the water, following James's view before his sudden demise. He sees Camryn swimming in the bright blue Caribbean water, unaware of his presence. He smiles, sits on the recliner beside his dead son, and waits for her to come up and join him.

***

Nova sits in the window well of the old house, watching the snow fall silently, wishing she wasn't cooped up in this facility, but at home, with her family, with her friends, with Luke. *Such bullshit being here. I was only protecting Luke from Jessica, protecting Tater Tot from those conniving bitches. They needed to be taught a lesson and I had to do it. For Luke, for my brother. Maybe I went a bit too far, maybe I didn't need to kill Cheyenne or Hannah, but they would have made it bad for Tater. And he didn't mean any harm. He was just looking for love and they gave it to him, and then they would have taken it away, made it look like he pushed himself on them. No, I did the right thing for him. And for Luke. Jessica didn't deserve him. She got what was coming to her. Now I have to sit here and play the games, go to the classes, go to therapy, tell them I did wrong, that I didn't mean it, that I'm better, while the fucking lawyers fight it out. Is it Friday yet? I get to make one call a week and I'm sure this week, Luke will take my call. He's just a little upset with me, but he'll see that we were meant to be together.*

***

Miles away in his bedroom at home, Tate watches the snow drift from the sky landing on the trees, the street, the front lawn. After Nova's confession to Luke, his relationships with Cheyenne and Hannah came to light and he has been held under a microscope, forced to go to numerous experts, be quizzed and asked questions about his childhood, his hopes, his dreams, his anxiety levels, his thoughts when he was with the girls. *I can't seem to make them understand that they wanted me. Cheyenne and Hannah wanted me. It's not my fault that Nova is such a bitch, that she went nuts and killed them. I would have made a good boyfriend. I would have been attentive, taken them out for a fancy dinner, made love to them. I don't need any help. Nova does. I'm fine.* He looks down at the exercise the therapist has given him, a worksheet to identify his feelings and actions. Today the assignment has him at a party, and the questions probe his feelings, his actions in that situation. *I would dance with the girls, they would love me, I would leave with one of them, and we would make love all night long, like Cheyenne and Hannah. But no, that's not the answer they want. Repress, repress, repress all of my feelings, and give them the answers they are looking for.*

323

***

Dylan stands looking at himself in the mirror of his new rental house, far away from Barrie. *My timing was right to leave that God-forsaken town. Got the hell out of Dodge before that bitch next door tried to pin something on me. Yup, the demons were getting a little too close again. Just like the last place. I'm going to have to be more careful here, make sure the girls can't ID me, make sure that I continue to be free. Free like a bird. Life is good here. Working as a mechanic, working on another muscle car in my garage, going to the bar to check out the girls on New Year's Eve. I'm sure there's someone out there that will be interested in this good-looking dude.* He smiles at himself in the mirror before grabbing his winter coat for his trip to the local bar, convinced he will meet someone hot, someone willing, someone he will be able to make his own.

***

Luke sits huddled over his computer in the school library, enjoying the quiet. He pounds the keys furiously, trying to capture the ideas that he wants to include in his paper due early in January. He looks up as a tall, lean woman, her strawberry-blond hair pulled back from her face, passes his table and smiles at him. He smiles at her before putting his head back down, reviewing the words that he has just typed, erasing a few, adding some more, saving the document, and sitting back to look out the large window across the room at the falling snow.

The same young woman passes by his table again, stopping. He looks up into her bright green eyes and smiles. "Can I help you?" he asks, unsure of who she is and what she wants.

"I think you're in my program," she starts.

"Police Foundations?" Luke asks, examining her closely. "Yeah, I think I've seen you there, usually sitting at the back of the class."

324

"Yup. That's me. Unlike you who sits in the front row, right in the middle," she laughs.

"Yeah, that's me," Luke grins. "What are you doing here on a night like this? Shouldn't you be out celebrating New Year's Eve with your boyfriend?"

She pulls out the chair across from Luke and sits down, chuckling. "No, no boyfriend. And I wanted to work on that paper for communications."

Luke looks down at his laptop and confirms, "That's what I've been working on too."

"Cool," she replies. "Done?"

"I think for the night, but not done as in ready to hand in," he clarifies.

As he ends his sentence, an announcement comes over the PA system, advising them that the library and the school will be closing within five minutes, to pack up their stuff, put the books back on the shelves and leave the building.

"Well, I guess that's a night," Luke says, closing his laptop. "Hey, I don't have a car but was going to order an Uber. Do you want a lift home?"

"Thanks for the offer, but my brother is supposed to be picking me up out front."

"No problem. We can walk out together if you would like," Luke offers protectively.

"Sure. That would be nice," she confirms.

The two pack up their stuff and move together out of the library to the front doors of the college. They stand on the sidewalk talking about their classes, their assignments and teachers that have made an impression on them.

As they talk, the rumble of a powerful car gets louder. Luke looks away from his new friend and watches as a Mustang rushes through the laneways of the college toward them. He holds his breath momentarily, catching his friend's attention.

The girl's eyes move in the direction that has Luke mesmerized and she smiles. "And that would be my brother. He just loves to make an entrance."

Luke moves his eyes back to the girl. "Your brother?" he questions. "Ziggy Tunes is your brother?"

"You know my brother?" she asks. "Sorry I should have given you my name. I'm Annie. Annie Lennox Tunes."

***

Alicia sits quietly in the Detectives' Den alone. It's New Year's Eve and having the least seniority in the department, she's taking care of things at the precinct while her colleagues are out enjoying the festivities.

This year has been quite a trip. Thank God Luke got Nova to confess to killing Jessica. We had her DNA on the blanket, but she could have wormed out of it somehow saying they were friends and oh so close. We did have the fingernail and the DNA for Hannah's murder, but she might have been able to wrangle out of that as well, been at the park at another time, just circumstantial. But then she confessed – confessed to Jessica, confessed to Hannah, confessed to Cheyenne. She caused a lot of havoc in such a short life. So glad we got her away from Luke. God only knows what she would have done to him.

Thank God things have calmed down. He's started his course at the college. Seems very quiet, very reserved, but I guess that's reasonable with all he's been through. Give him some time and hopefully he'll be able to put it all behind him. It just takes time, I guess.

Alicia's cell phone rings. She picks it up from the desk and answers it, "Happy New Year's," chuckling, thinking it's a well wisher from inside the building wanting to share some more spiked eggnog.

"Hey Alicia. Shots fired at the college library. I got a couple patrol officers enroute," Dispatch advises.

"On my way," Alicia says, hanging up the phone. *Didn't Luke say he was going to the library? Said it would be quiet, no one there to bother him, that everybody would be out celebrating. No way he would be involved in something like this.*

Acknowledgements

If there is a mistake or an issue with the story, whether a typo, grammar, the logic of the story, characters, their actions or the situations they find themselves in or issues with the book cover, that's on me, all on me.

To my fantastic family and friends – thank you for being there, for encouraging me and my writing. Thank you for showing up for me, for recommending my work and for every single expression of support and kindness. It means more than you will ever know.

To the team behind the story – I am so grateful to the fantastic group of people who took their time to read, review my story and offer thoughtful suggestions and constructive feedback to improve the plot, the characters, the credibility and the authenticity of Alicia and Luke's story. Their creativity, honesty and thoroughness is truly appreciated, and I am so incredibly fortunate for their counsel, their comments, their time, and their enthusiasm.

My incredible team: **Kathleen Chalmers, Mary Croteau, Cheryl Favot, Al Gilchrist, Heather Neilson, and Lisa Prentice.** I am so lucky to have each of you in my life and your support on my journey as an author.

And a huge thank you to my husband **William Bradley** for his love, and faith in me, his ongoing support for my writing (including telling random people in Canadian Tire that his wife is a murder novelist), listening to my ramblings about Alicia and dead bodies behind the Community Centre, and for your IT expertise. Love you!

Manufactured by Amazon.ca
Bolton, ON

26845098R00196